METAMORPHOSIS OF NORMAL

Book 2 of the Starlight Series

By: S C O T T   N E A L E

Word Widget

New Galaxy Date (NGD): 1 Year, 5 days:

The Black Asteroid Base:

Jaime Bordeaux:

The asteroid shook as the force of the weapon blasts slammed the surface. Dust fell from the ceiling, but otherwise nothing else happened. Another salvo, the room shook again.

"The place seems to be holding up" Jaime told the group.

"We've been lucky, they have not hit a weak spot on the surface" Allen answered, he then shouted out as he watched the next set of scan returns "Firing again."

"The material of the asteroid is really resistant to our standard weapons" said Jonathan.

Without warning, the floor of the room jumped, sending the entire command crew flying up, then back down. They all landed hard on the black-rock floor. A few scattered pieces of the asteroid fell from the ceiling.

"Okay, what just happened?" Jaime shouted out.

"It appears they made a lucky shot and hit a vein...they caused a fracture and we lost some atmosphere" Allen replied.

Otter ran in and looked at Jaime "Is there anything I can do? I'm aware of the situation."

Jaime pondered out loud "How did you..." the floor dropped, and once again they all flew up, until the artificial gravity took over, which pulled them back down once again. Jaime hit hard on her back side, causing her to show a frustrating moment of pain. "Damn! Yes, Otter...if you could get on Norm-Comm and tell everyone to put on pressure suits...just in case. Let's hope we don't need them."

She plugged the asteroid's communication antenna into the communication port implanted in the back of her neck. She felt a slight surge in her brain as the power flowed from the station into her system. She then pressed on her Norm-Comm device under the skin behind her left ear, and then announced

"Your attention please. As you may be noticing, we are under attack by a hostile force. Although we believe that the base will hold up, there are also possibilities that the attacking ship could find a flaw in the surface of our asteroid." She spoke with such a calming voice, Jaime could have sworn she almost heard music in the background that harmonized with her vocal tones. She continued "For this reason, we are requesting that all personnel put on pressure suits in the event of an atmospheric breach. Thank you for your compliance – do not fear...we will get through this. Command and Control out."

Her voice over the Norm-Comm sounded like a song. Jaime could feel the tranquility, and found she personally had lost any anxiety and was totally calm. Otter looked at her and smiled – she was really good at her profession Jamie thought. Despite the obvious attack and the damage taken, she was now receiving reports from all decks that personnel had calmly prepared and donned pressure suits. Within a few minutes, all areas of the base had reported that they were ready for any situation. *"Amazing!"*

Another round of blasts shook the base again. "They're just not going to quit until we're dead, are they?" Allen asked.

Jaime nodded "I don't think so. I'd hate to think that we've made it this far just to have them get the better of us now. Oomha, any chance for some Flaybah help?" She looked at the deer who was standing stiff and motionless, and seemed to be ignoring her – he was calm, there was no fear or panic in his eyes. His antlers glowed a bright shade of green. She assumed he was doing something to calm himself and even with his large ears, could not hear her over the noise.

Another shot and another pressure breach. "I don't think we can take much more" Allen called out. "Jaime, you should take the Blackbird and escape."

"What?" she yelled out "I will NOT leave during a time of crisis. What kind of Captain would I be if I did that?"

"A living one..." Oomha said calmly.

"No, I will go down with the ship...or in this case the asteroid. Allen, take Oomha out of here on the Blackbird."

"I prefer to stay, Jaime" the deer replied. "Besides..." The explosions on the surface stopped. "I think we are now safe."

Jaime looked up at the ceiling and raised her eyebrows "Hmm, yes they have..."

Boral Oldham:

The bombardment was going well, but in actuality, they had not made a dent in the surface of the asteroid. The Star Force Commander was a bit concerned that their sneaky raid was not having the desired effect on the Normal's base.

"Fire another round...try hitting a different spot" he ordered.

The Hammerhead launched hundreds of various weapons onto the surface of the asteroid – cutter lasers, plasma beams, accelerated particles, and spent plutonium projectiles. A flurry of colors emitted from the arrowhead shaped ship – the reds of lasers, green plasma, yellow particle flows, and the silver streaks of projectiles. Everything fired hit the surface with full force, but appeared to have no effect. By a stroke of luck, one stray laser hit a shiny vein of gold and melted it. The melted metal flowed onto the black rock and melded with it, which caused the new alloy to melt further. This in turn caused more of the material to melt in a cascade, which flowed downward until the cold of space finally hardened the new alloy. This time however, the cooling did not occur until the flow reached deep inside the asteroid, where it found a pocket of atmosphere – in this case, a storage compartment within the base.

Precious atmospheric gases vented out of the new crack and the force loosened more of the black rock and sent if flying out into space. Boxes of parts, and crates of materials followed the path of venting gas. Boral saw the ejected supplies and got excited – his fat lips formed a large smile.

"There...there is a way to beat this rock!" he shouted as he pointed to the small hole in the surface. "Shoot another laser into one of those shiny points, fire at will!"

More beams shot out of the arrowhead-shaped ship. The starboard edge of the ship was pointed at the asteroid with its hundreds of gun ports open and preparing to fire. The beams charged and lit up like a Christmas tree before they fired their deadly output of beams and projectiles. Once again, another beam hit another of the veins, which caused venting in yet another compartment. This time, two people were pushed out with the force of the escaping air. Cheers rang out amongst the bridge crew at the sight of the Normal victims who had been shot out from the protection of the dark rock.

"Can we focus all of our firepower on those points again?" he asked.

"It's difficult...they're small, and we have to hit one that is big enough to do damage. But I will try, my Star Force Commander!" shouted the weaponry officer. He ran his targeting glove over his target selection display, trying to focus the beams as best as possible. He fired and did manage to hit another small vein.

"Keep carefully aiming weapons...fire at your readiness." Boral ordered.

"Yes, my Star Force Commander... almost ready..."

The bridge holo-screen lit up with three bright flashes of light as they appeared in front of the ship. The flashes were so bright it took the weapons officer away from his aiming – which caused the next volley to completely miss the asteroid. Beams and projectiles flew aimlessly into space. Now taking up the entire holo-screen image were three large, brown ships – each one cigar-shaped, and each with a large set of metallic antlers that adorned what appeared to be the front of the ship.

The communication officer announced "They are hailing us, Star Force Commander."

"Well, put them on then..." he replied softly and got closer to the holo-screen.

A deer with a large set of antlers was now displayed on their screen. Boral looked at the creature confused, then mumbled "Why is this familiar?"

The creature began speaking in squeaks and honks. The science officer input the image into the computer. A moment later he announced "The computer says that this creature most closely matches a deer of earth – to be precise, the Mule Deer variety, my Star Force Commander."

"A what?" he asked as he stared at the screen.

Before Boral could get an answer, the honks and squeaks had become Alliance Standard English as the computer translators finally kicked in. "Vessel, this is the Battle Buck Marcole of the Flaybah, I am Commander Grazeel. You are trespassing in our space and firing upon an asteroid that is ours. State your reasoning and intentions."

"Uh..." he paused for a moment "Marcole, this is Our Supreme Commander's Spaceship Victory, of the Northern Alliance Order of Earth. We did not know this was an inhabited section of the galaxy...we are rather new here."

"We have heard of your intrusion into the galaxy..." the deer replied. "Will you stop your pointless attack on our asteroid?"

"Of course Marcole..." he pointed at the weapons officer to stand down, who in turn powered down all weapons and closed the gun ports.

"Are you aware that there are others of your kind on that asteroid?" he asked Boral.

He thought for a moment before saying "Why no...I did not...really? We wondered what happened to that colonization force – we thought they were lost. Could you give me a moment to contact them?" Grazeel nodded in agreement.

He motioned to the communications officer to shut down the communication with the Marcole. "Alright, contact that bitch Bordeaux..."

A moment later Jaime appeared on the holo-screen. "Hello Star Force Commander, did you forget we were here?"

"Umm, well yes, Alpha Starship Captain. Actually, your asteroid has moved from the position we were originally given by both you and the deep space probes. We arrived in your sector and found your base was not where we expected. I figured the Og had attacked and destroyed you. We detected life here, and I thought it was the Og...it enraged me that they had killed you, so I attacked. If I had known it was you..."

"I understand, my Star Force Commander" Jaime calmly interrupted. "It was an honest mistake. See, even Blessed make 'em." She had a small, sweet smile on her face – it enraged him inside as he knew she was mocking him.

"Yes, well now that we are here perhaps we can see your ship?"

Jaime waved a finger in the negative to him "Oh no...not until it is done! I would not want to disappoint you with only a frame. But when it is done, you will see it, and you will see how well it will be able to help the fleet."

He tightened his jaw before calmly saying "Very well. Perhaps you will come aboard the Victory? I would like to debrief you...say twenty one hundred?" Jaime nodded and shut down communications. He rubbed his stubbly chin while he thought, and at the same time he mumbled out loud "Now, what can I plan for her?"

Blessed Salvage Base Plug:

Lindy Light-Griggs:

The baby came quick and provided her with a swift labor and smooth birth. The birth was actually much smoother than the average Normal baby. She was also surprised as to how well she felt afterward – she felt almost good enough to go back to work. Instead however, she decided to take the time off and bond with her new son.

She looked at her newborn son – his face already showing signs of his new personality as he looked at her, and smiled. He had a look that appeared as if he knew exactly where he was, and who he was with. He had deep green eyes, brown curly hair, and large cheeks – the one feature he got from his father. But his skin was tinted a slightly off-shade of golden green, with just some slight hints of flesh tone. Also, when she turned his head she saw he had a full starter set of "wings" on his ears – the growths that many of the Normals had been developing as they spent more and more time in this new galaxy. She swore he even slightly moved them as he gurgled and laughed.

Even within the first moments of his life he seemed to be totally comfortable in this new environment. He looked around the room as if he was taking in all of the sensations of the moment – sights, sounds, and smells. He looked up at her, smiled again, and then did something she never expected – he pointed at her, and then moved his mouth. She wondered, was he so developed this early, that he was already close to speaking? She passed the thought as just her imagination.

A few hours later, Alpha Starship Captain Fitchburg Griggs was finally allowed to enter the room. He barged in with haste, and looked down at the mother and son with a look of frustration. "It's about time they let me in here...like I don't get the choice to see my son! So, this is him eh?" he bent down to look at his new son, and noticed his skin color and ears. "What? He's a freak! This cannot be my son...he would not have these defects."

"Get used to it" Lindy said with a dry tone in her voice. "Every child that your imaginary superior, genetically engineered male parts will create...will end up like this. It's what you deserve...to create a Normal from every Blessed."

"Why I ought to..." he raised his fist to strike her, then looked down at the child again. He realized that the infant did have some of his facial features. He lowered his hand and looked into the face of the newborn. "He does kind of look like me doesn't he?"

The infant turned his big green eyes to Fitchburg, and looked deep into his eyes. The big smile on the child's face turned into a frown – then to Lindy's surprise it turned into what appeared to be a sneer. Then the crying started – it was loud and high pitched. Fitchburg covered his ears, and ran out of the room. Lindy rocked the little one back and forth, and within moments the crying had stopped. The room was once again filled with the sounds of gurgling and giggling.

She looked into his happy eyes again. "You seem to know who is good, and who is evil...don't you little one?" The baby giggled and reached up as if to grab her chin. "Well, you will need that knowledge to survive here. But I somehow don't think that will be a problem. Hey, you know what? You are the first Human child ever to be born here. However, you and I may not be that Human anymore." She reached over to the nightstand and grabbed a computer film, unrolled, and then activated it. "Now, let's find you a name shall we? It sure as hell won't be Fitchburg!" Without thinking, she began her name search by selecting ancient earth history.

A Little Over Three Years Ago...

"Well, my son...I have decided to give you control of the Star Force. This is a great responsibility as you will be the guardian of the space ark we are building up there. As a matter of fact, you will take yourself and your Blessed brethren to find a new home for yourself. I will provide you with everything you will need – male Norms for the labor, female Norms for pleasure and reproduction, and any additional troops that your ship will be able to carry. I will pray for your success, but don't fail me. You are my first son, and I expect nothing but future news of your finding a new homeland for us."

He looked at his father and smiled. He was putting such faith in him and he intended to not disappoint him. His father sat in his motorized chair and smiled while he looked up at him. He reached down and hugged his father, then gave him a kiss on his metal cheek before saying "I will make you proud father, I guarantee it. We will talk more before and after we take off won't we?"

His father, the Supreme Commander nodded and smiled. "Of course, my son. I will want to know everything."

NGD: 1 Year and 6 Days:

The Black Asteroid Base:

Boral Oldham:

Boral sat on the bridge staring at the black asteroid on the holo-screen while a stream of thoughts flowed through his head. He tapped his fingers on the arm of the command console while he chewed on the finger of his other hand. No one on the bridge had spoken a word – none of them wanted to disturb his deep thoughts.

Finally he stood up, looked around the room, and then quickly walked to the ready room off the bridge. He sat down and activated his tele-vid console. Kip appeared in the image.

"Kip, is everything ready?"

"Of course my Starfleet Commander."

"Good, good...I have been thinking, how many people are still aboard Starlight?"

"Well, my last count was about two hundred thousand Normals and about seventy five thousand Blessed. Give or take a few thousand."

"And, how many Normals are frozen?"

"About another fifty thousand."

"How many children have Blessed produced with Norms to date?"

"Not many, sir. Maybe only a handful?"

"Hmm, that is not good – not good at all...Okay..." he once again chewed on the skin of his thumb while he thought. "When we get back instigate plan "C" and also start the awakening."

Kip had a surprised look on his face upon the receipt of those orders "C? Sir, is it that bad?" Boral nodded affirmative. "Also, you do realize we may not have enough supplies for the entire awakening. We may have to find somewhere to get more to feed everyone."

Boral nodded "Yes, yes...I realize that. Perhaps we will ration – take the food from the mouths of the Norms."

Kip gave a small smile. "Very well, I will send a message probe to prepare to start the awakening upon our return then."

"Oh Kip...I have also decided to use my authority as the substitute for the Supreme Commander to discontinue the use of Command Tri-Polyhedrons for selection and advancement of starship Captains. I will be the decider when it comes to who, and when one will be promoted or advanced in rank.

"Very good, Sir. I will make a note in the command logs for you then."

"Good, good...that will be all Kip. Oh also, have the kitchen prepare a meal for me and my guest."

Jaime Bordeaux:

"Jaime, let me take you over in the Blackbird ok?" Allen pleaded.

"No, Allen. First, they cannot see that craft...we don't want them knowing about that...not yet. Second, they instructed me to have someone fly me over in the Rebel Queen. Halley said she'd do that. Once the ship returns from rescuing our two lost comrades from the attack, she said she could turn the ship around and be ready to take me. So, don't worry...I will make it over there."

"It is the way back I worry about..."

Jaime chuckled slightly and patted him on the shoulder, and left the command center. She proceeded down the well-lit corridors to her cabin where she dressed in a full dress Captain-of-the-Order uniform. She checked her make up – or lack thereof, put her long strawberry blond hair into a high loose ponytail and made sure her ears were very exposed, noticeable, and outstanding. She wanted no misunderstanding that she had changed, and was now proud of it. She did a final check of her uniform then headed down to the launch deck.

Once she arrived at the launch deck, she checked the pressure in the gangway, opened the airlock door and crossed the gangway to board the ship. On the way through the gangway, she stopped and looked at the old transport. Still painted on the side in big pink letters were the words "The Rebel Queen". She was so determined to have that removed at one point – but it had been there so long, and life had changed so, that the name now seemed to fit the old girl. She no longer wanted to have those words removed, and had countermanded the order. She now liked *that* name painted on *that* particular ship. She stopped her reminiscing, continued down the gangway, and boarded the ship. Halley was waiting for her in the cockpit. She too had a worried look on her face. Jaime looked at her and scrunched her forehead "You too?"

"Jaime, I'm worried about leaving you there by yourself. Let me stay...okay?" she pleaded.

She shook her head "No...I'll be fine. They won't try anything this time. We've caught them at it too many times, and they would *have* to know we would be prepared for anything. Just get me over there. I promise to kick the crap out of Boral if he tries anything, okay? Besides, has Boral ever come up with a plan to get rid of me that's worked?" She gave her a small, reassuring smile.

Halley just nodded, and proceeded with the launch preparations, while mumbling "I just hope he doesn't get lucky this time..."

Once the ship was ready, the large doors that kept the space dock hidden and protected from the space outside were opened. The door was opened only enough for the smaller Rebel Queen to fly through before quickly being closed – they were taking no chances with the Blessed right outside.

Halley flew the ship to the Victory's space dock and landed. Once down, Jaime disembarked, and the ship quickly left and returned to base.

Jaime was met by Kip Gurrigan. "Alpha Starship Captain..." was all he said as he motioned her down the corridor to the officer's mess hall. Boral was waiting for her surrounded by a multitude of various foods.

"Ah Bordeaux, please join me!" he motioned her to a position opposite him at the table. "So, first report on your progress – will I have a ship by year's end?"

She nodded yes "Of course, my Star Force Commander..." she had to gulp that out without vomiting. "The ship is coming along fine, as scheduled, and will be ready to join the fleet by the end of the year you provided us for the task."

"And no details regarding the design? I hope you did not steal the design of this beautiful craft as I would have hated to now have disappointed you with the original version." He waved his hands around in the air to indicate the structure of the Victory.

"No sir, it is nothing like this impressive design" she lied. "It will be totally different" she told the truth.

"Good, good. Now eat something." He waved to the large banquet of food.

"Thank you, I must pass. I have been on space rations for too long and real food would not settle in my system."

"Your loss." He said as he grabbed a real turkey drumstick and sunk his newly implanted teeth into the flesh, tearing off a large bite. Jaime had to work very hard to maintain her stomach – she found it hard to watch the sight of his gluttony. He chewed for a minute, and then looked at her. She could feel the hatred in him, and it showed in his eyes – she knew he definitely had not forgiven her for the damage and loss in the Command Tri-Polyhedron game.

Finally, with a full mouth he said "Oh, I wanted to say sorry for the attack on your base. Your base was not in the location originally provided by the probe...we thought it was a dead rock."

"Of course, my Star Force Commander" she replied *"You are so full of shit..."*

He waved the turkey leg at her and continued to speak with a full mouth of the meat. "Very well, you're dismissed." She looked at him confused and he stopped eating – half-chewed turkey hung out of his large lipped mouth. He looked at her with a questioning look before saying "You are dismissed. There is a shuttle ready...go back to your rock now." He waved the turkey leg at her again as if shooing a fly.

She gave him a quizzical look then stood up, and saluted him. As she turned to walk away, she gave her head a slight fling to move the ponytail from one shoulder to another – for comfort. In the corner of her eye, she detected a slight flinch in Boral's face as the hair moved – a small, but painful memory from the game she surmised. She gave a very small smile at detecting the flinch, then continued to turn away from the Star Force Commander, and left the mess hall. Kip was waiting for her in the corridor to escort her back. She studied him for a moment before saying "No tour?"

"No..." Kip quickly replied, then continued "You were to report to the Star Force Commander, then return to your base.

That is what you are going to do." He motioned her back to the space dock.

They arrived at the dock and a small shuttle was powered up and prepared for her departure. "We will donate this ship to you. You can return it sometime...whenever we see you again." He saluted her, turned, and quickly stepped down the corridor. She looked at him wondering what was going on his head. She shrugged her shoulders, walked out into the space dock, and then boarded the shuttle.

It was a short-range, two-person shuttle. The craft itself was a small, silver box-looking ship that had a teardrop-shaped rear end that housed a low-speed ion drive. It had a single door and a single pressure window instead of an electronic view screen. She entered the craft, and shut the door.

She sat down at the pilot's seat and performed systems checks – she thoroughly checked pressure seals, engine output, and navigation. All appeared to be in proper working order. She looked around the interior of the ship – standard configuration for a Blessed shuttle – computer consoles on both sides of the compartment, atmospheric generator in the back, two seats and a full navigation and propulsion control system up front at the helm. She checked the safety systems – escape pod, and explosive door bolts which both were ready and operational. She could find no problems, so she took off from the Victory, and started on her return voyage back to the asteroid base. As soon as her shuttle departed, the Victory turned and left immediately.

As she approached the base she used Norm-Comm to contact the Control Center. "This is Jaime in the Blessed shuttle, approaching for landing."

Allen replied "Roger that Jaime, welcome back."

Something bothered her. "Why?" she kept asking herself "Why have me come over just for that?" On a hunch, she pressed the controls to stop the craft, but the ship did not respond to helm commands. She got out of her seat and started looking around the small craft, trying to find the cause of the navigation malfunction. She searched all around the craft for anything out of order. She began to suspect that there was something she had not found that had been prepared for her arrival at the base – a bomb she

14

surmised. She opened the small compartment that contained the ion drive and what she saw gave her a start. The compartment held the drive – and a device that she recognized would cause an engine overload – which would turn the shuttle into a thermonuclear device. There was also navigation and proximity sensors attached to the engine overload device. She now realized this was yet another plot to kill her – and everyone on the asteroid. *"Shit, he's an idiot...and so am I for thinking he would not try this..."*

She returned to the helm and examined the auto-pilot device – it was still active and guiding the ship to the now open set of space dock doors. She tried again to turn the ship around but the controls were frozen and no longer accepted commands. In addition, the escape pod launch controls had automatically become disabled. She looked around and lightly chewed on the tip of her finger while she thought of a solution. She quickly reached into her travel purse and took out two gloves and snapped them onto her hands. The glove material merged with the uniform and sealed air-tight. She then took a flexible helmet off of the wall cabinet and placed it around her head – the material wrapped around her head and sealed into the collar of her uniform. She looked at her legs uncovered by the uniform skirt *"Thank goodness for space transparencies...never leave home without them."* Now ready for anything, she began to work to disarm the auto-pilot device. Through her tinkering, she was able to slightly change the course of the ship – it might miss the space dock but would impact the surface of the asteroid, which would still substantially damage the base. She continued her attempts to manipulate the auto-pilot, which caused a slight spark in the controls, which in turn caused a beep to sound behind her. She turned to look at the detonator device – her eyes opened wide as she saw the timer had activated with only fifteen seconds on the clock. "Not enough time!" she said as she stood from the console, turned, and without thinking quickly hit the explosive bolts on the door.

The atmosphere vented from the craft, and sent Jaime out into the vacuum as quickly as the escaping air. Her head hit the doorframe of the craft as she was thrown out. The venting air also shifted the craft further away from the open space dock door and from the base. She was barely able to have grabbed onto the escaping pod hatch, and hung onto it for dear life. She only floated out in space for another brief moment before the concussion from the explosion hit her. She felt the explosion crush almost every bone in her body while her consciousness floated away along with her broken, freezing form out into the void of space.

Allen James:

The explosion rocked the asteroid but by a stroke of luck the small shuttle had turned away from the dock entrance at just the right moment to avoid any internal destruction. However, the shuttle Jaime was piloting was gone – and possibly her along with it. He activated every advanced scanner and SCADAR searching for any trace of her.

He looked at the scan returns while he activated Norm-Comm. "Prepare the Blackbird for immediate departure." He looked at Jonathan, and ordered "Continue scanning. I am going to go out there and look for her. Let me know the second you find anything that might be her." Holding back tears, Jonathan only nodded, and took over control of the scanners.

He ran to the space dock, boarded Blackbird, and flew out of the asteroid base the moment the doors had opened wide enough to pass. He projected the path of the doomed shuttle on his computer display, and estimated the most likely spot that she might have been able to escape.

He searched for three hours – slowly scanning every inch of space. He finally found her body – she had smashed onto the surface of the asteroid, only a few kilometers away from the base entrance. It was sheer luck that he had turned his scanners onto a small piece of debris that had impacted the surface, which ended up being the shuttle door and her body. Her body was resting on the shuttle door when it hit the asteroid – her hands firmly gripping the door handles – otherwise there might not have been anything left of her when they hit the surface of the black carbon asteroid. He put on a helmet, sealed his suit, and proceeded with an EVA to recover her frozen body. He cut away the handles from the hatch, brought her into the ship, and immediately activated the autopilot to return to base. While the ship proceeded home he removed her helmet and listened for any sign of life. She was frozen solid, only still in one piece due to her protective uniform, but she had no pulse and was not breathing – his fears were now turning to reality.

Getting on Norm-Comm he signaled "Max, prepare for Jaime's arrival..." he had to swallow his sorrow before continuing "She's dead."

The Year 2031...

"This blackberry tastes so good!" she thought as black stained fingers pulled another of the delicious fruit off the vine. There were sirens going off, and they scared her, but the berries made her feel better – made her brave. She pulled and ate yet another of the tasty fruit.

"There you are! I have been looking everywhere! Haven't you heard the sirens? We have to go!" Her mother was wearing a flowing cream dress covered with small printed flowers when she ran up to her through the long row of blackberry bushes. She breathed heavily due to running, and from fear – she realized her mother was as scared as she.

"But Maman!" she cried – she was so scared, but the fruit made her feel better. She just wanted to eat more of the sweet fruit. She wanted to forget everything else but the fruit – she wanted to not be scared.

"Come..." mother said as she grabbed her hand and started walking quickly toward the buildings of the chateaux. Loud swooshing noises were heard in the distance. Mother turned and looked up into the sky. She bent down, picked her up, and ran to the bunker entrance at the base of the wall of the main building. As her mother carried her, she turned and looked into the sky – round, bright red balls were flying by in formations on their way toward the distant city. She pushed her face into her mother's soft shoulder – hoping the scary objects would fly away and leave them alone.

She heard a beeping sound, and when she turned her head to look, she saw one of the red fiery balls as it changed course and headed to the nearby village. She watched as the ball floated above the town then dropped into the center of the neighboring settlement.

Her mother grabbed her face and turned her just in time to prevent her from seeing the bright flash of the exploding bomb. She ran them into the shelter, and quickly closed the door – large leaded panels quickly dropped from the ceiling, and heavy steel locks just as quickly bolted down the leaded door with only seconds to spare. The concussion of the blast shook the entire underground bunker.

The sounds of explosions filled her ears despite the distance from their vineyard. Mother held her close while she cried at the loud sounds that refused to stop their assault on her ears, and her fears. The explosions continued, and were getting louder each time. Only through her own tears was she able to weaken her mind enough to sleep.

When she awoke, she found the door of the shelter had been cracked open. Outside she heard her mother crying. As she approached the door, the sounds of her mother became louder. She called out "Maman...Maman, why are you crying?" As she stepped through the opening of the shelter she saw what was left of the estate – a barren burning wasteland. The building she called home was now a pile of rubble. All of her beloved berry plants were gone – what sat where her delicious berries used to grow were now only burning sands. The air above was glowing and burning, the wind howled with radioactive force.

Her mother heard the footsteps behind her and turned. "Get back inside and don't come out!" she screamed. Mother turned and picked her up and carried her back inside. She looked at her mother and noticed that her hair was now gone – she was bald. She began to again cry, she cried for her mother, for the chateaux, and for herself. Mother handed her to father. He took her and put her in the hovercar. He told her not to be afraid, that they were headed for Paris – the only place left where it was safe to live...

NGD: 1 Year 6 Months:

The Black Asteroid:

Jaime Bordeaux:

A bright light shined into her eyes as she heard "Ah, you're finally awake!" The light moved away and Jaime could barely make out the face of Doctor Max Sollix. He gave her a soft smile and rubbed the top of her head lightly "Jaime, do you remember anything?"

She shook her head no, but then a few thoughts came back to her "The ship...it was rigged...and was headed for the base...I...I..."

Max patted her lightly on the top of her head again, and shushed her. "Calm down Jaime...you made it...you saved the base. But you personally took quite a bit of damage." She looked at him confused. She could move her eyes and speak but could not feel her body. Her eyes darted around giving a look of panic – Max rubbed her forehead lightly "Don't worry, your body is not ready to move yet – we have it totally incapacitated. We're using the latest in large animal anesthesiology and electronic stasis fields." He gave an obnoxious smile and a small laugh.

"The base..." she muttered.

"Is safe. You saved us. Somehow, you got the ship to deviate course just far enough, and when you blew the hatch, the force of the escaping air sent the ship off on a course away from the base right before it exploded. You however, did not get away that easy – you suffered a lot of damage before you were frozen. Lucky that you put on that helmet, and had your space transparencies on. Between that and the pressure resistance of your uniform you survived the vacuum. You were however, quick frozen...but that amazing body of yours! The reactor in the back of your neck kept your brain cells energized despite them being totally frozen...otherwise, you might have been brain dead or had permanent neural damage. Once Allen retrieved your body he let me take over...it took me a little while to unfreeze your head, and get blood artificially flowing to it...I did a great job however, if I say so myself. Here's how I did it...I rigged this heart-lung machine that took warm blood and pumped it into your head. Then, it returned the blood from your head and oxygenated it. Once full of oxygen I..."

"Doc!" she blurted out. He looked at her confused "Please, not now?" He sighed, smiled, and nodded at her. She asked him "Why can't I feel my body? Why is it you are preventing me from moving?"

He looked down below her neck – she was encased from the neck down inside the stasis pod. "Well, it is still healing. You will need to stay totally still for another month."

"Month?" she cried out. "I can't wait that long. I have things to do..."

"It can wait..." he interrupted. "Besides, we have been running things just fine while you have been recuperating."

"And how long have I been recuperating?" she asked.

He gave a pained look and scratched his head "Well Jaime, I..." he took a small breath before blurting out "six months..." Her eyes opened wide. "It took a long time to thaw you out and repair you, and you still have a long way to go...so, be patient ok?"

She smiled and nodded at him. She gave a long look at the lines on his face – they looked less pronounced – he looked younger. "Did you do something? You look really good" she remarked.

He rubbed his chin lightly "I do look younger don't I? Although I would not go as far as being labeled "hot"..." He gave a small grin and a chuckle. "I do look much better than I did before we left, even I'll admit that. Also, you may find many of us are looking better now..." He looked at her and smiled while rubbing her forehead again. "Alright, I am going to go but will be back later. Now rest..." He turned, and walked out of the vitality ray booth and activated it. One of the base nurses came up behind him, and startled him.

She looked into his eyes and asked "Did you tell her?"

He shook his head "No, not yet...I couldn't..."

Jonathan Faraday:

The structure of the ship was complete and he was now in charge of getting many of the various systems installed and running. His pet project was the electronic bubble generator he found over a year ago on Stopper.

He ran down the inner passageways that snaked through the interior of the large black asteroid. He stopped at the lab where his friends were putting together the new computer configuration that would help to run the Dragon starship. He needed to see their progress before he continued on to his lab.

He arrived at to find Georgie Hayson and William Jergens huddled around a four foot by four foot black box.

Georgie looked up when Jonathan entered the lab. "Ah Jon, get over here – it's almost ready and you have to see this!" She had a large smile on her face that brimmed with excitement and enthusiasm.

Jonathan walked up and looked into the large black box. The two computer engineers worked as if they were mentally connected as they carefully plugged two inch-long, black, square rods into matching shaped holes built into the inside frame of the cube. Occasionally, they looked up at each other in unison, and smiled at each other. This caught Jonathan's eye and he wondered if perhaps there was now more than a working relationship. He looked down into the computer chassis and examined their creation. "So that's them eh?" The two looked up and nodded in acknowledgment.

William put another of the small rods into the supporting frame and snapped it into place. "Yep, this is it. This is one of three computers that we will be installing into the Dragon starting tomorrow. We hope to get the other two assembled, configured and installed in the next couple days."

Jonathan picked up one of the small black rods and examined it in the light. "Amazing that you came up with this. Are you sure it will work as expected?"

"Better!" Georgie blurted out. "That one module you are holding has the computing power of one terabyte of three-dimensional storage, along with an independent mega-core processor. It could probably run most of the ships systems by itself – but we will not want to work it that hard, so we will give it the other two thousand nine hundred and ninety nine modules to help it out. Then, if that is not enough we will give it another two more computer cubes to help if needed. This will provide all the processing power the ship will require to operate." She snatched the module from Jonathan's fingers and inserted it into an open receptacle. She then looked up at him with a raised eyebrow "So, do you want to help out here? We have another five hundred plus modules to plug in before we can power it up and start loading the operating system."

Jonathan held his hands up, and waved them at the pair "Ah no...I have my own work to do. I will leave you to your..." he thought for a moment before calling it "compucube." He looked at the cube again as the modules were being tightly packed together inside the compact electronic frame. "I have a bubble to blow...so, if you will excuse me."

"Yeah, get that bubble working so it can protect our little boxes here...Megacomps...eh?" William yelled out as Jonathan turned, and opened the door to the lab. He looked back at the two scientists – they went right back to their work, moving in unison as if they were mentally connected. Yet, they said nothing to each other while they worked. He shook his head, and proceeded out of the lab.

He began walking the corridors continuing on his way to his own lab. Behind him, a voice called out "Jonathan?" He turned to find Kate Grayson running to catch up with him. Since they have arrived at the asteroid, he had been noticing a different look about her. The gray streaks in her hair were fading, and were being replaced by a solid mahogany brown mane.

"I've been looking for you. How is the bubble coming along?"

"Great! I am going to do the final tests tonight. If that goes well, I will schedule two live tests. I'm confident I'll be configuring the actual unit in the Dragon in three days. I assume the support pylon I designed is ready and in place?"

"Along with the generator itself. All is ready for you...I anticipated you would have it running in just a few days."

"Funny, how you would know that..." he replied.

"Hey, how about we celebrate your success with the generator and our near completion of the Dragon? I'll buy dinner?"

"That sounds...fun..." he said with a little shyness in his voice.

"Great, then my place...say twenty five hundred tomorrow?"

"Ok..." he softly said as she placed her hand on his shoulder. He felt a tingle as her hand came in contact with his body – as if someone had turned on a light switch in his skin. The feeling of current on his skin surprised him, but he found he liked it.

She gave him a warm smile, and then ran off the other direction. He turned and ran the short distance to his own personal laboratory. He rubbed his shoulder again, still feeling the warmth and tingling on his skin. He put on a lab coat, and changed his glasses to a wrap-around pair that provided him with electronic measurements and readouts. He walked into the middle of the room and removed a white sheet that covered a small glowing elongated plastic bubble, inside this bubble was mounted a metallic bar with a wrap of fine silver-like wire. "Ok, let's see if we can get you working properly today shall we?" He attached two power lines to two matching terminals on the front of the unit – It began to give off a slight hum as it waited for activation commands. He walked over to the work bench and picked up a remote control.

At that moment, Max walked in and waved at him "Hello Jonathan, you wanted me for something?"

"Hi Max, how's Jaime doing?"

"Much better...although I could not tell her about the condition." He looked down at the floor in shame.

"I understand...that's going to be a hard one to explain. Well, I didn't call you over to add to your burden...I was hoping you could help me with an experiment. Mind giving me a little bit of time?"

"Absolutely! It will give me something to do and take my mind off of Jaime. What can I do for you?"

"Well, first...I need you to monitor me when I activate the bubble device. I will be standing in the center."

He looked at Jonathan grimly. "You think that's wise?"

"Yes, I'm feeling confident tonight. I just want to be sure I really have eliminated any danger items, such as suffocation. Remember what happened a while back?"

"How could I forget?" He thought back to a month ago when Jonathan had ran one of his first tests on the device. He had stood right next to the generator and activated the device. It worked – but it had an almost fatal side effect – it had cut off the flow of atmosphere to Jonathan, almost suffocating him. Only shutting down the power saved him. He hoped he would not need to do anything that extreme this time.

"Well, I am sure that will not happen this time...but...just in case..." he chuckled slightly as he continued to connect power cables to the device. The device was resting on a metal stand, the stand was firmly bolted down to a metal plate which sat on the black floor of asteroid material. "Ok, so this stand is big enough for me to stand on, which I have determined will allow me to become part of the structure attached to the bubble generator. I have surmised that this in turn will allow me to be part of the structure that will be protected by the bubble...this test will prove that."

He took one more look around the test area – he did a final check on the cabling and the support structure. "Ok, here we go..." he said as he pressed the activation button on the remote control.

Additional power was applied to the cabling that supplied power to the device. The amount of power was controlled by algorithms processed by the computer. This energized the coil inside the plastic bubble, which caused it to glow slightly as it began to interact with a gas that filled the inside of the tube. This was followed by a slight shifting of light as the bubble expanded around Jonathan and filled the test area with its field.

Jonathan took a deep breath of air and let it out slowly. He then took out a atmospheric pressure gauge and tapped on it to get a current reading. He looked up at Max while saying "So far, so good! We have good pressure and lots of breathable air. Now, if you could stand behind the safety screen and press that green button on the console, we can proceed to the next test."

Max followed his request and went behind the metallic panel. There was a small transparent window that allowed him to look into the test area while being protected from the testing. He looked down at the control panel and found the green button. Feeling confident, he reached down, and without thinking pressed it. To his surprise, a boom lowered into the room and fired a cutter laser at the bubble. He gasped as he realized what he had done. The beam fired from the emitter as the boom moved from the top of the bubble to the bottom.

Jonathan stood in the middle of the bubble unaffected and smiling. "Yes! I knew it would work."

"Crap Jonathan...will you warn me next time?" he yelled out from around the protective wall.

"Ok Max, now the purple button please?"

He looked again at the console, there was the green button, a yellow button, a red button, a blue button, and the purple button. He had determined that there would be no way he would press the red button. After the result of the green button however, he had some reservation as he slowly pressed the purple button. A hatch opened from the ceiling and a large proton blaster lowered on a mechanical arm. "Aw shit, Jonathan!" Max yelled out as the beam fired from the blaster. The beam hit the bubble and simply dissipated.

Unaware to Max, Jonathan had closed his eyes in fear. A moment later Jonathan realized he had not been vaporized, and he smiled. "Well, I think this thing is working...now one more test..." and in saying that quickly took out a blaster and fired it into the wall outside the bubble, and directly in front of him. The shot smoothly flowed through the energy bubble and hit the wall, which burned a one inch hole through the metal. Max yipped again in surprise, which made Jonathan laugh. "Ok, NOW it is fully tested" he said as he shut down the power to the device and stepped off of the platform.

"Ok my friend. If you want my help in the future, NEVER tell me to press the purple button, and never surprise me by pulling out a blaster!" He then muttered "I figured the red one would be bad...not purple..."

"Max, if I had made the red button fire the blaster you would have never pressed it." Max nodded his head in agreement. "Yes, as I suspected...so I made it the purple button. Next time, it could be one of the other colors. But more importantly, the bubble worked!"

"Congratulations my young friend" he said as he grabbed his small hand and shook it vigorously.

"Now...the next phase..." He activated his Norm-Comm "Allen, I have a need for a drone for testing."

"You got it working?" he asked.

"Yes, and I was able to get the voltage and amperage algorithms figured out so the size and strength of the bubble is totally controllable. We should now be able to make a bubble around any size of ship. The bubble should protect us from any form of beamed or particle weapon. If the drone test is successful, I will need a shuttle or the Blackbird."

"Blackbird? I warn you, if you blast my ship or even damage it, I will have your head"

"Don't worry, it will work, and the ship will be protected. I promise. From that test, I should have the specifications and requirements to configure the full-sized device, and have it ready for the Dragon in the next three days!"

He shut off his Norm-Comm, and took Max's hand to shake it once again. "Thanks again for your help. I could not have done it without..." he was interrupted by a small bell ring coming from his computer console – it sounded like a bell from an old style teletype. "Oh, the computer has discovered something..." he said as he dropped his hand, and walked over to the console.

"What is it?" Max asked.

"Interesting...Well, we were able to "obtain" the files from the computers onboard Starlight before we left. Ever since we have arrived here and set up shop, I have had this computer working on one task – to decrypt the Blessed cipher-coding and crack their files. Every so often the computer spits something out...this is one of those times. So, let's see what we've got..." He read the text that was being displayed on his readout. "Hmm, this is a record of the computer activity right before Starlight launched. So, what exactly is a reverse-trace scan transducer? It says it was activated right before launch...by Boral?"

Max gave a quizzing look. "Boral activated it? Why the hell would he activate a program at that time?"

He typed more commands into his console. "Not sure. I'm trying to locate this transducer program to see what...it's...all about..." A moment later, the computer dinged again. "There, the computer found the name of the file in the decryption. I have ordered it to try to decrypt it." He watched the thousands of characters as they flashed before his eyes while the computer performed its work. "Man, I wish I had that new computer cube for this...this decryption would have been done a year ago..." another typewriter ding "Ah, there it is. The computer has analyzed it to not be dangerous to our systems. Well, sometimes you just have to take a chance." He said as he activated the program. Klaxons sounded in the lab and all around the base as an imminent attack force had been detected. "Ah shit..."

Alan James:

The SCADAR showed it, but he could not believe it. He stared at it once again as the automatic defense alerts sounded – recently installed defensive weapons came on-line and targeting computers activated to guide the few installed external weapons in the repelling of the incoming attack.

"All right everyone prepare for battle. Otter, prepare a message to all personnel to put on pressure suits and batten down the hatches. Everyone get the base prepared for the worst!"

On Norm-Comm Jonathan buzzed him. "This is not a good time Jonathan, we have an incoming attack force... however, I am not sure where the hell they came from and how they actually got here..."

"Sorry to bother you Allen...but it *is* important. What's attacking us?"

"It's hard to believe, but we have a massive southern fighter attack force incoming. We showed three hundred fighters at first – but now the SCADAR computer is counting at least four hundred. This is a massive attack!"

"What kind of starfighters Allen? It's important that I know..."

"Century style. What's odd, is that there's no base ship. Where in the hell could they have launched from? There is no way they could travel all this way independently in deep space."

"One second..." he said and drifted off not saying anything further. A moment later the force disappeared off of the SCADAR, and the computer automatically cancelled the alert.

"What the hell?" Allen shouted out. "Otter, cancel the alert message. Everyone stand down...it appears they either had a change of heart, or the computer scanned something that caused a false alarm."

"So, everything is good now?" Jonathan asked.

"Yes fine. Jon, what do you know about this?"

"Yes, I would like to know too..." said Jaime who had come onto the Norm-Comm channel. "I was monitoring the situation. That was exactly what happened when the south attacked Starlight...right before we departed Earth. How could the exact same thing happen way out here? I want some answers now!" she demanded.

Jonathan tunneled a channel to Allen and Max on Norm-Comm. "So, I need one of you to do me a favor. Someone has to give her some bad news..."

Four Years into the Hemispheric Ground War...

The streets in the protected town were alive with the shouts of the happy inhabitants. A festival had just begun in the street, and she found she too had become washed up in the thick of the excitement. The singing and dancing was too much to ignore and she felt herself get caught up in the excitement as her body began to feel the rhythmic beats. She knew they had just taken this village, but the villagers were so happy to see them as they marched through the streets. They had even opened up the hatch to their protection wall to let them in. Shouts of "Welcome to our Alliance victors" and "We love you Alliance soldiers" rang out from all directions. They could not be any happier to see them, but she wondered why southerners would be so quick to want to join the Alliance.

Trays of glasses filled with delicious looking beverages were being passed out to every soldier. She took one but did not remove her helmet to drink. At just fifteen, she was still considered too young to drink, and thus had never actually touched the stuff. Even more important however – she was not trusting the people of this newly liberated village. Her comrades on the other hand, were taking the glasses of the beverage, and guzzling them down. One of them – it was Marc, took his helmet off and smelled the fluid in the glass. She watched as he took in the bouquet of the sweet liquid before finally taking a sip. He smiled and said "AH, delicious!" before belting down the remainder of the red fluid.

This got some of the other members of the platoon to also remove their helmets. A moment later they were all taking sips of the sweet wine. She still felt uneasy...she kept her helmet on and her weapon ready, as something did not seem right. For hours she sat and watched – more and more of the Alliance soldiers joined in the festivities. It was a celebration – their freedom had been won and they were free to become citizens of the Order. It was just what they wanted. So, why did she hesitate to join them?

Her paranoia eventually began to fade – the beats of the music and the laughing and singing were loosening her up. There were men, women, and children dancing and partying in the street, and it was wearing her resistance thin. She was wanting so bad to relax and let go – but something bothered her. She found she was not alone feeling this way either – five of her fellows were still fully suited up and ready for a fight – Sergeant Millie, Jones, Marcus, Fred, and Mel. The group searched for their XO – Lieutenant Broadmoor in the crowd. When they finally located him, he was a drunken mess – he had let go and was partying with the villagers as if he had lived there all his life. The Blessed officer had succumbed to the libations, was dancing, and was unable to hear anything she was saying when she spoke to him. He asked again "What?" – she told him something was not right. He asked her to repeat again, unable to hear what she was saying through her helmet speaker.

Finally, she gave up and removed her helmet to tell him that she was going to help him out of his stupor – she told him that in her gut, something was wrong. She began to administer a sobering medication. As she checked his eyes, she saw the targeting laser appear on his face – she pushed him away and looked up just as the blast came down from the church tower. She felt the pain through her cheek as she threw her helmet back on. The heat from the blast cauterized the entry point at the back of her left cheek, but the exit point between her nose and upper lip bled heavily. Blood spurted onto the faceplate from her cheek as she fully closed her faceplate and used her heads-up display to identify enemy targets. A powerful analgesic was administered automatically as her battle suit detected the increase in her pain level. A tacky mist covered her cheek to seal the blood – all while aiming and launching a small nuke toward the enemy sniper in the tower.

It was a trap as she suspected – only her and the other five had followed their instincts and were still ready. They took them out – all of them. By the time the small band of soldiers had finished, herself, the lieutenant she saved, and the five others were the only people left alive in the pile of rubble that was once a vibrant enemy town. The enemy had tricked them and taken the lives of thirty five members of the platoon before the six of them took down all of the enemy combatants – men, women, and children.

By the time the battle was over and all of the enemy townsfolk were dead, her cheek and jaw had locked up and she was having problems breathing. She would end up getting that first of

32

many medals for bravery and valor in battle – also, she would finally get that rest she deserved in one of the hospital domes back in the north.

NGD: 1 Year 7 Months:

The Black Asteroid Base:

Jaime Bordeaux:

She awoke to find Max staring down at her, a light smile on his face. "Wakie, wakie…" he examined the look in her eyes a moment before asking "Something wrong?"

"Only odd…I was dreaming…" she replied. He gave a confused look to which she answered "I stopped dreaming a while back – after the explosion however, the dreams have returned. Dreams of things I sometimes remember and sometimes I don't, but I feel I should…at least I think I should."

He scratched his chin "Hmm…I am not sure I am qualified to help you there. Well, in any case, are you ready to finally get up?"

She returned the smile "Hell yes, and it's about time…"

His face became serious as he looked to the control panel before he reached over, and turned down the stasis settings. "I have started the process of turning down the stasis field that is surrounding your body. You will start to feel your arms and legs as the field weakens, which will allow your nerves to function. While you have been sleeping each night, I have stimulated your muscles so when this day came you, would find no muscle degradation. Now, there is something else I need to speak to you about." His expression had become even sterner.

"Oh crap doc, don't tell me I only have one arm or something…"

He put his hand on the top of her head, rubbed her hair, and gave a light smile. "No, nothing that serious. However, almost every bone in your body was broken and damaged. We had to use every bit of serum to regenerate what bones we could. But we ran out of the compound, and then found we did not have the minerals – specifically carbon, to rebuild your remaining broken bones. So, I had to improvise with what we had on hand. We live on the largest supply of space carbon...both graphite and the black diamond form that we are using to build our ships. So, I found some of the asteroid material in powder form and threw it into the serum batch. I have since discovered that it was composed of both space graphite, and small amounts of space diamond dust. With the space diamond in the serum it worked even better than I expected to heal your broken bones."

"But there is something you are not telling me isn't there?" she asked as she felt the feeling come back to her body – her arms and legs experienced a slight tingle.

She was wiggling her fingers and toes as Max opened the stasis pod. "It has to do with the elements in this galaxy – they appear similar to the standard elements and minerals that we have on earth. The carbon here for example, has the same atomic makeup. However, when the scientists dug deep into the structure they discovered that the atoms despite their appearance are in actuality quite different from earth standards."

"Wait doc..." she interrupted "what scientists?"

He gave a slight chuckle "Since your incident, we have had quite a few Normals leave the main fleet and join us here...many of them are some of our best scientists. Anyway, they discovered protons that are in orbits where electrons should be, neutrons replaced by electrons, etcetera, etcetera. Not quite the same element as I expected it to be. Thus, when I used them for the serum...Well, I think it's just easier to show you..." he helped her up and onto her feet.

She found that he was correct about her muscles, she found no weakness or degradation in her legs. She came out of the pod naked and was surprised when Max did not offer her a robe – instead he rolled a mirror in front of her.

She was smiling until she looked into the mirror – her smile turned into an open mouth of shock as she peered at the reflection. The skin on her body seemed to give off a translucent appearance. She could not see muscles, but it appeared that her bones were showing through her skin – bones black as the deepest part of space. They seemed to shimmer as a floating blackness underneath her skin. She could see the bones in her legs and her pelvis. Every bone in her rib cage showed through her skin like they had been tattooed onto the outside. She turned to look at her back, and saw that her spine gave the same wavering black shimmer. She turned and looked at the back of her head then turned her head and looked at her face before saying "Well, I guess I should be fortunate that you were able to fix me however the outcome. I guess I should also be lucky my face didn't get smashed up in that explosion."

"Oh it did…" he corrected her "I used what little of the old serum I had on your face and head before I had to resort to the space carbon. For what it's worth, the bones in your body are now stronger than they have ever been before." He lowered his head and slightly shook it as he told her "In any case, I am so sorry Jaime…I hope you can forgive me someday."

She reached up and lifted his chin with her hand – dark bones shone through the skin of her arm and fingers. "Hey, if you hadn't done this I would probably be crippled or worse, dead. You did everything you could to heal me. Besides, I could get used to this…nothing a good black uniform can't cover." She peered at the dark bones again before furrowing her brow, then turning to look at Max with a needy look "Speaking of a uniform…could you find me one now?"

Max gave a weak smile "Of course…"

She dressed and headed back to her quarters. Her body was stiff, and she so badly wanted a warm massage and shower to stimulate her mind and body. As soon as she arrived she threw off her clothes and walked over to the cleansing bay. She stopped at the mirror and looked at the blackness emanating through her shiny alabaster skin. She did not know what to make of it – it seemed a little creepy to her, but at the same time she found herself fascinated with this new ability to view her structure. She looked at the blackened shoulder blades shimmering through her skin and rubbed them lightly. She noticed that her freckles still showed even though the darkness of the shoulder bone. It fascinated her to watch the fluctuation of darkness and light on her body.

She got into the cleansing bay, and turned on a deep, warm massage. She relished in the pulsating lasers against her skin. While she let the messaging beams soothe her body, she pondered on the program Jonathan had found. She now understood the "convenience" of the emergency that caused Starlight to launch – she now knew who killed Dex. She had a month to ponder and dwell on this thought – but she also knew that for now she needed to push it aside, and not let revenge get in the way of what needed to be done. She stood in the bay for almost forty five minutes as she worked to clear her thoughts. She focused on nothing but the soothing pulses. Her mind finally cleared and she began to meditate, which further cleared her thoughts.

She finally shut down the beams, stepped out of the bay, used a towel to remove any skin residue, and applied a soothing lotion to her translucent skin. She turned to walk over and get a robe when a noise in the corner of the cabin startled her. She froze all movement and looked around with darting eyes as she remembered hearing that sound in the past. Her eyes glanced around every corner and edge of flooring around the room. To her right, she finally spotted it – the space rat. It had crawled around from the back side of her bed and was now looking at her with hungry, dark eyes. Its mouth was open – sharp, venomous fangs stuck out in an almost threatening smile – drool dripped from its chin as it tasted the air in anticipation of its future meal standing before it. It was the biggest one she had ever seen – at least a foot long and at least eight inches wide. Its tail had to have been at least a foot long – it whipped the barbed end back and forth slapping it against the floor.

"Sorry my friend, but I really don't have the patience for you right now..."

She slowly moved her left arm slightly up and her eyes cautiously moved down to look at her wrist. A slight panic hit her as she realized she was not wearing her command weapon. Her eyes glanced around the room looking for the device. On the nightstand it sat – but she would have to step right in front of the creature to obtain the protection it provided. Unfortunately, she knew the creature would poison her well before she would be able to kill the beast. The paralyzing effect would take her down before she would be able to defend herself.

"Well, I guess it is your move..." she quietly said to the now growling rodent.

It took a step forward in preparation for the attack. Jaime looked around for anything to protect herself. She slowly grabbed a hair brush off of her make up stand and put the used towel in her other hand. She braced herself for the attack. The creature made a deep growl and flexed its muscles for the pouncing move. Jaime brought the towel up to her face in anticipation – but then she heard a animalistic scream, and then a loud thump. She heard another scream, and then another loud thump against the floor. She heard chewing as she lowered the towel from her face and took a look at the floor.

There was something – some creature – standing over the rat. It had its mouth wrapped around its neck, and was chewing through its spine with a set of small, but sharp teeth. It dropped the poisonous predator for a moment, then picked it up again with its mouth, and then jumped up and tossed it in the air. The rat hit the metallic floor again with a loud thump, and her savior jumped on it again, wrapping its small mouth once again around the neck. This time however, she heard a snap as the rat's spine broke. It dropped the now dead rat, and turned to look at Jaime.

It had oatmeal-colored fur on its back tapering into white down its four legs, which then turned into a jet black fur on each of its paws. Its face was similarly colored jet black, with a pair of sapphire blue eyes that stared directly up at her. On the top of its head sat two large pointed ears. Its head formed an almost perfect looking isosceles triangle. On its rear, a long, thin, black, short-haired tail stood straight up into the air. It licked the blood off of its chin, then used its paws to clean its face further – licking the paw then rubbing it to each side of its cheek. Jaime just stood and watched the creature clean itself for a minute before it stopped, and sat down onto its hind legs. It looked up and stared at her with those striking blue eyes.

"What are you my little friend?" she asked. The creature looked at her again, then gave a long and slightly shrill noise. A moment later, two more of the same type of creature appeared from behind the bed – both were larger than her savior. She watched the two look her up and down, and then they appeared to nod at her before turning away from her. The largest of the three picked up the rat by the neck and dragged it off – evidently to consume the creature in another part of the base.

Jaime crouched down to look at the smaller one still sitting in front of her. It watched her for a moment, then did something unexpected – it crouched down on all fours then jumped into her lap. Its claws slightly scratching her legs but not causing any real damage or pain. Her eyes lit up in surprise but she found herself wrapping her arms around the creature to prevent it from falling out of her lap. "What are you little one?" she asked, and was replied with a slight rattling noise from its throat as it rubbed its chin against her arm. She found herself involuntarily petting the soft, silky smooth fur on its back.

Her Norm-Comm gave a slight ping in her head. She tapped her receiver and heard Allen's voice in her head. "Are you ok?"

"Of course. Why wouldn't I be?"

"Something from you gave me a start...was a very odd feeling."

"Odd...well, I did have a space rat in my room. But the darnedest thing happened...I was saved by a small creature."

"Is it still there? Were there more?" he asked with some urgency in his voice.

"Why yes, I saw three of them. One is still here...quite the friendly little thing too!" She caught herself unconsciously petting it again before looking down and realizing what she was doing.

"I know you're tired, but can I get Jonathan and come over to your cabin? It's important."

She gave a sigh "Listen, I have slept so much there is no way I am going to bed tonight. Please, come on over."

He gave a slight acknowledgement and disconnected. She put the creature down, grabbed her uniform and quickly put it on just in time for the door annunciator to ring. She unlocked and opened it with her command console, which allowed the two men to come running in as if putting out a fire. Jonathan looked down at the small creature and his eyes lit up. "You're alive! Thank goodness!"

The creature moved behind Jaime's legs, and stood there while it stared up at the two men.

"So, you know what these are then?" she asked.

"Yes…" Jonathan replied "They are actually animals that lived on earth prior to the war. They are commonly known as cats. In this case, these are cats of the breed Siamese. In ancient times, they were considered a breed of the gods. They protected the ancient families from pestilence…likely from animals that carried disease.

"Well, I can understand their reverence for these creatures" Jaime responded. "This one saved my life." It walked in front of her, and looked up at her again. She crouched down and opened her arms, and it quickly jumped back into her embrace.

"Looks like you've got a friend" Allen said.

Jonathan looked at the cat sitting in her lap, and then grabbed and lifted its tail. "Ah, this is one of the males – the youngest one."

"Jonathan…" Jaime sternly spoke "how much do you know about these creatures, and more importantly…how is it you came to know this?"

"Uhhh…" Jonathan mumbled.

"These creatures were found in stasis containers in one of the alien craft salvaged on Stopper. We realized they were earth creatures, and thus had to save them." Allen replied.

"Well, I see no harm in this. As a matter of fact, if they will clear out *our* vermin…then they will be a blessing. Let's welcome them to our home." Jaime pronounced. She looked down into the cat's blue eyes while pondering "So, what do I call you?" She petted the animal, which replied with the rumbling noise in his throat while he rubbed his head against her hand. Finally, her eyes lit up and she announced "I know…Hero! I am going to call you Hero."

"Well, welcome to our home, Hero!" Allen announced. "You said you saw more of them?"

"Yes..." she replied. "I saw two more. They were larger..."

"Hero's parents, I would assume. Hero here is the youngest..." Jonathan told her.

"How many are there?" she asked.

"I had nine cases. Assuming they all lived, then there should be six more wandering the base" Jonathan replied.

Max walked in at that moment, and interrupted Jonathan as if he had been in the room the entire time "Umm, I hate to break this to you...but I checked the cases after you called and two still had animals in them, both dead...the stasis fields had failed in their cases. One was indeed a cat...the other..." Jonathan gave him a confused look, to which he replied "well, it is a species called a dog. Particularly a breed called Chihuahua. But it was similar colored and sized...so I could see how you might have gotten it confused.

"Dog? So you think there might be more?" he asked Max.

"DNA scans indicate one of the cases had a second Chihuahua in it." He rubbed his chin, thinking for a moment before questioning out loud "I wonder what an alien race would want with Chihuahuas? Well, in any case, all but the two cases were empty...so I would assume the rest of the creatures are running around the base."

Jaime smiled at the three men, then looked down at Hero. "Well, let's hope they are all alive and well, and living with us. Hopefully, Hero will stay here, and the others will find good homes too!" She looked at the little creature and it, in return gave a light meow that caused her to smile and say "Aww!"

About Twenty Five Years ago...

Her fist hit his face with a force powered by rage. It hit so hard that it caused blood to flow freely from his mouth. She may have even loosened a few of his teeth. She felt good, he deserved it. "Do you want to say that about my father again?" she yelled out to him. He just looked at her and shook. The pain in his mouth, and the fear she had placed inside him, prevented him from saying a word. "Maybe I should teach you again not to talk about people's parents?"

A hand on her shoulder stopped her threats. She turned to find her father, he had a stern look on his face. He did not say a word, only nodded toward the direction of the door to the building. They walked in silence until they were all the way inside the building, and safely in their apartment. Not until they were once behind the door and in the security of their home did he say anything. "What did I tell you? You should never make a scene like that. Do you want them to find us...to find me?"

"No papa, I'm sorry. But he said you were a traitor...I could not let him say that about you!" she said with tears in her eyes.

"What if he talks to someone? What if they ask why he is bleeding? You always have to hide your feelings...they give you away. You showed him that he got to you...that he was right" he scolded.

She knew he was right, and she had been a fool. The sirens outside their window drove his point right to their home. He peeked out the curtains "Damn, that kid told them. The Secret Police are right outside."

Father ran into the bedroom and returned wearing a thick jacket. He handed her a pouch "Tuck this inside your shirt and don't let anyone see it." She followed his orders and put the leather pouch under her shirt and zipped the shirt to the top of the collar. "Now, I want you to go outside. If the Secret Service asks you about me, act like I am a stranger to you, then tell them where I am."

"But father!" she cried out, then grabbed and hugged him.

"No, do what I say. I am not going to get away from this...but you will, and you will live and grow. Do you understand?

I have done everything I can to teach you and to keep you protected. You can do it on your own now. Tell them where I am, then do what they say. When you are somewhere where you are totally sure you are alone, open the pouch. Never tell them about me, or that you knew me. Tell me you will...promise me" he pleaded.

She cried and shook her head while trying to mumble out "I will papa. I will do exactly as you say."

"That's my girl. I love you...Jaime, my love...now go...and stay strong."

"I love you too father..." she left him in the apartment and ran out the front door. Two large soldiers in black uniforms were standing outside.

They looked down at her "You there. Someone reported a traitor in this building. He may be a mad bomber and needs to be stopped. Can you tell us where he is?"

She wiped any remaining tears from her face before she looked up at the soldier and said "Yes, I know who you are talking about. He is on the third floor...apartment 14."

"You have done the Order proud this day" said a man wearing a dark hooded cape. She could see his ghost white face and a slight smile on his face while he looked at her. "Who are your parents, young one?"

"I have no parents" she replied with sorrow in her soul "they died a long time ago..."

"Well, you have a family now. The Order will care for you. You are a hero now. You will learn to be a valuable citizen and member of the Order. You will grow with us, now come along." The ghost led her to a hovercar and took her away. As they left, the explosion rocked the vehicle. They stopped and she looked in the rear window at the pile of rubble that was once their home. The ghost turned back around and down at her once again "See, that person you turned in was a danger to everything and everyone. I wonder just how many people he killed today, and they call themselves pacifists...People Against War...Humph! Well, he eliminated himself and is no longer a threat...and it was all thanks to you."

She was taken to an Alliance base and registered in the Alliance Youth Corp. She was given a cot, food, and was then left alone to reflect on her heroism and what she will do in the future. That evening, she slipped out to a spot where she knew she was alone. She took out the pouch and opened it. Inside was a credit chip full of Alliance credits – enough to live off of comfortably for years – she later found a secure hiding place for that. Also inside was a holo-image of her mother and a small note that only had two words: "Stay Strong".

NGD: 1 Year, 7 Months and 4 Days

The Black Asteroid Base:

Jaime Bordeaux:

She breathed lightly as she jogged down the well-lit corridors of the base. Hero followed closely behind her – he knew better than to get in front of her when she was running. After jogging for miles of corridors, and countless flights of stairs, she finally arrived at the docking structure for the newly built starship. The Dragon starship was finally ready for its final test flight. She stopped at the viewing window and stared at the massive craft. She picked up Hero and pointed him at the window.

"That is what we are going to be riding in soon…" she told the little animal. Hero gave a small meow, and purred.

She admired the ship that sat out in the dock. It was clad in dark-black, reinforced, space carbon alloy panels. She examined from afar the three sections of the craft – the command module, the living connector and the rear engineering section. The command module in the front was a flattened, triangle shape, had rounded wing tips, and a flat backside. The module had a curvature that sloped downward from the center as if it had just motioned its large bulky wings downward in a flap. There was a connecting structure which was rounded, but covered with a curved skin of armor plating that covered the top and sides of the connector – this was the living section with quarters and crew entertainment areas. The engineering section was comprised of three hexagon shaped units, covered on both top and bottom by a similar curved-shaped, black plates of space carbon armor. The hyper-crawler drives sat in the middle of this module, a slight blue glow emitted from the large maw of the engine. Around these drives sat enhanced Pulsar drive engines. On each side of the ray-shaped cover of this module were two of the RFS engines for high speed travel. The engines were protected by the armor covering of similar shaped plates of space carbon alloy.

As she studied the ship she petted Hero, then asked him "Isn't it pretty?" The cat purred even louder.

"Why thank you! We worked hard to make this craft the pride of the future fleet!" said a voice from behind. Jaime turned to see Chief Engineer Kate Grayson emerging from the gangway. "Good to see you Alpha Starship Captain" she said while she gave an Alliance salute.

Jaime waved her hand at her in a manner of saying "no". "I decided earlier that the first change should be my title and that salute. Let's just call me Captain...no order ranks...and do an old fashioned salute, shall we?" She put the cat down, raised her hand to her forehead, and gave the engineer a quick snapping single salute.

Kate followed suit with a similar, albeit less confident salute while saying "Captain..."

Jaime looked across the dock. Two more ships were in various phases of construction – one appeared to be another Dragon class, the other a smaller version of a similar design. "So, another Dragon class, and...?"

"That is a Wyvern class cruiser, Captain" she replied. "Will hold a crew of four thousand and will provide support for the Dragon class battleships."

"They are beauties aren't they?" Allen asked as he walked into the docking station.

"They are Captain, everyone here should be proud of what you've accomplished. So, when do we depart?"

"Captain?" he queried.

"The test run, when do we leave?"

"Umm, I really think that we should first test the craft one last time before you come onboard."

"Nonsense!" Jaime barked. "I will come along. I have faith in this craft and all of the technology that has been developed. I see no reason not to personally take her out on her final test voyage."

"If you insist..." Allen softly said. Jaime nodded her head then returned to her viewing of the craft.

Jonathan showed up a minute later and was also surprised to find Jaime ready to board. He gave her a questioning look to which she replied "Me and Hero are going along. We would not miss this for the world!" He just nodded in acceptance.

"Well in that case, I should come along too!" Jaime turned around and saw Halley entering the room. She had joined them even though she was not on the official roster. She gave the young helmsman an approving nod.

Allen gave a pained look "So, now we have our most experienced helmsman, engineers and captain on the final test flight. Anyone else I should worry about?"

"How about a science officer?" said Katsumi entering the boarding room right behind Halley.

"You'll need someone to test the comm system too. There is no way I am going to let anyone else interface with this system first. "Said Otter who walked in right behind Katsumi.

"The same with weapons..." Said Yuli who walked in at the same time as Otter. Allen just shook his head.

"So, somehow everyone found out about the test flight..." muttered Allen.

"I think we have a test crew..." Jaime said "let's get moving."

"Wait!" Max called out as he entered the room. "I think before you go, you will need these..." he handed her a small box. She opened the box to find two small golden dragon-head pins "For your collars...Captain."

Everyone gave her a round of applause as she blushed, then took the two insignias out of the box and placed them on the side of each collar. "How long have you been holding on to these Max?"

He gave a slight chuckle "Ever since I released you from the sick bay...knew you would need them sooner than later."

Once she applied the insignias to her collar she looked around the room, and everyone gave her a sharp salute – even the civilians. She slightly blushed while she returned the salute, then said "Thank you, everyone! Now, let's get aboard."

They crossed the gangway while Jonathan reviewed the test plan to the crew. "So, first we will test the Pulsars for sub-light speed. Then activate the automated Gravitons. After that, we will make a run with the RFS..."

"Jonathan, what the hell does RFS stand for anyway?" Jaime asked.

"RFS...Really Fast Stardrive..." he replied which caused Jaime to raise her eyebrows then softly giggle. "We...we couldn't come up with anything snappier...In any case, after that test we will test the hyper-crawler and finally test the weapons and defensive systems."

"Defensive, so the bubble works?" she asked.

"We hope" replied Kate. "It has worked in all our other tests. I know Jonathan's calculations are correct for this size of ship. I'm positive it will work. It only protects us from beamed weapons so far though. Jonathan should have a gravity bubble completed soon, that will protect us from physical weapons. He will have it done very soon, I am sure."

Jaime looked at Kate who was giving looks to Jonathan. She saw the glimmer in her eyes when she looked at him. He blushed when he caught her giving him those warm looks. She suspected something was there – a May-December relationship perhaps. Then she looked at Kate's hand and noticed a slight blackening of the skin – she wondered if she had bruised it somehow, or was it something else?

They proceeded to the bridge. It was configured in a similar manner to the bridge of the Starlight. Jonathan told the group "We thought we would keep the configuration similar to the ships we have been working on up to this point. No need to retrain crew on operational stations..." Jaime nodded in agreement. She stepped onto the bridge and looked down at the floor – there were round metal plates behind every command station on the bridge, and one in front of her command chair. Jaime looked at the plates, pointed at them and looked at Jonathan.

"Future enhancements..." is all he said in reply to her quizzing look.

Jaime realized she had *her* bridge crew and this was *her* ship. This was going to be the first time she was going to command without reprise – and she was quietly excited to be in this position. She sat down in the command chair, Allen took the first officers station – which could assist any command position on the bridge. The rest took their appointed stations -- Halley took the helm, Jonathan the engineering station, Katsumi science, Otter communications and Yuli weapons. Hero jumped into Jaime's lap and joined her at command. She looked for the command interface to bind to, but it was not to be found.

"There is not an interface Captain..." Jonathan announced after he determined her confusion. "The command chair is DNA keyed. As soon as you sat down, it recognized you and, provided command control to you."

She looked at the command holographic interface and indeed, it had already recognized her, and had already provided detailed information about the ship's status. She nodded her head, impressed with the efficiency of the new interface. "Okay, well let's fire her up. Helm, put the controls in station keeping. Communications, signal the dock we are ready to leave. Science, fire up the advanced scanners as soon as we are clear of the dock, weapons in passive mode. Jonathan, are those Pulsars ready to roll?"

"Fusion reactors are high by five – they are at high output, reaction level five. All engines are ready at your command Captain." Jonathan announced.

"We are cleared for departure. Docking connectors and gangways are released and cleared" Otter announced.

"Ok...Halley, fire up the Pulsars, one-one hundredth speed – Take us out." Jaime found her palms sweating with excitement. It had been so long since she had taken control of a starship. The last (and only time) was when they ended up in this strange, new galaxy. But now it was finally happening – she was in command of a ship of her own.

The ship left its mooring and slowly proceeded to the opening space dock doors. The doors had opened sufficiently by the time they reached them and the ship glided out of the space dock smoothly and efficiently. The stars of outer space filled the imaging panels that surrounded the bridge command stations. The holo-display showed current front view with individual command information being provided to each station.

Once they were totally outside the dock Jaime commanded "Okay Halley, push the Pulsars to full power, let's take them to our first waypoint."

Halley pressed the power control lever forward engaging the Pulsar drives. The drives smoothly and quietly began their pulsing, which provided magnetic thrust to the ship and pushed it to one-tenth the speed of light. "Pulsars are fully engaged, running full and smoothly Captain."

Jaime turned to Jonathan "Give my compliments to Kate – the engines are running perfectly." He nodded in agreement.

Within an hour they arrived at the waypoint. Jaime examined the test plan on her command holograph. "Okay, now we engage the coils and add the Graviton drives for additional propulsion. Katsumi, I am told that the new Graviton control no longer needs human intervention, am I correct?"

"That is correct Captain" Katsumi replied.

"Very well. Jonathan, engage the Graviton coils and activate the computer controller."

He immediately followed her orders and activated the coils. They could feel the power being applied to the coils as a slight bit of static electricity filled the air – this static subsided within a minute of coil activation. The front field coils began finding attraction points while the rear collected and expelled dark energy for repulsion.

Halley watched as the computer maintained a constant speed while the Pulsar drives output was reduced. "Captain, Pulsars have lowered output but speed is remaining constant. I would say the Graviton is working."

"Captain..." Jonathan called out "our reactor output has reduced to fifty percent of what it was prior to activation of the Graviton."

"Good, good...maintain current course and speed then. So far, so good..."

After an hour of travel, they approached a system with a red dwarf star. Jaime examined her command console at the system ahead.

Halley called out "Captain, we are at the waypoint. I am setting course for the insertion point and will proceed with your word using the RFS."

Jaime nodded acknowledgement "Very good, proceed." Halley activated the two RFS engines, engaged the speed control on the helm, and the ship took off – within seconds they were nearing the speed of light. Jamie gave a slight gasp at the speed that was being delivered by the two high-speed ion drives.

Within minutes, they were at the insertion point for the test of the hyper-crawler drive. Halley deactivated the RFS and put the ship into a full stop as they arrived at the insertion point. She activated the navigational computers to calculate the sub-space flight. "Captain, computers are now formulating sub-space insertion."

"Very well Halley. Jonathan, how long will we have to wait before the computer finishes the formulations for insertion?"

Jonathan looked up from the console "Not sure really. We have the new computers doing the formulation. So, I am not really sure how long it will take. Normally on the Starlight, it would take two days to formulate the insertion for this trip, but with the new three dimensional processors who knows?" He looked down at his console again then looked back up with a confused look on his face "Umm, well the computer just signaled…"

Halley called out "Formulation complete. We have guidance computations for sub-space insertion."

"What? Really?" Jaime asked amazed.

"Impressive…" said Jonathan. "The new three dimensional computers really are much more advanced than what we ever had in the past. I am amazed at how quickly they can calculate sub-spatial navigation. We truly now have an advantage over the Blessed."

"An advantage we want to keep quiet" Jaime advised, to which Jonathan nodded in agreement. "Ok Halley, insert us into sub-space."

The enhanced ram beams fired and quickly opened a rift in the fabric of space. Halley launched a chaser particle, a door knocker ram beam shot, then activated the crawler drive. The crawler drive fired up, and quickly pushed the ship through the opening and into the void of sub-space. At the speed at which they entered the tear, they all felt the effect of entry on their bodies. Hero gave a slight whine in discomfort. Jaime petted the small animal while she herself gave a slight moan from pressure pain. The pressure equalized as the computer adjusted the thrust, the inertia dampers adjusted the gravity pressure inside the ship, and their bodies acclimated to the sub-space effect.

"Wow, ok I had not felt pressure like that in a while. I thought I was used to sub-space travel." Jaime admitted.

"Well, we are traveling faster than we ever have in sub-space, Captain" said Katsumi. "We should cross the void and reach the reentry point in…three hours."

"Three hours?" Yuli queried. "I thought this trip normally took three days?"

"It does…or did…" Jonathan answered. "With the new hyper-crawler however, we are traveling faster than we ever have in the void. With adjustment, we may be able to travel even faster in the future."

"Amazing…" Yuli admitted.

Three hours later the chaser arrived at the exit point. The door knocker beam followed the chaser particle and began to mark the spot where the ship would tear an opening for an exit point back into normal space. It struck the chaser and scuffed the fabric of space. Halley spotted the scuff and activated the sub-space battering ram beams onto the point of the scuff. It quickly formed a vortex in the fabric of space and within a few seconds had torn a hole big enough for the ship to pass. She boosted crawler output and pushed the ship out into normal space.

"Whew, that was quick!" Allen called out.

Jaime checked her test plan "Ok, next stop..." she was interrupted by klaxons indicating the approach of an unknown spacecraft. She looked at Katsumi who was analyzing the returns from the advance scanners and SCADAR.

"Captain, we have an unrecognized ship coming in at a vector that might be considered aggressive. They have activated weapons..."

The incoming ship was a long, pointed cylinder with pointed, wing-like protrusions coming out from each side of the body, and one on the top like a fish's fin. It had a single high speed engine in the back of the craft. It was about half the size of the Dragon, and the front of the cylinder focused down into a dull rounded tip.

"Yuli, fire up our weapons. Katsumi, give him fire points. Yuli place your targeting locks based on the analysis. Look sharp everyone..."

The unknown ship fired a volley of accelerated photon beams and proton bolts at the ship. The beams mostly bounced off of the space carbon enhanced hull. Some minor damage was recorded – mostly scuffing of the hull plates.

"Shit, fire back Yuli!" Jaime ordered. Another volley of beams along with projectile shells were launched against the mysterious craft. "Ok, Jonathan activate the bubble – let's see if it works."

He activated the bubble and the images on the star screens faded and blurred for a moment before returning to normal. "Bubble up!" Jonathan announced. The ship fired another volley – this time the beams bounced off of the bubble, and travelled harmlessly into space. The shells continued through the bubble but only caused minor damage to the armor hull plates.

"Yes! Ok Yuli, let them have it...fire what you need to disable the craft" she ordered. Yuli followed the order, and first fired a round of cutter lasers, which did some minor damage.

He selected p-accelerators and fired – some more minor damage. He switched to the rail guns and fired – more minor damage. "Crap..." he muttered as he looked at his weapons selector. He noticed something labeled "Ultras". He shrugged his shoulders before selecting the unknown weapon and firing. Purple beams shot from the ship and pummeled the attacker. The force of the beams ripped holes into the engines of the attacking ship. The engines sputtered and died – the ship slowed, and then started to drift. "Holly crap! Whatever those are, they kick ass!" He began to target for another barrage.

"Okay, stop Yuli" Jaime ordered. "Let's see who this is. Now they might be in a mood to talk..." She nodded at Otter who sent out universal hails. A moment later, a deer's face appeared on the main holo-screen.

"Hello, Normal craft..." It was Oomha.

Jaime stood up, placed Hero in the command chair and walked up to the display. "Oomha, what the hell are you doing?"

"It was a test...unscheduled of course. I thought you would want something realistic to test your new ship. So, I sent this drone. I was glad to see you acted as I expected and battled with restraint. You Normals truly are worthy of this galaxy's friendship."

"Thank you my friend...for not only this perfect test, but your trust, and the friendship of the Flaybah...and of your personal friendship." She looked around the bridge "Very good everyone. Stand down our battle status...deactivate the bubble and weapons, put everything into standby." Once again she looked at Oomha "Okay, we are headed back to base. Will we see you there?"

"Yes Jaime. I will be there soon. Likely in a few cycles. Until then." The deer nodded and disconnected.

She picked up Hero from the command chair and held him in her arms. She sat back down and ordered. "Okay, take us home Halley. Allen, when we get back, have a team paint Alliance flags on the sides."

Jonathan and Allen both turned and gave confused stares. Finally Allen spoke up "Captain, why put an Alliance flag on this ship? We are no longer Alliance and we definitely are not with the Blessed. They almost killed you!"

"As much as I hate to say this...but for the moment we ARE still Alliance. But only for the moment. SO, we have to play the part and be good soldiers – and put the flag on the ship...for now..." She looked around the bridge again "And this is a wonderful ship..." She thought for another moment before announcing "We still need to figure out a name for her however..."

Yuli Capsain:

As soon as the ship entered subspace after the practice encounter, Yuli ran over to the engineering station. Jonathan was busy completing final checks before shift change.

"Jonathan, you HAVE to tell me about those new weapons!"

The young man looked at Yuli and smiled "How about I just show you?" The weapons master gave a big toothy smile and a nod.

The two left the bridge, and took the lift down twenty levels to the middle of the command section. From there, they walked a long corridor until they could go no further. The pair stopped at a large door leading to one of the compartments located at the edge of the large manta ray-shaped command section of the Dragon starship. As they approached the large faratainium door, Jonathan stopped and took down two radiation sensors from a shelf next to the door. He handed one to Yuli "Just in case...It's safe...fairly..." he said, then gave a small chuckle.

Yuli smiled while hoping he really was joking, and attached the sensor to his uniform. Jonathan activated the hatch, and the door slid open which exposed a large room filled with various metallic boxes all attached to the far wall and pointed outward to outer space. All of the boxes nearest to him were closed but had hatches allowing access, and the ability to open each containment unit. In addition, each box had a multitude of cables, hoses and other power feeds, some of which he did not recognize – and with his knowledge of weaponry, he knew almost every type of starship weapon and virtually every connection that should be hooked up to those weapons.

Yuli whistled "Wow, I am impressed! I can tell those up there are the cutter lasers..." he then pointed to a box with a number of plasma conduits attached "these are plasma emitters..." He walked over to sets of large boxes with large round conduits attached. He followed the conduits to a machine that had racks of round projectile shells loaded into magazines ready to be moved through the conduits into the large boxes. "Rail launchers...no radiation shields however...also, does not look like plutonium..."

Jonathan shook his head no "These are off-line right now, but soon you will not fire spent plutonium any longer. We have discovered how to make heavy gravity projectiles. Much more...effective..."

"Ah, very good!" he responded. He walked over to another set of metallic boxes. More generic cabling fed the units inside "Particle accelerators I assume?"

"Yep, you have not lost it at all! Scoring one hundred percent so far" he acknowledged.

He walked over to a set of smaller boxes attached to the wall. These boxes had square conduits attached running across guides, which lead out of the weapons bay and in toward the middle of the ship. "What about this? Not sure I recognize these..."

He walked all around one of the ten foot long boxes. He eyed the sides – each side was three feet wide. He eyed the conduits leading out again. Finally, he shook his head "I have...no idea..."

Jonathan gave a short burst of laughter – quite unlike him Yuli thought – then said "Those are the latest in ship's weaponry...the Ultras."

"Ultras? AH! I fired those and I must say, they kicked ass!" He looked at the boxes again "What are they? Can we open one up?"

"Sure..." Jonathan said as he checked the seals on the weapon port, checked the atmospheric pressure in the containment box, then released the seals, released the locks on the bottom of the box that held it together, activated motors to open it like a clam shell, and finally activated actuator motors which moved the box up and out of the way. Now exposed was a polymer tube that was inserted into the wall of the weapons bay. The tube was coated in a metallic substance to prevent energy leakage, it had cables attached in the back and the square conduits attached to ports in the middle of the two foot diameter tube. "There you have it...the Ultra."

He looked it up and down then whistled "Man, that is a beauty. Did you design it?"

A voice from behind him gave him a start "No, I did..."

He turned to find a woman standing behind him. She was about three inches shorter than his six foot frame, was quite muscular, but still thin as shown by her tight fitting space-resistant uniform. Her hair was jet black and hung straight down around her head. She had bangs that were cut sharp and straight across her forehead. The bangs hung straight down covering her eye brows but stopped just a millimeter above her chestnut brown eyes. Where the bangs stopped, the hair fell straight down the sides of her face as if she was wearing a helmet. Her hair draped down below her shoulders, around the front and back, and was cut once again to a razor sharp straight line. She had a small nose that slightly curved up, and small full lips that lightly floated above her rounded chin and filled enough space between her full cheeks to not become lost. Yuli was not sure if he was more taken aback by her knowledge of starship weaponry, or her beauty.

"My name is Nova Jones. You must be Yuli?" She extended a small hand to greet him.

He paused for a moment before he replied "Yes, Yuli...Yuli Capsain. Weapons Master..." He reached out and took her hand, and was given a light but firm shake from the woman. He felt a light tingle upon her hand touching his.

"Ah, I am a Weapons Master too. I have heard a lot about you Yuli." She glanced down at her hand after releasing his shake.

"So, will you tell me what exactly an Ultra is?" he waved at the tube to his side.

"Of course!" she replied as she reached up and opened a viewing portal. "The technical name for this is the Ultraviolet Charged Matter Accelerator. However, that is a little too long to say quickly...so we shortened it to "Ultras"."

He peered into the portal at the purple glowing charged gas inside the chamber as she continued "It is a Deuterium exciter you are peering into."

He continued to look at the glowing purple gas inside the chamber. "So, you are using Ultraviolet? That isn't strong enough to do damage to a ship's hull. The beam I fired tore through that drone like it was made of paper. What else is going on here?"

"Ah, that is what these conduits are for. As you know, the Gravitons use dark energy for the repulsion that is used to help propel us around. Well, the field coils that we use to push that energy through also take in dark matter. Dark matter has the opposite effect on our drive, so we filter it out in the wave guides and store it in tanks in the most well-protected areas of the ship. Then these wave guide conduits move the dark matter from the tanks and inject it into the core here. The excited gas generates the ultraviolet, which is forced through the exciter exhaust into the injection core right above that viewing portal. The dark matter is injected into the exiting UV beam and voilà, we have an Ultra beam."

"Impressive. I would have never come up with that. You are a weapons genius." He looked into her brown eyes, and for a moment became lost in them. She also said nothing for that same moment. Without thinking further he asked "Perhaps, you would join me for dinner sometime? We could discuss weapon design and arrangement?"

She smiled and quickly said "I would love that! How about tonight?"

Her quick acceptance took him slightly by surprise "Why…why, sure…We'll be in subspace a few hours, so there's time to kill…Say eighteen hundred? I will come by to get you?"

"I look forward to it…" she reached out and shook his hand again. "Until this evening, Yuli…" she turned, and walked away – turning her head slightly to glance at him as she left.

Yuli stood and watched her walk away, slightly dumbfounded. "I didn't expect that…" he softly told Jonathan.

The young man smiled at him "What, a woman finally accepting your bold attempt at a date? Well, you're both Weapons Masters…perhaps there is something to having a talent in common? Or perhaps, when you shook hands you bonded somewhat?"

"Bonded?" he asked.

"Yes, it seems to be happening when two Normals touch and are compatible. They feel something between them. Later, if they are totally compatible, they find they start…changing…everyone is calling it reconfiguring. I will stop there and let you discover that for yourself."

"So, did you and Kate find that change?" he said with a shit-eating grin on his face.

Jonathan blushed, but then only said "Come on, let's go grab a snack. Since you mentioned food, I am starved!"

As they started to walk out of the weapons bay, Yuli turned and looked back inside. Nova was working on one of the launchers, but stopped and looked up. She smiled as she watched him turn to look at her before walking away. He smiled and gave a small wave. On the way out the door, he looked down at his hand. It still slightly tingled.

*   *   *

Eighteen hundred hours could not have come quick enough for Yuli. For the first time in years, he was so excited to be going on a date. Sure, he had dated many women before leaving Earth, but this felt so different, and he wondered why.

He arrived at her door a minute early. He breathed into his palm to give one last check of his breath, checked his uniform – a tight, black, casual, one piece suit – and then looked at his chronometer before finally ringing the annunciator. She answered wearing a light blue tunic top with matching short skirt, exposed legs to a pair of tight matching boots that stopped just below her knees. Her shapely legs were a thing of beauty to his eyes – he attempted not to stare, but had a hard time resisting the urge – he finally gave in to his desires, and took a good look up and down. She caught him, and blushed slightly before giving a small smile and giggle.

"You look lovely!" he said with excitement in his voice. She smiled again and nodded. He extended an arm "Shall we go? I have a picked a nice spot and reserved a table with a subspace view."

She took his arm "Absolutely, my Weapon's Master. Lead on!"

The pair enjoyed a wonderful dinner of freshly grown vegetables raised at the asteroid's hydroponics gardens, a perfectly cooked protein base sautéed in a mushroom-like sauce, and a sweet soy dessert. After the meal, they sat at the table, looking out at the various energy ebbs and flows that the ship caused during its voyage within the void of subspace.

"Beautiful isn't it?" he asked.

She nodded "It is. It for some reason took me so long to get used to it – subspace. I don't know why, it affected me longer than most. But I am ok now...I guess my body was just not as adaptable as most Normals."

"My dear, I see nothing that is not-adaptable when I look at you." She blushed. He gave her a moment to look out at the moving nothingness before he asked "So, where did you come from? What did you do before leaving with Starlight?"

"Well, for most of my youth I busted ass trying to get my weapons certifications. I knew since I was a child that was my destiny – my duty. I knew that would be the way I would become valuable to the Alliance, through my ability to learn and use weapons. It was my mother...she taught me to protect myself. When she died, I found myself alone and only had myself to depend on. I lived in sector one...I am not sure if you ever went there..." He shook his head no. "Well, it is NOT a good place to be a young girl with no parents. The hub of the Alliance, and yet one of the worst slums on the planet. I was stuck there for three years after my mother died. The pimps tried to get me – tried to force me to sell myself. Once a couple pimps tried to force me – they kidnapped me – but that only happened once as they found out that trying to force me to do anything was a big mistake. My mother taught me the use of a mini-blaster...and she taught me to aim straight and fire firm. If that didn't work, then there were the blades...I am good at using those too!"

She paused and looked pained as she thought about her past "You don't have to talk about it...its ok" he told her.

"No...no...it is actually good to have someone to talk about it with. Why do I feel so close and comfortable with you? I just met you?"

"No idea...but I feel the same...and I too don't know why. But I like the feeling..." He took her hand and felt the warmth and tingling again. "Please, go on..."

"Well, during those three years, I was able to land a job providing weapon cleaning and tuning services to the Secret Service soldiers that worked in sector one. I was surprised to find they preferred to not clean or tune their own weapons. I was good at it...and I made good money cleaning for them...good enough to be able to afford transport and to buy my way into advanced college. Of course, my choice of studies was..."

"Weapons..." he chimed in. "I had a similar childhood, except in the former Russia. My father survived the conflict but was injured in battle...so he got an honorable discharge, met my mother and had me. She died a few years later in a food riot, so he was left taking care of me. He too knew weapons and taught me what he knew. I managed to get into a placement testing center...ok, I forged an access card...in any case, it got me in, and I placed myself into weaponry school. I excelled, and eventually I ended up in Star Force as a bombardier over Mars. The rest is history."

"Somehow...I think history is just about to begin...here...now..." she said.

He reached up and touched her face causing a tingle on her skin. She closed her eyes and he slowly lowered his head and met her lips in a soft and tender kiss.

Later, he walked her back to her cabin, gave her one last very passionate good night kiss, and left her to return to his respective cabin. Sleep came quickly to him despite the tingling in his hand and on his lips.

*   *   *

The next morning he woke up fully rested and ready for his shift. He cleaned, dressed and quickly headed to for the bridge. He arrived on the bridge well before his scheduled start time, relieved the weapons officer on duty, and began his check list and preparations when he realized everyone was staring at him. A couple of them were slightly chuckling, but a couple other members of the bridge crew were looking at him with worried looks on their faces.

"Ok, I give...what's up? Do I have food on my face or something?"

Jonathan came across the bridge, and looked at each side of his face while adjusting the vision on his glasses. Yuli raised his eyebrows as if questioning him without saying a word. Finally, the young man softly said "Have you looked at yourself recently?" Yuli shook his head no. "Well, I think you should maybe go see doc Sollix. Looks like you ran into something...or did you get into a fight while on your date?"

"What?" he questioned. He took out his computer film, unrolled it, and turned on the facial camera so he could see himself. His jaw dropped when he saw his face on the screen. His lips were a dark, deep shade of a midnight blue. The rest of his face was normal flesh tone, however. He let the computer drop out of his hand before saying "I...think you...are right...I'd better go now. Can you get someone to fill in?"

"I will call in a substitute and inform the Captain. Go..."

He quickly ran to the sick bay. Max was behind his desk and attempted to hide his surprise when he walked in. Yuli wished he could somehow hide his deep blue lips, but it was impossible.

Max slowly stood up and looked at his mouth before saying "Let me guess why you are here..." He picked up his medical scanner, and waved it over and over across his face. He read the output before mumbling "Hmmm..."

"Doc! What is wrong with me?"

"Yuli, have you had physical contact with anyone lately?" he looked at his readouts again. "Contact with a female...or even a male? Hmm?"

Yuli nodded "Yes, I had a date last night..." then quickly added "with a girl."

"Ah! Did you kiss her?" Yuli nodded yes. "Ok, that makes sense. Too bad you didn't touch her a little stronger somewhere else." Now Yuli showed a look of total confusion on his face. "Ah! Well, lately as you know...or maybe you didn't...we have been changing. For example, we have all been growing these fine sets of wings on our ears. There have been a great many other changes in our DNA also. It appears that one of the changes that has occurred, is when we meet a compatible mate. On first touch, we notice a "feeling"...later, when we touch with more passion, the DNA of the cells of one partner seem to transfer, then bond with our own DNA in the area of contact. Most have noticed it happen from a casual but deep contact...a hand on the shoulder, or a contact when sitting close together. In any case, the DNA starts to change, and then the skin turns this dark color as the cells in our bodies begin to reconfigure – the color seems to match our home asteroid. I think the space carbon of the asteroid has somehow bonded into our systems and upon contact, the DNA mutates and the carbon comes to the surface. There is nothing harmful...as a matter of fact, the skin becomes more flexible, strong, and resistant to damage, but still soft and healthy feeling."

"Doc, I can't walk around with these lips!" He then pleaded "Do something!"

"Alright...give me a moment. Perhaps I can do some cosmetic manipulation. It won't change them...but it will cover them."

At that moment, the sick bay door opened, and Nova walked in. "Doctor, do you have something for a rash? I..." she stopped and looked at Yuli who put his hands over his mouth and turned his head. "Yuli, what are you doing here? What's wrong?"

"Please...don't...look..." he mumbled. She came up and moved his hand from his face and looked at him. She looked at his dark lips and smiled.

He looked at her and noticed her lips were plump and slightly darkened. Not black like his, but they looked slightly bruised. She then held up a hand – her palm was a dark shade of blackish-blue.

Max looked at the two and smiled. "Ok, so now I know who you kissed..." he took her hand and examined it. It looked slightly different than other's that had the DNA change which made him examine it even closer.

He took his scanner out and was about to wave it across her hand when she pulled it back and away. "Doctor, no...I don't...don't like to be scanned." She smiled lightly at him. "I was hoping you had something for this itch I have gotten on my hand for obvious reasons."

"Of course. You too Yuli...just a moment" he said as he left the room.

She looked at Yuli and blushed, then let out a small giggle. "So, what does this mean?" she asked him.

"According to the doc...it means we are compatible..."

"Yes" Max interrupted as he walked back into the room. "I have found this only happens to DNA compatible people. People that are meant to be together, and to eventually mate." He started rubbing the cosmetic manipulator on Yuli's lips. They started to lighten slightly as he worked. "As a matter of fact, the Captain has decreed that any Alliance law, or Order decree preventing sexual contact and reproduction has been deemed defunct, and has been lifted. Any couples who find themselves to be DNA compatible as you two are showing...have been given the blessing of all Normals to mate if they wish."

"Really?" Nova asked.

"Yep" Max acknowledged. "Anytime you two want...you can!" He worked a few more minutes on Yuli's lips until it was virtually impossible to see the blackness under the coverage. He then walked over to the dispensary and retrieved a tube of salve and handed it to Nova. "Ok, that will do it." He started to return to his desk, then stopped and turned to the two of them. "Anytime you decide, it will be welcomed. We have to grow to survive."

They thanked Max, and left the sick bay. Yuli stopped and took her hands into his, then looked into her dark brown eyes. She returned the deep stare, her mouth slightly opened, wanting to say something, but was not sure what.

Finally, Yuli broke the silence "How about we do a few more dates? I would like to really know you as best as possible. What do you think?"

She nodded her head "Yes, a few more dates. How about again tonight? Tomorrow, I actually will have weapons station shift after you."

"Ok then, tonight! Until then..." he gave her a light kiss before he returned to duty – a slight shade of black began to once again show as he returned to the bridge. But this time, he didn't care.

Starlight Space Ark:

Kip Gurrigan:

They stood in the space between the layers that made up the hull of Starlight. There was no provided atmosphere or heat in this level. Kip stumbled as he was not used to either wearing a space suit or walking in the lack of gravity. He walked with a group of technicians amongst rows of thousands of sealed tubes. Behind them was a train of fifty anti-gravity trailers, each had three brackets that were shaped to hold one of the tubes.

One of the technicians told Kip "There are one hundred and fifty rows of a thousand tubes. Each tube is capable of holding three sleepers, Alpha Starship Captain. Thus, we have a total of four hundred and fifty thousand frozen sleepers. About fifty thousand are Norms, we have another seventy five thousand more Blessed and the rest...well you know. I am curious however, my Alpha Starship Captain...as much as we are honored that you are accompanying us...we are however, curious as to why?"

"The Star Force Commander requested that I personally select the first of these tubes for retrieval." He went through his command computer and selected a name and tube. "Yes, this one...find tube 5Z-894."

The technician acknowledged and began to lead the group to the specific tube. After walking for twenty minutes they came upon a tube with the same identification number painted on the end. "This is the tube you requested my Alpha Starship Captain."

"Take that tube and load it separately. After that select this tube – 2A-231, and load it along with this tube. Once that is done, separate this mover and take it into the lab. Then start the awakening as ordered by our Star Force Commander."

"I will do as you command my Alpha Starship Captain!" the technician shouted.

He waved off the technician "Yes, yes..."

Once back inside the standard temperature and gravity of the controlled environment of Starlight, Kip removed his space suit. After he was back in a standard uniform, he was joined by his first – Stanford Massey. The two of them proceeded to the laboratory where the two tubes had been brought into the ship and now sat held above the floor by mechanical arms. Frost covered the two tubes, and they steamed as they slowly thawed in the controlled temperature. As he entered the lab, he immediately barked orders to the technicians "You there! Open tube 5Z-894. Pull out number 2 and begin the thaw process."

Large mechanical arms were secured on the end of the tube. Locking bolts on the tube were loosened, then removed, and finally the arms slowly opened the tube. Frigid air escaped as the pressure changed inside the tube. The two peered inside the tube

– it was divided into three segments. Inside each segment was a human body, frozen solid.

Kip and Stanford looked closer into the tube at the three bodies. Kip pointed at the body in the tube he wished to be taken out and repeated "Remove number two...Do what you want with the other two...they are only Norms...probably not worth anything...although, one appears to be a pretty girl." He tapped a finger to his lips before ordering "Do not dispose of them, go ahead and thaw them out too. Let me know once *she* has been thawed out."

The technicians nodded in acknowledgement, then pulled the body of a male out of slot number two. He was an older man – a Normal, with scars on his lips, above his left eye and one on his cheek. As the two men looked at the frozen man, Stanford asked Kip "Who is this number two?"

"A fighter pilot...Benedict "Messiah" Marsh. Bah, everything about this man is blasphemous...and because of that, he is going to fly through the Devil's Throat for us."

Six Years Ago...

Her injury forced her to convalesce in the sector 10 recovery center, near the border of the battle zone that encompassed the whole of Central America. She had a hole in her leg that was now healing, and radiation burns from the blast of a nuke that she herself launched against the enemy. Once again, she sacrificed herself for the benefit of her fellow Alliance soldiers. Her heroism had saved not only herself, but the lives of the men that fought beside her

She was laid up in the hospital ward, her leg supported in the air by a magnetic field to immobilize it while it healed. She was not allowed to move it at all until the doctors decided she was ready for therapy. So, she just lay there and watched the Alliance News Network that was playing across the room – more propaganda for the masses, but it kept her from going totally stir crazy.

"You look bored to death, just like me" said a voice to her side. She turned her head to find a man had quietly walked up and was now sitting in the chair next to her bed. He was handsome she thought – brown wavy hair that slightly hung down across his small forehead, a strong chin, smooth, clean shaven skin on his face, brown eyes with thick eyebrows, and a wide but not large mouth that housed a perfect set of teeth.

He looked at the news imager and shook his head. "What's it all for?" he asked. She started to open her mouth but he interrupted "don't answer...you just looked bored so I thought I would say hi." He took out a pack of cigarettes "Smoke?" he asked and tipped the package at her.

"Are you kidding? Blech!" she blurted out.

He smiled, took one out of the pack, and popped between his smooth lips.

She gave him a look of disgust "You are not going to light that in here are you? I would rather smell burning flesh than one of those. Please leave..."

"Aww, come on..." he said as he blew into it and a puff of smoke-like powder ejected out the end. She tried to not take a breath but he caught her by surprise. She gave him a look of

surprise as she realized she could not smell anything. He laughed, took it out of his mouth, turned it on end so she could see it, and pointed at the pink end. "Bubble gum..." he said with a chuckle as he unwrapped the white paper and popped the pink stick into his mouth. "Sure you don't want one?"

This time she nodded her head yes and laughed as he handed her one of the bubble gum cigarettes. "Who the hell are you anyway?"

"Ah, we've broken the ice...finally! First off, I must tell you that I've had only minor training in this, but they are short of people to work the hospital beds...but I promise, I will do the best I can." He smiled, stood up and offered his hand to her. She now noticed he had a medical staff ID badge on his shirt. "Dex Morgan, I am your physical therapist. Nice to meet you!"

NGD: 2 Years:

Starship Ladyhawk:

Jaime Bordeaux:

For three days, they slowly travelled through sub-space – a trip that would have normally taken the Dragon starship six hours. Jaime had ordered that the crawler drive be ran at the slowest speed – a speed that would simulate the speed at which a Blessed craft would travel in the void between the layers of normal space.

The crew had taken the time in sub-space to do final preparations of the ship prior to the presentation ceremony. Computer tweaking, engine tuning and other tasks were performed during the time they travelled the void. Some of the crew also caught up on sleep during the voyage. Jaime was in the group that got caught up on some well-deserved rest.

She awoke and did some light stretches as soon as she got herself out of bed. Afterward, she took a relaxing shower, and then selected her dress uniform for the christening ceremony. She looked forward to getting this ceremony over with, as it was all for the pomp of the Blessed and had nothing to do with Normals.

She looked at herself in the mirror before she put on her uniform – the coloration that highlighted her bones had spread. Her calves, knees and thighs had now taken on the shade of deep midnight blue that once only highlighted her bone structure. The shade was dark enough to appear black, and her skin shimmered even with the new dark pigment that now colored her flesh. She found it quite interesting to watch the slight fluctuation of light in the darkened appendages. She was concerned with what else might be occurring with these changes. In addition to her legs, she noticed where her spine ran up her back, the dark color was creeping out and spreading the same dark shade of blue. She reached down and touched the skin of her leg, and it surprisingly felt normal – the skin felt soft to the touch, and quite pliable. Hero walked up and looked at her now darkened skin. He sniffed the skin, then started purring and rubbing his chin against her darkened calf. She smiled at the feline, reached down and petted him, which caused even more purring. While down there she rubbed and poked at her legs for another moment before she shrugged her shoulders, stood up straight, and began putting on her uniform.

Today's uniform would consist of a tight black Alliance dress uniform jumpsuit. One that would cover her entire body completely – she did not want any Blessed to see the changes going on in her body, and this suit would prevent that. The shiny black polymer suit had shoulder epaulettes, but no insignias to indicate her rank level. She placed captain's insignias on her collar, and an Alliance logo patch on her breast, over her heart. She once again checked her uniform, and then proceeded to the bridge.

She entered the bridge to find her level one crew was on duty and ready for exiting sub-space. Halley was at the helm, and was making navigational preparations for activating the beams and opening a rift in the fabric of space.

"Good moment" she greeted her crew as she sat down in the command module. Everyone replied and proceeded with their preparatory duties. Katsumi was making scans of the void, Jonathan was checking engine status, Otter was monitoring ship's communications, and Yuli was performing a count of rail launcher projectiles. She looked over at the first officer's station and the empty seat – she felt bad leaving Allen at the base, but he could not be seen by the Blessed as they thought he was dead. Also, he had plenty of work to keep him busy with the construction of the three ships in the dock, along with managing the day-to-day activities of the base.

"Halley, are we close to leaving sub-space?" she asked.

Halley nodded in acknowledgement "Yes, Captain. One minute to beam activation and exit."

"Very good" she replied. "Remember, we will not be using anything other than standard Blessed technology while we are with the fleet. They must not know we have anything more advanced than them."

"Captain…" Jonathan queried "what do we do if they tour the ship? Won't they see our technology and question it?"

"Let me handle that" she answered. "I have a sneaking suspicion they will not be touring this craft. Even if they do, I have a very well-planned tour just for them."

The ship emerged out of sub-space almost to the exact spot of the Blessed fleet – just far enough away to not cause a navigational hazard created by the tear in sub-space. This caused a bit of a stir over the Blessed comm channels, as they had not expected anyone to be able to pilot a ship from sub-space with such accuracy – however, their ships did not have Halley as a helmsman.

The fleet had expanded to five ships: Starlight, and the smaller version of Starlight – Ultimate. Two Hammerhead class battle cruisers – Victory and Triumph. Finally, the new Super-Hammerhead battleship, Conquest. The Conquest had four ion drives instead of two, and was loaded with twice the number of weapon arrays as the standard Hammerhead cruiser. It looked like a formidable weapon and Jaime wondered how it would fare against the Dragon.

"Bring her into parking position Halley, then prepare the Rebel Queen for me to transport over to Starlight."

"Aye, Captain" she replied.

Twenty minutes later, Jaime found herself standing in the launch bay of the Starlight. She wore a pressure suit, as she would be required to go out into space for the christening ceremony. She would be joined by Boral and his entourage, they would all exit the controlled environment of the ship and stand on the ceremonial platform on the side of the ship. Once there, they would go through the ceremonial process of speeches, which then would culminate in the tossing of a bottle of champagne against the new ship.

Boral walked into the bay along with Kip. Both wearing black and silver pressure suits which were adorned with epaulettes and dangling cords of gold and silver. They gave Jaime traditional Alliance salutes, and to her surprise even shook her hand in apparent acknowledgement of her accomplishments.

Boral cleared his throat before speaking "Well, shall we get outside and see what you built for our fleet?"

"Absolutely, my Star Force Commander. I think you will be impressed" she replied.

"Hmm, we will see…" said Kip.

They exited through the air lock and stood on the platform mounted on the side of the ship, just under the large bank of engines in the rear of the craft. Slightly below them was Jaime's Dragon starship.

"Hmm, an interesting design…" said Kip as he looked over the ship. "However, it seems too sleek to really be effective. You would not want to go up against a Super-Hammerhead in that."

"Probably not, Alpha Starship Captain…" she said while thinking *"You would be so embarrassed to have your ass kicked by her."*

Boral cleared his throat again "Well in any case, let's begin the ceremony."

For the next twenty minutes, a long and drawn out speech had been prepared and was being presented to the fleet by Boral. Jaime found it hard to maintain her composure through the lies. But even worse for her, the whole speech was simply boring.

Finally, it was time to complete the ceremony and toss the bottle of champagne. He reached down and picked up the bottle of simulated wine – it was flash-frozen solid. "As the Star Force Commander, and loyal representative for the Supreme Commander, I now am privileged to christen this new weapon of the Alliance, and the Order. In the name of the Supreme Commander, I bless this starship..." he localizes the communications to just the three of them for a moment "Umm, what is the name of this craft?"

"Ah!" Jaime replies "Well, as you may know...it was built by a wide variety of people. Eighty three percent of everyone who built, and now operate this vessel are women. For that reason, we decided...by opinion poll by the way...that the name of this craft shall be His Supreme Commander's Ship, Ladyhawk."

He looked at her "What? Ladyhawk?" She nodded in reply. He bowed his head and shook it slightly, then handed the bottle to Kip while saying "Banquet, cancelled..." He then turned, and walked away without saying another word.

Kip looked at Jaime "Well...it appears you did it again..." he said as he handed her the bottle, turned to follow Boral, and walked back to the air lock.

Jaime smiled, and announced to whoever was left on the open channel "I christen thee, Ladyhawk!" and tossed the bottle. It floated to the Dragon, and smashed against the hardened hull.

She went back inside, boarded her shuttle, and immediately returned to Ladyhawk. Upon departure from Starlight, she signaled Jonathan on Norm-Comm and announced "See, I told you they would not want a tour..."

*   *   *

Jaime was back on Ladyhawk, had gone through a vigorous exercise session, and was now ready to relax in her cabin. She put down a plate of previously frozen space rat for Hero, who gobbled it down. She sat on the bed and stretched – she realized that she was feeling relaxed and tired once again. Perhaps she would get a good night's sleep this time period – at least she hoped. Right before she was about to lay down and go to sleep, her Norm-Comm buzzed in her ear. She let out a loud moan of mental agony, then answered. "What now?" she snapped.

Who was on surprised her – it was Lindy. "Hello Captain. I have heard that is what you want to be called now...Captain?"

"Lindy, my god! Where are you?"

"That's not important right now. I'm fine, let's leave it at that. I needed to contact you because of something that is about to go down. I don't have details, but I have a feeling you will be interested. They are going to broadcast it to the entire fleet in 10 minutes, I have been told you don't want to miss it."

"What is it?" she asked.

"I have no idea..." Lindy answered "I was just told by a reliable and anonymous source that you will want to see it. I have to go..."

"Please take care...we miss you."

"I miss you too. Goodbye my Captain..." Jaime felt her leave the Norm-Comm channel.

She sat up and activated the Alliance News Network – or at least the Blessed version that is transmitted for the fleet. On the screen was an announcer in a courtroom.

"In a few minutes, the accused will be brought before the tribunal and be judged. Ah, here comes the accused now..."

Jaime's eyes opened wide as she recognized the prisoner being brought into the courtroom. It was her old friend and wingman Messiah. Boral entered the room and took the adjudicator position at the front of the courtroom. He glared down at her friend and adjusted the light on him while he spoke to the accused.

Benedict "Messiah" Marsh. You are accused of actions against the Alliance and blasphemy, the evidence against you has been presented and reviewed. How do you plead?

Messiah looked at the Starfleet Commander confused "I don't understand...I have never done anything against the Alliance – and what blasphemy?"

"Really Marsh..." Boral answered "your name is Benedict for god's sake. You take yourself to be one of the Blessed while you use the sacred name of our lord when you fight. I think you can understand why you are blasphemous. Very well, you have pleaded..."

"Don't I get to post my defense? I have not even entered a plea for Christ's sake!"

"Again, you do that in this court! Benedict Marsh, I find you guilty of acts against the Alliance, and the Order, and I also find you guilty of blasphemy. Your sentence will be to fly through the Devil's Throat on a mission for your fleet. Before you go through, you will launch a communication beacon, then fly through the throat. Once on the other side, you will launch a matching beacon. Your choice then will be simple – either stay where you are, in which case you will die of starvation...or you can try to come back to the fleet. The first beacon on our side will be attuned to the beacon you launched on the other side – that will provide us with a tunneled communication link through the gravity well. Should you make it back, then it will be deemed that you have atoned, will be forgiven of your sins, and allowed to live. The sentence will be carried out in two days. Prepare yourself and may God and the Supreme Commander have mercy on your soul. Court is dismissed." He rapped the gavel, got up and quickly walked out of the room.

Jaime turned the video screen off and activated her Norm-Comm to contact Jonathan. "Yes Captain?"

"Jonathan, did you just watch the broadcast?"

"Yes, I did. You flew with him right?"

"Yes. What the hell was that all about?"

"Well, they came up with every bogus rule in the book to force him to fly through the throat" he answered.

"Damn! I always warned him about using Messiah as a handle..."

"No, it is the fact that he is named Benedict."

"I don't understand..." she admitted.

"Benedict...it is old earth Latin for blessed..."

"Oh crap..." she sighed. "Ok, is there anything we can do to help?"

"I will try to get over there and make sure the coils on his ship are properly tuned. Captain, they are going to send him through in a Wolf Pack fighter. It is doubtful it can handle the trip, especially both ways."

"I understand, do what you can..." she said as she signed off.

Nova Jones:

Another wonderful evening had been spent with Yuli. They had dinner, then went to the entertainment center and watched a movie from the early 20th century – The African Queen. The film depicted a man and woman of two totally different worlds coming together in a small primitive boat for a common cause, the destruction of a heavily armed German steamship. They travelled through the rivers of Africa while they searched for the steamship that they would attack against all odds, all while coming together as a couple and falling in love.

"Could you imagine living in those times?" she asked him as they walked to her cabin.

"In some ways, it's not that much different. We Normals are struggling to survive a larger and better armed Blessed population and fleet. We have our weapons...our homemade torpedoes..."

"Mister, they did not have Ultras...or heavy gravity projectiles. If they did, that movie would have been over in five minutes."

"Yes, but they would not have fallen in love either..." he pointed out.

"True, very true..." she admitted as they reached the door to her cabin.

"Well, here we are again...another wonderful night that's now ending..." he said with some regret.

"Yuli..." she said, and looked up into his blue eyes "we don't have to end this evening. I think we have dated long enough, don't you?" she said as she pleaded to him with her eyes. "I think it is time you finally come in...for the night..."

"Ahh..." he had no idea what to say.

She reached up and kissed him passionately. "Come on...we're done dating..." she grabbed his hand and pulled him inside her cabin.

*　　　*　　　*

They awoke that next morning, but did not get out of bed. Yuli had the next shift, but he knew he had time and was in no hurry to get up and leave. They spent another hour in bed before she finally came to her senses and realized it was time for him to get up and go to work. "Yuli, if you don't get moving you'll be late for shift. You DON'T want to keep the Captain waiting." She sat up and started to stretch in preparation to stand, and get up out of bed.

"I suppose you are right..." he admitted. Without warning, he spun around and grabbed her and pulled her back down. He lowered his mouth to her neck and bit it lightly, moving up her neck to her ears. He moved the thick black hair out of the way to nibble on her ears but then stopped. He looked at her ears – there were only small nubs of flesh where the large fleshy wings were growing on most other Normals.

She pulled away, and quickly pulled her hair back concealing her differently shaped ears. "They have been growing...slowly. I don't know why..." she turned to look him in the eyes. He saw she had gotten slightly teary. "I hope you don't think me a freak. I don't know why these things are growing so slowly. I have the coloration...I am reconfiguring with you. You know that don't you? Please say you love me...that you don't think poorly of me!" she pleaded.

He put his hand to her face, and softly stroked it. "I could never think badly of you. I think more of you every moment I spend with you. I am more in love with you than I was last evening...or even a minute ago." He thought for a second before suggesting "Perhaps we should go ahead and make it official?"

She opened her eyes wide, and looked at him questioning. "I think we should join...we have bonded and are reconfiguring, so why not go all the way and make it official."

"Do you really mean it?" he shook his head yes. "Okay, yes...please...that would make me the happiest woman in this universe!"

"I am sure that after my shift the Captain will do the honors. I will ask her once I get to the bridge. I'll comm you if she agrees."

"I'll be waiting" she promised.

He got up, got dressed, and went to his shift. More of his face had turned the deep shade of blue since their passionate encounter of the previous evening. When he arrived at the bridge he immediately went to the Captain and asked her to do the ceremony. Jaime instantly agreed, and promised she would perform the ceremony after they finished their shift. Yuli contacted Nova and gave her the good news.

After the shift the three met in the command conference room along with Jonathan, Kate, Halley, Otter, Katsumi, and Max. Nova showed up in a long flowing ivory flexi-polymer blouse and a matching ivory skirt that fell down to her ankles. She had the computer attach intricate tubes of fabric that formed the petals and leaves of flowers into the material. On her head she wore a matching ivory headband with simulated daisies attached to the front, this band held her hair tightly against her head.

Jaime performed a short ceremony, and then congratulated the newly joined couple. Afterwards, they all sat down for a good meal and camaraderie.

Max looked at Jaime "So, many of us have bonded. What about our captain?" he asked.

Jaime shook her head no "I think not...there is an anchor embedded in my heart, it has a chain, and that chain goes through the Devil's Throat. There used to be an anchor on that side, but it is now lost. But I still feel the attachment...and I don't think I will ever be released from that attachment."

Max looked at Halley who had a slightly pained look on her face, then realized what happened to Jamie, and how it still pained her. He looked down at the table feeling awful for bringing up such a painful topic for his captain. "Sorry…" he softly said.

"No Max, it's ok…really" she reassured him. "I have come to terms. This is my destiny, it allows me to be strong, and prevents me from straying from my purpose. It allows me to be strong for all of you. Besides, there is no one who has DNA that is strong enough to bond with me!"

The group laughed, but it did make Max wonder – was she correct, was there no one that could bond and mate with her? They could use a child with her abilities to command and lead. He gave up the thought and instead concentrated on the happy couple.

Nova looked at her new mate – she was the happiest woman in the universe. There would be nothing that would stop her and Yuli any longer. She was no longer alone and he and she were now a single entity, they had each other. Nothing would ever tear them apart.

Six and a Half Years Ago…

The neutron bombs were exploding overhead – the enemy hoped to catch one of them in an unguarded moment – with a battle suit deactivated or an open helmet. This time the enemy was not going to succeed however, as their suits were powered up, helmets locked and electronic shielding was activated. They had one more mile to travel to get to the base – rest and recuperation would be waiting, if only they could make it that one long mile.

He looked at the other two that was all that was left of this patrol – himself, Jaime, and this guy they ran into during a battle. They had been running from the moment the enemy attempted the ambush., This was the first time he had a chance to look at this soldier who just came charging into the battle – and who may have saved their necks. When he tried to look at his face however, he could not – he had a reflective tint on his helmet faceplate, which prevented them from seeing the face inside.

The hell started as they tried to cross a small valley – the enemy was waiting in ambush. Of their squad, only two of them were still alive and fighting, but they in return, had taken out a good portion of the ambushers by the time this mystery soldier had showed up. He and the other three of his fireteam entered the valley and fought by their side. By the time they were able to evade the enemy fire and take the remaining twenty southern soldiers out, only the three of them had made it through the battle.

The southern bastards had been waiting for them – they knew it would be a potential trap when they came to this valley, but they were running low on ammo and supplies, and needed to get back to base as soon as possible. People he had fought with for years were blown away in a flurry of photon mortars, neutron pods, and blaster cross fire. As more of his men and women went down, he thought all was lost. But then this guy showed up – he had a fireteam, full sets of ammo packs, and the skill to use all of the weapons he had on his person.

He looked at this man he had somehow been teamed up with since then. He never showed his face, but that didn't matter as he fought hard, and had already saved his ass a few times. Jaime seemed to trust him also, and that was more than good enough for him. He decided the two of them were lucky to have found him, or for him to have found them.

The three looked out of the foxhole at the final flat ahead. It appeared clear, but they all knew better. They all knew that there would be southerners just waiting to take them out. He called on his comm "This is it. How much ammo do each of you have?"

"I have enough..." replied Jaime "I have two full charge bolts still...and a surprise for them if they should be so stupid..."

He wondered what she had up her sleeve, but that was the Jaime he knew and had fought beside for so long. He looked at the mysterious soldier by his side – he was checking his power reserves and ammo.

"I have a full bolt, a few piercers and my solar batteries are full. I am good to go."

He nodded to the hidden faced man, then checked his own weapon reserves. He was not quite as fortunate – he only had half a charge in the bolt that powered his suit's blasters. He had no missiles and his solar panel was damaged, and thus was barely charging his suit – he only had a quarter charge in the pack. "I guess we are ready then...shall we?"

The three jumped out of the foxhole and began running north to the base. As soon as they started the final sprint, alarms sounded in his helmet as every nearby enemy weapon had been targeted on them. His heads-up display lit up as targeting lasers were piercing through the smoke as the enemy tried to get a bead on him and his two comrades.

"Guys head west, now!" Jaime yelled out. He started to question her, and she yelled "GO!". This time he only reacted, the two men followed her order, and took an immediate left turn and started running.

On his radar, he saw that instead of going with them, Jaime had turned to the east. She bounded for another two hundred feet before stopping, lowering her back and firing a missile. Her having a nuke surprised him – she must had loaded the weapon before they went out, it was the last missile she had in her pack, and she obviously had been saving it. He turned to see her fire, then she turned and ran back toward them. A host of return fire missiles and mortars followed her tracks as they tried as they could to take her out before the missile hit. He saw a blast hole that he knew would be a good place to ride out the explosion. He jumped in then turned to see Jaime's progress. Shock came to his eyes as he saw her lying on the ground – a lucky shot had disabled one of her suit's leg servos. He increased magnification and saw blood dripping out of the damaged leg, she was injured inside the suit as well as outside. She fought off the injury however, and had gotten up and was hobbling trying to get to their location.

He jumped out and ran to her aid. She yelled and screamed waving her arms as she tried in vain to keep him away. He grabbed her arm and began to take some of the pressure off of her damaged leg. He felt her become lighter and when he looked to the other side of her saw the other guy – he too was helping her escape.

When she yelled "Down!" she pushed the two of them down near the hole as they all hit the ground. The two men were barely far enough away when the nuke hit. They slid down the hole and the radiation blast pushed Jaime the remaining distance across and down into the hole. A few moments later, the mushroom cloud was high in the air, and to their surprise, all was quiet – no enemy activity was detected or present. Jaime's suit was burnt, and he could tell she had taken the brunt of the radiation from the explosion. By pushing them down so close to the foxhole, she probably had kept them from a hospital visit – too bad she was not as lucky.

He realized however, that neither of them would have made it had he not had help from this mysterious soldier. He looked at the masked man and smiled through his visor and said "Thanks for helping us out and saving our asses. We owe you friend. I would however, like to know your name."

He simply said "I am just known as Perfecto..."

NGD: 2 Years, 1 month and 2 Days:

Blessed Starfleet, Currently Orbiting Salvage Base Plug:

Benedict "Messiah" Marsh:

He was given a meal of real chicken the night before. If he had any doubt that he was just experiencing his last night alive, then that meal was his proof. The real meat upset him slightly, but he figured he might as well enjoy it – not like an upset stomach would make any difference this morning.

The cell door opened, and four black uniformed men marched in. Two of them walked over, and hauled him up by his armpits. He looked at them with surprise "Secret Service? On board this ship?"

The largest of the four servicemen ignored his comments. "Benedict Marsh, you are to come with us to the launch bay" he said with a slight mechanical tone in his voice. He motioned for him to follow the first two soldiers.

As he walked out into the corridor, he noticed that one of the black uniformed soldiers was actually a woman. He looked at her chest then at her black helmeted head before commenting "So, they are now recruiting women into the Secret Service eh?" She ignored him and kept prodding him to continue their march toward the launch bay.

It was a slow death march to the launch bay. They took a long dark corridor that traversed most of the length of the ship. The corridor had been emptied of all activity while they walked him on their way. No personnel were to be in this corridor while they passed – it was as tight of security as could be made possible. He felt the constant prodding of a stun stick against his side by the woman behind him. She had not used it yet, but he could tell by the way she poked it into his side that she was really wanting to stun him with it. He continued to follow the two soldiers in front without thinking – only noticing the occasional prod from behind. That is until he realized that the prodding had stopped. He looked through the corner of each eye and noticed that both of the soldiers behind him were now missing. He then heard a ruckus behind him and as he started to turn, he heard the sound of multiple blaster shots, saw the beams fly by him, which was then followed by the tumbling over of the soldiers in front. As he watched them fall, he heard the sound of a blaster firing again – he felt the heat of the beam on his back, then blacked out.

Jeremy Ponds:

He had been running transports since Jaime won the last game of Command Tri-Polyhedrons. He knew the other trainers were after him and he needed to disappear. The death threats if she won would be carried out and he had to hide away until he could find some way to join the rest of the Normals on their new base. After a while, he decided it was easier to hide in plain sight.

He sported a large set of wings on his ears now. To hide them, he had grown his dark brown hair very long – long enough to cover the side of his head and his ears. On his face, a long dark, thick beard and mustache concealed his features. Along with his forged documentation, no one on board any of the ships recognized him and that was good. He found that running supplies and hiding groups of escaping Normals was not only making him good credits, but it also felt really good. He found he was as good at smuggling as he was at training.

Today's run was no different – he had some contraband copper wire and platinum bars, along with about a hundred changed Normals. All he had to do was make it through inspection and he would be off and running. Three black uniformed Secret Service soldiers boarded his ship and looked at him through dark screened helmets.

"Papers!" the shortest of the three ordered.

He handed them his computer film which listed his ship's manifest. They looked over the list of supplies that were to be delivered to the Victory from Starlight – food stuffs, tools, and construction robots. They wandered around the cargo bay looking at every crate. They randomly opened a crate every so often, examined the contents then moved on. The tallest and bulkiest of the three stopped at a crate nearest to the cargo bay airlock door. He pointed at a crate he did not recognize – he wondered if someone had put something on board to get him arrested. The guard looked at the crate's label – it was labeled "food stuffs, rations M-5344". A small amount of sweat started to form on his brow – he was not sure what to do if that was something he had not properly hidden.

"I have seen enough..." the larger soldier said to the other two. He walked up to Jeremy and he could feel him looking at him through his darkened helmet "You are cleared for takeoff. Proceed with your mission. Glory to the Alliance, and to the Order."

He gave a half salute to the departing servicemen – he had not heard anyone give the glory motto in a long time. Must be a throwback soldier he thought.

As soon as the three had left and he had secured the hatches, he took off and started his normal flight path. He would start to head to Victory, then detour just slightly around Cork and finally head in an opposite direction to Bung, where he would drop off his cargo. From there, his cargo and people would be transported to the black asteroid base for the advancement of the Normals, and the pursuit of their common goals. He hoped that soon he could join them, but for now he was doing something – something that would help the cause, and further the future of Normals like himself.

After he started his run around Cork, he decided to go back and look inside the crate that somehow appeared in his hold. He hoped there was not a tracking device he might have missed – or worse a bomb. When he opened the crate he was shocked even worse by what he saw. Inside the crate was the body of a man. He was in a fighter pilot's space suit and was lying unconscious in the box. He recognized the man as Benedict Marsh. He checked his vitals – he was alive and well, just knocked out.

He closed the crate and went back to the cockpit. He turned on the fleet video channel and the fighter ship that Messiah was to be piloting had already been launched and was headed for the Devil's Throat. He wondered out loud "So, if Messiah is in my hold...who is flying that spacecraft?"

Perfecto:

He was flying to the Devil's Throat. He checked the field coils and verified they were properly working. He would need them to provide the gravity field needed to pass through the throat and the flypaper-like void in the middle between the passageways. The Starlight kept signaling him to verify his status, but he ignored their calls. He did not want them finding out that Messiah was not on board. It had not been long enough, and sneaking him aboard that transport in the crate could be discovered if he gave away his plan too soon.

He flew to the small blinking light where Stopper used to sit when it blocked the way back to his home galaxy. He slowed the ship down, and came to a stop in front of the entrance to the passageway. In his ear, the commands of the Starlight bothered him like a buzzing insect "Go on, enter the Throat. Be a man...be brave..."

He launched the first beacon, and then took a deep breath and pushed the ship forward. The blinking light became a large brightly lit maw that opened up and gobbled his ship. The ship travelled at a tremendous rate of speed. He adjusted the field coils hoping to maintain some control over his motion. After a moment, he felt the opposite force on the front of his craft – he was rapidly approaching the void. He increased the gravity fields on his craft, hoping to cancel the effects of the opposing forces that seemed to ebb and flow in the well. Finally he emerged into the cavernous void at the end of the tunnel. He was only half way and yet he could tell his ship was expending way too much energy to get through. He knew this was not going to bode well for him.

In the massive void of the center of the throat was a graveyard of giant spacecraft. The void was filled in the center with every size of starship imaginable. Some were huge – he was surprised by the size of some of the behemoths that were trapped here. He wondered how races of beings could build such massive ships, and yet not have the technology or capability to repel and escape the gravity forces within the void. His thoughts were interrupted by his computer alerting him of the passageway on the other side. He guided the ship toward the exit, while he at the same time readjusted the field coils to continue to repel the forces acting against his ship. Through the ITZee, he felt a slight stress crack form on one of the fins in the tail of the craft. He made a computer note of the stress forces and continued on. As he approached the exit he noticed to his side another opening in the void fabric. He became worried that perhaps he might be picking the wrong tunnel. He made a silent prayer and pushed the craft forward to his selected passageway.

The ship rocked and bucked while it fought the gravity pushing and also pulling him through a vortex of forces. Finally, he emerged from the Devil's Throat – through his partially damaged star screen he saw stars. He took a moment to relax then instructed the computer to attempt to get a bearing of his location. Within a minute the computer returned its estimated location – he was in *his* galaxy, *his* Solar System had been spotted by the computer. He smiled as he activated the launching sequence for the communication beacon. The beacon, moments later launched from one of the rail guns and deployed itself a few thousand miles from the entrance of the throat.

He examined his ship's damage readouts. He had substantial damage to the structure of the cradle that held the pod, the engines were damaged and would probably overload on the way back, and the ship had major structural damage and stress fractures along the entire fuselage.

"Ah, what the hell..." he said as he pushed forward and turned the ship to reenter the passageway. He fought the forces into the void once more. He looked at the void and noticed even more openings around the cavernous void in the center of the throat. He activated his recorder and started to record a message as he entered the passageway that would return him to the fleet.

Jaime Bordeaux:

Jaime watched the Wolf Pack fighter as it entered the gravity well and disappeared. A tear came to her eye as she realized that her good friend had just gone off to his death. "Goodbye my dear friend..."

One hour passed, then a second hour. Finally, to her surprise the Devil's Throat opened and spat out a ship – a Wolf Pack fighter. It made it far enough from the gravity effect that she thought he made it. With his mission successful, Boral hoped that the two beacons would provide a way to communicate with the Alliance on the other side of the gravity well. As soon as the ship was ejected from the throat, it exploded from hull fractures and overloaded engine failure. The ship, and its pilot went out in a fiery blaze of glory.

"Damn…" she whispered. A tear started to form in her eye.

"Captain?" interrupted Otter. "I just received a message specifically to you – from Perfecto…"

"What? Put it on!" she ordered.

"Jaime, it's me, Perfecto. First, please forgive me for my actions in the game…I don't know what I was thinking. I would never have gained my status, and I really do not know why I even thought about that. Especially, since it meant turning on one of the only friends I ever had. We have been through so much – our battles in war and our fights in the air and in space…well, I hope you will somehow forgive me. I also hope you will forgive me for deceiving you and not telling you about my Blessed heritage. It was both an embarrassment and yet something I wanted to be proud of. It was a paradox for me, as I am sure you now understand from what you have seen in the actions of the Alliance and the Blessed, and what they are capable of doing. I am almost about to exit the passageway, and I do not think the ship will make it. I have programmed this message to automatically transmit to you once I am clear of the interference. So, please take care and thrive…you and all Normals. I wish you the best. Oh, say something nice about me to that goldbricker Messiah…tell him I saved his ass again. Goodbye Jaime."

Tears flowed freely from her eyes, and when she looked around she saw everyone on the bridge had tears falling as they all had just lost a friend and ally.

Six Months Prior to Starlight Launch...

You are so great Marigold! You have the ability to do so much for the Alliance and the Order. When you wake up, you will be in a different place, probably a different world. You will provide so much to your Blessed kin. Your father and I are so proud of you!

NGD: 2 Years, 6 Months and 9 Days:

Star System D-893, Aboard the Starlight Space Ark:

Marigold Minford:

She awoke to find the face of a pretty brunette nurse starring into her eyes.

"Ah, you're awake, good!" the nurse said to her in a soft but happy voice.

"Where...where am I?" Marigold managed to mumble out.

"In a totally different galaxy..." the nurse replied "We are so far from earth now. We are looking for a new home...but we need you."

"Me? Why?" she asked confused.

"Remember my dear Marigold...you are one of special ones. You are female, AND you are Blessed. That makes you and me very special." She looked at the middle aged nurse – she wore a bronze bead with the number "432" engraved on it. She reached up to her own neck with a weak hand and felt around until she found a similar choker. She found the bead and tried to feel the number. "You are 98...very special. Now, let's try to sit up. You have been on your back for such a long time."

The nurse helped her to sit upright. She sat, but wobbled as she was not yet used to the artificial gravity – it tried to pull her body back down onto the cot. While she worked at sitting up, the nurse wandered away for a moment, then returned with a pink gown. "You will want to get up and stand in a moment. Then, I know you will want to clean up. The cleansing bay is right over there. I will have some clothes for you as soon as you come out. Now, give standing a try...come on."

She was able to slowly stand, and with weak legs took her first step in outer space. It was wobbly, but she found after the first step, the second was much easier. Three steps later she stood at the cleansing bay. She took off her robe and stepped in. She felt the messaging lasers soothe her tight muscles, and relaxed both her body and her mind.

When she finished and stepped out of the bay, she found a black Alliance citizen's uniform laid out neatly on the cot. She slipped on the tight outfit and checked the fit. She noticed the bead connected to the platinum choker around her neck – it was wooden and had the number "98" engraved in the dark polished ironwood surface.

The nurse returned and handed her a computer gel. "You are assigned to the Conquest. That's Kip's ship – it's an honor to be assigned there!" she said with real excitement in her voice. She then leaned over and whispered into her ear "You do remember your duty as a Blessed female, don't you?"

Marigold thought for a moment "Ah yes. We are to help our male Blessed as required. That includes...umm, mating?" She wondered where that thought came from, as it just somehow popped into her head.

The nurse smiled and nodded "Yes, you have it right! It is our duty as female Blessed citizens of the Order. We are to help to expand and improve the Blessed race. We are rare in the Blessed...and we are treated as special because of it. Don't forget that..."

"I won't" she replied.

The nurse gave her a warm smile "Alright, let's get you on the shuttle. Don't want to keep them waiting over there!"

They left the recovery room and entered a large laboratory filled with rows of dark tubes. Many of the tubes were covered in frost – some had just been removed from cold storage and the frost coating them was solid. Others that had been sitting for a while were now starting to melt – water beaded and dripped down the curved sides. The air here was filled with moisture, and this room was much warmer than the recovery room. She noticed that some of the tubes were open, and there were both men and women that had just been pulled out of the tubes and were now laying on stretchers. IV's and other tubes had been inserted into their bodies. They were lying motionless as they were being brought back to room temperature, and eventually back to life. They all had metal plates imbedded in their heads – both the males and females alike. In addition, there were blinking lights, and electronic implants in various parts of their bodies.

She looked confused at the thawing humans, then looked at her own body and touched her head in the same spot as the ones lying before her. The nurse smiled and took her hand "You don't have any of the implants like they do. They are Secret Service – they have been enhanced in a different way…a way that will help them in battle. You are not one of them, you are Blessed. Now come…"

As they continued through the lab, something else caught Marigold's eye. On the far wall were clear tubes. Inside these tubes were human forms – but that was all they were, forms. They did not seem to have developed faces, and only had a glimmer of what a human should look like. Also, their body form looked human shaped but seemed to her like they were missing features. She stopped and stared at the tubes, trying to get a better look at the forms inside. It appeared to her that the forms had wires inserted into their misshaped heads – as if they were plugged into something.

She felt the tugging of the nurse on her arm "Those are ones who did not awaken properly. We are trying to save them, so don't worry. Now come on…let's not keep Kip waiting."

They boarded a ship-wide travel shuttle and began the journey to the launch bay. She took in the sights of this new world she had awoken into. The Starlight was magnificent, she was awestruck at the wonders that her kind had built. As they rode the shuttle she got to see the various areas inside the open living habitat section. There were green parks below her, she saw people playing games and taking walks in the man-made open spaces. She saw the exercise areas, and the open-air restaurants that this magnificent ship had to offer. She felt very lucky that she had been put to sleep and was now awake in this wonderful ship during this amazing time of human expansion. She felt so lucky.

They arrived at the launch bay and were greeted by a dark haired Blessed shuttle pilot. He looked her up and down, then gave a clicking noise with his mouth. "Wow, you are beautiful!" He reached up and looked at her number choker "...and Blessed in addition. Someone is going to be lucky. Is there a raffle for her?" he asked the nurse.

"That has not been decided. Check with your Alpha Starship Captain about that."

He gave her a look of disappointment "Well crap..." he then looked at the nurse "How about you, hmm?" He reached out and stroked her dark hair.

She took his hand and pushed it away. "You know I have already been reserved for duty at least into the next three years. Get in line pilot, get in line..." She looked at the young Marigold and smiled. "See, you will be in high demand over there. Good luck, provide us some fine new Blessed!"

Marigold waved at the departing nurse then turned toward the pilot. He smiled and bowed as he pointed her toward the shuttle hatch. A few minutes later, she got to see the beauty of outer space, and within minutes found herself onboard a different ship. This one looked like it was ready for battle – armed soldiers wandered everywhere. Everyone had some form of side-arm – and she was handed one the moment she stepped foot off of the transport.

The guard that met her pushed the weapon into her hand "It is mandatory ma'am ...all Blessed must carry a sidearm."

"But, I don't know how to use one" she told the man.

"You will be given training. Please, take it for now" he said as he pushed the weapon at her again. She reluctantly took the blaster and holster, and attached it to her uniform belt. He then handed her a microchip – it was an inch long and had a plastic foam covering sharp terminals on the bottom of the device. "This is your identity chip, ma'am. You will need it to order food and supplies. It will also register you for the mating drawing. Although, I have heard through the gossip web that you will probably be the Alpha Starship Captain's mate for at least the first month." He then turned slightly red, and looked around the room

"I ask that you not repeat that...I could get in big trouble for telling you that. Umm, you will need to put that chip on your forearm when you arrive in your cabin. Our Blessed scientists just developed it, and all Blessed personnel must have one aboard this ship. Once you place it on your arm, it will embed itself and activate. He then handed her a small square plastic patch "Your communication device. You will need that to receive information and instructions by command. You will apply it behind your right ear. Now, unless you have any questions, follow me to your cabin."

She shook her head no, and was escorted to her cabin. It was a small room, it had a dressing table, a wardrobe, and mirror on one wall. On the other wall, a large and surprisingly comfortable bed. She also had a small private latrine and cleansing bay. It was small, but yet cozy she felt. She sat on the bed and felt her rump slowly sink into the foam material. It was warm and cozy feeling to her backside.

She took the communication patch and looked at it – it was a small quarter inch patch of plastic – flat and not very remarkable. She peeled the protective coating and stuck it onto the area behind her right ear. She then held the identity chip in her hand and looked at it with a slightly worried look. "Well, I might as well get this over with..." she said out loud to herself as she removed her uniform top, and extended her arm. She removed the protective backing on the chip and held it on the sides with her fingers. There were hundreds of small terminals – as soon as she removed the backing they started moving back and forth as if trying to find her arm to burrow into. She took the chip, closed her eyes and set it on her forearm. Burning pain extended all along her arm as the chip buried itself underneath her skin. She gave a yelp of pain and then a moan of agony as the chip finished its burrowing and then connected itself to her nervous system.

After about five minutes, the pain had subsided. She gave one last moan of remaining pain, then shook her head to clear the burning sensation from her mind. A moment later, she felt a buzzing in her right ear. She pressed on the little plastic patch, it felt like she had pressed a button.

"Marigold, this is Conquest command. We are about to go into battle alert. Because of this status you are to immediately report to flight section two-seven for shuttle simulator training assignment within the hour. At twenty four thirty report to command quarters A-one. Our Alpha Starship Captain wishes to dine with you tonight."

Doctor Max Sollix:

The alert had been sent, there was another Og battle fleet in a nearby system and the Star Force Commander had decided to go after them. Jaime suspected that the Ladyhawk would once again be sent into the thick of the battle and wanted Max to have everything in the sick bay ready – it had not been needed yet, but he always needed to be ready, just in case.

He was organizing equipment into emergency packs for every situation he could think of. He looked around the room and pondered on what he might be missing. "I will never be ready for battle..." he said out loud.

Behind him a voice he did not recognize asked him "Well then perhaps you could use my help?"

He turned to find a woman standing in the doorway. She had medium length brown hair that curled up at the ends, bright green eyes with thin eye brows, a small up-sloped nose, rounded cheeks and small lips that formed a relaxed smile. Her eyes lined up with his nose, thus she had to slightly point her head up to look him in the eyes when she spoke to him. Hello Doctor...so,can you use some help getting things ready? I am Doctor Annette Starling. I am on temporary assignment to the Ladyhawk to assist you in setting up the sick bay for battle triage. Captain James thought I could show you some tips and tricks. I am a battlefield medical support specialist, and I offer my assistance to you So, Doctor. How can I be of help?"

He looked into her eyes and for a moment became lost as he found something about them very mysterious and attractive – he snapped back to reality, hoping she did not catch his momentary day dream. "Um, well of course! I can use all the help I can get, thank you! I really could use some guidance as to what needs the sick bay will have in the event of numerous battle injuries. So far, I have not had any serious injuries…but with all of the attacks we have been thrown into it is bound to happen sooner or later.”

"Well, then I think the first thing we should do is go over all of the med-packs you have so far. Then determine what is missing and prepare those. I have the listings for general starship battle triage – med-pack requirements, equipment and diagnostic needs, and can check the staffing roster to make sure you have everything and everybody you will need to help your injured, should the need arise.”

Max smiled "That sounds great! I do not have the battle expertise or experience as you do. I really appreciate all the help you can give.” He extended his hand to her and she gladly took it with a light grip and shook it.

As she prepared to get to work she said "All right, let's get started…first your med-pack situation…” She turned and started to examine the preparation he had already completed. He stood in the same spot for just a moment and looked at his hand. She turned and asked him "Everything alright Doctor?”

He shook out his hand as to get the blood flowing back to it. "Yes, yes…everything is fine…sorry. Now how have I done so far?” he walked to her still shaking his hand. For some reason it started to tingle and he is not sure why the tingle had not yet stopped, but he had his suspicions.

Jaime Bordeaux:

The alert had been called by the Star Force Commander. Jaime activated the secured command communication network of the fleet. After a moment, another alert tone sounded, then Boral Oldham's voice came across the channel.

"All starships of his Supreme Commanders fleet. This is a general battle activation command. This will be logged as Og battle number thirty-five – star system D-893, no record of a name is listed in the star maps, and as of yet unnamed by Blessed cartographers. Prepare for battle, HSCS…” he paused for a longer than normal time to simply look up a ship registry "Ladyhawk…prepare for battle. You will lead the spearhead and protect the rest of the fleet from harm. Acknowledge.”

Jaime rolled her eyes in disgust "Acknowledged. Ladyhawk will protect the fleet from approaching Og battle fleet...Over." Then muttered "Again..." She waited while she received the official battle orders over the Blessed battle-comm on her command console. She read over the attack command, then acknowledged the orders. "How many times have we been sent out into the front of the battle while they sat in the rear watching?"

Katsumi checked the computer records before responding "This will be the thirty fifth time we have taken front line battle position, Captain."

Jaime shook her head and thought for a moment before calling out "Ok, we have our orders. Katsumi, scan the approaching fleet. Look for anything unusual.

She heard the sounds of construction work and a vibration on the floor plates. She activated Norm-Comm "Jonathan, stop what you are doing and get to the bridge. We're in battle status...Acknowledge." A moment later she heard him reply and within another minute he was running onto the bridge. He took his station while checking his black uniform jumpsuit. He took one more check of the console then gave Jaime a small salute.

She smiled at the young man then ordered "Jonathan, prepare all damage control parties and energize the hull armor. Do not activate the bubble unless I specifically instruct." He nodded in agreement. "Halley, set the course and use only the standard drives if possible – Pulsars, Graviton, and keep the RFS down to a level as to appear to be a standard ion drive."

"Aye Captain, as always, I will only use standard thrust and maneuvering in battle unless you specifically order. All drives are ready to go. Fusion reactor is high by five."

"Thank you. Yuli, only use Alliance standard weapons. Lasers, p-accelerators, protons, rail guns, missiles, whatever. Do not activate or fire any of our new weapons. No need to tip the Blessed to anything they don't have, right?"

"Acknowledged, Captain." He gave her a slight jaunty salute to which she smiled back at him. He activated the weapon arrays that would give him only the necessary standard weapons at his disposal.

"Otter, please monitor the Og frequencies for any communications. Translate if possible and let me know of anything unusual."

"Yes, Captain" she said as she plugged the ship's communication array into the port in the back of her neck. Her eyes slightly lit up as the power flowed from the antenna into her brain.

Hero came onto the bridge and jumped onto Jaime's lap. She looked down at the furry creature "You, just stay calm and don't claw my leg like last time..." Hero replied with a small squeak.

"Captain, sensors are showing twelve Og battle cruisers. They all look the same, so I cannot say if any of them are different from anything we have fought in the past" announced Katsumi.

Jaime nodded to the young science officer. "Ok, let's go get them...take us in Halley...look sharp all. When you get close, initiate battle maneuver...Zulu three-three-five" Halley nodded and entered the navigation commands into her console. A display of the enemy fleet and probable battle maneuvering paths were calculated by the three-dimensional computer and projected onto her portion of the holo-display.

Halley accelerated the ship directly into the front of the enemy fleet. Right before they engaged, she made a hard turn to starboard. The Og fleet was caught off guard by the quick movement tactic of this still unknown ship.

"Okay Katsumi, give Yuli fire formulations and targets. Take 'em down Yuli. Fire at will."

The young Russian quickly examined the targeting points being provided by Katsumi at the science station, and he began poking his gloved hands at the various lock location identifiers. As he pointed, he also tapped on various command buttons to select desired weapons. He tapped on the holo-display and tactile sensors picked up the motion, which fired the various weapons systems. Lasers, and p-accelerators fired out of the port side and top gun port arrays into the oncoming fleet. Two of the round Og ships were taken by surprise and were solidly hit by the blasts. Secondary explosions followed – one of the ships exploded, and the second immediately became disabled. The force of the explosion of the first ship sent fragments into two of the other Og ships damaging them without a shot. Those two ships retreated, but were replaced in the formation by two other ships. They fired their beam weapons, which caused pinging noises on the hull, but otherwise did not cause any real damage to the space carbon armor hull plates.

Halley took the ship into an opposite turn, keeping the port and lower weapon arrays pointed at the enemy fleet. Yuli took the cue and fired a burst of the rail guns, which sent spent plutonium projectiles tearing into the ball-shaped ships. Those two ships exploded as the fierce force of decompression tore them apart. Halley had now turned the craft in the other direction, which gave Yuli the fully-charged starboard side weapon arrays to be fired at his discretion. His display gave him new target locks – he selected a combination of each standard weapon and began poking his fingers on the displayed locks. Each time he tapped on a target indicator, a set of weapons opened fire. This time he took three of the attacking ships out.

Alarms sounded as impacts were detected on the engineering section in the rear of the ship. Two Og ships had managed to come around to the aft end of the craft and were attempting to take out the engines. Halley immediately turned the ship and accelerated with just enough speed to escape the attack and yet not appear to be traveling faster than any other Alliance starship. She spun the ship in a turning-corkscrew maneuver which brought the ship along the side of the two Og ships. Yuli took the moment to send a massive volley of weaponry to bear on the two hapless Og ships. The Og had no way to escape as the weapons tore holes in the heavy metallic materials that made up both the ball section and rectangular drive modules. Both vessels went totally dead well before Yuli completed his pummeling of the two ships.

The last Og ships turned and began a hastily retreat. The bridge crew cheered as the Og fleet shot out of the system.

"Very good job all. Stand down our battle status and go to low alert." Jaime called out. She looked at Jonathan "Damage?"

Jonathan looked at his ship's status display and shrugged his shoulders "None, Captain." Jaime nodded her head in agreement and astonishment. The ship and her crew had done well this day.

"Captain" Otter called out "I did pick up some transmissions from the Og command vessel prior to them leaving system."

"Really? Were you able to decipher and translate?" Otter nodded yes. "What was the message and who was it to?"

"To whom, I am not sure...but it was not Og. The message was – "We cannot defeat these beasts, we need your assistance. Please help."

"Did they get an answer?" Jaime asked.

She continued to listen to the computer translations before answering "Yes – The reply to the Og was...We will help."

Kip Gurrigan:

He sat on the bridge of the Conquest and watched the battle, secretly astonished by how efficiently and quickly this ship of Norms were taking out an entire fleet of Og battle cruisers. Blessed salvage crews were already in route to collect valuable materials for future ships. He watched the Ladyhawk return to the fleet and come to a stop in perfect formation. He thought for a moment before he finally slammed his hand down on the arm of his command console. "There is no way they could have done that again...they must have had some knowledge of a weakness. That, or the Og are now soft and are easily beaten." He stood up and walked around the bridge while he pondered the battle he just watched. He stopped at the science station, and then queried "What type of weapons did the...Ladyhawk...use this time?"

The Blessed science officer looked over SCADAR historical returns for a moment before answering. "All weapon signatures were standard Alliance type weaponry, Alpha Starship Captain. Lasers, p-accelerators, rail guns and proton beams."

"Then the Og have become even weaker than they were before. We must be wearing them down! Communications, get me the Star Force Commander, now!"

A moment later Boral appeared on the main holo-screen. Kip walked up to the screen "Sir, the Og have become weak. We cannot be sending those Norms into battle every time. It would be bad for morale."

Boral thought for a moment "Yes, perhaps you are right. What do you suggest Alpha Starship Captain?"

"I suggest that the next battle we send the Conquest in. We will defeat them soundly and bring the thrill of victory to all of the Blessed who man these warships. I will take credit for the victory in your name my Star Force Commander."

"Me and our Supreme Commander you mean?" Kip nodded in agreement. "Very good, next time the Og attack, we will send in the Conquest...Boral out."

Nova Capsain:

She looked at the display on the bathroom console again. The latrine disposal unit served a dual purpose – it eliminated human waste, and it analyzed the waste prior to disposal for any medical abnormalities that might be present. If the analysis found something, it would notify the user of those issues. She had just finished urinating when the computer console beeped – there was something unusual in her urine.

She nervously watched as the screen flashed "abnormality discovered, analyzing" while it worked. Without realizing it, she was lightly chewing on her fingernail while she waited. Finally, the display turned green and a message was displayed "Congratulations, you are pregnant."

A tear came to her eyes as she read, then re-read the message. She was going to have a child – Yuli's child. She was so excited that she had to comm Yuli and let him know.

Without thinking she pulled her finger from her mouth, but had not yet let go of the nail that was between her teeth. She felt a slight pain, a warmth in her mouth, and then detected an object between her lips. She ran over to the sink and spit out the object. Blood followed the object as she spat it into the sink. She looked down and in the sink, sitting in a small pool of blood was her fingernail. She then looked to her hand and saw the nail-less finger, blood dripped from the exposed nail bed onto the countertop. As soon as she saw the injury, she cried out in pain.

She shrieked again and grabbed a towel to wrap around her finger. She ran to the cabinet and took out an emergency med-kit. She applied an analgesic spray to the nail bed, then wrapped a flexi-pad to the finger sealing off the flow of blood from the injury.

She looked at the injured finger. *"What the hell has happened to me?"*

12 Years Ago...

She looked at her mother, blood flowed from her abdomen onto the bed. The stab wound was deep – the burglar she caught was for once faster than she at wielding a blade. "Oh mother, I can't lose you, I can't!" she cried.

"My sweet, sweet love..." she barely managed to mutter. She lifted her head just enough to look into her eyes. "I have done everything I can to prepare you for this. Now, it is your turn to make something out of your life. Don't do what I did, don't fall into my trap." Her head fell back down onto the pillow she smacked her lips in a vain attempt to moisturize her dry mouth. The young girl gave her mother a small sip of water, then propped her head on her arm.

She looked deeply into her daughter's eyes. "You came from two worlds. You are special, and I hope I have done everything to prepare you for what is to come in your life." She coughed and gasped, it was almost her time. "You are the bright point in my life. You brought the only thing that made it worth living for me. You are my star...and because of that I named you Nova. Please leave this place and live a happy life..."

The young girl cried as her mother exhaled her last breath.

NGD: 2 Years, 11 Months, 5 Days

Planet Queek:

Nova Capsain:

She received her orders on Norm-Comm. She was needed in the starboard side weapons bay to analyze a problem with the rail gun magazine. She acknowledged the order and started getting into a uniform.

While dressing, she bumped her arm against the dresser. The pain that accompanied the slight bump surprised her, and when she looked down at her arm, surprise turned to shock. The skin on her arm had sliced open where she bumped into the dresser. Blood was flowing freely from her arm onto the floor.

She cried as she ran over to the cabinet and pulled out the med-kit. She applied analgesic and a flexi-wrap onto the wound. As the flexi-wrap started to tighten around the wound, the skin where the flexi-wrap was bonded started to tear.

More pain flowed up her arm, and she screamed in agony. She fell to the floor and cried as blood dripped onto her legs. Her tears stopped for a moment as she realized that she now had a pain in her legs. She looked down and the skin on her knees were torn, it appeared as if it was just flaking off.

She screamed again and activated her Norm-Comm "Doctor, please come quick...please, I hurt so badly!"

When Max arrived, he opened the door with his emergency medical code, and ran in. He saw Nova laying on the floor in a pool of blood, unconscious. He looked over the torn skin – he touched the skin near her knee and to his surprise a large flake came off and stuck to his finger.

"Medical team, this is Doctor Sollix – prepare the emergency center for triage. Send a sealed transport here stat! Prepare for treating patient as a burn victim." He looked at her again. "What the hell is going on with you..." he said as he pulled out his medical scanner and began waving it across her body. Reading the scan results all he could mutter was "Oh shit, this can't be..."

Jaime Bordeaux:

Finally, they had been released to survey star systems for habitable planets. Yes, the Star Force Commander expected them to survey for the benefit of the Blessed, but at least they would be able to first determine if a world was suitable for any human life before the Blessed made a jumping conclusion. Their star maps listed this planet as designated name – Queek.

They had been circling the planet for the past hour as they performed surface scans and looked for signs of population centers. Jaime watched her crew work while they determined the best spot to send a landing party. Queek was the fourth planet in a five planet system that surrounded a yellow class G star. This planet was also the only one in the system that had an atmosphere capable of sustaining human life.

"Captain, we have determined the best site for an exploratory landing" announced Katsumi. "There is a spot large enough to land in the middle of a forested area. This forest is near a spot that we suspect may house civilized life. We cannot be sure, but it is the best possibility, and the bio-sensors are indicating some form of life down there."

"So, pretty much we are going to go down and verify we can't live there, eh?" Katsumi nodded in agreement. "Ok, well prepare two transports. Well, at least it looks like the weather is good and we can enjoy a little time planet-side. Let's go down and log the population so I can make the Star Force Commander's day."

Within three hours the transports had landed on the surface of Queek. After checking for air quality and breathability – the hatch opened to a brightly lit field of green, tall grass. The ships were in a clearing surrounded by a thick forest of ponderosa-type pine trees. The air was thick with pollen and various smells of pine and other flora. Small insects flew in the sunshine. The air was warm, sensors indicated it was seventy six Alliance standard degrees.

Jonathan sneezed as soon as the air hit his nostrils. He had to remove his wraparound sun filtering glasses, as tears were flowing down his cheeks from the swelling in his eyes. Doctor Starling had accompanied them, she came up to him and gave the young man an anti-histamine shot to ease his allergic suffering.

Jaime giggled at him slightly, then stepped out onto the transport ramp. She closed her eyes and relished in the warm sun on her face. She reopened her eyes, but then had to cover them from the bright sun – she was definitely not used to the bright light of a real sun. She went back into the ship and returned with a half-coverage, Alliance soldier battle helmet. She placed the helmet on her head and lowered the protective screen, which provided polarized control of the light to her eyes.

Upon recovering from his sneezing fit, Jonathan went back inside and returned a moment later. He handed a pair of spectacles to Jaime. She looked at the glasses now in her hand. "Try them Captain..." he advised. "They will filter the light and give you much better freedom of movement for your head and eyes. It will definitely be much better without that bulky, Blessed helmet. I styled them based on an images I found of spectacles designed in the late twentieth century."

She removed the helmet and put on the aviator shaped glasses, the gold coating on the outer side of the glass reflected the scene in front of her to everyone else. She looked around, testing the filtering ability of the glasses. Then, she noted the digital displays and indicators that activated as she looked around. She nodded her head as she was impressed with not only how they filtered the sun, but also the various identifications and measurements the glasses were providing. After testing the glasses out for a minute she smiled at Jonathan "These are great. May I have a pair?"

"Those are yours. They have no vision adjustment and are perfect for you. They look stylish too!"

"Well, thank you then." She turned and tossed the helmet to another of the crew who was squinting their eyes at the bright light. "We may want to make more pairs for the rest of the crew. OK, let's head through the forest and see what is over where we think there is civilized life. Everyone bring weapons, but let's try not to use them ok?"

"Captain?" said Otter over Norm-Comm "the Conquest just arrived in-system and is coming into a parking orbit around this planet. Orders?"

"Crap, that's all we don't need. Do nothing – we are one big Alliance family after all. Let's hope they just don't start anything while we're down here." She lowered her head in frustration for a moment, then turned to the team "Okay, we have to get moving...our time here just became shorter. Thanks Otter, Bordeaux out."

The landing team walked for five miles to the edge of the forest. Beyond the forest was a knoll that overlooked what they thought, based on their scans, was a habitation. What was in that habitation, if anything, they were not sure. They quietly crept up the knoll and crouched just below the crest. Indeed, there was some form a habitat or village as there were buildings down below them. The buildings appeared to be mud huts – round mounds with openings in the sides used for entry and exit.

106

Creatures wandered amongst the mounds of mud, but Jaime was unable to tell much about the beings. Jonathan reached over and showed Jaime a button on her glasses that allowed her to zoom the view of the glasses. With this adjustment, she was able to see with great detail into the center of the city.

She saw creatures wandering around what appeared to be a central marketplace. The creatures were covered with dark brown fur, they had round black eyes – three of them, and long elephant-like proboscises which hung down past their fanged mouths. Below their heads were four furry arms – two in front and two on the side of the top of their torso and below that six small legs that they used to skitter around. Their backs were curved, so much so she was surprised they could even move at all.

"This is amazing…" Jaime said as she watched the activity in the village below. "They are nothing like us. So totally different. I could just watch them all day…" She then turned away and looked back to the forest "But…we can't stay. We have no idea about this race, and this is their planet. We need to leave. Science teams take your scans and images, grab what samples you need or want to take, and prepare to return to the ship."

"A primitive race? Perhaps we should just kick them off?" said a voice from lower on the knoll. Jaime looked down and saw Kip Gurrigan coming up the slope followed by at least a hundred black uniformed Secret Service guards. They had parked their transport in an area just a mile away – not a care about being detected – and were already upon them and the village below. He joined the team on the crest, opened the visor of his half-helm, and took out a pair of binoculars. He gazed down into the village and watched the activity. "Interesting…" he says as he continued his scrutinizing of the creatures. "We should be able to take this planet pretty easily" he finally said.

"No, that won't be happening" Jaime sternly told him. "This is their planet and we will not be trying to conquer them or this place. It is not ours to take. Let's not be stupid about this…"

"Did you call me stupid?" he yelled out. "I think you overstep yourself, Bordeaux!" he shouted.

"Actually..." she interrupted "I think it is *you* who has it wrong and is overstepping your authority. I AM the number one Alpha Starship Captain you know."

"Oh really? Care to wager that with your consciousness and your position? I think one shot from my stunner will teach you a lesson, and put you down one notch in the ranking order."

He lifted his left arm and aimed his command weapon at Jaime. She stood up and moved about ten feet away from him, smiling the whole time. "Are you really thinking of using that on me?"

"As a matter of fact...yes" he said as he fired. He however, did not anticipate Jaime just as quickly raising her left arm, and being able to fire a return stun bolt. The two electrical bolts hit in the middle and each dissipated into the air as they each fought to gain control. The air filled with static electricity as the two captains fought to get the advantage.

Kip concentrated and was able to increase the flow of power from the embedded reactor in the base of his neck. The power flowed freely and started to push Jaime's bolt back toward her own command weapon. Jaime began to sweat as she fought off his increased attack. He pushed again and the bolt moved even closer – it was now only two feet away from her.

"See, you have no chance...no chance at all little girl..." he said as he pushed even more amperage and voltage through his weapon, forcing the meeting of the bolts another two inches closer.

"Oh my..." she said, her arm shaking slightly as she fought off his increased onslaught "whatever shall I do?" Kip pushed again, but this time he could gain no more ground in his attack. He looked at her and noticed she was smiling. She said to him "I know...I think this little girl will end this now." Suddenly the power emitting from her command weapon tripled and completely reversed the advantage he had into a disadvantage favoring her.

"What? How can this be?" he shouted as he pushed more power through to his weapon. He smelled smoke and felt heat in the back of his neck as his reactor was pushed to the limit and had started to overheat.

"Take a nap, Kippie" she said and pushed one more increase in the power of her bolt. The pulse reached his command weapon and blew it apart with a loud pop. He was shocked into unconsciousness, and his body was flown down the slope from the force of the electrical bolt hitting him. He landed sprawled out on the ground convulsing, foamy saliva spat out of his mouth. Mercifully after a minute of convulsing, the muscles of his body finally stopped the involuntary constrictions, and his body calmed, leaving him a limp mass of flesh lying on the ground.

Jaime looked at the lead Secret Service guard. "I think I have proven my Alpha status. Take this Captain back to your ship and leave."

"Yes Alpha Starship Captain" snapped the guard who turned and pointed at Kip. Four other guards opened a folding stretcher and placed him upon it. The lead guard then nodded to the others to follow. A minute later they had retreated around the back side of a nearby hill and out of sight.

Halley looked at Jaime with amazement. "I didn't even think you could fire that at him, much less overpower him to THAT degree!"

Jaime chuckled "Yeah...My Blessed reactor was failing, and Max discovered the limiting circuitry while examining me. He and Jonathan designed a better reactor for me...without the limitation circuits. He installed it quite a while back and I did quite a bit of practice with it. Really had not had a reason to use it until now..." Hearing her words, Jonathan raised his chin and glowed with pride.

Jaime turned back to the village to make sure the small internal battle had not alerted the village to their presence. They were still wandering around in the same manner – they still did not know they were up there. "Ok, let's head out and get back to Ladyhawk" she ordered.

Kip Gurrigan:

By the time they arrived back at the transport he had started to regain consciousness. He found himself on a stretcher being carried up the ramp and into the ship. With a weakened voice he called out "Put me down!"

The guards followed his command and softly set him on the deck of the ramp. He sat up and relaxed there for a moment, then looked at the guard towering above him. "Are we ready to leave? Are all our troops accounted for?" he asked.

"No, my Alpha Starship Captain" he replied "we are awaiting one last patrol."

"Very well. Fetch me some water then...I thirst" he commanded.

The guard returned with a flask of water and as Kip drank it the guard called out "Look, they are returning from patrol, and it appears they have found something..."

Kip's eyes opened wide as he saw they had some living creature surrounded and were escorting it back to the transport. As they got closer he could see it was a humanoid female. She appeared to be a little over four feet tall, had dark brown hair that flowed down her head and covered part of her naked body. He stared at her and took in her features – she seemed human enough. Breasts and her lower parts appeared to be human, her two legs seemed strong and shapely, she appeared to have the proper amount of eyes, a slightly larger forehead, small nose, and a shapely mouth. He licked his lips as they brought her in front of him. Her hands and feet had five digits each, and her skin was both very tan and slightly covered with dirt. He assumed she had been living in the wild for quite a while. Despite his weakened state, he found a slight arousal from being near her.

"Where did you find her?" he asked.

"We investigated a cave, my Alpha Starship Captain...and she was inside. She gave no resistance which surprised us. We were ready to take her by force."

He found he had enough strength to stand. He looked down at her and ran his fingers through her dirty hair. He looked into her eyes as she stared up at him. "So, I wonder if you are intelligent at all? I wonder if you can speak or if you even have a name?"

"Paa…" she said softly.

"What?" he replied.

"Paad" she let out again.

"Is that your name? Paad? I don't like it. I am going to call you Patti."

"Patti…" she replied, then surprised him with "I like that. You may call me Patti."

His eyes opened in surprise "So, you DO have some intelligence then. You are coming with us. I have a nice warm bath planned for you. Then a visit to the doctor. Then…we will see…"

They boarded and she came along willingly. The transport lifted off and returned to the Conquest. Upon arrival Kip ordered Patti to a containment cell and commanded the doctor to clean and examine her. He then proceeded to the bridge where his crew was ready and awaiting his next order. He sat at the command console and thought for a moment. The helmsman finally queried "Course, Alpha Starship Captain?"

He looked at the holo-screen and pointed to the next planet in the system while ordering "There, take us behind that planet and put us in a parking orbit. We will be waiting there until Bordeaux leaves the system. Then, we go back and take over…"

10 years ago...

He handed the card to the guard, who scrutinized it more than he expected. He looked him up and down, but finally relented, handed the card back to him, and nodded his head toward the door – he was being allowed access.

He walked down the long hallway until he found the sign labeled "Recruit Evaluations". He turned and entered the large room. There were hundreds of others waiting for their chance to convince the headmasters to take them in as students. He was handed a number the moment he walked in the door, and was ordered to find a seat and not make a sound while he waited. He did as he was told and sat in the uncomfortable wooden bench for the next five hours.

Finally, his number was called – he followed the lights down a hallway and into yet another room. Here however, was only a desk. A woman sat at the desk – she scrutinized him as he slowly walked in. She motioned him to sit down, then continued to look him up and down. He began to perspire as she kept looking at him without saying a single word. Finally, she broke the tension and said "So, what is it you can do?"

"I can handle a weapon really well..." he replied.

"You think so huh?" she said as she pressed a button then pointed at the door. "Go prove it, follow the lights."

He followed the lights to a dark room. Only a single spotlight shone on the floor. A voice boomed from somewhere in the room. "Stand in the light..." the voice ordered. He complied and waited, and waited. Finally, a table slid in front of him – on this table was a hand blaster. "Pick it up. Fire when you see a target."

To his left, a hallway lit up and standing in the hallway was a soldier. He was carrying an enormous blaster rifle. As soon as the soldier saw him he lifted his rifle to shoot him. He did not wait or hesitate, he quickly lifted his blaster and fired. His shot was deadly and accurate as he took down the soldier with a single shot to his unprotected throat.

A moment later the table appeared again "Place the gun on the table and sit at the console ahead of you" ordered the mysterious man. A light appeared on a console that seemed to look like a spaceship command console. He followed orders and sat at the console. A moment later, it lit up and began giving him details about a space battle. There was an attacking force incoming, and he was receiving orders to take them out. He took the fire control, and quickly wielded the weapons. There were five ships inbound toward him – he aimed quickly, and fired. He quickly downed two, then three, the fourth, and finally the fifth incoming fighter craft without wasting a shot.

The mystery voice spent the next four hours running him through a battery of scenarios. Each one became deadlier and deadlier. He started to wonder if these simulations could hurt him if he failed. In the knife examination, he discovered the deadly reality of the tests as he misjudged and felt the sharp edge of his opponent's blade against the skin on his arm. Blood flowed but he did not stop – he fought off that attacker, and killed him. He realized at that moment, that everyone he fought and killed had actually died. He wondered if they were being tested also – if so, he assumed they failed.

Finally, the lights came on and behind him sat a man smoking a cigarette. He wondered about that smell and now he knew where it was coming from. The man stood up, put out his cigarette on the floor, and walked over to him. He looked him up and down before finally giving a small smile, extending his hand, and saying "You lived. Welcome to the academy Mr. Capsain."

NGD: 2 Years, 11 Months, 6 Days

Planet Queek:

Yuli Capsain:

Max called him to the sick bay with no information other than "Come quick!" Based on Max's lack of information, he assumed that an accident happened to Nova. When he arrived, he realized it was even worse than he though.

He ran into the sick bay and yelled out "Where is she? Where's Nova?"

Max ran up to him, and grabbed him by the shoulders. His strong grip stopped Yuli from moving any farther. "Yuli, something has happened to Nova. She is in the isolation bay."

"Isolation?" he questioned "Why is she in isolation?"

"For her own good..." he answered. "Did you know she was pregnant?"

"Yes, she told me the good news. Is the baby...the baby alright?" he started to cry slightly.

"Yes, both baby and mother are alive. However, Nova appears to have a...condition..." he stopped speaking and looked behind him into the burn treatment bay. "Her skin is deteriorating at an accelerated rate. What has she told you about herself?" he asked.

Yuli looked confused. "She grew up in sector one, her mother died when she was young and had to survive alone."

"Did she tell you about her mother? What her mother did?" Yuli shook his head no. "Well, I looked into it. It ends up her mother was a prostitute...a prostitute for Blessed customers."

"So? Her mother was a Normal correct?" he queried.

"Yes, but she was an exclusive for the Blessed. She became pregnant by a Blessed. And thus, her child has Blessed genes. This is why she always avoided being medically scanned. She knew I would see the enhancements in her DNA."

"So, why is she suffering? Why would this happen to her now?"

"You two bonded and started to reconfigure. Then she became pregnant...it caused her to reconfigure even more. But now, her Blessed DNA is fighting the change...she is rejecting the change in part of her genetic make-up and accepting it in the other. Thus, without being able to control it, she is tearing herself apart."

"Is there anything that can be done?" he asked Max.

"Right now, I am keeping her in a sealed chamber. Her skin is deteriorating at a fast rate, she will be prone to infection or disease at this point, and I have to prevent that. Also, if the deterioration continues, her skin will fall totally away – she will have nothing to keep her insides contained. Jonathan and the engineers are building a robotic shell for her. As soon as it is done we will seal her inside the shell. This will prevent her from turning into a mass of un-contained muscle and organs. After that however, I am not sure."

"So basically, when I mated with her, I killed her..." he said somberly.

"No, it was not your fault..." Max replied.

"But had I not mated with her, this would never have happened" he muttered.

"No, it would have happened sometime. The moment she found anyone she was compatible with and had contact, the process would have started. It could have been anyone. Now, quit blaming yourself and go on over to the console. You will have to speak with her via the internal comm channel as her Norm-Comm appears to have shut down. Use the intercom, she will be able to hear you. Talk to her...she needs you."

He went quickly to the console and pressed the comm button. "My love...I am so sorry...this is all my fault..." Tears flowed from his eyes as he saw the sealed tube where her body lay. He could not see her, but he knew she was in there, he could feel her presence inside.

From the console he heard a weak voice "No, it was my fault. I didn't tell you. I didn't think it would matter...did not think..."

He looked at the console, the display showed a heart rate, but she no longer spoke. "Doc, what happened?" he yelled out.

"She drifts in and out of consciousness. She needs rest now. If you want to stay, I'll prepare a bed for you." He nodded yes. "We'll do whatever we can for her. But at this point, the Normal in her needs to beat the Blessed that is trying to kill her. Her genetics need to battle it out – let's hope the stronger side is the Normal side."

Kip Gurrigan:

It was a long twenty four hours before the Ladyhawk finally left the system. He was still drinking recovery drinks when the Normal vessel finally zoomed away. "AH! They have finally left! Okay...Helm, take us back to Queek and put us into orbit. Captain of the guard, prepare your soldiers for a conquest party." He looked to his first, Stanford Massey "You go down and conquer this planet for us. You will be a hero and will give the Alliance a reason to promote you to a Captaincy"

"Thank you, my Alpha Starship Captain!" he snapped to attention. "I will conquer this planet in the name of the Supreme Commander, the Alliance and Order, our Star Force Commander, and of course for you."

"Do us proud First Officer...do us proud."

Stanford Massey:

Stanford took five hundred crack Secret Service soldiers down to the surface in three large transports. He boldly landed the craft in the clearing just outside the habitation. The creatures in the village began gathering and slowly moving toward the three spacecraft.

The shuttle ramps were lowered and hundreds of black armored soldiers came rushing out like swarming locusts. They quickly began to setup perimeter defenses, ground station blaster platforms, and automated mortar launchers.

Stanford walked bravely and boldly out into the sunlight, he raised his hand over his eyes to shield them, then finally put on a full coverage battle helmet, and lowered the sunscreen. He approached the command Sergeant "Is everything in order? Have you assessed the battlefield? Are we ready to attack?"

The Battle Sergeant snapped to attention. He stood seven feet tall and was a solid tower of muscle, his black armor pushing his large chest even further out as he stood at attention. He spoke through the speaker in the neck piece of his dark black helmet. "We are ready my First. I have analyzed the inhabitants of this village, and have determined a frontal attack is the best course of action. They have no weapons, we have nothing to fear. All that is required is your order to attack."

He looked out at the habitation again. The creatures were just standing at the edge of the village – they appeared to be just watching the invaders out of curiosity. He looked back at the Sergeant "Yes, you may begin the attack."

The soldiers lined up in two equal lines of two hundred and fifty soldiers each, one line in front of the other. They began to take slow steady steps toward the village, weapons drawn and aimed. As they got to almost point blank range, the Sergeant took aim and commanded the force to open fire. Blaster beams shot across the open field, some hit the staring creatures, which tore holes through their bodies. The creatures immediately scattered to hide behind their mud huts. Blasts continued to fire from the muzzles of the soldier's guns, and tore through the huts, killing many more of the concealed creatures.

Stanford watched the encroaching force from a safe distance behind the perimeter defenses. Helmet open, binoculars glued to his face, and smiling with the taste of victory in his mouth. "Yes, this will be a bloodbath. It's like taking candy from a baby." He then noticed balls rolling from behind the mud huts. They slowly rolled toward the approaching army. "What is that?" he asked.

His bodyguard, also viewing through binoculars shrugged his shoulders "I am not sure my First...but they seem to be rolling to our troops."

The balls approached the Battle Sergeant and stopped. He looked down at the ball. Each ball was about four feet in circumference, they seemed furry, but at the same time looked like leather, and when he poked at it with his rifle it was hard as steel. He looked closer at the ball with curiosity. As he got closer, he noticed little sharp thorn-like protrusions beginning to poke out slightly from the surface of the ball. He never expected the needles that shot out of the ball without warning. The needles pierced his armor, flying straight through his body and out the other side. Those needles continued from his body into the soldier standing directly behind him. The Sergeant's eyes were taken out by even more needles shooting out of the ball a second later. He screamed in pain as the needles not only pierced right through him, but at the same time left a trail of acidic syrup that burned the insides of his body. Over his own screams and moans, he could hear the screaming of the soldiers all around him.

Stanford, at his observation position dropped his binoculars in horror. His troops were being attacked and slaughtered before his eyes. The air was now filled with the smell of acid on burning flesh – his army was melting away while he watched. More balls rolled over to the next line of previously approaching men. They started to flee, but the needles shooting out of the rolling balls were too quick for them to escape. They fell as quickly as the first line, screaming and melting – the chemical payload of the needles were doing their damage to the flesh and meat of the attackers. As the second line went down, the creatures from the village skittered out to the first melting line of soldiers. They stopped and began to consume the dying soldiers, his troop's screams of agony continued to fill Stanford's ears as the creatures bit through armor. Sharp teeth tore into the melting flesh and bone of the hapless men and women. When the creatures would hit an imbedded piece of tech, they would tear it from their bodies, chew on it for a moment, then spit the worthless piece of circuitry onto the ground.

"Sir, we should go…" said his bodyguard.

He nodded "Yes, leave everything behind. Get anyone left aboard, and give the order to take off immediately!" He ran up the ramp and his remaining soldiers followed. He raised the ramp and closed the airlock door. He ran to the cockpit and started up the engines. Outside he heard the pops of the automated defensive weapons – beams and mortar shells were launched as the native defenders approached. "We have got to leave, NOW!" he shouted.

The engines fired up and he could feel the bulk of the ship lift off of the ground. He started to feel a moment of relief, that is until he heard screaming behind him in the cargo hold. He turned on the bay monitor to see thousands of small rays of sunlight beaming in through the same amount of small holes in the hull. He heard pinging as another volley of needles hit the hull of the ship. The navigational controls began smoking and sparking as the small needles pierced the electronics and melted them. He

119

then felt the needle hit his leg – he cried out in pain as the appendage started melting away before his eyes.

The ship started to waver and plopped back onto the ground with a jolting thud. Stanford reached down and touched his leg – or what was left of it – as most of it had melted away and was now a stub. Flesh and blood dripped from the remaining bone fragment and plopped onto the steel floor plate. He heard the engines die a slow death as the needles penetrated the ionic condensers and thrusters. Then, he heard bodies climbing the hull of the ship – and they were climbing up to the cockpit. In the cargo hold, more screaming and in the monitor, he saw the creatures on top of the passengers viciously tearing their fanged mouths into them, devouring the leftover flesh. He heard scratching on the hull above him and he slowly looked up. Fear now took everything from him, he was unable to move – frozen solid in panic. On his communicator, he could hear Kip screaming, but he was too scared to answer him – he only mumbled in tears.

Finally, the hull plating was torn away from above his head and one of the three-eyed creatures looked down at him. The thing's trunk lowered and wrapped itself around his neck, then with a smooth motion pulled him out of his seat, and up out of the ship. It dangled him with its trunk while it looked at him with its three dark, black eyes. Stanford whimpered, and tears started to flow freely from his eyes. The creature looked more curiously at him and made a sort of light squeaking noise, then a cooing sound. Stanford relaxed just slightly at the sound and looked into the three eyes, thinking perhaps they might show him mercy – right before it sent a volley of needles from its torso into his belly. He screamed out in pain as he felt his body start to melt. The creature then lowered Stanford near his fanged maw and shot out a burst of digestive acid onto his head. He was still screaming as his head had started to melt. He did not stop his painful cry until the creature popped his softened head into its mouth, and chewed it off with vigor.

Patti:

She was taken from the holding chamber to the bridge. Kip was standing at the holo-screen with tears flowing freely from his now darkened blue eyes. He turned and looked at her, sorrow was now being replaced with anger. She was not sure what to think or was not sure what he was about to do.

He looked down at her and said "Did you know they would do this? Did you know and allow us to die this way?"

She looked at him slightly confused, then looked at the holo-screen and understood. "Oh, you attacked the Queek."

"Yes, and did you know they would do this?"

"You attacked the Queek, and the Queek killed you. I would not have attacked the Queek."

"Shit, take this bitch back to the cell" he ordered. The guards began to push her near the bridge door. She stopped and saw Kip turn away from her "Weapons..." he said as he turned to the weapons officer "activate the nukes. Lay waste to that planet. Full carpet spread of smart bombs – make sure everything burns. Also, prepare wide angle lasers and fire those right after the bombs hit. I want nothing left alive on that planet before we leave."

"That might take a while to fully accomplish, Alpha Starship Captain. But I will make it so." the weapons officer replied.

The guards on Patti poked her in the back with their blaster rifles, but she resisted and turned toward Kip again. He heard the scuffle, turned, and she said "Queek now will kill you, and now will kill me. They will now kill all of us."

"Take her out..."

Kip was interrupted by the science officer who screamed in panic "Sir! A large number of objects are rising from the surface of the planet. They appear to be missiles of some form. I am picking up high levels of various forms of radiation. Based on these readings, if one hits us, we will be destroyed."

"Shit!" he cried out. "How long before impact?"

"Two minutes..." the science officer replied.

In the holo-screens they all saw the multitude of bright green lights headed up from the surface toward their location.

"That is enough time then. Helm leave orbit NOW...push the ion drives to maximum and get us out of here." He looked at her again and pointed at the hatch "And get her out of here!"

The guard looked down at her then froze in his tracks. The second guard also looked down and followed suit in becoming stiff as a statue. Kip turned and saw her still standing there, just staring at him "If we are going to die, then I choose to die here and not in some cell..." she told him.

The ship zoomed out of the system, with hundreds of missiles following in pursuit. Kip looked at the small bright green dots following them on the rear bridge view screen. He steepled his fingers while he watched their continued pursuit. "Damn, they have to run out of fuel soon...Weapons, fire the rear rail guns..."

The officer followed orders and fired a spread of spent plutonium shells toward the oncoming pursuers. Most of the missiles however avoided the shells – only four actually hit a target.

"Shit, that isn't going to do it..."

Patti sat on the floor and watched the events with a smile.

*   *   *

Three days had passed and the missiles were still following them. The crew was weary and worried that they were indeed going to die. Kip now bit his fingernails trying to come up with a plan. Patti was still sitting on the floor, watching the events unfold. Two days ago, Kip ordered that the fission reactors be brought on-line as they needed the additional power.

Kip looked at his command display, even with the fission reactors on line, the engines would fail eventually as they could not handle being driven so hard for such a long period of a time. He thought for a while before he finally came up with an idea. He ran to the science station which peeked Patti's interest. She jumped up, leaving the two guards still frozen in place, and ran over to see what they were looking at. Kip glared at her as she approached but otherwise ignored her. "So..." he said to the science officer "what we need is a very busy asteroid field. One that may give us enough distractions for those missiles."

"Yes, I understand, my Alpha Starship Captain..." replied the young officer as he studied the readouts from the computer analysis. "I think this...might be a good place. It is a nebula, and our maps show it to be a highly concentrated mass of gasses, dust, and asteroids. It just might work."

Kip slapped the officer on the back. "Of course it will work! Helm, set a course that will be computed for you by science and head there flank speed."

Patti sat down and waited another three days for them to reach the nebula. She looked in the rear view screen and saw that the missiles had actually gotten closer in their pursuit. She was impressed by the Queek weapons.

"Sir, we cannot fly flank speed through there..." the helmsman called out.

"Well, I guess either you fly us into that before you slow down or be nuked by the missiles behind us. Your choice as to how you die. Personally, I want to die trying to achieve victory. So, either you fly us in there at flank speed or I will shoot you, and do it myself. Your choice..." He aimed his command weapon at the pilot, but then realized it was destroyed in his fight with Jaime. So he got up, walked over to one of the guards, took a blaster from his holster, and aimed it at the helmsman.

He nervously eyed the blaster pointed at his head while he began to slowly change course. "Yes, my Alpha Starship Captain. I am heading into the nebula at flank speed..." he gulped and held his breath as they entered. He was able to avoid the first few asteroids but figured he would hit one he had not seen at any second.

Kip however, gave him some faith when he ordered "Ok, slow us down so you can maneuver."

In the view screen behind them, a few of the missiles were hitting various asteroids and objects as the nebula interfered with their targeting systems.

"Now, Weapons...fire the rail guns again..." Kip ordered.

Another volley of shells fired out in a random pattern. This time many of the missiles were hit and taken out. The

Conquest swerved around two, then three more floating bodies of rock. Many of the following missiles could not determine the proper path around them, hit the asteroids, and detonated. The ship was rocked by the force of the explosions.

"Shit!" Kip cried out. "If even one of those hit us with the explosive power they contain, we will be taken out." An alarm took him from his thought. He ran over to the engineering station, and his eyes opened wide as he saw that the engines were overheating. "Damn, is everything against us?"

Patti replied quietly "Yes…"

"Another spread from the rail guns!" Kip barked "Helm, take us to port…over to that set of asteroids. You had better be good at steering, as you will be turning fast and hard…Weapons, fire!"

Another round of rail gun shells and more explosions. The ship sharply turned as the helmsman managed to snake the ship through the thin opening between the tumbling asteroids. Then he made a small turn to port and then back onto a straight path. The ship shook again as more of the missiles hit the tumbling asteroids.

The science officer looked up from his SCADAR readings. "Alpha Starship Captain, there is only one missile left pursuing us!"

"Good!" he shouted as he ran over to the weapons console, and took the firing glove off of the station officer. "I will fire the final shot. I will be our savior!" He placed the glove onto his hand, and allowed the targeting computer to gain a lock on the incoming missile. "Slow the ship down Helm" he called out. He took one finger, and pointed it at the incoming weapon of death. Then he made sure the computer had a good target lock, and then poked the one finger at the target on the screen. A single shell was launched and hit the oncoming missile. The target was much closer than he anticipated and the explosion pummeled the ship, which sent everyone flying across the bridge. Kip hit his head on the far bulkhead, the injury caused a flow of blood to pour down his forehead. He sat up slightly dazed, but then looked at the remnants of the explosion on the view screen. He jumped up and lifted his fist in victory as he shouted "Yes!"

Patti was still sitting in the same place on the floor of the bridge. She gave a small laugh, causing Kip to turn his attention toward her. "You were lucky…" she said. He walked up with a closed fist and began the motion to strike her. She looked into his eyes and he stopped his swing in mid-air. "I don't think you will be so lucky the next time…" she said as she stood up, turned, and left the bridge. She returned to her holding cell and closed the door herself.

Six Months Prior to Starlight Launch...

We are so proud of you. You will be traveling out into space to help preserve the Blessed race, and spread the goodness that is the Alliance to the stars. You are going to be so happy, you will be the first to wed and have children on a new world. Your father and I are so proud of you my darling Dahlia.

NGD: 3 Years, 1 Month and 23 Days:

Starlight Space Ark:

Dahlia Marteen:

"Good morning Dahlia, did you sleep well?"

Dahlia could barely keep her eyes open as they were not used to the bright lights, it had been so long since she went to sleep. She squinted and put her hands in front of her eyes to shield them from the light.

"Is it too bright? Here, let me turn that down some..." The lights dimmed and Dahlia found it much easier to open her eyes and look around. Standing next to the bed was a nurse. She was smiling fondly at her. "Better?" Dahlia nodded yes.

"Where are we?" she asked.

The nurse smiled "We are in a totally different galaxy. A place no Blessed human has ever been before. We are going to conquer this galaxy and make it our home. That is why you have been awakened, it is time for you to prepare, and to become one of the community again."

"Are we on a space ship?" Dahlia asked. The nurse nodded yes. "Are we going to a planet? Are we going to a colony?"

The nurse shook her head no "Not yet...but soon. In the meantime, you will be staying on a temporary colony. One where we are building great ships to explore and conquer. As soon as you are up and around, I am going to take you to a ship. That ship will take you to one of our bases on the asteroid Plug. You will be happy, and can perhaps start to raise fine children for us. We will be at the asteroid in just a couple days. This will give you time to adjust to being awake and to acclimate to outer space. Do you think you can be ready by then?"

"I am ready now…" Dahlia softly replied.

Blessed Salvage Base Plug:

Lindy Light-Griggs:

She looked at her child and wondered what was going on in his head. He had grown so quickly, he was already walking, and even talking. He was already four feet tall at only a little over two years old. She wondered what all he was going to be capable of.

She had named him Janus. To her, it seemed to fit as Janus was the Roman god with two faces. To her that felt right – he had the genes of both Normal and Blessed. She hoped that the Normal in him would be the dominant force in his life. It appeared to be the case, at least outwardly as he had been developing the winged ears like most Normals since coming to this galaxy. And his growth and learning, it had to be the Normal genes. The skin color however, was different from both Blessed and Normal as it was that greenish-gold shade. Not flesh pink like his father, or the slight blue tinting that had appeared on his mother.

The one thing that was a little worrisome to her, was that Janus went from loathing of his father, to putting up with him, and now was actually starting to like him. This day, Griggs was not on board a ship, and the fleet had gone off on an exploration mission without him – so he was in their quarters, and was playing starship battle with his son. They each sat on the floor holding starship models in their hands. Fitchburg was gliding his ship down toward Janus in an attacking manner.

"I am firing on your helpless ship…zooooommm! Bam, bam, bam" he yelled out in a childlike tone.

Janus looked up at Fitchburg and shocked him by opening his mouth and saying "Boom, cobalt mines, hahahaha!"

Fitchburg looked up at Lindy, who had a shocked look on her face. "He said that? And more important, how could he know that?" he asked her. "Those mines are classified, much less something that an untrained two year old boy should know. Where did you hear about those and why did you teach him that?"

Janus reached up and grabbed his father's arm "No, I knew..."

"How little one?" he asked softly.

"I just knew it."

"What else do you know?"

He looked down and grabbed his starship toy again "I don't know...things...stuff. I just had a feeling I could say it, so I did."

He looked back up at Lindy who was on duty station, monitoring the new communication relay with the home galaxy. "When did you teach him to speak anyway?" he asked her.

She raised an eyebrow at him. "Me, never...he seemed to be able to learn to talk without any intervention on my part. I figured it was one of the gifts he had received from this galaxy."

"Maybe...for once...you are right..." he grumbled.

She snorted at him, and returned to her monitoring as he returned to his play with Janus.

Fitchburg left them after an hour. Janus continued to play with his spaceship toys. He waved them around in various patterns as if they were chasing each other. She wondered what else was going on his head, what else he might know. Her thoughts were interrupted by her Norm-Comm.

"Hello Controller, this is Allen..."

"Well, hello there stranger. Going to Plug for another pick up?"

"Yep, Jeremy said he has quite a few escapees – and he said he has a surprise for Jaime. Are we clear for approach to Plug?"

She checked the SCADAR and listened to Blessed communications for a moment before replying "Yep, you are clear for far-side approach. Have a good trip back."

"Roger that, and thanks. Lindy, are you and your son ready to join us?"

"I can't. Janus needs his father, no matter what I think of him."

"Okay, your decision. We'll talk to you next run. Allen out."

She disconnected from Norm-Comm and looked at Janus. He looked back up at her, then smiled and shocked her by saying "Allen...Recruiter..."

*   *   *

Three hours later, an indicator light came on her console. SCADAR had picked up activity at the Devil's Throat. She quietly activated the video monitor of the area, and then watched as it opened, and spat out a starship. Her eyes opened wide and didn't blink as she watched it float out of the gravity well, then just sat there for a minute. Without warning, it lit up like a candle, and disappeared. She reached over and plugged the deep space antenna into her communication port. "Otter..." she thought on Norm-Comm. "This is what I just saw..." she thought an image of the alien ship "Tell the others..."

Starship Ladyhawk – In Transit to the Black Asteroid

Nova Capsain:

She no longer had any feeling in her skin. She was still in the sick bay, but Max had taken her out of isolation. He told her that she was no longer in danger of infection or disease. She was happy about that one piece of good news. The next good news was walking through the door – Yuli.

He looked at her with tired, sad eyes. He reached up and touched her face, but for some reason she could not feel his touch. "Hello my love. I'm glad you're are out of danger. I've been so worried about you." His hand kept stroking her face and her hair – but she still could not feel the warmth of his touch.

"I have thought of nothing but you Yuli..." she replied. "I wasn't sure I would see you again." She thought for a moment of the belly she could no longer feel. "The baby!" she cried out "What about the baby?"

He shushed her "The baby is fine. Max told me the baby is still healthy and growing despite your problems. The baby is fine..."

"Oh, thank the stars. When I could not feel anything, I was worried that something had happened to...to our child." She calmed herself for a moment then asked "Yuli, why can't I feel anything? You touch me, but I can't feel it. Why?"

"The doctor had to put a coating around you. The coating is protecting the inside of your body. Without it, you would have to stay in isolation." He stroked her face, but she still felt nothing.

"Bring me a mirror...I want to see" she asked.

"I don't think that's a good idea..." he told her.

"Yuli, bring me a mirror" she demanded.

Reluctantly, he picked up a mirror from a nearby table, and brought it to her. He looked over and in the window saw Max who was mouthing "Crap!" when he saw him with the mirror. Max ran into the room, and immediately prepared an injection.

She tried to reach for the mirror, but for some reason could not lift her arm. He took her arm and lifted it slightly to put the mirror into her hand. When he lifted her arm far enough, she saw her body, and for the first time noticed a difference in the way it looked. She stopped her struggle to reach for the mirror and just looked at her arm. The skin was not skin at all – it was a polymer of some form. It had a coloration of Normal flesh tone, but it did not look like flesh. It looked unreal and fake to her.

Max came up and took her other arm and began into inject a medication. She looked at him and he smiled, and said "A sedative...you are going to need something to relax."

She allowed him to give her the shot, but once again she did not feel anything. She looked at the arm that just got the injection and noticed a small port on the underside of her wrist.

Once again, that same flesh-toned polymer covered that arm. "I think you should give me that mirror Yuli..." she ordered.

He handed her the mirror, helped hold her arm up, and she looked at her face. It resembled her face, but it too was fake and plastic. Her eyes had a clear covering over them and plastic eyelids. Her hair was made of black strands of polymer formed and styled to look like her natural hair, and her mouth was only a slit in the plastic.

She dropped the mirror and put her head back. All she wanted to do was cry. Instead she yelled out "I just want to cry...but when I try I CAN'T!"

Max tried as best he could to give a reassuring look as he told her "No, you can't cry because you no longer have tear ducts. You also do not have eyelids...or any skin on your body for that matter. The Blessed DNA in your body tried to kill you. The Normal in you fought it off finally, but not before you had lost every inch of skin on your body. I could do nothing to stop it, it just started falling off. I had Jonathan develop this skin suit for you as otherwise your muscles would just hang loose and eventually weaken to the point they might just fall off the bone. He is developing some micro-servos that will provide additional strength to your muscles as they are having a hard time staying strong even with the polymer skin suit. Your body is fine on the inside, just everything that faces outside is gone or degraded. Your skin, teeth, nails are all gone. Fortunately, your eyes did not degrade..."

"I wish they had..." she interrupted "then I could not see what a monster I've become..."

"I am trying to come up with a plan...I am working on a possible process to graft new skin on you" he told her. "However, with your body missing one hundred percent of your skin...it will take a while to formulate a process and a plan. But I am working on it. I'm sorry Nova..."

She was starting to feel tired from the shot, but managed to reach up and take his hand and say "It's ok doctor...you did what you could...this is my fault. Could you two leave me alone for a while? I need to think about this..."

Yuli kissed her forehead – she did not feel it, he moved her eyelids down over her eye covers, Max dimmed the lights, and then the two of them left alone in the room to rest. Nova lay in the dark and contemplated her death.

XOXO "Otter" Otterdon:

Otter was surprised when she received the deep space message from Lindy – she had no idea she was capable of such long-range communication. What surprised her even more, were the images she sent of the unknown spaceship that had just arrived in their new home galaxy.

She captured the images herself, and then transferred them to the computer of the Ladyhawk. She signaled Katsumi at the science station. "Kat, I just got a video transmission from the Devil's Throat. I have saved it in the computer...you should take a look and have it analyzed.

Katsumi nodded, and then instructed the computer to do the analysis. She then replied "Otter, will you also notify the Captain? I think she will want to know about this, I will continue the analysis."

"Will do..." she said as she activated her Norm-Comm to Jaime. "Captain, we received an image transmission from Lindy on Plug... we think you should see it."

"Lindy? Plug?" she queried.

"Yes, but don't ask me how. Anyway, Katsumi is going to display the images for you. The computer is analyzing it now." Katsumi activated the image for Jaime.

A moment later Jaime came running onto the bridge. "Katsumi, put that image on the main holo-screen please."

The image appeared on the display in the middle of the bridge. It showed the throat opening up and spitting out a large starship. It had three large engine pods at the rear and two engines in the middle section, projecting from the sides. There was a central command sphere and an engineering block in the rear of the craft. It sat in space for a minute after it had been ejected out of the throat – then it lit up and disappeared.

133

Katsumi checked the computer readouts before announcing "Captain, the computer has completed its analysis of the craft..."

Jaime interrupted her "I can tell you what that is. It's a starship of the Southern Hemispheric Union. It appears the south has found us."

Thirty Four Years Ago...

Becky Bursbury was the most beautiful girl he had ever met. He and she took walks through the park, played ball or house all day long. He tried to spend every waking moment with her. She was everything he ever wanted or needed in a girl.

As they sat together on the soft green grass, he analyzed the love of his life. She had her strawberry blonde hair tied into two pigtails, each one flopping down the appropriate side of her head. Rounded freckled cheeks, big bulging blue eyes, a small upturned nose, and large red lips with a perfect set of small teeth.

At his mature age of twelve, he knew she would spend the rest of her life with him.

They sat and looked up at the sun shining through the protective dome of sector one city. The filtered heat of the sun felt good on his face. He was so happy, and was going to let her know. He reached over and took her hand in his. He squeezed her hand and felt her lightly squeeze in return.

"Becky, I have to tell you something..." he said with a wavering voice. "I have decided you are the only girl for me."

"Are you saying?" she asked softly, and looked over at him before looking down in embarrassment. "Do you want to go steady? Is that what you are going to ask?" She was never one for mincing words.

He gave a slight look of disappointment, but managed to continue on "No, a little more than that..." he reached over and took her other hand into his and pulled her body around to face him. "I am thinking that you are the one for me...that we will be together as long as I see fit. You are going to be my bride, and we are going to make a large and wonderful family."

She gave him a look of surprise. "Umm, a family? Don't you think that is a bit too much, too quick? Don't you think we should go steady and maybe even date?"

"No" he interrupted "I think we should start a family...start it now." He reached over and planted his lips against hers in a passionate kiss. At first he thought she was kissing back, but then

felt her push on him as she struggled, and then she bit his lip. A slight bit of blood flowed from his mouth down his chin.

She pushed him away again "I thought you were a nice boy, but now I think you're a jerk! After all this time, and you do this?" she lashed out. "Family? I don't even want to see you again. What do you think I am anyway?"

"A Norm..." he softly said.

She slapped him across the face. His cheek turned a bright, beet red. "I hate you, I hate you!" she screamed. "Leave me alone, I am going home. My mom said you were a pervert! I hate you!" she turned her back on him, and started to run.

She never saw the blaster beam that hit her in the back. Would never know that she had a hole through her chest. She would never know the red blood that now stained her pretty pink dress. She would never know that her now, former boyfriend had shot her as she ran away.

Two Secret Service soldiers came running to his aid, and stood by his side. He stood over her and stared at her dead form as it lay in a growing pool of dark, red blood. He finally expelled saliva onto her dead body "Once again..." he dryly said, then sighed. "Father was right...the only good Norm, is a dead one..."

NGD: 3 Years, 2 Months, and 4 Days:

Starlight Space Ark:

Boral Oldham:

He woke up, and slowly got out of bed. He walked over to the dresser, while letting out a very large yawn. He scratched his face while he looked in the mirror with bleary eyes. He stopped and looked more carefully in the mirror. *Have my sideburns grown longer?* He rubbed the skin on his cheeks and indeed his sideburns had grown down his cheeks and onto his neck. Also, his forehead looked a little longer today. Then there were those two bumps growing in front of his armpits. He definitely would need to visit the ship's doctor sometime soon.

His self-examination and thoughts were interrupted by the bridge trying to contact him. He walked over to the display and activated it. The ship's communication officer was on the line. "My Star Force Commander, I have Alpha Starship Captain Gurrigan on the line, wishing to speak with you."

Finally, Kip was contacting him. He had not heard from him in weeks, and had feared the worst. He cleared the transmission for forwarding. Now, Kip's face was on the holo-display. "Report Kip, where the hell have you been?"

Kip gave a cocky smile. "We ran into a slight bit of trouble, my Star Force Commander. We overcame, but had damage to the ship's engines and communication system, which prevented me from contacting you. The ship has been repaired, and we are headed back to the fleet."

Boral gave him a concerned look "Trouble?"

"Yes, my Star Fleet Commander..." he replied sternly "we had found a planet. It was inhabited, I felt we could take out the indigenous population. I am embarrassed to report that I was wrong. I lost troops and even worse, I lost Blessed under my command...and I lost my First. I will return for punishment."

Boral sighed and spoke with disappointment "Yes, you will be punished for your incompetence." He would have to come up with some form of punishment, it would be light for him in any case, but discipline would have to be maintained. He thought for a moment. "What is even more disappointing Kip, is that once again we have not found a new home to help the Blessed flourish. We have explored so many systems, and yet, we have found nothing."

"I am sure we will find a home soon, my Star Force Commander" Kip stiffly said.

"Report on the Norms..." Boral queried "Were they with you when you attempted the conquest? Did they see you fail? Were we lucky enough for them to be destroyed in your attempt?"

"No, my Star Fleet Commander" he replied with disappointment in his voice. "They left before we attempted the attack on the planet. I have since marked the planet as uninhabitable for Blessed. We should not venture there again."

"Well damn…" he sighed "I guess I will also have to read and acknowledge Bordeaux's report on that planet then…"

"What about the Norms?" Kip asked "What are we going to do about them. It appears they are gaining strength. My analysts suggest that her ship is more powerful than we may realize. We will need better weapons to prevent a revolt. I don't trust her, I think she will eventually become the enemy we have always anticipated she will become."

"I agree, Kip" he replied. "I have made arrangements…I have a spy in her base, and I am getting reports on a daily basis. My agent will do what they can to disrupt any progress they might make. If they can find any technology we do not have, they are to steal it, and send it to me. I have faith they will succeed in their mission. Very well, carry on Kip…Boral out" he said, then terminated the transmission. He looked down at the computer screen. Jaime's face was in the display as part of her planetary discovery report. He looked at her freckled face. *"Damn you Becky…"*

Black Asteroid Base – "Haven":

Jaime Bordeaux:

The Ladyhawk had just returned from exploration patrol, and had just docked at the asteroid base, now called "Haven". Jaime made all final command checks, and released the first crew for some downtime, while at the same time transferring command to the second bridge crew – there was always to be a shift manning the bridge and critical ship's stations. For her crew however, rest and relaxation was now the order of business.

Halley was making her final docking checks. Ensuring that all moorings were properly connected, all drives were in total shutdown mode, and that there was no way the ship would break away from its harbor dock and float into the open space dock. Jaime walked up to the young helmsman "Halley, want to join me for dinner?"

She looked up at her captain with her dark brown eyes through bangs of matching colored hair. "Sure, that would be wonderful!" she said gleefully.

She completed her final checks, then she and Halley left the bridge together. As they walked out, Jaime said "Let's take a walk first shall we? I want to see more of the ship."

They wandered through the many levels of the command module and admired the clean passageways – well labeled hatches, computer assistance indicators everywhere. The ship was the apex of modern technology and advancement.

"It is a thing of beauty isn't it?" Halley asked.

Jaime shook her head yes "Indeed. Let's take a look at the engineering section shall we?"

They walked through the connector section, looking at the modest living areas, recreation rooms, gymnasiums, and artificial open areas. Jaime looked impressed over the condition of her ship. They reached the end of the connector section and took a lift as soon as they entered the engineering section of the ship. Upon entering the lift, she ordered the lift to the lowest level.

Halley looked at her with a confused look. "You want to go to the low levels? Why?"

Jaime had a stern look on her face "I want to see the lowest, most hidden, forgotten levels of this ship..." she said with a serious tone.

The lift stopped at the bottom level of the ship. The door opened to a quiet, cool passageway. The two stepped out and looked around. There was a slight hum reverberating in the passageway, the reactor noise in this section would be intense during full power runs. The passageway was clean and new. She touched the wall then checked her fingers as if looking for dust. She nodded her head in acceptance "Let's go to the rear of the ship..."

They walked down the long corridor, occasionally stopping at random hatches. Jaime opened the hatches, looked inside, and inspected the room behind the doors. A half hour later they reached the end of the corridor, a stairway led from this point up into the other parts of the engineering section. She turned and looked at Halley seriously, then smiled at the young woman. "I'm satisfied."

Halley gave her quizzical look "What exactly were you looking for?"

"Crap...garbage...scum..." she said seriously. "I never want to have any of that on board this ship. When I was on Starlight, a number of times I was asked to meet...the Recruiter...in some place as far away from other people as possible. Those meetings took me to the lowest levels of that ship. I saw some of the most despicable and disgusting areas that a ship could become. Every type of scum was down there and that part of the ship reflected that. It was neglected and run down...something that should never happen to a modern starship. I committed myself... if I ever got a starship...that would never happen aboard any ship...under my command. If I have to come down here and make sure personally, I will. That will NEVER happen aboard this ship...or any ship under Normal command...if I can help it."

"Then I will do what I can to help!" Halley told her with enthusiasm in her voice.

Jaime gave her a warm smile "I knew you would understand. Okay, let's go eat..."

The pair walked through more of the engineering section, inspecting the engines on their way to one of the connecting gangways, then made their way to one of the dining halls that overlooked the space harbor dock. Jaime's position got the two of them a table right at the external transparencies. They dined on a wonderful meal of fresh grown plants, protein base in a roast format, and a gelatin desert hosting a delicious flavoring of ripe blueberries. Jaime tasted the last spoonful of her dessert and let a small "Yum" escape from her lips.

"This flavor so reminds me of when I was a child..." she said.

Halley took another spoonful of the clear jell, but thought of other things while she savored it.

Finally, Jaime put down her spoon and looked deeply into Halley's eyes. "Halley, there is something I want to ask you…"

Halley was not sure what to think. She blushed slightly, but just looked at Jaime with interest, hoping she would not notice her mental struggle and agitation. "What is it?" she finally asked calmly.

Jaime smiled "Well, Ladyhawk is a very large ship as you just found out…it really takes more than one person to command her. I was hoping that you would consider becoming my first. Allen will never be on board as he is close to having a ship of his own. You are closest to being next in line for a command…at least I would hope you consider command as some point. Will you consider this? Will you be the first officer of the Ladyhawk?"

Deep inside, Halley was full of disappointment. Confusion wracked her soul – she replayed the request over and over in her mind, not knowing what to think or do. Jaime looked at her with concern. When she finally had overcome her inner thoughts and fears, she said "I can't…"

Jaime scrunched her forehead. "But why? We work so well together."

Halley shook her head lightly "I just can't…and I can't explain…"

Jaime gave her a disgusted look. "It isn't what everyone says is it?" she asked sternly.

Halley was overtaken by shock. "What? What do you mean?" she asked. Inside she was mentally panicked.

Her fears came true when Jaime said dryly "Everyone says…That you have eyes only for the Captain? Is that really the reason why you won't take this position and work with me?"

Halley could barely keep her tears from flowing – it was all coming out now. She gave up trying to be formal with her and just blurted out "That's right. I can't be your first. It would not be right. I think we were meant to be together Jaime, I can feel it. It wouldn't happen if I was your first. I could never properly serve with you."

Jaime gave a light but worrisome smile. "Halley, we were meant to be the best of friends. But as my friend I think you know about my heart and feelings. I am like a Swan that used to live on earth...that is, before they became extinct. Just like that Swan, when I mate I mate for life. I promised myself to Dex and that was it...and now he is gone...and yet I am still promised to him. I cannot give what you want. Besides, don't you think this is just an infatuation? Look deep into your heart and know I am right."

It was too late now, she was going to let it all out. "I don't believe that. I think you are just hanging on to the past, and won't allow anyone to join with you." She knew it was now or never – regardless of the outcome, she was now going to tell her. "I love you, we were meant to be together...I know it!"

Jaime gave her a stern look. "Ok, if you think we were meant to be more than friends, take my hand. If we were meant to be together as joined, then our DNA should bond...we should start to reconfigure. Go on, take my hand" she ordered.

Halley reached out with a shaking hand. Jaime took it and held onto it firmly. Then Jaime did something Halley would never had expected – still holding her hand, she stood up walked around the table, lifted her face with a finger under the chin and gave her a light, tender kiss. After Jamie broke away from the kiss, she went back around the table, and all while still holding her hand sat down. She then took her other hand and held it tightly. She looked into her eyes and gave her a soft smile while they held hands. Halley could still taste the light flavor of her kiss on her lips – she could have sworn she had just ate a ripe, sweet berry. After a few minutes, Halley looked down at her hands still being held by her captain...nothing was happening. Her hands felt normal, her lips felt as if nothing happened.

Jaime's look softened "No tingles, numbness, or dizziness?" she asked. Halley shook her head no. "See, we are friends...and the best of friends..." she said as tears started to drip from Halley's eyes. Jaime reached up and wiped them with a light touch. "I think you are meant to reconfigure with a command rank member of our people, Halley...I can feel it...it's just not me..." She smiled at Halley still wiping tears from her cheeks "I am...different...Max said I am like the catalyst for the rest of the Normals. I seem to change, then everyone else follows. I think

142

between that and my locked up heart, I will never be able to reconfigure with anyone. I hope you can understand that. But out of any of the Normals, I trust you the most…I trust you explicitly. No one else would have ever admitted their feelings like you did. And now, you have gotten it out of your system." She gave her a moment to regain her composure before asking "So, let me ask again, will you be my first?"

The young girl felt so confused, she was so sure that it was love, but now – maybe not. She tried to regain her composure and to actually analyze what she felt, and what had just happened. She still had no reaction to any of the touching between her and Jaime. She felt nothing else happening – now she realized that her captain was right. There was only the strongest friendship between the two of them. She started to look back to all of her feelings, and realized it was pure friendship all along. The deepest, richest friendship two people could have *without* becoming lovers. Halley took another moment to get more of her composure together before finally saying "If you will still have me…alright, I will be the First Officer of the Ladyhawk. I will serve my captain well."

"That's my Halley!" she cheered softly. "Of course I will still have you. You are my best friend after all…you were just confused, and as you can see, it was that easy to work out! Okay, well you have a lot to do then." She tapped on her command module entering commands and receiving acknowledgement through her holo-projection. "There, you now have access to all command files. This will give you command access to the ship, the ability to read all technical libraries, and the authority to issue commands." She then reached into a pocket in her uniform and took out a small box – she opened the box and exposed two single gold bar insignias – the insignias of the First Officer of a starship.

With newly found pride Halley took the box and stood up in stiff attention while saying "I will do my best my captain!" she then gave her a swift salute.

"I know you will. I will expect you to be the captain of one of those new battle cruisers being built there in a very short time…" she pointed to the frames of two Wyvern class cruisers being built in the space dock. "Learn well what it takes to command thousands of crew, and how to keep them safe. It's a lot of responsibility..."

Norm-Comm buzzed in Jaime's head. She answered and was surprised to hear Oomha's voice. "Jaime, we have a problem..."

"Oomha...how did you get on Norm-Comm?" she queried.

"Your controller, Otter..." he replied "she is quite talented at using communications devices."

She raised an eyebrow while admitting "I guess so..."

"Jaime, You need to take an unmarked shuttle and rendezvous with me immediately..." he commanded.

Jamie furrowed her brow "Immediately, as in right this instant?"

"Yes, I must respectfully tell you that you must leave now, this instant. Do you have an unmarked shuttle vehicle?"

"Yes, the Blackbird is unmarked..." she replied.

"Good, then take that vehicle and come to the location I will transmit momentarily. I will board your vehicle, and ride with you to our destination."

"Why the sudden urgency, Oomha...what is going on?" she asked.

"There are war drums in the air, Jaime. The warriors beating those drums are preparing to come after the ones they think started the aggression. They think YOU started the war...and only YOU will be able to stop this war..."

She disconnected with Oomha and looked at Halley. She was giving her a questioning look. "Looks like you will be taking the duties as the captain of the Ladyhawk right away. I am leaving immediately and you will need to take command while I am gone." Halley gulped quite loudly without realizing it. Jaime gave her a light smile, a soft chuckle, and then replied "You'll be fine. I know the ship is in good hands with you."

Nova Capsain:

She was not even able to move her arms. For now, all she could do was lay around and watch the entertainment hologram. Just weeks ago, life was so hopeful and so exciting. Now, all she was doing was laying around, waiting to die. With everything that made her soul, she inwardly wished for death. Life was nothing but darkness now.

Yuli was always there when he was not working, but that no longer brought light to her life. She was embarrassed for him to see her in this condition – the polymers that made her artificial skin was just that, artificial – fake. It had a phony pigment, a phony look, phony feel, and her face – well, there was no hope for that. Her eyes were visible through the clear plastic shell, there were polymer eye lids, and they had attached micro-servos to move them as if she was blinking them – but otherwise everything about her looked artificial.

She saw it in his eyes every time he looked at her – the pity. She could not blame him, he had no way of knowing that she would degrade in this manner when they touched, and started to reconfigure. Who would have guessed that combining the DNA of a Normal and a Normal/Blessed hybrid would cause this battle inside of her. She could not blame him for pitying her, and it hurt her to know he was blaming himself.

The door annunciator rang. "Enter" she said coldly. Not as if she told them to stay out they would.

In walked yet another doctor. This one carried a small box that jangled with each step he took. She did not recognize this doctor. "Who are you?" she asked.

"I am Jacob…" he replied. "I am your therapy doctor. Today we will be installing servos under your skin to help you stand and walk." He opened the box and with a pair of tweezers took out a small electric motor, no larger than a small screw head. "We are going to install these under the polymer skin and then activate them in a patterned manner. By the time we are done, you will be able to at least fully move your arms and legs."

"How come I have never seen you before?" she asked.

"Ah! I am new here. I just snuck in on the last transport. Because of my bio-electrical knowledge, Max thought I would be perfect for fitting the servos under your skin. I would also be perfect to start the training and therapy process once all servos have been installed. Also, once we have completed installing the muscular servos, I will also be doing some surgery on your lips – I will put some servos under the skin of your lips, and then tighten the flexi-skin around the mouth muscles and attach it to the inside of your mouth. It will get rid of that motionless slot and give you a facsimile of a mouth with real lips."

"Well, alright…" She said and slightly relaxed to let him work – not as though she could stop him in any case. He worked for the next few hours, installing the micro-servos under her skin. Cutting small incisions in the polymer, inserting a servo, wiring it into her nervous system, attaching the servo motor gearing to the invisible, internal skeleton that was attached to the skin, and finally melting the polymer to seal the incision. He inserted the small motors in her arms, then her legs, then in her neck, shoulders and even her buttocks. Every time he activated a servo, she felt a slight jolt in that extremity. Finally, he numbed the tissue in her mouth and did the surgery on her lips.

He finally stood up and looked at her. "Well, that should do it. For now, let's just have you work on the simple movements – raising arms and legs. After you get used to that we will try harder motions, like standing and finally walking." He motioned with two fingers "Come on now…raise your arm. You can do it….just an inch or two."

She struggled to find what it took to raise anything. She had no idea how to control her body now. She closed her eyes and concentrated on her arm. She heard a slight mechanical sound and opened her eyes. Her arm was an inch off the bed.

"Yes! There you go!" Jacob cheered. "Now, add a finger raise to that arm lift…"

She closed her eyes again and thought of her finger. Once again, a slight noise from a servo and she looked down to see her finger pointing slightly in the air.

"Yes! The servos are linked to your nervous system. They will respond to your impulses that you naturally send to your muscles that are right now fully atrophied. They will assist your muscles in movement. The muscles are being held by the plasti-skin, but the polymer is not a substitute for real skin…thus, the muscle is unable to properly flex. The servo will assist in that flexing. You will be feeling a little stronger every day now. Soon, I would not be surprised if you were not stronger than you were before this all happened. Maybe this will work out for the better? Maybe you will be better than before."

This thought enraged her. "Better than before?" she mumbled out, very loudly. "You call THIS better? Perhaps you would like to be permanently encased in plastic? Perhaps you would like to never be able to feel the touch of your loved ones, to be able to feel and touch someone, anyone? Better? Bullshit!" Somehow, she found using her lips was easy and natural – unlike her attempts to use her extremities. By the time she was done yelling at him she noticed was speaking quite clearly.

"You can get mad at me…" he said in a dry, calm voice "but I was not the one who mingled Blessed genes with Normal genes and thought nothing would happen. I was not the one who messed with fate and reconfigured with someone knowing I was different." He stopped sneering and now smiled at her. "I'm sorry, but someone had to tell you the truth…it might as well have been me. Again, I'm sorry. We'll get you through this…we will get you as normal of a life as possible. But you have to realize, you will never be the same again. I just have to be honest."

"I'm sorry too…" she said in a sad, weak voice. "I should't take this out on you…"

He gathered up his tools and put them into the small box. "Don't worry. I don't take it personally. I know you are hurt and angry right now. If it was me, I would be figuring out what I was going to do. I would be very angry too…I would be plotting my revenge on the ones who did this to me…regardless of who they were. I'm glad I don't have Blessed genes inside me…as I have found the Blessed like revenge, and can at times take revenge on anyone…even the ones they thought they loved. In some ways, I don't blame them…they've had to endure so much hatred from us Normals. Well, in any case, fight it off. Fight off what makes you both Normal and Blessed. I don't think one side will win without your help. You may have to pick which side will be of better benefit to you."

She sighed. "Yes, I really am fighting off those feelings and confusions. Thank you doctor...thanks for your help with my body and being honest with me to help clear my mind. I think I know what I need to do now."

He made a smirky smile as he turned to leave. "Then, I will leave you with your thoughts...you will figure out what needs to be done. You will know how to best correct what has happened to you."

Eight Years Ago...

The missile barely missed that time. She swerved just enough to cause the proximity sensor to activate and explode without actually hitting the ship. The explosion rocked and almost caused them to fly out of their seats, despite the strapping. "Hang on...here we go again!" More quick turns and more explosions. Even in the upper high atmosphere, the g's of acceleration were having their effect on the passengers.

She turned and looked at the green faces sitting behind her cockpit seat "I want all passengers to get into the escape pods, now!" she barked. The twenty people unlucky enough to be aboard that day obediently followed her orders, and boarded the escape pods. They wiggled and shook their way to the open pod hatches, and threw themselves in. Once safely inside she announced on the the pod intercoms "I will be making another pass, at which time I will eject you while we are skimming the lower atmosphere. The pods will open their chutes and you should land fairly softly. If you hit harder than expected however...well my apologies. Here we go."

She ran full speed down through the thin air of Mars. The friction on the hull was bad, but nothing like that of trying this maneuver in earth's ionized atmosphere. She pressed the ejection button and the pods were released. They flew down the opposite direction while she zoomed the craft back up into the path of the attacking southern fighters. "Hang on!" she yelled again as she did evasive maneuvers to avoid more shots and missiles.

"Ok, we're going to have to ditch."

"Ditch?" asked her copilot Vanda Marshall "We can't do that. We are obliged..."

"To live to fly another day!" she interrupted. "Get in the escape pod. I'll be right there..." she ordered as she steered the ship to avoid some more shots. "We're not a fighter...I can't shake them. We can only take the heat for the rest of the ships. If they can make it, then the base will get the needed supplies to continue the fight. If not, then the fight up here is lost. Now, get in the pod!" Her copilot obediently followed her orders.

She entered the commands into the auto-pilot, validated it was active and on, then ran to the escape pod. She quickly jumped in, closed the hatch, and ejected. They watched as they spun wildly away from the now circling cargo ship. A moment later, it exploded in a fireball that tumbled past their slowing pod.

"I can't believe you would lose your cargo like that, Halley. How did you make it so far in the marines?" her first officer asked.

"Because I AM willing to sacrifice, for the good of the whole. Our ship being destroyed allowed for the safe landing of the other shuttles...besides, there was cargo onboard that was valuable, and some that was not. Didn't you notice I shot all but one escape pod out during that run?" Vanda shook her head no. "Didn't think so...very few of those pods contained people. The rest...our valuable cargo. Thus, the bulk of the important supplies got through to our troops. I hope you understand, Vanda that I will always sacrifice one ship, or even one crew...including myself, for the good of the whole."

NGD: 3 Years, 2 Months, and 7 Days:

Normal Starbase Haven:

Halley Cet:

She stood at the mirror in the Captain's ready room inspecting her new uniform. The dark blue command uniform looked pretty good on her, she thought. She wore a semi-tight fitting uniform tunic that hung down below her hips, a black belt held the top in place right above her hips. To round out the uniform was a pair of matching slacks which hung down to a pair of smartly polished black shoes. A pair of single gold bars adorned each side of the upright collar that wrapped around her neck – the insignias of a First Officer of the new Normal fleet. The tunic had gold piping running down the front of the tunic to the beltline. She turned to look at each side of the tailored outfit – she was glad she had finally lost some weight as the roll she had developed over the years would not have looked good in this tight fitting outfit.

What a first day! It was her first day as First Officer, even worse it was her first day filling in as captain of the Ladyhawk, and now her first alert. SCADAR had picked up five objects on a direct intercept path with Haven. She was preparing to take the ship out to investigate. She adjusted her uniform top again, took a deep breath to calm herself, and then confidently walked out onto the bridge. She looked at the crew and nodded at each of them while taking her seat at the command console. The console immediately recognized her DNA and activated all command systems.

She examined the command holograph – so many status displays and condition reports. She was slightly overwhelmed by all of the information being provided to her. She wondered how Jaime managed it. She also had a new found respect for everything her captain did for her crew and the ship.

"Captain?" the helmsman, Marcella Stone called out. Halley looked at the young woman and she continued "All docking and moorings have been disconnected and cleared. All gangways are cleared. We are ready to depart at your word, Sir."

"Ah, ok...very well... Umm, communications clear us for departure with dock control. Jonathan, reactor and engine status?"

He checked his console "Reactors are high by five, engines are ready to fly, captain."

She had a hard time hearing him call her that, but attempted to ignore her lack of comfort. "Thank you" she replied "OKAY... Helm, take us out on Pulsars, one-one hundredth." She wiped the sweat from her palms onto her uniform pants as discretely as possible. She then looked down and saw Hero calmly sitting at the base of the command chair, cleaning his face. *He knows what's going on...*

The ship slowly departed the space dock, zipped out through the space doors which closed as soon as the ship cleared the four moving plates of space carbon.

"Location of the objects Katsumi?" she queried.

"About a light hour to an approximate intercept point. If we use the R.F.S. we should be able to intercept them just outside of our sector, captain."

"Do it...kick in the R.F.S. helm, maximum speed" she ordered.

The ship sped to the intercept point. As they approached the oncoming unknown intruders, they saw that the approaching craft were five small, powered capsules. They were still ahead of them, but were gaining on their position rapidly. The front tip of each vessel glowed in a light shade of green. Telemetry reports were showing they were speeding toward the asteroid with a speed that amazed everyone on the bridge as scans also reported that they did not appear to give off any engine thrust.

Katusmi carefully analyzed the data coming in from active advanced scanners, and SCADAR. The computer validated her theories – she looked up at Halley with a worried look on her face and said "Captain, those are missiles. They have a high yield warhead that I or the computer is not able to fully analyze. However, I can safely say that if even one of those hit the base, more than likely, Haven will be destroyed."

She nodded at the science officer "Very well, give weapons station targeting points. Yuli, as soon as you are provided the points, set target locks and fire at one of those missiles. We need to stop them!"

The helmsman turned the ship to pursue the five weapons, while the computer provided Yuli with targeting options. He locked the weapons on the computer-provided points. He activated the Ultras, and pressed his finger at one of the missiles now being chased by the ship. The beam fired out true and straight, but somehow missed. He fired again, same results. He switched to rail guns and fired. The projectiles approached the target, but once again missed – they seemed to just go right through the speeding weapons. He gave Halley a look of utter confusion, and then shrugged his shoulders.

"Captain..." Katsumi called out "the missiles seem to be shifting out of phase as soon as our weapons are about to hit. I don't think we will be able to stop them that way."

Halley looked at the five speeding warheads on the screen. She bit her finger while she thought about how to defend against these apparently impossible-to-stop weapons of mass destruction. Finally, she stood up and announced "When you signed on this ship, you knew there would be risks. Well, we're going to take one of those risks right now. Helm, accelerate so we are once again ahead of the missiles. Yuli, shut down the target locks...they will not do us any good at this point. Everyone, we're going to do what we can to protect Haven."

The ship and the missiles were quickly approaching the base – Ladyhawk had once again gotten ahead of the incoming weapons. In the rear view screens, Halley could see the five speeding green lights. In the front screen the marker lights of the space dock doors were rapidly approaching. She stepped over to the helm and put a hand on the young pilot's shoulder. "Helm, once we reach five thousand miles from the base come to a dead stop. Turn the craft to the side..."

"Captain?" the young helmsman interrupted "We'll be right in the flight path of the missiles if we do that...they'll hit us...destroy us."

"I realize that. It's the only thing we can do to prevent the base from being struck. The people aboard Haven are the reason we are here. We are here to protect all of those thousands of people trying to live. It is our job...our duty..."

"Yes Captain..." the young woman said. A tear was in her eye. Halley looked down and saw the tear dripping down her chin. She put a hand on her shoulder and squeezed it lightly.

Halley looked around the room – all of her crew were looking at her. Each one nodded in agreement – the crew was with her. She hoped Jaime would someday agree with her decision, that she had indeed made the right choice. As she looked at her loyal crew, she felt the pride that she assumed every starship captain must have had whenever they discovered how loyal and dedicated their crews were. She smiled back to them, then turned and walked back to the command chair and gently sat down. She looked down at Hero and softly said "Sorry..." the cat looked up and gave a single meow. He did not seem to be worried at all she thought – but then again, there is no way he would know the danger they were currently in. She then looked around the bridge again before she said "Well, it was a short stint at command..." she sighed then ordered "Helm, all stop, turn the craft now – put our exposed side to them."

Halley looked up at the ceiling in anticipation of that moment, when it would all be over – only another second now – then nothing. She looked back at the holo-screen and saw the five weapons had stopped just short of their apex point of destruction. Instead of hitting the craft, they simply had stopped, and now maintained a stationary position to the side of the ship. They were definitely still active – Katsumi validated their energy levels were as high as when they first encountered them, but for some reason they stopped their attack.

"Shall I place a weapons lock on one, captain?" asked Yuli.

Halley nodded yes at him and he applied a single targeting lock on one of the missiles. Immediately, the green glow in the front of the warheads increased their intensity. The brightness filled the bridge with the green glow. "Shut it down, now!" Halley ordered. Yuli immediately followed orders and removed the target lock. The light dimmed and returned to the previous state of brightness – the weapons were also standing down.

"Well, it looks like we have a stalemate for now. I don't know what it is doing or why it did not destroy us or the base...but for now we seem to be at an impasse. Might as well relax, but stay sharp. We may be sitting here a really long time..."

Near Planet Queek:

Jaime Bordeaux:

She had rendezvoused with the Marcole, picked up Oomha, and they were now exiting sub-space. When he had boarded the ship he immediately gave her the coordinates of their final destination, and as soon as he told her the course to take, she knew exactly where they were heading. When they left sub-space and entered the Queek system her suspicions were confirmed.

She looked confused at the deer. "Queek, Oomha? Why are we here? You said someone was about to go to war with us."

"Yes, war is about to be declared on you...by the Queek" the buck replied. "We are here to stop this war from occurring. They say you came and attacked."

"We attacked? We only observed from a distance then left! We never..." she thought about everything that happened. "It was the Blessed wasn't it? Kip was also here...he never left. He came back and attacked!" Oomha shook his head yes and snorted. "Damn..." she mumbled. She thought for a moment "Ok, what's it going to take to stop this?"

"AH!" he quickly replied "Simply convince the Queek you did not attack them. They will either believe you and stop aggressions, or eat you then attack your kind."

Jaime gulped slightly "Eat me?"

Oomha slightly nodded his head "Yes, the Queek believe in eating their enemies. They feel it makes them stronger. So, they will either accept your explanation, or eat you. I hope they believe you personally..." She nodded her head in agreement. "I run the possibility of being eaten too, if they find you guilty" he added.

She looked at him quizzically. "Then why are you here? You could of just given me the coordinates and told me what to do. Why did you come on a mission that could kill you?"

He gave her a deer-type of smile. "A few reasons my friend. First, you ARE my friend. I know you would do the same if I needed your help. Second, I speak Queek...I am one of only a few that ever learned their complex language. I will interpret for you. Third, having me with you will strengthen your position. They are more likely to believe you with me at your side. Thus, I am a valuable support buck to have around."

"You are always valuable, my friend. Thank you, for everything you have done and everything I know you will do in the future – no matter the outcome today." She patted him on the neck and rubbed his mane. He closed his eyes as he felt the touch of her blue-skinned fingers on his hide. After a moment, she stopped and turned her attention back to piloting the ship. "So, did they give you a specific landing site?"

"Yes, they did...let me enter the landing coordinates into your navigation computer. If I may?" She nodded and waved her hand in presentation of the navigation console. He extended the small extremities from his hoof and entered the landing coordinates into the computer. "There, you may now approach and land."

Jaime turned toward the helm controls to start piloting the ship down to the surface, but then stopped. "Oh, shit..." she softly said. The deer turned and looked at her with raised eyebrows above dark, black eyes. She turned and activated the computer next to her helm controls. Oomha looked at her again and once again raised one of its fur covered eye brows in a questioning way. She finally admitted "I just realized, I never certified myself on the landing procedures of this craft. There are no landing thrusters on my console...I need to figure out how to land this thing!"

"This might be a short trip then..." the deer softly said, while she called up the operational manual for the Blackbird. She began to scan the manuals furiously.

After a few minutes of studying the design manuals, she provided herself with enough information to give a hearty "AH HA!" She now had a look of confidence on her face. "This will be a piece of cake" she announced.

"I hope cake is good?" Oomha asked.

Jaime nodded yes "Cake is very good. We'll be fine. This craft has anti-gravity plates that are used for landing. A very advanced design actually...I just need to make sure I deploy the heat screens at the right moment..."

The ship began its decent through the upper layers of the atmosphere. Right before the friction of the air against the hull would begin to heat the craft, Jaime activated the heat screens. Two flexible, ceramic, folding panels extended out across the bottom of the ship, protecting it from the friction forces. They sank down through the upper layers of the planet's atmosphere, dropping like a rock. Jaime then increased the thrusters and began a controlled decent through the remaining layers of the upper atmosphere. Once the heat subsided, she retracted the heat screens and activated the anti-gravity plates for final approach and landing. She skillfully maneuvered the ship right to the edge of the Queek habitation before turning the craft around and softly landing on the surface.

She shut down the engines and peered out the view screens at the remains of the three Blessed transports. The ships had been reduced to three melted mounds of titanium. Where the ground based defensive systems had been, mounds of steel and plastic were all that remained. Circuits and computer chips had been strewn all over the area around the former ships and weapons.

She shook her head at the destruction "The Queek did this?"

Oomha nodded "Yes, they are quite formidable. I must warn you, it is worse outside. Where they did battle with the Blessed will not be pleasant."

"I'm sure..." she agreed. "Okay, let's get this over with..." then stopped "Wait!" Oomha looked at her with a deer-like look of surprise on his face. "You said I need to convince them I'm not Blessed right?" He nodded yes. "Okay then..." she said as she ran to the back of the craft and entered some commands at the uniform computer. A moment later, an outfit was produced at the dispensary alcove. She grabbed it and began to take off her uniform. Oomha turned, looked, and watched as she removed her clothes and started to get dressed again. He looked over her naked body, she had changed much since he first met her – every inch of her skin from the neck down was now a mixture of black and blue coloration. With her darkly colored back side that faced him – and even in the low light of the back of the craft, he could see how her skin shimmered with some form of energy. He finally got bored watching her and returned his attention to the view screen. A moment later she had finished changing and said "Okay, think this will help?"

He turned to see her in the outfit she wore in the last Command Tri-Polyhedron match – a tight, two piece, light blue outfit. It was composed of a pair of tight shorts, and a sleeveless crop top which, along with her exposed belly, showed the full midnight blue coloration of her exposed skin. The freckles on her shoulders now showed as small white spots on her dark, shimmering skin.

Oomha clopped up to her and looked her up and down. "This might work..." he said as he looked at her neck. "The coloration is even starting up the neck I see" he said.

She gave him a confused look, and then walked over the mirror. She saw that indeed, the dark pigment of her skin was now creeping up her neckline. Streaks of bluish-black pigment had moved up her neck, and were progressing to her face and head. "Damn, I am going to be this color everywhere soon aren't I?" Oomha nodded yes. She then took a hair tie and put her long hair into a high pony tail, exposing her winged ears. "Alright...let's get this over with..."

She opened the hatch on the port side of the craft. As soon as the air from the outside rushed in, she smelled the stench. The warm, humid air reeked of burned, rotting flesh. She coughed at the odor while she adjusted to the smell of death in the air. She put on her aviator sunglasses and stepped out into the carnage. In front of her were the remains of hundreds of humans – she went over to the closest corpse and looked at the dark uniform. Only slight traces of meat and flesh now filled the hole-riddled suit. Tossed all around the body were steel implants, computer chips, and circuitry.

She recognized the uniforms and the tech implants. "This was Secret Service..." she said. "So, the Blessed have been hiding the Secret Service from us all this time. I guess they needed backup help." She gazed out at the field of carnage "They lost a lot of people this day. What a waste...what fools they are. What makes them think they should attempt conquest of every race they find?" She shook her head downward in disgust. "Maybe they will think a little longer and harder the next time they consider attacking another race...at least I hope they will." She shook her head again, then took a single step further into the lines of what remained of the troops. "Okay, I have to do this..." she said as she started to boldly walk through the field of butchery toward the village.

As she approached the first mud hut, one of the long trunked creatures came skittering out from behind one of the mounds. It moved quickly on six shuffling legs, and was upon her in seconds. She stopped as it approached. It stretched its body to look straight into her eyes. Now right in her face, it stared at her with its three dark eyes. Following immediately behind the trunked creature was one of the round creatures. It rolled out from behind the hut, and over to Jaime – it stopped right next to the Queek who was examining her. Oomha caught up, and stood to the side of her. "Now it begins..." he said "They will now judge you."

She glanced down at the round creature, it had a slime forming on its skin. There were also little sharp spines slightly poking out of its hide. She looked again at the empty, hole riddled uniform just to the left of her feet, and had a bad feeling about those spines. The Queek with the trunk now looked at her almost black legs. Her translucent skin was shimmering in the bright sunlight, which caused it to color shift from a midnight blue shade to almost black – the creature sniffed and examined the skin of her legs. Then, to her surprise, it stuck out a long tongue, and licked her leg. It then moved its examination of her upper body – it looked at her arms and tasted them, then looked at the black streaked flesh of her neck, and finally moved up to her head as its three eyes stared at the wings on her ears. It made slight squeaks and honks the entire time while it examined her. Finally, it lowered itself and made some loud honks and grunts, then appeared to lower itself onto its belly in what appeared to be a relaxed position. It honked again and the round leather-like creature moved away, and back to the village. It made a few more honks, loud snorts, squeals, and then stared up into Jaime's eyes once again.

Oomha also looked at Jaime while giving a few matching honks and snorts. Then he said "They recognize you from your visit the other day, when you watched from the hill over there." He moved his head in the direction of the hill where they had observed the village. "They knew you were there the entire time it seems." The Queek gave a few more honks and a snort. "He said you fought the other one bravely, and showed you were a warrior."

"They could see that?" she asked amazed. "I could have sworn we were well hidden..."

"Don't be fooled by their looks" Oomha corrected her. "They are quite advanced. They only appear this way as a defense." The Queek gave another snort and a honk. "It appears he does not think you would be worthy of eating. The Queek have decided you are not to be warred with at this time. They have chosen peace with you...but he said the Blessed will be dealt with in other means. He said he will personally feast on their leader if given the chance."

She raised an eyebrow. "So, they know who their real enemy is also? Amazing that one would miss any technology that would give them that much detail without us knowing!"

More honks and squeals, then Oomha said "He said I was right to be your friend, that my description of you being kind and intelligent is sincere..."

"You said that?" she asked.

"I did..." he replied.

"Well, thank you..." she softly told him.

He nodded in acknowledgement "You're welcome."

The Queek honked a few more times, then turned and began skittering back to one of the mud huts. Oomha translated "I guess there were weapons waiting for their decision at your base...they are being recalled at this moment. They told me your starship commander is brave and should be commended." She gave him a raised eyebrow of suspicion. "It is safe, he will keep his word, and the weapons are probably already gone. He now wishes to show you the habitation. He said you will gasp in shock, and be in awe when you see it."

"Well, we'll see..." she muttered.

The Queek leader led the pair to the closest mud hut. When they came around to the other side, she realized it was not a hut at all, but an entrance shelter. Inside was a shiny, steel, spiral staircase that led down. The pair were led down what appeared to be an almost endless stairwell that emptied to a large underground city. The city was housed in an enormous cavern dug out of the rock of the planet. There were magnificent cylindrical silver steel skyscrapers that towered from the base of the cavern to the very ceiling. For hours they were shown the advanced technology and abilities of this race. When they finished the tour and were led back up the stairs, the Queek honked a question to Oomha, who translated "He wants to know what you think."

All she said was "I...I'm speechless..."

"He thought you would be..."

The Queek honked a few more tones. Two Queek came out from around the mud hut entrance carrying a large plastic case.

He squeaked a tone then gave a long honk. "He said to please accept this as a gift of the Queek." A few staccato tones and a squeal. "It is an insect that produces a sweet fluid he thinks you will enjoy." More honks. "He said that once the creatures leave the hive, you will find that the hive can be turned into very durable clothing...as it appears to him you need to wear outerwear to protect your skin." Three short squeaks and a coo "He warns however, to hang this hive in a secure, sealed area." Squeaks and many short honks. "They will move every two of your weeks to create new hives and will abandon this hive as useless." More honks. "The insects are deadly to most living things during the time of moving, so avoid contact when they are locating to a new hive location." Some snorts and a squeak. "However, when not moving in search of a new hive location they are quite harmless."

She looked through the clear surface of the case. The insects were flying around inside the case. A large rubbery, round hive hung from a support in the middle of the case. "Thank him for the wonderful gift, and for his offer of peace and friendship." He translated her wish for him. He honked very loudly, then turned and skittered back to the village.

Oomha turned toward her. "It appears, you have a new friend, and the Blessed have a new enemy..."

Aboard Ladyhawk, in front of Haven:

Halley Cet:

They had sat in front of the five missiles for hours. Neither the missiles nor the ship made any moves, or instigated any aggression toward each other since they all came to a standoff in front of the base.

Halley wiped more sweat off of her brow with a cloth while she sat in the command chair and stared at the deadly weapons ready to strike.

Jonathan turned toward her and asked "Think they will ever give up? Or will they finally tire of this, and kill us all…or they could leave anytime…"

Halley smiled at him but then returned her attention to the view screen. Then without any warning, all five missiles simply turned and flew off into the opposite direction, into deep space. No message, no apology, nothing. "What the hell just happened?" she asked rhetorically.

"Captain, the missiles have activated their near-light speed drives. They are now totally out of this sector." Suddenly, large explosions filled the screen with light. Massive green flares appeared far out in space. Katsumi looked up from her scans and said "It appears they have self-destructed…"

"Guess they had no purpose?" Halley surmised, then questioned "Why the hell were they here?"

"Captain…" said Otter "I have Captain Bordeaux on sub-space transmission…"

"Transmitting via sub-space? Put her on Otter…" Halley was amazed that Otter could pick up a signal that far away. She wondered what else she could do with that communication port.

Jaime came on the holo-screen. "Captain, everything alright there?"

"Yes, captain" she replied. "We had a minor run-in with some very odd missiles, but we survived, and are now out of danger."

"Excellent, Halley" she said formally. "I too have had one hell of a day. I hope to tell all of you all about it once I return home. Glad all is well…and good job all. Especially YOU First Officer Cet." She gave a snappy salute. "See you when I get back, Bordeaux out."

Halley was now beaming with pride as she looked around at her crew. Hero looked up and meowed, then jumped in her lap, and started to purr. "Guess I passed the test, eh?"

Six and a Half Years Ago...

"In signing your enlistment agreement, you will also be volunteering for this experimental communication procedure...do you realize this?"

"I do, and agree to the procedure with no hesitation" she replied.

He looked at her with some confusion. *"Well good...but I must say I am surprised. Most Normal communication recruits do not want to put themselves through this, and end up bailing before signing the enlistment document."*

"Well, I'm not! I want this...more than anything. I'm ready, give me the pen." He did, and she signed.

"No turning back now..." he told her. *"If you will follow me..."* He led her back to a surgical center. There awaited two doctors and three nurses, all in the surgical gowns, wearing masks and gloves, and ready for surgery.

"Wow, you don't waste any time do you?" she asked. He shook his head no.

The doctor handed her a gown, and pointed her to a dressing area. While changing into the gown, the doctor spoke to her. *"You will be the first to get this new implant. You will notice changes in a number of your senses. For example, your hearing will at times change, it will become more sensitive. You may find that you will communicate with computers better than with people. Also, you will notice changes in your mood. You will go from happy, to angry depending on the amount of stress imposed on you from external sources. You will find that you will at times be revengeful or spiteful towards others. But don't worry, most of the time you will be your Normal self. Do you have any questions?"*

She thought for a moment, and could only ask *"Will this hurt?"*

The doctor chuckled and said *"Not at all, we will put you out for the procedure. We will need to wire the socket implant into the communication sectors of your brain. Also, we will need to wire into certain logic and reasoning areas...in this way, you will be able to better communicate with the communication computers in the function of your job. Because of the work we need to do, we will put you out."*

"Ohh...okay..." she softly said as they led her to, and helped her to sit onto the cold, steel surface of a surgical table. They flipped her onto her belly, put her head through a small hole in the table, and then strapped her body down to prevent her from moving. Then without warning they shaved her. She watched with tears in her eyes as the blond locks fell to the floor and were just as quickly vacuumed up.

She began to shiver from both fear and the cold of the steel table. The doctor put a hand on her shoulder, bent down below the table, and looked up into her face. He smiled at her, lowered his mask, and then said "Don't worry, it won't hurt..."

He lied...

NGD: 3 Years, 2 Months, 9 Days:

Salvage Base Plug:

Lindy Light-Griggs:

Lindy sat listening to all of the conversations across all of the communication channels. She listened to Normal traffic (lightly) and Blessed communications (intently). Occasionally, she would relay something that might seem important to Otter, who would forward it to who she thought could use the information at Haven.

Today, a few messages caught her attention – first, despite the scrambling, she was able to hear some of the conversations of the Star Force Commander. He mentioned something about someone on the inside. If that was not concerning enough, she heard a garbled segment of the conversation regarding a new shield technology.

She immediately contacted Otter on a tunneled protocol sub-space carrier. "Otter, I was barely able to decipher it out, but I think you have a spy amongst you."

"Oh, that is definitely a problem…" Otter replied. "Very well, I will let the captain know once she returns. I will let Max and Allen know immediately."

"You may want to monitor the communications out of there…he or she has a way of contacting the Star Force Commander from there. Also, you might want to let Jonathan know that it sounds like the Blessed have developed or found some form of shielding for their starships. It might make a difference if they ever decide to come after you again."

"Message is being composed, and sent to him as we speak!" she replied.

"Thank you Otter. Everyone doing ok there?" she asked.

She could almost hear the sympathetic smile in her voice. "Yes, everyone is doing fine…except Yuli's wife, Nova. They joined and started to reconfigure when they discovered she was half Blessed! Well, that made a mess of things…everyone is really worried about her, as she started physically breaking down."

"I will keep her in my thoughts…" she told her with sadness in her heart for Yuli, he did not deserve this.

There was a brief moment of silence while Lindy thought of her friends so far away. Then Otter broke the pause "Well, I had better go. The captain is due back from some mission she and Oomha were on. I will get you details once I hear them myself…but it was quite exciting around here. Oh, wait! I will forward you a mental synopsis." A moment later Lindy saw the memories of the missiles threatening the base and how Halley heroically threw the ship in the way of the speeding weapons of mass destruction.

"Oh crap!" Lindy replied to the images in her head. "I can't believe how close everyone was to biting it! You all out on the frontier…you get all the excitement."

Otter laughed. "Okay, I really need to disconnect…unless you need something else. You know, you sound a little uneasy…"

Lindy thought a moment before saying "Yes, there is one thing…let me remote it to you…" she put her request into her thoughts and sent it.

Now Otter had a tone of worry in her voice "You really need that? Okay, I will get it to you. Take care my friend…" and Lindy felt her leave the circuit.

She sat there in the silence of the room, the communications in her head were the only noise she could hear. Finally, she put her mind back on her duties – her Normal duties. *"Okay, what else is going on…activate Jonathan 145"* she thought, and through her communications port attempted to activate the Jonathan 145 – a special program that scanned and monitored computer communications channels.

An image of Jonathan appeared in her head. *"Hello Lindy, I am Jonathan 146."*

"Did 145 already get discovered and eradicated?" she asked.

"Yes, it did not hide well enough that time. This version has done a much better job. They will not find me…for a while at least. What can I do for you?"

"Just a standard scan of events and communication logs. Better check duty rosters, rotations and possible salvage finds we would want to know about" she ordered.

"Very well, I am on it now…"

While Jonathan 146 worked, she went back to listening in on Blessed communications. After a few minutes Jonathan 146 alerted her to some ambiguities in the various shuttle flight plans.

The image of Jonathan reappeared in her head. *"Hello again Lindy, I have found something of both far above coincidence, and also of interest. Let me show you…"* The program transmitted all of the shuttle flight plans into her mind.

As she mentally scanned the plans, something piqued her curiosity and made her dig deeper. *"Jonathan, show me the duty rosters, please"* she thought to the program.

Sure enough, she found something very peculiar when she started looking deeper into the duty rosters – at first look, it was only the pilots, but then upon further investigation she found others scattered around the base area: Marigold Minford, shuttle pilot for the Conquest…Daisy Milton, shuttle pilot for the

Ultimate...Petunia Morris, shuttle pilot for the Starlight...Dahlia Marteen, salvage operations team member, salvage base Plug...Oh, and Tulip Maxwell (someone named her that?), engineer on the starship Conquest. She looked at the rosters and noticed something else – every one of them was on a shift where they would never be in the same place with one of the others. That was something that never happened between the crews. At some point, crews and pilots would always run into one another or bump into a friend somewhere during the course of daily work.

She thought more about the names on the duty list she had separated out from the rest of the crews. *"All named after flowers...and there are at least 60 flower-named, female, Blessed crew members...and none of them ever are scheduled together..."*

"I think you will find this of interest..." the program told her as he presented medical records of the flower-named Blessed.

"Your right..." she thought to the program *"I find that of great interest!"* She pondered for a moment on what they had found, then requested. *"Jonathan 146, do you have access to all of the previous Jonathan programs?"*

"I do" he answered.

A smile came to her face after hearing that. *"Good, an older Jonathan found weakness 78...can you find that?"* she asked.

"Already located..." he replied *"I cannot activate it however."*

"I know and understand" she acknowledged. *"As long as we have it, I think we might have a use for it."* Her eyes lit up in excitement and a smile came to her face when she came up with an idea. *"OHH! I think we need to have a garden party!"*

Tulip Maxwell:

It was odd for her to be called off ship in such an unknown manner. She was now assuming that some lucky Blessed soldier had won the lotto and it was his turn. She didn't care, that was her purpose in life until they found a suitable planet to colonize. She went to the docking bay, and found the shuttle waiting for her as promised. She obediently boarded the shuttle and was quickly flown from the Conquest to Plug.

Once the shuttle arrived, she was met by a Secret Service soldier, and was escorted to a waiting room. It was a small room, in which there were two doors – the first, was the one she entered – the second was located on the opposite side of the room and was closed. Along the wall was a couch that took up the entire length of the wall on the one side of the room. A small table adorned the other side of the room, there were glasses of water, and a locked liquor cabinet that could be used for guests if desired.

After a few minutes of waiting, the other door opened and Tulip was met by a blonde woman. She reached out a hand. "Hello, I am Lindy Light-Griggs. Welcome to Plug. I hope your flight was smooth."

"It was..." she replied, then asked sharply "Exactly, what am I doing here?"

Lindy smiled at her before replying "An interesting thing was brought to my attention. I thought perhaps you would like to be made aware of this...coincidence." Tulip gave her a confused look. Lindy reopened the door. "Please, follow me...this will explain everything." She motioned her toward the open door.

She followed her suggestion and passed through the doorway into a much larger room. The room was filled with women softly talking. When Tulip entered, the room went hush and all eyes turned toward her. She stopped in her tracks at all the faces that were now staring at her – eyes that looked exactly like her own. As she let her eyes wander about the room she saw why she was there – every woman in the room was an exact duplicate of...her...or, was she an exact duplicate of them?

"Odd, isn't it?" Lindy asked her. "How is it there are so many copies of you...or copies of one of you?" She looked around the room with her arms stretched out. "How is it there are sixty of you?" She rubbed her chin for effect while she looked around before continuing "Every one of you seems to be an exact duplicate of the other. The real question is...are any of you the original?"

A soft rumble reverberated through the room as they started to discuss the question posed by Lindy, who now had a soft evil smile on her face.

Finally, one of the women – she thought it was Dahlia said "So, how do we tell which one if any of us is the real one? If any of us are real..."

Lindy rubbed her chin again. "Well, have you discussed any common themes that you all might have? A dream or a memory that each of you remember?" She knew exactly what to tell them – the Jonathan program had discovered the pre-awakening memory programming they had been given. They began discussing amongst themselves again while she took a seat in the corner and watched.

After a while the discussion died down and it was Dahlia who once again spoke for the group. "It appears that we all had this same dream right before we awoke...our mothers' telling us how great we were and how important we would be on this trip." She lowered her head for a moment and shook it lightly before saying "Funny...that is ALL I remember prior to being woken up. They told me all about how I was put to sleep and the things I did before we left earth...but other than that, I can't remember a thing."

"Oh, you mean this?" Lindy asked, then activated a view screen where the Jonathan program re-ran Dahlia's pre-awakening program.

"That...that's my dream!" Dahlia cried out. "What the hell is going on? So, are you saying I was programmed?" Lindy nodded yes.

The room went into an uproar again as they all started to shout in agreement with Dahlia – everyone but Tulip. Finally Lindy stood up and waved and shouted for quiet. She looked at Tulip and walked over, put her hand on her shoulder and said "You remember more, don't you?"

Tears welled in her eyes, her lips began to tremble, and she nodded her head in agreement. "Yes, I remember everything...my childhood, growing up, going to school, joining the space program, everything. Am I...am I the original?" she asked.

Lindy nodded yes. "According to the computer records, you are the original "flower". You joined the space force, and were put to sleep. While you slept however, your stem cells were extracted from you, and used as nuclear material for an egg donor...we could not get a name, only a number – 432.

"I know her!" shouted one of the women. Lindy thought it was Marigold from the Conquest.

"You're on the Conquest?" Lindy asked her.

"Yes, and she was the nurse who woke us, and took us to our assignments" she replied. "I never realized that I was put there as a manufactured sex toy!" she yelled out, which was followed by a rousing yelling of "YEAH!" and "Those sons of bitches!" and other colorful metaphors. Marigold continued once their yelling calmed down. "Somehow, they managed to keep all of us apart. Tulip was on the same ship as myself, and I never even knew!"

"Well..." Lindy interrupted "I think you can see why they kept you all apart..." Marigold and Tulip nodded yes.

"So, I am the original. Did they take genetic material from me?" she asked.

Lindy queried Jonathan 146 before answering "Yes, probably from your spine." Tulip quickly removed her top and turned her back to Lindy before asking "Are there any marks or scars?"

Lindy looked and just below the base of her neck, between her shoulder blades she saw numerous marks where it appeared she had been punctured over and over again. Tulip turned and she nodded to her before saying "You have had many, many samples taken from you. They likely harvested your stem cells from your spine to use as genetic primer, then syphoned the nucleus of the cell and injected it into the empty egg cell of the nurse you met. From there, they would need a tube for growth and processing – but from what I am being told, it would have to be different from a normal gestation tube. The nutrients and growth fluids would have to be special for growing...clones." She let that sink in for a few minutes before continuing "All of you but Tulip are clones. The Blessed produced you hoping you would be able to mate and reproduce with them."

The yelling and swearing started again. Lindy started to worry they would get out of control. If they did, she would have to come up with some explanation for them being there, and then explain their actions. She determined she would figure it out...somehow. Fortunately, they all maintained control and after a few minutes calmed down when Marigold started asking for quiet, and waving her arms up and down to get their attention. They did finally settle down, and then Marigold said to Tulip. "Well, I don't know about you...but I am not going along with this any longer. I am not going to be a sex toy for those pigs again. As a matter of fact, I am thinking of maybe just..." she stopped and thought about it, and Lindy could see her slightly choke down a sob in her throat before she continued "I am just thinking of ending it all. I am not real...I do not deserve to be here, and I really don't want to be here. Although, when I think about it I don't really want to die. DAMN, I don't know what the hell to do!"

"I do..." Tulip softly said "I am going to get back at those bastards who cloned me without my permission"

"REVENGE!" they all started yelling.

"Ah, typical Blessed for sure..." That was the moment Lindy was waiting for. "If it helps, I was also used by these bastards for sex. I ended up getting married to one of them, since he finally succeeded in getting me pregnant. However, before that I was raped over and over by the Blessed captains. Now, I have nothing but revenge in my heart. If you feel the same, I am here for you...and I have some ideas."

Tulip came up, looked into Lindy's eyes, and then reached out and gave her a strong hug. "I think I can speak for the rest of my-selves...I...we are with you." Lindy looked around the room at all the eager faces wanting blood for their situation – she had them. "What can we do to get back at them?"

Fitchburg Griggs and Janus Light-Griggs:

Fitchburg just stared at the drawing. It was scribbled out in crayon colors, but it was definitely a real drafted drawing of –

a weapon he thought. He rubbed his chin while he continued to stare at the colorful blueprint-style drawing. "So, do you know what this is?" he asked him.

He looked up at his father, smiled, and said "Incindiator…"

"Hmm" he mumbled. He pointed at the drawing of a large tube with other tubes going into the larger tube. "So, what are these smaller tubes for?" he asked.

"Inject gold…" he replied. Then looked up at him and gave a stern, serious look – much too serious for someone his age – and then said "Only gold though, daddy."

Fitchburg was amazed. Not only could his son speak coherently at his early age, he also seemed to have a knowledge of advanced weapons. Now it appeared that he could also design advanced weapons. All he could do was stare at the drawing and shake his head in amazement.

"Do you want it daddy?" he asked.

"Can I have it?" Janus shook his head yes, hit the print command on his drawing tablet, and then gave him the colorful drawing.

"Someone can make it…" he told him.

Fitchburg quickly got up off the floor and rubbed his son's head, which brought a smile to Janus' face. "I have to go now son" he said. Janus smiled again, then nodded as Fitchburg turned and started walking out of the room. He activated his communication device. "Science lab, this is Fitchburg. Drop everything, I have a priority project for you to work on!"

Janus opened a fresh drawing on his tablet. He looked at the color palette in front of him. "This time, blue!" he shouted as he selected a dark shade of blue. He drew two circles and filled them with color. Then, he selected black and drew a large black dot between the two blue circles. Finally, he selected yellow and drew two arcing lines that paralleled on each side of the black filled circle. "There, all sealed up!" he said to his new drawing while he clapped his hands together, and laughed.

Starship Conquest:

Kip Gurrigan:

He was deep in thought while sitting in his ready room when the message came in. He had been put at the top of the list by Tulip. She wanted to be with him – tonight.

He read the message two more times, just to make sure he read it correctly. Yes, she said tonight – she had moved him to the top of the mating list. *"She is wise…she wants the best genes for her child. I too would make the same decision."*

He activated his vid-comm and a moment later, her face appeared on the screen. In his eyes, she was radiant – her blonde hair was perfectly styled. Her face was wearing the best make up available in the fleet. Her thin cheeks were covered in a soft warm rouge, her eyes were glowing blue and her eyelids a shade of power blue to accompany her eyes. She wore a bright red lipstick that showed off her large luscious lips. She saw it was him and gave him a warm smile before saying "So, you got my invitation?"

"I did…" he replied "and I assume you have determined that being the captain's bedmate is the best choice you could make?" He raised an eyebrow at her in questioning manner.

"I thought about it, and after having failed with so many others the only choice I could make would be you. Your genes…I looked them up. They are so…strong and interesting. I must have them inside me. I must have them in my next child. Say you accept, please?"

"Ah she begs me!" He smiled at her while he thought of those luscious lips pleasuring him. He let her sit for a moment as if he might reject her. She gave him a slight worried look, and he decided she had suffered enough. "Very well, I accept your offer. Come to my quarters…say in an hour?"

"Oh, so soon?" she said with a giddy voice.

"Why put off the inevitable? You have made the wisest choice possible, and I see no reason to put this off." He then thought *"Finally! I shall have a child. A prodigy that will be as strong and capable as only myself. One to take my legacy!"*

She smiled at him and licked her lips before saying "Very well, an hour it will be..." and disconnected.

*   *   *

It was the longest hour he had ever experienced. His body was so longing of what was about to happen, and he was secretly so impatient. But finally, he completed his duties and it was time – time for him, and his pleasure.

He left the bridge, and went to his quarters. As he expected, she was already there. She had two drinks poured and was waiting for him. He entered the room and looked at her – she was sitting on the couch, wearing only a very sheer nightgown, it did not conceal much to his prying eyes. She stood up and grabbed one of the glasses and handed it to him, she then returned to the table and picked up her glass before returning to look up into his eyes.

"I thought a small cocktail would liven the mood?" she said with a small impish smile on her face. She raised her glass to his and clinked it before taking a taste of the clear fluid.

He followed suit, taking a much larger swallow. It was Vodka, with a slight addition of lime – one of his favorites. *"She has done her homework..."* He took another swig then looked down into her blue eyes. He could feel her body almost touching his, she was that close. He had now become way too aroused to continue any further discussion. He put the glass down on a nearby counter then turned back to her and placed his hands on her shoulders while he looked deeply into her eyes. He said "I think I will stop my drinking at this point. I have so much more to take care of...I think the pleasure will start here, now."

He grabbed her, then kissed her passionately. He then took her hand, and walked her into the bedroom. They would remain there until the orders came in from the Star Force Commander to prepare for departure.

Patti:

She could feel them, the Og – they were getting closer. She knew she would have to leave soon. First, she needed to get out of the cell she was occupying, and do it in a way that no one would

176

see. She looked at the plate of food the guard brought. It was so unappetizing, but she did need some sustenance.

Then, as if knowing her thoughts, the guard peered into the cell through the small slit in the steel door. He saw the food still sitting on the tray, untouched. "So, you are not going to eat again, eh?" he asked her. "I don't know you survive without eating, but whatever…"

It was now or never she decided. She walked up to the door and grabbed the handle. With a light tug she pulled it open to the surprise of the guard. He started to reach for his blaster, but she stopped him with a light touch of her outstretched hand. She looked at him with a sly smile, and said "Food is really not what I need right now…" She took a firmer grip of his hand, and led him into the cell. The guard now had a very big grin on his face as he realized, then anticipated what he hoped were her intentions.

She let go of his hand, reached around, and removed her top. She immediately followed up by removing the black, wrap-around skirt, exposing her now totally naked body. She walked over to her cot and sat down, keeping her legs slightly spread as she looked at him. His gaze became totally fixated on her body, he could barely even look into her eyes he was so engrossed by the nakedness in front of him. She began to release sex pheromones to enhance his excitement. Finally, she said "So, I think you now know what my hunger really is. Are you going to satisfy me? I warn you however, I am kind of a barbarian…I like it…rough."

He said nothing – he only started to remove his clothes. She licked her lips at him, and he undressed even faster. Once fully naked, he said "Don't worry, most Blessed are not gentle…we are known for our aggressiveness in bed. I WILL be rough, and you WILL enjoy it." He walked over and sat next to her on the cot. He ran his rough hand across her body, exploring every part of her. Finally, he grabbed her hair, pulled her head back, and kissed her roughly. He pushed her down onto the cot, jumped on top of her, and mounted her.

"Yes, that's it…" she softly moaned. He was now on top of her and moving in hard motions as he forced himself onto her. She allowed him to become enflamed in passion. She released more pheromones as she heard him grunt and groan as he took her. He was in a mad frenzy by this time – so much so that he never realized that her body cavity had opened up, and the skin of her torso was now wrapping itself around his body. He kept his furious lovemaking at a rapid pace until he finally felt the sharp stings of thousands of bony cilia as they pierced into his flesh, absorbing his life-force, and digesting his muscles.

Finally, he began to ease up on his passion as he realized the pain he was now experiencing. She rubbed the hair on his head and shushed him as he began to let out small cries of pain and suffering. "I'm sorry, but it is necessary. Please, keep making love to me...it will make it easier...less painful. Keep going..." She released more pheromones which took his mind off of the pain and caused him to continue by instinct. She was telling him the truth as the pain turned to pleasure, he stopped his whimpering, and instead continued his passion to her. He finally stopped moving as his head was swallowed into her chest. His hips were also brought into the lower part of her torso, followed by his legs as she completed the absorption of the remainder of life-force, and the consumption of his flesh.

She relaxed for a minute while she finished the process of digesting him. Now with that process complete, and her hunger satiated, she stood up and put her clothes back on. She reopened the cell door and looked up at the video cameras in each of the corners of the room. With a slight flash the cameras became non-functional. She left the brig and stopped at a computer information center. Manipulating the inputs, she analyzed the docking logs and found a Normal transport ship preparing to depart.

She ran from the terminal and as fast as she could headed to the loading dock. Upon arriving at the dock, she discovered a sentry guarding the open door. She walked right up to the sentry and looked at him. He froze in place as she smiled at him, rubbed his cheek with her hand, and then proceeded into the open area of the loading dock.

She looked around at every surveillance camera and disabled them. They would eventually notice, but the alarms that announced the launch preparations of the Conquest would distract them from noticing the missing video feeds for now – by the time they did notice, she would be long gone.

Over across the cargo dock, in one of the loading bays was the Normal freighter. She snuck quickly behind a group of crates, then ran to another grouping, and then another. Finally she managed to get to a set of crates that were sitting on a pallet, ready to be loaded onto the freighter. She opened one of the crates, got in, and then sealed it behind her. Finally, this set of crates was loaded and the cargo hatch sealed.

Jeremy Ponds:

He was having a slight disagreement with the dock chief over the cargo that was to be loaded onto his ship.

"Look, my orders are to take all of those crates over there and ship them to Plug. Are you saying that is not what this says?"

The cargo chief looked at the computer film again. The orders were clear, he just didn't want to read them. "I don't see that. I see nothing that says you can take those crates with you."

About at that moment, the alarms sounded – the Conquest was preparing to depart. He realized he needed to take off, and do it now. "Look, what's it going to take for me to get those crates onto my ship? Those supplies are needed by the bases…I just want to get them delivered and get my rewards for a job well done. You can understand that can't you?"

"I might be persuaded to understand…" he said as he rubbed the fingers of his right hand together.

"Oh, I see…" he said as he realized the only way he was going to get this group of refugees off of this ship was by bribing him. He tapped on his computer film and transferred a large amount of credits to the chief's account. "Will that do?"

The chief looked at his account on his computer. "Yes, I think that will do nicely." He smiled, then the smile changed to a sneer. "Better get those crates loaded, or you and your cargo are taking a ride with us. Get moving Norm!" he barked.

"Whatever…" and turned away *"asshole…"* He signaled the forklift to load the final pallet of crates onto the ship. The computerized machine followed orders and he quickly sealed the cargo hatch. He boarded and sealed the boarding hatch before the cargo chief changed his mind, and would extort even more credits off of him. He requested and was given clearance, and he departed the ship as fast as possible. He watched the Conquest kicked in their ion drives, and zoomed off to who knows where. He transmitted his flight plan to Blessed starship control. Once confirmed he activated a computer program, and then changed his flight path. He would make his normal slingshot past Plug, and once outside of Blessed detection would make a beeline to Haven.

As he set the coordinates for the slingshot however, the computer rejected his calculated route. "What the hell?" he said as he rechecked the computations. There was a problem – a problem with the weight to thrust ratio calculations. He had the computer analyze the calculation and the computer replied that the problem was in the cargo weight. His ship was much too heavy for the normal slingshot trajectory. His eyes opened wide when he saw the actual weight of his cargo.

He ran back into the cargo bay and began opening up crates. Inside were hundreds of Normals – all in a state of suspended animation. With them in that state, they could be stacked on top of each other, allowing for even more refugees to be smuggled onto his ship. As this was the third cargo load in such a state, he wondered if there were any Normals even left on Conquest. As he inspected the crates, he heard a noise in one of the crates in the far back of the hold. He took out his blaster, and walked slowly to the large metal box. With shaky hands, he entered the code to unlock the crate, held his blaster near the lid, and opened it. She fell out rolling onto the floor. She yelped as she hit the cold metal floor, and bumped her head

She looked up at him and rubbed her head. "Owww!" she cried. She then smiled, and giggled at him.

There was something about her that made him put his blaster away without thinking. She wore nothing but a black, wrap-around skirt and matching bikini top made out of Alliance uniform material. Her brown skin showed that she had spent quite a long time in the sun, somewhere. She had a slightly larger forehead and sunken eye sockets that held a pair of eyes that were a color of deep, dark brown. He stared into them, and became slightly lost. A moment later he regained control of his thoughts, and squatted down next to her.

"So, who are you?" he asked.

She replied simply "Patti…"

"Ok Patti. You are not Blessed, and you are not Normal. So who or what are you?" he queried.

"Does it matter?" she replied.

"Well then, are you with the Blessed or the Normals? You need to choose. Choose wisely…" he advised.

"I am here. I was with the Blessed. I think I have already chosen…I am with you." She looked at him and smiled before asking "What is your name?"

"Jeremy…Jeremy Ponds…" he answered.

"Jeremy, I like that" she responded. "Now, will you take me to safety Jeremy Ponds? I am requesting sanctuary."

He sighed "I don't see why not…" she gave him a big smile, then reached up and touched his face. He felt the soft touch of her hand on his skin and could have sworn he felt a slight bit of electricity jump from her fingers to his face – in any case, it felt good. He stood up and reached out his hand to help her up. She took it and his assistance gladly. He pulled her up and looked down into her deep brown eyes again, he once again became slightly lost staring into them – this time however, she seemed to be in the exactly same trance. Once he regained his composure, he shook his head to clear it, then he suggested to her "Come on up front. No need to ride with all of the sleepers back here."

As they walked she took his hand and squeezed it while she said "Thank you Jeremy Ponds…I will never forget this."

Normal Base Haven:

Jaime Bordeaux:

She docked at Haven and departed the Blackbird. She was surprised to find Max waiting for her at the end of the gangway.

"Welcome back, Jaime. I take it your trip was successful? Based on what happened here, I must assume it had something to do with what you were also doing?"

"Yes, we were close to annihilation...very, very close. Somehow we convinced them we were not involved – but the Blessed certainly were."

He gave her a stern, serious look. "Jaime, don't you think it's about time we broke with them?" he asked.

She shook her head no "Not quite yet. We're not there yet, but close." She looked out the window across the space dock. The two Wyvern space cruisers were almost complete and the second Dragon starship now had all of its black armor plating in place. It would be only a week or two before the three new craft would be ready for their initial test flights. Farther across the dock, she could see the start of yet another craft – she was unsure what type it was however. "After those three are ready to protect the base, then we can consider breaking away. But we don't want a repeat of what Boral attempted in our first year here. No, we cannot start up any rebellion until we have a fleet...one that can stand up to the Blessed." She started walking away from the docking area and Max followed in tow. As she continued to walk she said without even looking "You didn't meet me just to say hello...is there something wrong Max?"

Max shook his head no "Nothing wrong, but there is something I wanted to show you. Can you make a detour to medical? It will only take a moment, but I do not want to discuss it here."

Jaime now stopped, turned, and looked at Max with concern "What's up?" she asked.

"We received a report from Lindy. There's a spy in our midst. We're trying to figure out who, but with all of the Normal refugees we're taking on a daily basis, it's going to take a while to figure out who it is. But you know we will find him or her. Until then, there are certain things I do not want spoken in public. This is one of those things."

Jaime nodded in agreement. Behind her a voice called out "Captain! Jaime!" It was Halley. The young woman ran up, and stopped right behind them. She was panting when she greeted them with a wave of her hand, and then a small snappy salute. She was dressed sharply in a blue uniform suit – matching tunic and slacks. Her hair was perfectly styled, the brown hair going from a part on the left side of her head to the right side, but not draping in front of her dark rimmed glasses. "I wanted to catch you before you went to your quarters. I wanted to be the first to tell you what happened…" and she explained the situation that occurred with the threat of the missiles.

Jaime looked at her sternly and then said dryly "So, you put the ship in front of the missiles. Putting everyone on board in danger, and possibly destroying the only protection this base has against the Blessed…is that correct?"

Halley gulped slightly and admitted "Yes, it was what I thought was best. But now that you put it that way…"

"That is exactly what I would have done!" Jaime interrupted. Halley gave her a look of astonishment. "I knew I had picked the best person to take over while I was gone. I knew you would be the best choice for the next starship captain, and I was right! Excellent job First Officer Cet, excellent job!" She saluted Halley, and the young girl returned the salute. Before Halley had a chance to recover, Jaime grabbed her and gave her a big tight hug. "Thanks for protecting the base. You will have one of those Wyverns soon, so take a look and pick one my friend."

Halley pulled back from Jaime's hug and had tears welling in her eyes. "Thank you, thank you my Captain. Now, if you will excuse me…" she said as she quickly saluted and ran off.

Jaime had a warm smile on her face as she watched her friend depart. She was so proud of her.

"That was the best thing you could have done for her." Max said.

Jaime nodded silently, then turned and returned to her walk to medical. About halfway there she stopped, and leaned against the wall. Max started to reach for her, but she waved him off. Shooting, small pains ran up and down through her nervous system. It was if her reactor was malfunctioning and sending excess current along her enhanced system. She was finally able to ignore the small currents shooting across her body, she straightened herself up, and returned to her walk. By the time they reached medical the current flowing along her nerves had doubled. She somehow had managed to push off the pain however, and was showing no signs of trouble to her doctor.

They entered the medical unit and she looked around. There were a few new people she noted. She walked up to a man working at a computer terminal, programming a number of small servo motors. He looked up and gave a small smile, then returned to his work. She looked down at him, the wings on his ears appeared fresh and new – she assumed he had just grown them. "So, you are new..." she said to him.

He stopped working, and looked up at her. "Yes, I just arrived here a while back. I am Jacob...my specialty is muscular and nervous recovery and enhancement."

"Really?" she replied. "What is it you are working on there?"

"These are servo motors that will be used to assist Nova Capsain. She is now my patient and I am implanting these to help her be more mobile...eventually to be fully productive again. It is the only thing that will heal her completely. She has most of her movement and locomotion back...this will help to give her additional strength" he replied.

She nodded at him. "Ah, that is great. Nova is such a wonderful person. To have such a tragic thing happen to her and Yuli. I'm sorry to have bothered you, nice to have met you Jacob...please carry on."

He nodded, placed the servos into a box, stood up, and left the medical lab. She looked over at Max, who nodded to one of the research labs. She followed him into the lab and he secured the door behind her.

"So, what is this discovery Max? What is it that is so important to keep secret?" she queried.

"These..." he pointed to the wings on his ear. "I have figured out why we have them and what they do."

He stopped for a moment – she looked at him, then cocked her head before saying "Well, don't keep me in suspense..."

"The wings seem to give us some ability to resist heavy forces. They keep our equilibrium and balance in check when massive forces are placed upon our bodies..."

"You mean like when we're in sub-space?" she interrupted.

"Yes, exactly" he replied. "These wings are the reason we're not only able to withstand sub-space, but are able to travel faster and faster in the void each time. Because we have these wings, and the Blessed do not, we are able to travel at the fantastic rate of speed through sub-space, where they are barely able to crawl."

She walked over to the mirror and stroked the fleshy wing of her left ear. "Amazing. So, we have changed to adapt for the conditions of sub-space. That's hard to believe."

"Isn't it? I am going to continue my studies of the changes we...and you are going through. I bet we'll discover so many more amazing changes that are helping us to adapt."

She felt yet another burst of voltage surge through her nervous system. She turned her head to hide her discomfort from Max. "Well, please keep me informed Max. I think I need to call it a day as I am feeling a little tired."

She took the long journey from medical to her cabin. She plopped herself onto the bed and despite the tingling in her nerves, was tired, and felt like she would immediately fall asleep. When Hero jumped into bed and curled up with her, she found herself quickly drifting into a restful sleep. A few hours into her sleep however, she was awoken by the emergency ping on her Norm-Comm. She answered and it was Halley. "Captain, sorry to disturb your sleep. We just received a priority message from the Star Force. We are to depart immediately and meet the Blessed fleet. They have detected an incoming fleet of Og ships."

"Og, really? It has been a while." She sighed then continued "Very well, prepare for departure. Halley, once we are under way, I will want you to take the bridge for a while. I am beat, and I definitely did not get enough sleep!"

"Very well, captain. Crews have been recalled, preparations for departure are under way" she said, then signed off.

"Come on Hero...time to go to work." She stood up and started to change her uniform. As she took off her top, she noticed some more changes had occurred – the skin on her neck was now the same shimmering black as the rest of her body. Only her face remained flesh colored. Also, she had forgotten to remove her command weapon before she fell asleep – and now it had changed – it was different. What once was a black, polymer, magnetically-attached module was now a fleshy appendage of her body. While she slept, her skin reached up and over the device, and encased it in dark, blue flesh. She looked at it both in curiosity, and shock as a new part of her body. The four beam ports were still exposed however, so it was still useful as a weapon – almost as if by design. She shook her head, not knowing what to think. She then finished getting dressed, and then contacted Max.

"Doctor, are you headed to the Ladyhawk?" she asked.

"Already on board, Captain" he replied.

"Good, once we are underway...I need you to look at something..."

"Very well" he acknowledged, then asked "Want to tell me what? Are you having problems with your nerves firing again?"

"Yes, but there is something else...something very odd..."

Nova Capsain:

Jacob had come by to install some advanced servos into her body. He told her these would make her stronger and faster than a normal, Normal person. With the installation of the new motors, he invited her to try them out. She at first took some small steps, then walked around the room with a fast paced gait.

186

He opened the door to her cabin and motioned her out. "Now, I think you should give it a real test. Try running down the corridor. Show me how well they work for you."

"No, I think it's better that I don't..." she insisted. He shook his head no and motioned her out the door. She sighed, but then stepped out and looked around. The corridor was empty, no one would see her, and that was a good thing. She took a few fast steps and stopped. She looked around and she discovered that in those few short, quick steps, she was already out into the main concourse of the base. She quickly turned and returned to her cabin.

Jacob was waiting for her at the door. "Better, stronger, and faster eh? Between those new servos, and your synthetic skin, you are more resilient than any other person here. I bet you could even survive the vacuum and cold of space, if you were wearing a helmet for air." he told her.

"I'm amazed, doctor!" she admitted.

He motioned her inside again. "Well, there is nothing you can't do. You could maybe even go back to work."

"NO, I couldn't" she demanded.

"You are letting that stubborn Blessed half of you take control. Or, is it the inhibited Normal side that keeps you from being seen?" he asked.

"I'm not sure...maybe the Normal side I think."

"Then you need to use your Blessed side to get you out the door." He walked her back into the room and to the couch. On the way, he stopped at the mirror on the wall and turned her. "You have to give up trying to stay put in this cabin. You need to go out. The Blessed in you I know is still fighting your Normal side. If I was in your place, I would be inwardly fighting constantly. However, in the end, the stronger side must win. You may have to choose the side you want to control you and I hope you choose the stronger of the two. In your case, I think it is your Blessed side...that is what must prevail to get you out the door."

She looked at herself in the mirror and clenched her fists in anger. Jacob looked down at her closed fists. "You're angry aren't you? Use that anger to power yourself out of here. Let that anger push you out the door" he urged.

At that moment, a signal came through on Norm-Comm. It was the boarding call for the Ladyhawk, she was preparing to get underway.

"You want to go aboard don't you?" he asked. She shook her head yes. "Then go" he urged. "Let the anger of the Blessed side of you push you to the ship."

"But I don't have orders to board!" she said with frustration. "Grrr, it just makes me want to wreck something...I feel so angry and revengeful!" she yelled out.

"Well, then get aboard that ship. Do something that will make you feel better. It will remove the anger and calm you. Doesn't matter if you don't have orders. Tell 'em your doctor sent you. Now go!"

She ran to the dressing bay and quickly put on a uniform. Returning to the main room, she checked her outfit in the mirror. "Your right, my anger is giving me strength. I have this need...I need to be on that ship, with the people that did this to me. Yes, I have to go. If you will excuse me now..." and she quickly turned and ran out the door.

Jacob smiled, shook his head, and left her cabin to return to medical.

She ran to the gangway and looked at the boarding scanner. She thought for a moment *"if I use the scanner, they will know I'm aboard and may stop me. AH!"* she realized a weakness in the gangway security and jumped over the scanner and into the gangway. She ran the remaining length of the gangway and onto the ship. Once there, she ran as fast as she could into one of the weapons bays. She knew she could hide there until they were well underway. After that, if she was discovered it wouldn't matter as they could not send her back.

Twelve Years Ago...

"You WILL come with us, bitch!" he yelled as he pointed to his hovercar. "I have a client that would just love to get some of your delicious brightness. Now, get in!"

His assistant Milo reached out to grab her. But he didn't see the blade she had hidden up her sleeve. She swiped out at him, cutting his arm. He screamed in pain, but then jumped at her in an attempt to wrap his bloody arm around her, while at the same time going for the knife in her hand. She moved back, and quickly slashed out again. Blood shot out of his neck, onto her face and across her body, staining her once-white dress. This time, he crumbled to the ground – a pool of blood began to form at her feet.

"Damn you bitch!" the pimp said as he pulled out a blaster. She just as quickly answered his threat with one smooth motion – she slid a small pen knife out of her sleeve and flung it into the fleshy meat of his neck. The blood spurted out of his Jugular as he began to bleed out across the sidewalk. The other pimps now were aware of Ferchan's trouble and began running from their cars to where the two men lay bleeding. They drew weapons and prepared to fire, she turned and ran.

She ran and ran, turned corners, ran down street after street, quickly passed through dark alleys, all in the hopes that she could evade her pursuers. They continued to follow however, as they were not going to give in. She knew she would die if they caught her – they were no longer interested in her body or the money she would make for them – they just wanted her dead. She only could run, but as she ran, she started to come up with a plan. If only she could keep them far enough away until she could get where she would need to be for her plan.

More turns, more streets, and through more alleys she ran. She on occasion jumped over obstacles and pushed people down who were just innocently walking. She did anything she could to slow them down. She hopped over a moving hovercar as it slowly passed through an intersection – this gave her a few more seconds. Finally, she reached her destination. Now, she just needed a few more precious seconds to get inside.

The gang caught up to her, though she was now hidden inside – but she had left the door open. It seemed like a trap to them, but they cared less as they were now out for blood. If they killed her inside or out, it no longer mattered – she just needed to die. They could clean, cover up, and bribe for silence later. They entered the building through the open door. It was a surplus store, it was filled with various items of clothing and equipment from the days before the global war.

They recklessly started knocking over racks of uniform clothing – no sign of her. One rack however gave one of the pursuers a start as it had a mannequin amongst the clothing. It jumped out at him – he shot at it, killed the already dead plaster cast, and then laughed. Another rack, another mannequin. He knocked over another rack, but this time the mannequin attacked and shoved a large knife through the soft flesh right behind his chin. The blade went all the way into his brain, killing him so quickly he had no chance to react or scream out.

His repeater blaster was then used to take out the other five pursuers. It was fast, only slightly noisy, and they died quick. She had done her work, cleaned herself up, and left before anyone outside had reported the noises of the blaster being fired. She had enough time to clean the blood off of her face, take clothes off the rack, change out of her blood stained wear, and casually walk back onto the street.

NGD: 3 Years, 2 Months, 14 Days:

Starship Ladyhawk:

Nova Capsain:

She had successfully snuck onboard the ship and had been hiding in the weapons bay during their trip into sub-space. She tapped her fingers on the deck while she thought about what she should do next. She was confused, and there was a battle going on inside her mind – she was fighting herself: The Normal in her said to just hide and do nothing while the ship was on its mission. The Blessed in her said to take revenge on the Normals...Yuli...who caused her this agony. She thought she could control herself and maintain her logical composure, but in reality was not at all thinking of her own accord.

She tapped her fingers more and harder. When she finally stopped the loud tapping, she looked down and saw she had caused dents in the hardened metal of the deck floor. She made a small laugh as she realized the power she held in her hands. Power, that was being caused by the pain and suffering that she was now going through. Pain and suffering she finally decided was caused by being part Normal. That part disintegrated with her darkened skin, so she had decided that she was now more Blessed than Normal.

As the ship left Haven and entered sub-space, she felt it on her body. She felt the strain that the void placed upon her. She felt how it made her feel, how bad she felt in sub-space. This strengthened her decision that she was indeed more Blessed than Normal, it was time for her to act as the Blessed that she was. Her kind needed her now more than ever.

Fighting the forces the void was placing against her polymer skin and body, she slowly made her way to the dark matter containment center. She had determined how she would take revenge for the pain and suffering she was going through – she had determined a way to make them all pay. Upon arriving at the containment center, she put on a clear polymer helmet for atmosphere – this would be the only way that she would be able to breathe inside the chamber. She then entered the control room, then proceeded to the control panel. She deactivated the security protocols, the notification system, and then overrode the safety policies. Once all of her reprogramming was completed, she walked over to the access panel, entered her code into the hatch leading to the containment room, and entered the tank chamber area through the multi-layered isolating hatch system.

The containment room was filled with energy, some of those forces were the electronic shields that were active around the containment tank to hold back the forces within. Other powers were emanating from the tank itself, the dark matter trying to escape its captivity. On top of those forces, she could also feel the force of gravity, dark energy, fighting its way into the tank. At any time, any of these powers could win the battle and destroy the containment – the automated computer force field adjustments were the only thing keeping everything in check. She felt all of the various forces being exerted on the tank, these forces seeped out of the containment area and affected the entire room surrounding the tank. The air itself was being warped and misshapen into visible bizarre patterns. There were hums, crackles, and snapping of power all around her.

She sat on the floor and examined the control panel located near the bottom of the tank – the one spot on the tank where the pressure exerted was the lightest – this was where she would do her work. She felt the forces on her body, but her skin was strong – it repelled even the forces trying to warp matter itself – all being exerted from the battle of containment occurring within the room. The space helmet would keep her lungs filled with air. She would survive this, and show them all how strong she had become. Then, she would take her revenge on them all.

Jonathan Faraday:

Something was odd about the readings in containment room 3. The dark matter containment system did not look right, and to him it did not feel right – but at the same time, the readings were still within normal parameters. He never could explain why he got those feelings, but they would come to him at any time – and this time they were telling him something was not right. He logged off of his engineering station on the bridge, and took his leave from duty with the captain. Yuli, had a look of concern on his now dark blue face and asked if he would need help – he declined his kind offer.

He took the lift down to the mid-section of the command module of the ship, then walked the distance from the lift to the containment room. This was the area of the ship where he had built the dark matter containment tanks. He stepped inside the entry area, then into the command room and looked into the containment room through the coated transparent viewports. He did not see anything, but it was always hard to see inside the room as the containment tanks were constantly fighting the forces that were held within. The battle of dark matter vs dark energy caused the air to warp and also forced the manipulation of the tank and the walls of the room – thus, what was seen one moment, might be totally different the next. However, he could have sworn he saw someone moving inside the chamber – *impossible when the tanks were full and actively storing!*

However, he saw the movement again. He adjusted the focus of his glasses to overcome the fluctuation of visible light in the room and was then able to see her – it was Nova. She was sitting on the floor at the base of the tank, manipulating the controls on the containment fields. He not only wondered what she was doing and why, but how she was able to maintain herself in there. The forces inside the chamber were too great for a person without a stabilizing suit and without lowering the amount of matter contained. But there she was in a normal uniform suit, and no added protection except a helmet for breathing. He realized the new polymer skin they had developed for her was stronger than any skin that would be found on a human. It was what was keeping her together, and now it was allowing her to stay in the containment room, while still keeping her alive.

He tapped on his Norm-Comm "Nova, what are you doing in there?" he called out. She ignored him and continued to work. He tried again "Nova, I am seeing fluctuations in the containment field in there. Are you trying to stabilize the fields?"

"Go away, Jonathan…" was her only reply.

He continued to monitor the fields and realized that instead of stabilizing them, she was actually causing them to fluctuate at an accelerated rate. Based on his mental analysis, she was manipulating the fields to the point of degradation. The field would fail, and containment would break down. If she continued at the current rate, she would allow the ship to be destroyed. He ran over to the containment controls on one of the command consoles and began to attempt to reverse the sabotage she was causing.

For a brief second, he could remove his hand from the control computer just long enough to tap on his Norm-Comm. "Captain, I need you down here and I need you here now."

Jaime Bordeaux:

Max had come to her cabin at her request. "So, what is so wrong that you need my services?" he asked.

193

She raised her left arm, he did a quick glance, and then took a double-take. He took her arm and held it closer to his view. He examined the command weapon now embedded into her skin. The black flesh completely covering the device.

"Well, this is interesting..." he said as he continued his inspection. "Hmm, the firing ports of your module are not blocked by the flesh. You can still use this weapon. There would be no interference of the beams from the device" he assured her. He pulled out his medical scanner "OKAY, I need to do a full scan on you...at least as complete of a scan as possible aboard a starship. When we return to Haven, I want to do a full, complete analysis scan of you."

He ran the device along the front of her, moving the device from the top of her head to the tip of her toes. Then he went around the back side and performed the same motions.

He examined the readout with such a level of concentration that it brought concern to Jaime. "Okay doc, what the hell is wrong with me now?" she asked.

"Actually, nothing I didn't expect" he replied. "Here's what I'm now seeing..." he said as he activated the holographic display of his scanner, then continued "as you can see, your command weapon has now become part of your body. It actually has turned organic."

"What?" she blurted out. "How can that happen? It's made of polymers, metal, and circuitry. There is no way it could become part of me, unless my body is changing..."

"Nope, it changed" he corrected her. "The polymers have turned to some form of cartilage, and the metals some interesting modification of bone. But, there's more. Your nervous system...it was modified with the superconductors when you were given the command implants...well, they also are now organic. And, the rest of your nervous system has followed suit. All of the nerves in your body are composed of superconductive chained nerve cells...and I mean EVERY nerve."

Jaime looked at him with concern. "OKAY doc, that really scares me..." she admitted.

"I don't suppose you want to know that there's more..." he said with a slight bit of sarcasm.

"Not really, but I have a feeling you are going to tell me anyway..." she replied.

"I am..." he said and gave her a small smile and a chuckle before saying "I don't think it is that bad...really. However...ready for this...your reactor...it has also turned organic. I'm not sure how, but it's now an organ of some form, an organ that is able to create the massive amounts of power needed to feed your newly modified, supercharged neural system. Then there is your Norm-Comm implant..."

"No..." she sighed.

"Yep, organic. It is now part of the hearing structure of your left ear. I would not be surprised if eventually you would not even need to speak to use it..."

She thought a moment. "I think that might explain a few things" she told him.

He looked at HER slightly confused now. Now SHE was able to give him a smug little smile. He was about to reply to her comment, but before he had a chance to say anything else, Jaime's Norm-Comm buzzed. She held a finger up to him while answering. "Bordeaux here."

It was Jonathan. "Captain, I need you down here and I need you here now. You need to get to containment room three...we have a problem, it's Nova."

"Right Jonathan, we're on our way." She quickly turned to the door of her ready room, then stopped and turned back to Max. "Come on, I might need you on this one."

The pair took the lift and ran to the containment room. They found Jonathan, working the computer with all of the skill he could muster. He looked quickly over his shoulder at them. "Captain, Nova is trying to shift the containment to cause a breach. I am fighting with readjustments, but I can't keep this up much longer. She has become quite fast at manipulating the controls."

Jaime looked into the tank room through the high density glass. The air was being shifted by the waves of conflicting gravimetric forces – the air had formed waves and was crashing around all sides of the room. Nova was inside, sitting on the floor, and was manipulating the main containment control with furious fingers. "Jonathan, is there any way we can remove control of the containment from the panel in there?"

Without looking he answered "Yes, but I cannot leave this station and the command console is across the room. She will breach the containment before I have a chance to deactivate the console in there."

She ran to the command console across the room and yelled out "Just tell me what to type, I can do this!"

"OKAY, control A-47…switch to manual…" he told her.

She looked around the console until she found a rotary switch with the same label. She turned the knob to manual and yelled out "Done!"

"Ok, you will now have to log into the computer and enter your command code. Once logged in you will have to enter the command 'XJC2233, then OVERRIDE"

She activated the command console and entered her logon and password. It rejected her password. She tried again, with the same results. "Shit!" she yelled as she tried once more. Now the console projected a warning that she was about to breach security protocols. Max tapped her on the shoulder and pointed down at the command console. She saw a small metal pad, shook her head in embarrassment then smiled. She then yelled out to Jonathan over her shoulder "Blessed command pads on my ship?"

Jonathan replied without looking "Did not have time to install DNA readers on every piece of command equipment, so we had to make do with what he had. I will upgrade those later…provided we survive. The new ships will have all DNA readers."

"Hmm, okay…" she said before she placed her palm near the pad. Her command module wiggled loose, and then flew from her palm onto the metal plate. With a loud clink, it attached itself securely, and a moment later the terminal gave the message *"Good morning, Captain"*

Max looked at the console and nodded his head "See, always a way to do something..."

She nodded then entered the code exactly as Jonathan had instructed. The console beeped, and with that she heard Jonathan yelp in excitement – a few more commands were typed in by the young man, then finally he let out a very large and loud sigh. "Okay, I have control and have deactivated her station. She cannot cause a breach now. That was very good, captain! For a..." he stopped himself from continuing.

"For a soldier?" she asked, finishing the sentence for him. Jonathan said nothing, just looked to the ground, and blushed.

With the containment back to normal, the forces in the room were still in a state of flux, but now in a way that was totally controllable by the computer. Jaime looked into the room and saw Nova just sitting on the floor, her back against the tank, and her head pointed down looking at the floor. Max walked over, looked in, and then went over to one of the computer consoles. He activated the computer and initiated a medical scanning program.

Suddenly, Jaime felt that feeling again – as if someone was overloading her neural system with an excess of electricity. She gave a slight gasp as the shock hit her system. She heard a similar noise from Max and Jonathan. She turned to look at them – they were both rubbing their necks. She wondered for a moment, then turned back to her real problem.

Jaime activated Norm-Comm. "Nova, why? Why were you trying to breach containment? You knew that would destroy the ship. So, why?"

Still sitting against the tank, she looked up at Jaime through the window. "Because, you Normals did this to me. You destroyed my skin and turned me into a mechanical freak...you made me into this...this monster. I will never have a life again...and it is all because of you...you Normals!" She had such spite and hatred in her voice. Jaime could not believe this was the same person she had met just a few short months before. Jaime stood at the window, not sure what to say.

She deactivated her Norm-Comm. "Is this true? Did we cause this pain in her? Did allowing her to stay with us cause her demise?" she asked of the other two men.

"I don't think so..." Max said as he continued to peer into a holographic display on his computer terminal. "Look here..." he waved Jaime over to the console. He pointed at a small red dot in her elbow. "Look at that..."

Jaime looked at the display. "Okay, it's a red dot. So?"

"So..." he stopped and pointed at the red dot again "That, appears to be a servo motor...however, it is emitting beta waves and increased electrical energy." He rubbed his neck again. "I think it is over stimulating parts of her brain via her neural network. In particular the Amygdala – the fight/flight part of the brain. In other words, this is stimulating fear, anger, and revenge in her. In a Normal, this would cause some problems that could be overcome...but in a Blessed..."

"A real need to destroy anything that caused him or her pain...like us Normals..." she interjected and Max nodded his head yes. "OKAY...so...what do we do about it?"

"Well..." Max thought out loud. "If we could somehow deactivate that servo..."

"It is under a centimeter of ultra-strength flexible polymer" Jonathan interrupted. He then thought for a moment, ran over to a storage locker and pulled out a small silver gun. In his other hand, a sharp tipped projectile. "This is to be used in the event that we need to send current into the tank in case of an emergency. We fire this at the tank, it will slightly pierce the shell and we can then pass voltage or other types of power through the tip into the tank. If we could fire this into the servo, we could take it out with a blast of voltage. But someone would have to run up and attach a cable to it for the voltage...that is after we shot it into her skin in just the right spot to affect the servo. Don't think she would let us near it...don't think we could make a shot like that...not like she would just stand there and let us shoot her in the arm."

"Don't be so negative…" Jaime said, causing Max to give a look of surprise. "It has a laser sight…I can hit her with it…I am a soldier after all, and am a crack marksman. If I can get a clean shot and hit her, then I can use my command weapon to energize the probe."

"Might work…" Max added. Jaime gave him a dry smile.

Jonathan went back to the command computer. He called out while entering commands into the console "I am draining this tank. It will not be a threat to us in just a few minutes."

She took the gun from the table where Jonathan left it, and loaded the projectile into the chamber. She examined the fire circuit, and then waited. She peered through the window – the forces inside the chamber were now leveling off into a normal state. Nova was still just sitting on the floor. She assumed she was planning her next move. A moment later, she got up off of the floor and looked up, then jumped into the air and grabbed onto a pipe that was suspended from the ceiling. This particular pipe ran from the tank into the body of the craft. She started furiously wiggling and pulling on the pipe with her ultra-mechanically enhanced arms and hands.

Jonathan yelled out to Jaime "She's pulling on one of the Ultra feeds. If she loosens that up, or breaks it, this compartment will be flooded with whatever remaining dark matter is left in that pipe. If she manages to damage the conduit structure it could leak into the entire ship."

"I guess it's now or never then…" she said as she released the safety locks on the compartment air lock doors. Then entered her override command code and hit the red button that released all of the doors simultaneously. A hissing sound filled the room for a brief moment followed by the clanking of the doors as they unlocked. Servo motors opened them all simultaneously, giving Jaime a perfect line of sight to Nova, now hanging onto the conduit with all her might. Jaime took careful aim at her elbow with the gun's laser sight, and slowly squeezed the trigger. The projectile probe shot out the barrel and flew straight and true to its target. It hit her in the exact spot, just above the elbow joint – the ultra-hard space carbon tip piercing the polymer flesh and embedding itself into the muscle.

Jaime immediately dropped the gun, raised her left arm and fired a powerful electrical bolt to the probe. It struck Nova's arm in the precise spot and dissipated across her polymer arm. Jaime could tell it also got under her skin as her arm convulsed and twitched, causing her to release her hold on the conduit above – but not before she was able to have dislodged the pipe at a joint, causing the section to break away from between the tank, and the conduit that continued into the body of the ship. She and a piece of the pipe came tumbling to the floor. Jaime keep her weapon aimed true and continued her assault on the servo inside her arm. Nova screamed in pain as the electricity caused her to lose the feeling in her arm. The other servos began breaking down in her arm as the voltage coursed through her system. With what little control she had left in her body, she reached down with her other arm, picked up the fallen pipe segment, and heaved it at Jaime with what remained of her strength – but the strength that remained was still ten times that of a normal human. The pipe flew quickly through the hatchway and struck Jaime square in her chest, knocking the wind out of her lungs. She fell to the floor, gasping for breath.

Nova took that moment to run to the door, Max came up to subdue her but with a quick movement butted her shoulder into his chest, and sent him flying into the wall. Without hesitating, she gave Jonathan a quick side kick – he was totally unprepared for the attack and had no defense prepared. He bounced into a console and keeled over onto the floor in pain. She opened the hatch, and ran out into the hallway and was gone.

Jaime recovered quickly, but by the time she was back on her feet and ready for pursuit Nova was nowhere to be found. She helped Max get back to his feet, then Jonathan.

"Guys, we have to find her. There is no telling if we did the job or not" she told them.

"We did…" Max corrected her. "I took a reading right before she attacked us. The servo was damaged and was totally disabled. The beta waves were gone, she should be returning to her normal self."

Jaime thought for a moment about how she felt. "Funny, but I am feeling better myself. Max, do you think that servo was causing the misfiring of my nerves also? It seemed to have started as soon as I arrived to Haven and again when I got near Nova. Could she have caused that?"

"The servo...or whatever it was could definitely cause that" he replied.

"It was a neuro-manipulator" Jonathan interjected. "I saw a plan for one of those once. It is a Blessed design of course."

"Then, someone put it into her" Jaime surmised.

"And I think I know who..." Max added.

Jonathan looked at the command console. "Captain, Max...I think we have a bigger problem."

The doors to the containment center suddenly closed and sealed shut. Alarms started blaring inside the room. Jaime held her hands over her ears and was yelling to Jonathan. He looked at her with confusion, and started waving his hands in the air. He turned and input commands into the terminal, the alarms stopped instantly. "There, now I can hear you. What did you say?"

Jaime rolled her eyes. "I was trying to get you to turn those alarms off!" she said yelling.

"They're off, you don't have to yell anymore..." Jonathan replied, then realized who he was speaking to "Umm, Captain."

"SO, why did the alarms go off?" she asked.

Max, checking the hatches added "And why are the hatches locked?"

Jonathan checked the readouts "Because, this room is full of dark matter...the computer locked and sealed the hatches automatically. The room has containment fields to hold anything that escapes in the event of a containment tank leak. So sealing the room may prevent the escape of the dark matter into the ship."

"Oh shit..." Max mumbled, then turned around from the door and said "Oh, double shit..."

"What?" Jonathan said then turned from his console, his face or expression could not hide it *"Oh shit!"*

"Would someone mind telling me what the hell is going on...what is with the oh shits?" Jaime demanded. Jonathan pointed at her, but could not utter a single word. Max walked up and activated his medical computer, pointed it at Jaime and allowed her to look at the video reflection of herself. She saw her eyes – they were now the brightest shade of blue, like a pair of finely polished sapphires – they actually seemed to glow as they were so bright. In her hair were streaks of red flame and strands of gold, which glowed like the fires of the sun. But it was her skin that was the most surprising – it was now the darkest shade of midnight blue, practically black – small white spots that were once her freckles now dotted her cheeks. Her skin glistened like reflections on water and seemed to shift with random patterns. She stared at herself in the output, ran her fingers across her smooth dark face and said "Oh shit..."

Nova Capsain:

Nova had escaped her potential incarceration at the hands of the captain, but her mind was still trapped in a battle – the battle between Normal and Blessed thinking. She reached over with her other hand and pulled the probe out of her elbow. Her muscles beneath the polymer skin hurt like hell, but otherwise she was undamaged. She squeezed the two torn folds of her plastic flesh together – the material melded together, and within seconds showed no signs of even being damaged. The neuro-manipulator however had done plenty of damage – it did its job well, she was mentally mixed between the former thoughts of revenge, and the sorrow she felt for trying to kill both friends and loved ones. She realized that she almost killed Yuli, the one person who gave her nothing but love and respect. She was torn, and had no idea what to do about it or where to turn. A sign on the wall however, gave her the way to go – "Weapons Bay 3".

She looked at the hatch and put her hand to the locking mechanism. She knew it would alert the people that were looking for her, but at this point she didn't care. She now had an idea, a plan was now in her mind that nothing or no one could stop. The final victory over her pain and suffering would end here, in the place where it all began, where she met Yuli.

The hatch opened and she quickly entered her code to secure the hatch, then smashed the locking mechanism once it had done its job. No one would use that to open the door again. She leaned against the wall, then slumped down, and finally slid down the wall and onto the floor. She sat there and whimpered – she could not cry, she no longer had tear ducts, but she wanted to. Her heart was so filled with sorrow. The more she sat there, the longer the effects of the beta waves dissipated. The excess voltage was no longer flowing through her system – no more stimulation for anger existed. Her revenge and anger were being replaced by loneliness and sorrow. The Normal side of her was once again taking over the battle – she was becoming more human than machine. Within minutes, the need for revenge was almost totally gone.

The final remnants of anger subsided when she heard the all too familiar voice over the weapons bay speakers – it was Yuli. "Nova...Nova honey, please answer." She could not reply, only mumble incoherent words that no one would hear or understand. He tried again "Nova, please say something. We were all so worried about you. We didn't know you were being manipulated, and were in such pain. Nova, please...I love you. Open the door so we can help."

She stood up, looked around, and finally found the direction to walk to her fate. "No, I won't open the door my love. I know what I have to do. I cannot be with you, any of you...I am no longer one of you." She walked over to the corner of the bay. On the floor was a hatch, labeled airlock. She reached around and removed the air cartridge off of the space helmet she was wearing, and replaced it with a fresh, full cartridge. She bent down and pressed the button to open the first hatch. She stepped in and closed the first hatch, then opened the second hatch. "I know what I have to do" she said as she climbed down the second hatch. She now felt the missing effect of the artificial gravity generators – she was weightless.

"Please Nova, don't...I can't live without you!" Yuli pleaded, then added "Nova, the baby! You remember the child? Remember when Max told me you were pregnant, you remember that don't you?"

She did. She looked down at her belly, she rubbed it and wondered how something could live inside a shell of plastic. A slight sob escaped her polymer lips, she told him "I'm sorry my love...but you also can't live with me, and who knows what would be produced by my body. The Blessed know my weakness, I cannot be here, as I would be a danger to you and everyone else. I am going to go where no one else has ever gone...I am going to the one place that hurts me so. I am going into the void. Take care my love, I will think of you for my time remaining. I hope you will not think ill of me...please, remember me as I was. Goodbye."

And with saying that, she pressed the red button, which opened the airlock door in emergency mode. The door flew open, which caused the atmosphere in the airlock to rush out into the nothingness in a gust. The force of the rushing air took Nova along in the evacuation, which moved her quickly away from the ship, and into the void. Now out in the void, she found she felt nothing – no cold, no pain, no feeling at all. For a brief part of a second she saw the usual lights of sub-space travel, then everything went dark as she left the energy field of the ship. She looked back and for only a brief instant saw the Ladyhawk as it zoomed away leaving her in nothing but pitch black. There was absolutely nothing that she could see. The flashes and lights of sub-space travel were reserved only for those on the spaceships – for her floating in the void, nothing but darkness.

"So, this is what it's like..." She thought as she floated in the nothingness, awaiting death in the final seconds of her existence – then she saw the bright light she always expected when one was about to die.

Max Sollix:

He could not believe his eyes, the skin on her face now matched the skin on her body – blue, but almost black as midnight. Her skin now had a glossy sheen that shimmered in the light, and seemed to make her skin appear fluid. He walked up and put his hand to her face, the smoothness of her skin was both amazing to view and pleasingly soft to touch.

"This is amazing..." is all he could remark. He continued touching her cheeks, feeling if there was any difference in the white spots where her freckles used to be. Then he examined her chin, lips, eyes and finally her forehead. "It feels and looks perfectly fine, just now it is a different pigment. I suspect it is also a totally different cell structure make-up. I was detecting that when the skin on your lower body started to change. Your face now matches that cell structure I bet." He got his medical scanner out of his shoulder pouch and started to scan across her face. "Hmm, yes..." he mumbled to Jaime's annoyance. He then scanned her entire body once again. He looked at the readings on his computer then turned the scanner on himself. "Hmm, makes sense..."

"Doc..." Jaime called out but was ignored.

He walked over to Jonathan and ran the scanner around him. "Yep, as I thought..."

"Doc!" she shouted, clearly annoyed.

Finally, he looked up from his computer and into Jaime's glowing blue eyes. "Well, I think we can say that you have completely transformed. You are complete." Jaime looked at him confused, raising an eyebrow then scrunching her forehead. Max put his hand to her forehead to stop her "That is still going to be permanent if you keep it up, regardless of the changes to your flesh." She stopped, then he continued "As I told you before we left...you were changing and appeared to be the catalyst for these changes in everyone else. I may have been a bit premature in my statement. Instead of being the catalyst, you are instead the precursor...the view of our future. Being exposed to the dark matter only accelerated the process of your changes. And, in scanning Jonathan and myself we are changing also, albeit at a slower rate. As a matter of fact, take a look at his eyes."

Jaime walked up to Jonathan, removed his glasses and looked at him. "Well, I'll be damned..." she exclaimed. His eyes were now a glowing shade of green.

"My eyes should follow in the same manner very shortly. And eventually, our skin will follow. As a matter of fact, there is a small growth in our necks – I would suspect we will soon have small reactors similar to your organic generator. Also, I noticed some small changes in our Norm-Comm devices...I suspect those will be organic soon too."

"So, basically you are saying that our exposure accelerated what was going to happen anyway?" she asked.

He nodded yes. "It would have happened to us in any case, yes. Just not today. I wonder…" he removed his gloves exposing his dark black-blue hands.

Jaime looked at him with surprise. "How long have you had those?" she asked.

"A while now…"

"Since you met doctor Starling?" That question caused him to blush – he said not a word. "Thought so…" she surmised.

Finally getting over his embarrassment he rolled up his sleeves, then cleared his throat. "Well…when I first…met her…it only affected my hands from our first handshake. But I have a feeling…" As he rolled up his sleeve it revealed a midnight blue arm. "That the change had progressed…" he looked down "Yep, I only had the skin change three inches up my wrist. As you can see, after our experience it is now up my arm."

Jonathan was lifting his shirt to look at his belly…now a similar shimmering shade of midnight. "It was my shoulder only, it started moving down my chest of late, but now…well, you can see…and now you say my eyes are different?" Jaime and Max nodded their heads yes.

"Kate?" she asked, knowing the answer. He nodded his head yes and blushed.

"Well, how long will it take to vent this room so we can get out of here?" Jaime asked.

Jonathan looked at the command console and requested scans from science station. He read the reports before saying "New problem…when she pulled on the conduit, she released dark matter into the general ship superstructure. I figure by now everyone will have come in contact with dark matter."

Max went over to the hatch and entered his medical authority code. "Jaime, use your command code to unlock the door. The ships been saturated with dark matter, there is no real danger, no need to stay in here." He thought for a moment while Jaime went to the command console and entered her code – she then reached out her hand and gave the release command, causing the metal command plate to fly from the console back to her hand. He then continued. "What's important now, is that we stop Nova. With the neuro-manipulator destroyed she is going to need our help, now more than ever."

Jaime shook her head in agreement "Despite what she did, she has always been our friend…up until an hour ago at least. Can she be helped Max?" she asked.

A buzzing on her Norm-Comm interrupted her questioning of Max – it was Halley. She could tell she was upset and trying as hard as possible to maintain her professional demeanor and composure. "Captain, Yuli found Nova. She went to the weapons bay…he tried to stop her…but he couldn't. She ejected herself into the void. She's gone…"

Seven Years Ago...

The ship fired another volley, this one took down the armor of the opposition. He looked at the status displays again, then ordered. "Initiate plan XY-37."

His first officer gave him a look with a mixture of confusion and worry, but then said "Very well. Communications, signal fleet ship 3 to initiate battle plan 37." The communications officer gave the same confused look, then complied.

Moments later a star ship entered into their view screen displays. They began pelting the enemy carrier with various forms of weapons fire. It was an amazing display of firepower, worthy of the viewing of the Supreme Commander. The ship however, could not take the opposing continual broadsiding from the two enemy vessels as it was now burning.

"You may now fire your missiles weapons master..." he called out. The weapons master followed orders immediately and sent a massive flotilla of nuclear armed missiles into the mass of the three ships. They slammed into the enemy vessels, detonating into multiple bright bursts of light. The missiles also slammed into the friendly vessel, lighting it up and causing massive gaping holes in the superstructure. "Better get us away from these wrecks...:" he ordered. The ship veered off away from the carnage.

Moments after they quickly moved away from the three ships they all exploded in a massive fireball. He squinted at the explosion, it was so bright that it almost took out the view screen sensors. "Glad we moved away when we did..." he said softly. "Science, do we have any more enemy ships to worry about?"

The science officer looked over his SCADAR returns before saying "No, my captain..."

A moment later the lights came on in the simulator. The war games were over. He stood up and let out a bellowing laugh. "Good job all, good job!" he belted out.

Over the intercom a voice echoed his pride "Yes...that was an extremely good job. Very good strategy and use of available resources. I can see why we picked you for this position."

He recognized the voice, and replied "Thank you, my Supreme Commander."

As the crew began their wrap up of the games, the weapons master came up to him and asked "My captain, you sacrificed one of your ships to get the kill? Is that ethical?"

He gave the young man an annoyed look, then smiled and answered "Yes, a captain should use every asset available to him, and any strategy necessary to win the battle. Everything or everyone is worth the sacrifice for a win." What he had not realized was that his father had the same strategies for battle and winning as he did – and that was his plan for colonizing outer space – at all costs.

NGD: 3 Years, 2 Months, 16 Days:

Sector L, System 74 – Starlight Space Ark:

Boral Oldham:

He looked over the fleet operations schedule. *"Good, as expected, Ladyhawk had joined the task force."* They would be the first to go out...as was always the case. He activated the task force assignment roster and put the Normal ship in the point position in the fleet assault org chart. "Science, give me status of the invading Og fleet."

The science officer looked over his SCADAR readouts, then called out. "Og fleet is in sub-space approach, based on last position before sub-space insertion. Computer estimates they will arrive in ten minutes, my Star Force Commander."

"Very well, communications prepare the fleet annunciator" he ordered.

At that same moment the young communications officer announced. "My Star Force Commander, the captain of the Conquest wishes a tunneled communique with you prior to deployment."

He looked slightly annoyed at the young man, who looked down into his communications console, hoping to not attract Boral's ire. "Very well, put him through." A moment later, Kip appeared on his command holograph" He gave the officer a stern look "I hope this is important, Kip."

"My Star Force Commander, I hate to bring this up at this time, but we discussed for the morale of the Blessed..." he stopped speaking and looked at his commander so he could remember. Boral had a slightly confused look on his face, he continued so he could be reminded. "We discussed that a Blessed battleship should lead and take this victory...so that all Blessed and Normals could see how advanced and superior we are in both battle tactics and technology."

Boral thought about it a moment, then remembered the conversation. He thought for another moment and realized that Kip was specifically enhanced for battle tactics, a natural to lead the assault on the Og fleet. *"Yes, he would make the battle look even easier than the Norms."* He smiled at Kip "Yes, I agree. This is our chance to show the Norms just how pitiful they are. Do you have a battle plan in mind?"

"Yes, my Star Force Commander. I only need the Conquest and one Hammerhead as a backup. I really don't think they will be needed, but just in case."

"Very well, we will have the rest of the fleet as a willing audience to your soon to be impressive victory. You have the Supreme Commander's, and my blessings. Go give us victory Alpha Starship Captain Gurrigan!"

"Thank you, my Star Force Commander. To Victory!" and with that cheer signed off.

He called out to his bridge command. "Communications, a change of plan..."

Kip Gurrigan:

His chance had finally arrived, he was to command his first battle against an aggressive enemy of the Blessed. He would lead the charge to yet another victory by his Supreme Commander's fleet. He would be the triumphant captain of this battle. He would be the hero of the Blessed. He was ready and knew exactly what needed to be done to exterminate this threat once and for all. He inwardly also hoped they would be as weak as they had always been – he needed a quick and decisive victory. He looked down and realized his palms were sweating – most likely in anticipation of the upcoming victory, as there was no way he was worried or nervous.

He wiped his palms onto his slacks and looked around the bridge. He had a young crew, all Blessed, but all seemed very worried about the upcoming battle. He gave them a cocky smile in confidence and said "You all look worried. Don't tell me you are worried or scared? If so, I will have to ask you to leave the bridge. I have no place for a cowardly Blessed on my command bridge. Do I have anyone that feels the need to leave?"

They all shook their heads no. The communications officer then stood up and did the traditional Alliance double pump salute, pushed his fist into the air, and shouted "TO VICTORY!" The rest of the bridge crew followed in his cheer. Kip also stood, and over and over they shouted "TO VICTORY!"

After a few minutes of rabble rousing, Kip stopped, and sat back down into his command chair. He heard the bridge door open, turned, and saw Tulip standing within the mantrap – force fields glowed on both sides of her, which prevented her from either entering or leaving the bridge – lasers at the ready to cut her into small pieces should the captain deem her a security risk or threat. She stood at the force field facing the bridge with an expectant look on her face. "Permission to enter the bridge?" She asked with a confident smile on her face. Kip looked at her – her blonde hair was perfectly styled, her blue eyes glistened in the lights of the bridge, she had applied rouge to her small cheeks, making them appear larger than reality, and bright red lipstick highlighting her small but plump lips. She was wearing a standard Alliance uniform skirt, albeit the hemline may have been a bit higher off the knee than regulations.

He looked her over, licked his lips at the sight of her, deactivated the interior force field, and motioned her to enter. She walked up to him, and whispered in his ear "I'm pregnant with your child. You have done it! The two of us wanted to be here for your first of many victories my Alpha Starship Captain...and my lover."

He smiled at her. "Of course, that is understandable…" he was having a hard time concealing his excitement. Finally, he was going to bear a child, a child of Blessed origin only. He nodded his head at his first officer to vacate his seat. The young officer had a slight look of rejection on his face, but quickly took a chair in the back of the bridge at a secondary computer station. "You may sit at my side and witness our victory…" he said as he motioned her to the chair.

She took her seat and looked around the bridge. The crew looked at her with some suspicion, which did not surprise her. She gave a beaming smile as she turned her head to look at each of them. She was going to show her pride and victory this day – she was going to watch the father of her child – and her lover do his job.

Kip regained his composure and activated all command systems, lowered the bridge lights, and like his mentor, activated lights above his head. "Position of Og fleet, science?"

The science officer was a older Blessed officer, with straight brown hair that was styled in a bowl cut. His droopy eyes took in all of the sub-space buoy's SCADAR returns, and he concentrated as he analyzed what he was seeing. Finally, he announced "Enemy fleet will be exiting sub-space in fifteen seconds. Sub-space SCADAR is indicating fifteen ships, ten cruisers, four ships we suspect are carriers and a large unknown configuration of a single ship"

"Unknown?" he asked. The science officer nodded yes. "Hmm, ok…" He transferred the SCADAR readings and studied them. His enhanced genetics were developing various scenarios of battle, he tried to determine what that large ship might be. Finally he looked up from his holo-display. "Very well. Communications, contact the captain of the Victory, have them take out any of the cruisers that might be launched against us. We will take out the carriers and the unknown ship. I am going to assume that ship is some form of new battleship. I will also assume that they will be launching fighters the moment they exit sub-space. Launch our Wolf Packs now…first. Helm, prepare to engage the first carrier once it exits sub-space." He looked over at Tulip again, smiled, and then said "Look sharp everyone, prepare for battle."

The tear formed in the fabric of space and the ships one by one emerged from the dark rip that had been formed ahead of the two ships. The first of the ships to come out of the tear were the cruisers. To Kip's surprise, they immediately launched Streamer fighters – each one a smaller version of the larger cruiser – small white balls with dimples, a small square silver rectangle in the back that provided propulsion. The shape of the ships reminded Kip of the balls he used when he first learned the game of golf – a sport exclusively reserved for Blessed and members of the Order. He also knew however, that the dimples all contained small beam emitters, however in the front of each of the craft, in the ball section was a large dimple. Obviously a weapon, he surmised. The ships flew out of each emerging cruiser like swarms of angry bees flying out of their hives to attack the invaders.

Kip shook his head at the sight on the holo-screen. "OK, so the cruisers are also carriers...so much for that crappy intelligence staff...they will have to be replaced..." the first officer cringed at that statement – he was the leader of the intelligence section. He sighed before ordering "Victory, launch Wolf Packs. Launch any of our Wolf Packs in backup...let's make short work of these."

The Wolf Pack fighters had been already shooting out of their launch tubes and into open space. They immediately began to converge on the enemy ships. Hundreds of dogfights ensued – Human fighters and automated pups versus the slower streamer fighters. At first, Kip thought it would be a bloodbath – the streamers were no match for the faster and more powerful Wolf Pack fighters. Then something changed – the fighters started attacking the Victory. Small green bolts emitted from the large, front dimples in the streamers. The green bolts were slow and small, but when they hit the hull of the Victory, they went right in one side and out the other. Kip could not tell exactly how much damage occurred, but with the bolts going all the way through the ship he knew it had to be causing major structural damage to the ship. He wondered how many brave Blessed souls had already died from this battle.

The realization of the situation finally hit him, and his enhanced genetics of wartime strategy told him what was happening – they were committing suicide to take out the engines of the much larger starship. They were preparing his fleet's cruiser for the incoming enemy cruisers. He turned to his helmsman and shouted "Keep us back away from those fighters – let the Wolf Packs take care of them." He looked at the holo-screen and saw the largest of the fifteen ships emerge out of the tear – it was configured exactly the same as every other Og vessel – but it was just so large. Four times larger than any of the other Og vessels. The ship moved slowly out of the tear in sub-space and immediately turned to head toward the Conquest.

Kip felt somewhat confident at this prospect. "Helm, continue to keep us away from the fighters and take us to the side of that craft. We are going to attack it on its weak side. We know the smaller weapons can't hurt our hulls...we can take it out by attacking there and avoiding that large emitter in the front. Really a poor design..." he said with as much confidence he could muster. He inwardly did not feel quite the same. "Prepare all weapons. Science, have the computer select fire points and transfer to weapons station when ready." He looked at the large ship again, it was not making any moves or aggressions, it lumbered along in a straight line path toward the fleet. Kip definitely did not like that they were being ignored and that they were obviously targeting the fleet still off in the distance. "Look sharp everyone...Helm, prepare to turn the ship for maximum weapons focus. Weapons prepare to fire on my mark..." he waited until he felt they were at optimal position, then yelled out "Fire, now!"

The weapons master followed orders and let loose a barrage of every weapon he had at his disposal. Laser cutter beams, proton arcs, p-accelerators, and rail guns all fired their deadly forces toward the large Og craft. To Kip's surprise, every beam and projectile bounced off the ship and out into space. Also to Kip's surprise, was the force of the beam that ricocheted back into the Conquest, taking out a weapons array.

He turned and gave a look of fiery hatred to the weapons master. He screamed out "What the hell? What kind of weapons master are you? You just hit our own hull! Idiot!"

"Sir, our weapons have no effect against their hull. We scored direct hits, I swear with my life. The beams did no damage, my Alpha Starship Captain!"

"Humph..." Kip grumbled. He thought for a moment, using his genetically enhanced abilities, he came up with a new plan. He entered commands into his console, then looked at the science officer. "I have entered some calculations for weapons fire that will not reflect back into us. Put those into your targeting system, arrange new fire points and fire again."

The science officer nodded and did as commanded. He then looked to the younger weapons master and gave the young man a similar nod. As instructed, the young man looked at the firing points, and selected targets with his fire glove. Once again, all weapons arrays lit up creating a multi-colored light show as the ship emitted its deadly beams and projectiles. Like before however, they did no damage, only bounced off the reflective white body of the large Og ship.

"Damn!" Kip sighed. "Fighter status?" he called out.

The first officer behind him called out "We have sustained major losses with the Wolf Packs we sent out. What is still out there is protecting the Victory, I can call them back."

"Yes..." he agreed "call them back. We need..." he was interrupted by a large flash in the holo-screen. The communications officer and Tulip yelped at the bright light and noise that followed. On the other side of the large Og ship was the remains of an explosion. "What was that?" Kip called out.

The science officer read his SCADAR outputs, and said "THAT, was the Victory...she has been destroyed."

"How can that be?" Kip asked, then stood up from his command chair and looked at the burning remains of the former Hammerhead battle cruiser. He turned back to his communications officer. "Order the launch, get our fighters out there to clear out any remaining enemy fighters. Contact the Star Force Commander, tell him he may want to prepare the fleet for disengagement." The communications officer was scared to death. He had tears dripping slowly out of his dark brown eyes, his small mouth was shaking in fear. He looked up at Kip, who in

216

return gave him a look of anger. Kip tilted his head threateningly at the young man, which finally brought him back to reality. He finally wiped his eyes, and nodded while he began the process of contacting the fleet.

"Victory...She took out all but one of the enemy cruisers, sir" the science officer reported without looking up from his SCADAR readout.

"Well, that is at least a minor victory..." Kip softly muttered.

"Alpha Starship Captain..." the science officer called out again. Kip turned toward him, and he simply pointed to the holo-screen before saying "The large Og vessel...has changed course...it is headed toward us." Kip turned and saw that indeed it was now slowly headed in their direction.

He turned to the helmsman. "Evade, get us out of the path of that large emitter...who knows what that will do. Turn now!" he screamed.

The helm followed his command, and turned the craft, while engaging the faster ion drives to move the ship to the side of the large Og vessel. Now on the side of the enemy craft, they could see the side of the large ball section again, and the silver metallic rectangular propulsion section. Kip yelled out "Weapons, fire at their propulsion section, now!"

The weapons master followed his command and fired a volley of every weapon available to him. The beams and projectiles had a similar effect, they simply bounced off of the metallic hull doing no damage.

"How in the hell...they were never resistant to our weapons before..." Kip said softly. As he looked at the image of the ship, he noticed that even though the ship was traveling in one direction, the large ball section had pivoted in the direction of his ship, and the large emitter was now pointed right at them. A moment later, a large green blob of energy was released and was floating in their direction. "Shit, helm get going...evade that weapons fire!" he ordered.

The helm put the ion drives into full speed and the ship zoomed away. In the rear display however, the green blob was still in pursuit. As Kip watched, he saw it get larger and larger, until it was almost to them. "Helm, give me a ninety degree turn now!"

The helmsman did as instructed and did a sharp turn of the ship. The blob grazed one of the engine pods as it sped by – the pod dissolved into molten metal where the green mass hit. Once it contacted the ship, the blob faded into nothingness.

"That's one engine down, Alpha Starship Captain..." said the science officer. "We will not be able to perform that maneuver again."

"Understood." Kip softly said as he examined his command console. "Helm, take us out of here. In the opposite direction of the Og vessel."

"The vessel is in pursuit, but slowly, my Alpha Starship Captain. We now only have three engines. If they fire again, we may not be able to outrun the blast." He manipulated the helm controls, which turned the ship in a direction away from the battle. "Evasive maneuvers away from the battlefield, sir"

"You're running?" Tulip yelled out.

Kip gave her a look of poison. "Never speak to me in that way again. For if you do, I will have that child ripped out of you and put into a tube, then I will have you spaced. Am I clear?" he said with dryness and distain in his voice.

"They have fired again at us. Weapon fire will be upon us in ninety seconds" yelled out the science officer.

"Adjusting our escape course, sir" said the helmsman. Without warning, the engines shut down. Alarms sounded throughout the bridge.

"What the hell just happened?" Kip called out.

"All power is down, sir" replied the science officer.

"How? How did this happen?" Kip cried out.

"I just happened..." replied Tulip as she raised her hand showing a small command pack. "I shut down your power. You will not run like cowards!"

"Get that from her..." he dryly said to his first officer. "Wait..." he stopped him. "I will do this..." he said as he raised his command weapon to her head. Before he had a chance to fire however, the familiar "zwak" sound of a blaster rang through the bridge. Kip felt a burning in his arm, he smelled burnt flesh, and when he looked down at his arm, he found that his hand and wrist were gone. He screamed in agony as the pain from the burning beam finally hit his brain. The first officer jumped to his feet and was also quickly taken down by a blaster beam to the chest.

Through the pain, he realized that another shot had been fired. He turned behind him and saw his first, now laying in a growing puddle of blood. He then turned to the bridge mantrap and saw Tulip standing at the archway, holding a blaster in her hand. The mantrap was disarmed, and allowed for full and open access to the previously secured bridge. Confused he shook his head and looked toward the first officers console – sitting there was Tulip, still holding the command pack. He felt a sting in his neck and immediately, the pain in his arm was gone. He looked up to see – Tulip – holding an medication injector in her hand. He gave her a confused look.

"Are you that stupid?" she asked him. "You made us all the same. You made all of us out of the same clone material."

"You made them out of me" Tulip added. "You took my cells and cloned me, over and over."

"Over and over...just like when you and your captain buddies raped me" said a voice over the communications channel. On the holo-screen was the face of Lindy. He looked at her with total confusion. "You cloned them and raped me, and now, you will pay..." she said as the green blob hit the ship in the engineering section, taking out the remaining engines. "With our help, the Og will score a victory in eliminating one scourge of this universe. They will take you out of existence Kip Gurrigan, and we will never have to see or hear of your abuse of women again."

"They have fired again, my Alpha Starship...aw shit, who cares..." said the science officer. Kip looked at him and he stood up and spat at him, then walked off of the bridge. None of the clones stopped him. A moment later, Kip heard the sound of an escape pod fleeing the doomed ship. A moment later, the escape pod exploded – it was rigged to blow up upon launch.

Kip looked at the holo-screen and saw the large green blob of energy floating toward them. It was getting bigger by the second. Then he looked at Tulip and said "The Norms...you will be killing all of the Norms on this ship. Is that really what you and your Norm turncoats want to do?"

"There are no Normals on board. I had them removed..." Lindy said smugly.

"The only people manning this ship are Blessed, and us...flower clones." Marigold added. Kip's eyes open wide in surprise, his lip began to tremble, and he started to shake. "Not so brave anymore are you, Kippie?" she asked.

He looked to the star screens, the green blob had changed direction and was now headed directly toward the fore section of the craft. He suddenly had a thought – he moved his right hand to the command console and started to reach for the emergency ejection button. A quick blade to the middle of his hand from Dahlia stopped the motion of his hand. His hand was now firmly pinned to the console, far enough away to prevent the escape pod button from being pressed. He cried out in pain again and was once again administered a pain killer.

Dahlia whispered in his ear "We can't have you running off...not in your time of ultimate glory..." He looked at her and she had an evil smile on her face. "Besides, all of the escape pods are booby trapped. No one will run away that easily."

"But your child...our child..." Kip muttered to Tulip "you will be killing him also."

"This is not a child, it is a monstrosity. A spawn of you." Tulip spat out to him.

"My child is even more of a freak" said Marigold. Kip looked at her with total surprise and confusion. "Could not even tell the difference between us could you? Well one night, you were with me. I too became pregnant."

"And another night you were with me" said Dahlia. "And yes, another pregnancy."

"Then, don't you all want to live? To have these children?" He smiled at them, with a look of pleading in his face.

"Are you kidding?" spat Marigold. "We're lab created. These things growing inside us are just more splicing. The Normals call you Frogspawn...we are even more Frogspawn than you...and these embryos in us are even more Frogspawn than us! No, we are all better off ending this here and now..."

He turned back to the star screen, the blob was almost to the ship. He heard Lindy shout out "Say goodbye, enjoy your eternity in hell!" as the bolt of plasma hit the ship and began slowly melting its way through the front hull. He watched as entire sections of the ship melted into atoms before his eyes. Finally, he felt the pressure change and he now realized it was his time. The front star screen melted, then took out Lindy on the holo-screen, then the helmsman, the weapons officer and Tulip. He heard her scream as she melted into nothingness. It was if the bolt was surrounding him before it took him out – everything around him was now gone, nothing but green surrounded him. It was if his life was being taken from him in slow motion, like the Og wanted him, and him personally to feel the end of his life as slowly as possible.

Mercifully, the plasma began to touch his skin. He felt what remained of his arms melt away, and then his legs followed. The plasma slowly moved its way up his torso, he saw his intestines explode and melt away. He finally felt it reach his head, his brain recorded the last milliseconds of his life, and the pain that he felt as his face melted away. He finally died as his brain exploded out of his skull and disintegrated into the nothingness of space.

The universe would no longer hear, or fear the name Kip Gurrigan ever again.

Starship Ladyhawk:

Jaime Bordeaux:

"Yuli, I know you probably don't want to discuss this, but I have to...as your captain."

"Yeah, I know. I'm fine..."

"I know, but I also know what it is like to lose someone you love."

"Really? I didn't know that..."

She activated the holographic statue of Dex. "This is Dex. He and I were to be joined. He died the day Starlight left Earth. The Star Force Commander killed him with a phony emergency."

"What? Shit...er, sorry captain." He spat out. "And yet you still serve under him and haven't tipped your hand that you knew what he did? I don't see how you can still treat him as your superior officer."

"I have to...for all of us" she admitted.

"I think I understand. Thank you, captain. You CAN depend on me. Really..."

"I know. I just wanted..."

She was interrupted by Norm-Comm – it was Otter. "Captain, they have engaged the Og. You might want to get out here."

"Very well." She looked at Yuli and smiled. "I'm here if you need anything. I know what you are going through, and will go through in the future. I'm here to help...so don't hold back, okay?" He nodded at her. "Come on...let's go see what is happening. And hey, for once the Star Force Commander didn't try to kill us...that's different!" He turned to leave the ready room – she got up to leave, then stopped for a moment, turned back to the holo-image, looked warmly at the image and tried to touch it. The image just wavered as her fingers passed through. She smiled again at the image, turned it off, and then stiffened herself up for the walk onto the bridge.

They left the ready room and entered the bridge. On the holo-displays and star screens were the images of the battle. The moment they looked at the images on the screens, the Victory exploded. The bright flash caused Jaime and everyone on the bridge to squint or cover their eyes. Jaime stood at the screen and just watched as the large Og vessel started its pursuit of the Conquest. A minute later it was damaged, and minutes after that it was torn in half by the new mysterious weapon.

With a slight look of confusion on her face she asked Katsumi "What the hell just happened?"

The young Japanese science officer reviewed the returns from SCADAR and advanced scans, then replied "It appears that the fighters and the cruisers were able to take out the Victory with various forms of weapons fire. The Victory did take out all but one cruiser. As far as the Conquest – the large Og ship took it out with two shots fired from that large main emitter in the front of the craft. My scans are indicating that the bolt fired was a form of anti-matter plasma. It was created in such a way that it would coat the surface of its target and disintegrate it upon contact. It appears to have coated the ship like a slime, then it simply destroyed the molecular bonds of whatever it contacted."

"Plasma slime..." muttered Jonathan from the engineering station.

"Good name for it..." Katsumi replied. "It does seem to match its composition and modus operandi..."

"Captain..." Otter interrupted. "We're getting a tunneled message from Blessed battle operations to you."

"Put it through..." Jaime responded.

"Ladyhawk, battle command. Our Star Force Commander has ordered your ship to take point in protection of the fleet. You will eliminate the opposing force, while providing the opportunity for the bulk of the fleet to escape. Battle operations out."

"Well, there's a surprise..." she said softly. "Otter, get me the Star Force Commander on a tunneled protocol, please. And mask my appearance also, please."

A moment later Boral appeared on her command display. "Star Force Commander...this new weapon is unknown and obviously dangerous to the fleet. I suggest instead of fighting we retreat and determine a defense to counter this weapon."

"Stay on duty. Protect the fleet, captain" was his only reply.

"Sir, it is stupid to stay and fight a weapon that we have no idea about or any way to stop..."

"Are you calling me stupid?" he asked. Jaime shook her head no. "I thought not. Protect the fleet Ladyhawk. Star Force Commander out."

Jaime sat in the command chair trying to figure out what was going on in Boral's mind. Hero jumped into her lap and curled up into a ball. She looked down at the kitten, bright blue eyes staring up at her. She wondered how he somehow always managed to be on the bridge during times of stress.

"Captain..." Katsumi interrupted her thoughts. "The fleet, just crawled into sub-space...they are gone."

"They left us?" said Halley.

"Does that really surprise you?" Jaime replied. "Okay...well, we're not going to sacrifice ourselves or commit suicide for them. Halley, take the helm, determine a point, and prepare for sub-space insertion. Jonathan, fire..."

She was interrupted by Otter. "Captain, I have an emergency transmission from two remaining Wolf Packs that were engaged in the previous battle. They are requesting pickup."

"Damn..." Jaime let escape from her lips. "Do we have any idea who's out there? Please tell me they are not Blessed pilots."

"Doubtful, that would put them in harm's way..." said Jonathan.

"I am getting the message via emergency beacon..." said Katsumi, then continued "It's War Bitch. Her pack is destroyed, she was able to eject her pod. But, she is stranded."

"We should just leave her..." Jaime said, not really meaning it. Both Jonathan and Halley turned to give her both quizzical and scorning looks. "I'm just kidding...jeez..." she said with a smile while she held her hands up in an imaginary defense.

"Captain, I am getting a second transmission from another Wolf Pack...It's a pilot with the handle of Star Child. She too is requesting assistance and pickup."

"What? She's out here with us? Damn, well I guess that seals the deal...we have to stop and save them." Another look from Jonathan. She smiled at the young man. "Helm bring us around...Otter, signal Star Child to grapple cable Eva's pod and drag it in. Somehow, I think we are going to regret this..."

The ship made a sharp turn and headed toward the location of the two pilots. Star Child had already attached a grapple line to the ITC pod of Eva's former craft and had dragged it slowly toward the rendezvous point with Ladyhawk. In pursuit was the lone remaining Og cruiser. The large Og battleship was slowly following the cruiser in additional pursuit, but as yet had not activated their main drives.

"Captain..." Katusmi called out "The large Og battleship is moving much slower than I would expect. I am not sure why...scanning for more details..."

"I think it is a power conversion issue" interjected Jonathan after he analyzed the incoming scans. "I can see energy emissions from the large weapon emitter in the front. I think they cannot engage their main star drive as long as the plasma slime projector is energized. I think that weapon takes all of their available power. That might be their one weakness."

"The only problem is..." Katsumi interrupted "that we have to somehow take them out when their weapon is down. To do that we would first have to be close enough to fire on them...which would also mean they would probably have their weapon on-line, AND we would have to be able to penetrate that hull. From our scans of the battle, standard weapons had no effect on that new reflective surface."

Jonathan shook his head yes. "True. So, what do we do?"

Jaime thought a moment, then shook her head in frustration before saying "Honestly, I am not sure. We run for now. How long till we have those two pilots on-board?"

"One minute till pick up..." Katsumi called out.

Jaime looked at the advancing cruiser. "Ok, we will have to fight this one and hope they do not have the same armor or weapons. Yuli, you up for this?" He looked at her and gave a confident nod of acknowledgement. She continued to watch him prepare, he was moving and wiggling his fingers inside the targeting gloves as he stretched and warmed up for battle. He was more than ready, and anxious for a fight. She hoped he really was mentally prepared for the battle ahead. "Ok...Katsumi, give Yuli targets. Yuli, don't spare anything. Use our better projectiles and the Ultras as needed. Jonathan, bring the bubble on-line. Prepare for battle everyone"

"Captain..." Katsumi yelled out. "They've launched fighters. Not many, only ten...but based on scans and the battle records those ten could do quite a bit of damage if left unchecked." She continued to scan then announced. "For some reason, War Bitch's pod has been released from the tether. She is again adrift, near the ship but still adrift."

Jaime nodded to Otter, who opened a communication tunnel to Star Child. The young girl appeared on her command display. Jaime was amazed by seeing her face again – she had not aged a day since they left earth. "Star Child, what are you doing?"

The young pilot had a playful smile on her face. "There are enemies out there, and I have fighters. I'm taking them out."

Jaime was going to protest, but instead just smiled at her and said "Go get 'em kid!" The young girl gave her a return smile, a nod, then let out a loud yelp of excitement as she charged into battle.

Jaime was amazed at how her dogfighting skills had developed and improved. She quickly took out two of the Og streamers within the first few seconds of battle. She closed in on three of the enemy fighters with a matching number of pup drones. After a few seconds of shifting positions, weaving, and swerving, the drones finally took them out – this all occurred while she took out two of the enemy in her own manned ship along with a single escorting pup. There was a point in the battle where three of the enemy fighters managed to avoid her detection, and were able to take out one of her pup drones. Jaime heard her scream and cuss as she felt the loss of her drone inside her ITC. It was a furious five minutes of battle. However, after those five minutes the enemy had lost all ten of their remaining fighters, while Star Child had only lost one of her four pups.

"Damn, I lost one...shit!" she yelled over the common battle channel.

"Don't worry Star Child, unlike the other Alliance ships...we will not downgrade you for a loss. Better to have lost a pup than a good pilot like you!" Jaime thought for a moment, then asked "Star Child...why haven't you picked a new handle?"

"I've decided I kinda like this handle...I'm going to keep it!" the young girl replied.

Jaime smiled and nodded "Very well. Now, gather your War Bitch and get aboard. We have a very large ship approaching and I want to get out of its path!"

"Yes captain. Will be aboard in two minutes" she replied and signed off.

"Unfortunately..." interrupted Katsumi "the cruiser will be here in a half minute."

"Then, I guess we get ready to fight" she sighed as she reopened the channel and told her fighter pilots. "Star Child, hold your position for pickup after battle." She closed the channel and the ordered "Halley, you control the direction on my command." She paused for a few seconds before announcing "Take us into battle, everyone prepare for a fight..." she paused for another moment to verify everyone was ready, then called out "Let's get 'em!"

Halley quickly accelerated to the side of the inbound Og vessel. The round ball of the cruiser let forth a large volley of various beamed weapons. With the activated bubble, the beams bounced harmlessly off into space. Yuli, received his targets from Katsumi, and began tapping onto target lights with quickness and ease. A volley of plasma bolts, heavy gravity projectiles, and ultraviolet accelerated dark matter pummeled the various spots of the enemy craft. The round Og hull could not take this assault and quickly developed cracks in its shell. It veered off, but instead of allowing for a retreat, Halley turned the ship to expose the lower racks of weapons for further attacks, and glided the ship in closer. Yuli took the cue and fired his weapons at will. He tapped at the target locks with fierce abandon. His anger showed now, and he was about to take all of it out on the hapless Og cruiser. Within seconds more cracks appeared in the hull.

"It's about to lose integrity..." Katsumi called out.

Halley took her to word, and maneuvered the ship away from the weakening cruiser. A moment later, the ship exploded.

Halley turned the ship onto its previous course "Returning to previous heading toward our rendezvous with the star fighters.

"Captain, the Og battleship has powered down their main weapon. They have increased speed to our position" said Katsumi.

"How long till we pick up the fighters?" she asked.

Otter replied "They are signaling that they are landing now."

"Should be secure in twenty seconds..." added Katsumi.

Jaime looked at her command console and analyzed the heading of the Og vessel. She brought up the navigational display and used her fingers to draw lines across various points. Finally, she entered a command to send the display to Halley. "Halley, take a look at this. Entering this as maneuvering plan 43a...Can you pull a maneuver off like that? Might be a little tricky..."

"That maneuver? Could do that without looking." She lied, but she figured if anyone could do it, she could.

Jaime saw through her deception, but ignored it. "Very well, you make whatever adjustments you need. Then, figure out some vectors for a sub-space insertion immediately afterward. Just in case." Halley nodded acknowledgement.

"Captain?" Jonathan asked softly.

"If this works, we might have a way to battle them. If not, well...I am hoping for a way out. Can you put priority on the computers for navigation calculations? We will need a quick insertion into sub-space at a moment's notice."

"A moment's notice? No...the computers still need time for computation of pathways and exiting. I can only prioritize it...cannot guarantee anything else."

"Then that'll have to do..." she acknowledged.

"Landing bay reports both Star Child's Wolf Pack and Eva's pod have been brought aboard and secured. Landing bay is closed down and secured, captain" Otter reported.

"Okay...ready Halley?" Jaime asked and got a slightly worried smile and a nod from Halley. "Kasumi, please provide fire points for weapons. Yuli, you are going to have to fire as soon as you get green lights...won't be time for any fire approvals. If you get a lock, use it...and use everything we have, don't hold back. Jonathan, put the bubble on full. Here we go...execute maneuvering plan 43a Halley, now!"

Halley engaged the ion drives full-power, which zoomed the ship into near light-speed within micro-seconds. She almost as quickly disengaged the drives, engaged reverse thrusters, and steered the ship to a near perfect stop on the side of the Og battleship. "Maneuver executed, captain" she called out.

Yuli instantly received his fire points from the computer and without any delay began pummeling the large round section of the craft with every weapon at his disposal. Halley took the ship into an outer turn so that the lower deck of weapons were now facing the Og vessel. He immediately fired another volley, this time into the propulsion section of the craft.

"No effect!" Katsumi yelled out. "Captain, they are turning their large emitter toward us and it is powering up. It will fire in seconds."

"Halley, now!" she ordered. With that Halley kicked in the ion drive again. She powered the craft to a considerable distance away, then as quickly stopped, and then started the computing program for sub-space insertion.

"They have fired the weapon. Will strike us in thirty seconds..." Katsumi called out.

In the rear star screen, Jaime could see the green blob of plasma gliding its way toward their ship. "Halley...are we ready?"

"Computers are not done with computations...no end point yet. Safeties are still active..." she replied.

"Damn the safeties. Activate the crawler now!" Jaime ordered.

"Okay..." she muttered as she shut down the safety protocols and activated the sub-space ram beam. "Here we go...hope we don't exit into a planet or star..." she quietly said as she sent the chaser and door knocker ahead, then pushed the ship into sub-space.

A few moments later, the door knocker created a scuff in the fabric of space, and then the computer activated the ram beam again.

They quickly exited the tear and returned to normal space. Jaime called out "Position?"

Halley looked at the astrogation display, then turned and gave a Jaime a sheepish look, and then looked at the rear star screen before she said softly "We travelled one light second..."

Jaime turned and looked at the rear star screen. In the distance was the Og battle ship. It had turned and was headed in their direction. Fortunately for them, the green blob of plasma that had been fired on them was drifting away in the opposite direction.

"Og battleship has deactivated their weapons and are in quick pursuit, captain" announced Katsumi.

"Shit..." Jaime muttered. "Halley..."

The young helmsman needed no further words as she was already activating the navigation computer for another sub-space insertion. "Fifteen seconds and I can force another insertion..."

Jaime looked at her command console. The Og ship would be on them in thirty seconds. They would barely have enough time.

"Here we go again..." said Halley as she activated the sub-space ram and opened another hole in the fabric of normal space.

This time, the ship stayed in sub-space for an hour. The chaser particle finally burst, marking the spot where the door knocker would follow and burnish the fabric of sub-space to normal space for the ship to create a hole and exit. Halley activated the beam and tore into normal space. They could not see outside sub-space through the tear, so she closed her eyes, hoped for the best, and pushed the ship through.

Only when the star screens had filled with the bright dots of distant burning stars, did they realize they had safely entered normal space. Halley engaged the Pulsars and pushed the ship away from the tear. Jaime looked at her command console and asked "So, where are we?"

Halley examined her star charts, searching for any reference point. Finally, she spotted a familiar star system. "Ah, okay...sector "E", near star system B-345. We travelled five light years. Where to now, captain?"

"Can we get a course to Haven?" she asked.

"Captain, might want to think twice about that. Something is coming through the tear" Katsumi announced.

"What?" she asked dumbfounded, but then looked at the scan readouts on her command module. Indeed, it showed the Og ship, still in sub-space, but would emerge in just a matter of moments. "How the hell are they following us?"

Jonathan answered "It appears that they are a more advanced in astrogation than we are. It seems they can use OUR sub-space rifts, and follow us through the void. We had better not go home yet..."

Jaime tapped on her lip while she thought about the situation. "Halley, make another blind insertion and take us...somewhere."

"Aye, aye captain..." she acknowledged.

Thirty seconds later, the large ball of the Og battleship began to emerge in the sub-space tear. The Og battleship was much bigger than the rip created by the Ladyhawk, and because of the size difference, it struggled to get through the hole. The fabric of space wrapped around it tightly, only the large plasma slime emitter was exposed to normal space. They could tell it was pushing its engines to the limit to force its way through the tear in space. Watching it gave the impression of an egg being laid by a chicken. Finally, the ship somehow managed to push its way through and emerged whole into normal space. It immediately powered up its main weapons emitter.

"I suggest we leave now, Halley..." Jaime told the first officer/helmsman. Halley followed orders, overrode the computer navigation safeties, opened another hole in the fabric of space, and then pushed the Crawler drives full power into the rift.

Jonathan started to tap commands on his engineering console. "Captain, I believe we can reduce the size of the sub-space tear. Make it just big enough for the Ladyhawk to fit through. That way..."

"The Og ship might get stuck?" Jaime interjected. He nodded yes. "Do it. Maybe we can catch them on the next exit point and strand them in here."

Katsumi added "I hope so, because they have just entered sub-space and are in pursuit."

An hour later the chaser provided the stream of particles marking the exit point. The door knocker scuffed the fabric of space and Halley followed up with a ram beam just big enough to push the ship through.

After a minute Halley called out "I have our position...and am starting the computers on calculating a new safe route. Question captain, is where do I take us?"

"Pick something simple and quick. Just something the computers can calculate navigation for quickly. Get us into sub-space as soon as possible."

"Very well, captain. I have found a system, should be a fairly short, easy hop in sub-space. Computers estimate we will be ready for insertion in two minutes."

"Og vessel will attempt to enter normal space in a minute and a half. Let's hope Jonathan's idea works..." added Katsumi.

In the last thirty seconds before they inserted themselves into sub-space, they saw the Og ship attempt to leave the void. It was struggling and fighting the small tear in the fabric of space. They did not get to see how successful they were however, as they were now entering sub-space into yet another tear.

After a few minutes of quietly holding her breath, Jaime finally asked. "Any sign of the Og battleship?"

Katsumi watched and watched her advanced scans and SCADAR. She finally started to shake her head no, but was interrupted by a small alert on her monitor. "Sorry captain, the Og ship just entered sub-space. However, they are quite a ways behind us now."

Jaime sighed loudly. "Very well, keep me apprised of their position and timing." She looked at Halley "Start to determine another insertion point and execute the computer calculations the moment we reach normal space. Activate the rams as soon as the computers give you the go ahead. Maybe we can just keep putting more distance between us and them."

$$* \qquad * \qquad *$$

"What is this, thirteen or fourteen, Halley?" Jaime asked.

"This will be number fourteen, captain. Insertion into sub-space in fifteen seconds."

"Og battleship is about to attempt to enter normal space. We should gain another one minute by the size of the tear" Katsumi announced.

"Yes, but they will still come out and continue their pursuit, won't they?" Jaime added dryly.

Jonathan walked over to Jaime and softly said "Captain, the ship is only setup to do fifteen continuous insertions into sub-space. Any more after that and we will run the possibility of tearing the Crawler drive apart. We will need maintenance after number fifteen."

"Understood, engineer." She thought for a few minutes while the ship entered sub-space for its fourteenth voyage into the void. She sighed and looked down at Hero sitting quietly in her lap. She petted him while whispering to him "Sorry, my friend...I am not sure WHAT to do at this point. We may have to stand our ground and fight."

The kitten just looked at her with his deep, bright blue eyes. Then to her surprise, he stood up, jumped down, walked over to his bridge cat box, and used it. As soon as he stepped out a force field went across the opening of the covered box, and a vent opened in the back. A vortex formed in the box, sucking all waste products out the vent and into sub-space. Hero looked up at her again and gave a squeaky meow. She looked at him, then at the box – still being cleaned by the vacuum vortex of sub-space. She continued to stare at the vortex – every small particle was being sucked out and into the void. He looked at her again and gave one more squeaky meow before walking back to the command chair, and hopping once again into her lap. She just kept staring at the cleaning vortex, her mind suddenly was filled with possibilities.

She turned and looked at Katsumi, and ordered "Put up the star chart of the section of the galaxy that we will be entering when we exit sub-space please." On the holo-screen in front of her was the chart – there were various dots indicating star systems, other dots showing the locations of stars without systems, and red circles and polygons highlighted in various locations on the map. "What are those areas marked in red?" she asked.

Halley replied "Oh, those are navigational hazards, based on Flaybah explorations. They had deemed those areas unsafe for travel and navigation, and had put them off limits to their spacecraft. We have always gone with their judgment regarding those zones."

She stared at the chart for a moment, and then thought another moment before ordering "Jonathan, will you and Katsumi join me in the ready room?" The two followed her in and she motioned for them to sit at the table at the side of the room. "I've had a thought that I want to run by you..." She brought up the star chart on the holo-projection in the middle of the table. She then expanded one of the off-limit zones. "I want to go to this area..."

They both looked at the area on the map. Jonathan was the first to speak up "Why?"

She zoomed the map in and said "Because of this..." in the middle of the danger zone was the image of a black hole.

"Captain, first I don't think I need to remind you of the danger of getting anywhere near one of those. Second, are you just planning on flying into that area?" warned Katsumi.

"Not really...I was thinking of exiting sub-space there."

"Umm..." gulped Jonathan "there has never been a test of a sub-space tear anywhere near a black hole. That could cause something that...well, we have no idea what could happen if we tear space there."

"How close were you planning on going to that?" the science officer asked.

"Well, that is why you are here. I need to know the absolute closest we can get to that without losing our ability to escape. Also, based on what you know of the Og battleship, how close can THEY go?"

Jonathan replied "Well, there is the event horizon...the point where nothing can escape from the pull of the black hole. It is supposed to be a fixed spot, however I have read that although it is in a fixed area, the ability of the ship can actually increase or decrease that area of escape."

"So, what you are telling me is that a starship with more powerful engines will have a better chance of escape?"

"Kind of..." he answered. "If the ship is capable of light speed travel, then it theoretically should have the power to escape easily. What I am considering however, is for ships that cannot reach true light speed."

"Like ours" Katsumi added.

"Exactly. We cannot achieve light speed yet...but we can get really close. Our drives are very strong and powerful. We could probably get a lot closer to the event horizon than say...."

"The less powerful engines of the Og ship!" Katsumi surmised. Her eyes lit up "Of course! We have to just get close enough, and go fast enough to catch the Og off guard! In sub-space they will not know where they will be leaving the void, as we are the ones designating our direction and path. All we have to do is exit near enough to the event horizon and with enough speed that we can avoid falling in ourselves. They will exit at normal speed, and with the problem we have been causing by cutting the rift too small, they will more than likely exit extremely slowly. They will squeeze out and get caught in the gravity well and fall in. It could work..."

"Well, we do have a few issues to consider..." Jonathan added. Jaime looked at him with a raised eyebrow. "Well, for one thing...what would tearing a hole in the fabric of space cause when near a black hole? What would happen if we activated our main drives in sub-space? Would it crush us before we left the void? We know the effects sub-space used to have on us. Have we changed enough to take the added pressure?"

Jaime looked at the two scientists...they both showed their physical changes. Katsumi had light blue streaks on her neck, and Jonathan was now sporting dark, shimmering, midnight blue, almost black skin.

Katsumi looked at her, then him, and thought for a moment before saying "One other thing we have not taken into consideration...humans really have no idea about them, we really know nothing about black holes. One scientist assumes that the event horizon is in the outer area of the vortex, but others surmise that it is in actuality inside the throat of the hole. The only things we can be assured of...is that there are jets emitting from the hole, and that there is a point of no return where we die. We don't really even know that if we are lucky enough to get close to guessing the event horizon that we will still have the power to escape. We don't have faster than light propulsion, and even Hawking stated we would need that to escape. Plus, there is that estimation of the horizon...I sure as hell can't guess where the actual horizon is..."

Both Jaime and Jonathan turned to give her a quizzical look...that was the closest to an actual curse word they ever heard come out of her mouth. Jonathan raised a finger before saying "Actually, I can tell you the event horizon is here." He pointed to a spot on the image about halfway between the edge of the vortex and the center of the black hole. The two women gave him a quizzing look before he continued "The Flaybah have done extensive research on this, and have sent probes into this and other black holes. They have a 99.99999 percent confirmation rating on the location of the event horizon of this black hole. I studied their computer files in bed for a few evenings..."

"You must be real exciting to live with..." Jaime said with a joking smile on her face – he gave a pained look in return. "Well, what do you think now Katsumi? I will not bring Halley into this unless we three are one hundred percent in agreement."

The young Japanese girl looked first at Jonathan, then at Jaime, and finally nodded in agreement.

Jaime activated her Norm-Comm. "Halley, come to the ready room, please." A moment later the young first officer entered the room. She saw the three of them and raised an eyebrow. "Sorry to leave you out of this until now. I wanted to get scientific estimates of survival for what I am wanting to try." Halley looked at Jonathan and Katsumi again. Jonathan shook his head yes, Katsumi just looked down – still not one hundred percent convinced. "We have a plan that might shake the Og battleship off our tail, once and for all."

Halley looked at the holo-display and her eyes opened wide at the image. "Why do I have a feeling I am not going to like what I hear?"

Jaime smiled "You are my best starship pilot..."

"Why can't I just be a first officer, hmm?" she said as she shrugged her shoulders and looked up at the ceiling.

Jaime gave a light chuckle. "So here's the plan..."

*   *   *

"Preparing to leave sub-space in three minutes." Halley announced.

"Very well, is our next insertion plotted and ready to go?" Jaime asked.

Without looking up from her helm console, Halley replied "Assuming the computer got everything correct on our last insertion. If we are off even a slight bit, we will have to run the computations again. The Og might catch up again in that case."

"The computers will not be wrong...we will end up where we expect." Jonathan said with a defensive tone.

"Yes, but I have to be exact in our insertion point, and even more exact launching the chaser and door knocker..." she retorted. He silently nodded in agreement.

She opened sub-space and pushed the ship out. A moment later, the star screens showed the bright lights of the distant stars. A nearby nebula glowed an eerie green, as radiation created phosphorescent lights from the cloud of gas. Halley looked over all of the astrometric readouts on her navigation console. She activated the computer controls, turned to Jaime, and smiled. "We are exactly where we should be. The computer is calculating our next insertion. Will be ready to go in two minutes." Jonathan gave a glowing smile to the room like a proud father. Jaime chuckled.

"Og battleship will attempt to exit the rift in two and a half minutes. I expect them to exit the tear in three and a half minutes..." Katsumi announced.

Jaime replied "Good, plenty of time." She nervously stroked the soft fur on Hero's back as he calmly sat in her lap.

Halley called out "Computer has already started sub-space navigation calculations for insertion into sub-space."

"Thank you. The moment the computer signals green, put us into sub-space, don't wait for my approval or order."

The computer notified Halley the computations were complete, and as she activated the ram beams and sub-space crawler she said "Well, here we go...where no woman has gone before..."

Jonathan spoke up at this "I think the saying was "where no man has gone before..."''

Jaime looked around the bridge. Next to Jonathan was Otter, on the other side of him was the vacant first officer station, then her command chair behind them, back to the control circle sat Halley at the helm, Katsumi was still manning the science station, and in the weapons position was Naomi Watson – who had taken over for Yuli. He had been on duty almost continuously and needed time off to recuperate and prepare. Naomi was a young recruit, recently brought into the Normal space force after escaping from the Conquest. She was trying to concentrate on being as professional as possible – checking readings and verifying weapons systems and settings. She had medium-short, black hair, cut in a shag style hairdo. Her green eyes were still of normal color, her rounded face had not started to change to either blue or black – she obviously had just arrived. Jaime turned once again to the others, then turned back to Jonathan and smiled before saying "No, it is where no woman has gone before." The young man looked around the bridge, gave a small chuckle, and shrugged his shoulders in defeat. Jaime returned the smile.

A moment later, they had entered sub-space. Halley announced "This will be a short hop…only an hour in sub-space…"

"Then all hell will break loose…" Jaime interrupted. She looked around then nodded at Otter who activated the ship-wide Norm-Comm and attuned it to Jaime's personal frequency. *"My I have your attention. As you may have noticed, we have just entered sub-space. Anyone familiar with the ship and its capabilities knows that we could only make one more insertion before we need to do maintenance on the craft and engines. If you did not know this, then I will explain. The crawler drives have a limited lifespan on their ion emitters. This is due to the materials used in their manufacture, and this is why these drives are so much different from our standard ion drives – this is also why they are able to propel us through the void of sub-space. Because of this, the material of the emitters break down after fifteen uses. So, we would have no more insertions after this. We will be forced to stop and replace the emitters. Unfortunately, the Og have not stopped their pursuit – they still want us dead, and they show no signs of having to stop their pursuit. For this reason, we have come up with a plan, albeit dangerous, that we hope will shake the Og and allow us to return home. This plan involves us flying extremely close to a black hole. We are only guessing that we will be able to escape the vortex and come out of this alive…but that is the risk in this plan. I am sorry if you are being dragged into this without warning, but it is the only way we think we will be rid of the Og battleship threat. When we are about to exit sub-space, we will be activating all of our drives in an attempt to achieve a speed sufficient to escape the forces of the black hole. This may cause discomfort, bodily injury, or even death due to the pressures that will be exerted on our bodies by the void, and the possible forces in trying to escape the gravity vortex.*

We will give an announcement prior to our departure...please secure yourself as best as possible. Crews will be available to make sure everyone has a secure place to ride this out. The sick bay will be available for your immediate use once the emergency maneuver has been completed. Once again, thank you for your courage, we will get through this. We will create history that will be handed down to our offspring. Stay strong, captain out." She nodded back to Otter, who closed the channel.

She looked around the bridge again...the various shades of blue, black, and Normal flesh eagerly awaited her next command. Instead, she just scratched behind Hero's ear and said "Carry on..."

*   *   *

"We will be opening the rift to normal space in five minutes, captain" announced Halley.

"Very well, helmsman. Make any preparations necessary for the exit...no need to check with me for my ok." Jaime looked over at Otter "Open a Norm-Comm channel..." she realized it was already open – somehow Otter anticipated her needs.

"Attention all crew, this is the captain. Prepare for exiting sub-space and emergency acceleration to escape velocity. Secure yourself now...we will be exiting in less than five minutes. There will be no more warnings. Good luck to us all, captain out." She shut down her Norm-Comm channel. She looked down at Hero sitting between her thigh and the arm of the command chair. He had flattened his body out as much as possible – his front legs pointed straight out in front of him, and his head was tucked in between the two outstretched arms. "I see you are ready..." she said softly to the small animal. The sound of the ram beams took her attention away from her companion and back to the reality of the moment. *"Shit...here we go...."*

The hole in the fabric of space showed no indications of anything ahead of them. The ship slowly moved toward the exit point – that is until Halley pushed all engine controls to full. The ship bucked and gave a horrendously loud mechanical groan as engines not meant for travel in the void kicked into play. Jaime felt enormous pressure on her body – pressure that only increased with each nano-second. The pain became almost unbearable and she groaned as she felt her body being squeezed by unseen forces. Amongst the noise, she could barely hear the sounds of her bridge crew crying out in pain and agony. Even Hero was giving soft crying moans of pain as the forces pressed on his tiny, fur-covered body.

The ship lurched forward, and into the tear in space. The speed toward the tear, and the pressure on her body increased at the same time. Blood flowed from her nose, around her lip, and down her cheek – she was unable to move a muscle to wipe up or clean any of the now-flowing red fluid. The pressure increased once again, and she now knew they were not going to survive, she was about to die.

Then the ship lurched again and the pressure stopped, but was replaced by a blur in reality. Through her blurred vision she could see Halley moving her hands over the helm controls, she looked down and saw her command holograph. It showed that the computer had taken control and was piloting the ship in the prescribed path. She looked to the side at the port star screen – in the distance she saw the swirling mass of light flowing to the center point of darkness – the black hole. She looked ahead and only saw blurs of bright light, on the starboard star screen she saw the same blurs.

She heard a scream to her left. She looked over and saw Otter – her hand was grasped onto her communication port connection. She was attached to the antenna array of the ship, and now appeared to be getting feedback from all the interference in the vortex. She pulled and tugged on the antenna feed, trying desperately to remove it from the port in the back of her neck. Finally, with a final surge of strength she ripped the plug from her neck taking the attached socket with it. Blood flew out of the now open hole in her neck, and splashed against the wall behind her. The blood flow slowed to a dribble as Jaime saw her slump her head onto the console, then she blacked out. All for the better she thought.

The ship lurched forward again and shook even harder and more violently, she wondered if it would stay together. She now worried they would end up as nothing but floating debris, sinking toward the gravity well of the black hole. She wondered if they would just become part of the fuel for this mysterious force of space. The ship shook and jumped again, the blurs in her vision became even more pronounced. She looked down again at her command console and saw the speed indicator – it was just a tiny second slower than the speed of light now. This was the fastest any human ship had ever travelled.

Then she passed out...

Six and a Half Years Ago...

The trainer was in the seat behind her, she was about to take the stick solo for the very first time. The ship sat in the docking port, prepped for launch. Her palms were sweaty, but not as much as her trainer – she wondered how many times he had actually done a pilot's solo flight certification. She noticed that he was sweating even more than herself. He was nervous and anxious, and appeared to not want to be in the trainer seat.

Finally, the clearance came through from the star base, she was clear to launch. She instructed the computer to clear the bay, evacuate the atmosphere, and once that was completed, open the launch doors. When the doors opened, she for the first time was seeing the stars from a solo pilot's perspective – and she liked it.

From the back seat she heard "Take it out...nice and easy!" The voice behind her sounded to be getting more and more nervous by the second. She assumed it was because his flight controls were missing on this craft. Live or die, his life was in her hands – he had no control over the situation.

She was kind to him – once the doors had opened, she slowly slid the craft to the space doors and into the open vacuum. She thought she heard a sigh of relief over her comm channel. Then she decided to punch the accelerator while still exiting the space dock. The ion drives kicked in and the ship zoomed out of the star base. She heard the gasp of the instructor behind her as she punched the throttle. The engines roared with the raw power of thrust as she quickly entered into orbit.

"Ms. Bordeaux, I will ask you to stick with the flight path and programmed protocol for the solo exam!" the instructor lashed out.

"Very well" she replied as the she kicked the thruster in again. She quickly left her orbit and was now very close to the atmosphere. She heard something from behind her, but with the engines at full throttle, she just somehow could not hear him.

Taking the craft into a steep dive she raced toward the first layer of air that surrounded the planet. She saw the shimmering of flames on the sides of the ship as it dove down toward the earth.

Then, she blacked out – when she came to, it seemed like it had been minutes, but she quickly realized it was only a second or two. It was now time for phase two, the ionization layer would be coming upon them fast. She pulled up on the stick and brought the craft into a steep climb out of the edge of the atmosphere and back out into space. She felt the tug of gravity on her body, and passed out again. Another second passed before she returned to consciousness, then leveled off the ship into gradual climb.

She thought she heard a moan behind her, right before she punched the throttle again. Within minutes she was preparing for a tight low level orbit of the moon. With the ion drives at full power, the ship had quickly accelerated to a speed that would take them to the moon within minutes.

As she started her orbit of the moon, her SCADAR detected the multitude of weapon locks on her craft. She was a little too low and knew she was seconds away from being blasted to bits, so she punched it again. She heard the screaming of the trainer in the seat behind her as she pulled into a higher orbit for a minute, then streaked away on their way back to their home. Within fifteen minutes, they were approaching the star base.

She obtained her clearance and began a speedy approach and landing sequence. She deftly landed the craft without even a bump or a nudge as the craft softly touched down. She removed her helmet, then turned and looked at her instructor. He was passed out, his body hunched over, and his head resting on the control panel in front of him.

She jumped out of the craft – she was invigorated and really wanted to hop back in for another run. Her trainer had different plans as he remained passed out for another minute. He finally regained his awareness and exited the ship five minutes later. He jumped down, and threw his helmet to the ground. He had the remains of digested food and bile on his chin, the smell of vomit emitted from his space suit. His hands were shaking as he walked slowly up to her and pointed a finger in her face. He started to say "That flight, did you bother reading the flight plan? You will never..."

She shrugged her shoulders and interrupted him by saying "What? I followed the flight plan explicitly."

He turned beet red and prepared to yell at her, but was stopped by a voice over the intercom – it was flight command. All that was said was "Excellent job Bordeaux, you are a perfect candidate for a fighter. Solo flight pass."

She smiled at the instructor, patted him on the shoulder and said "Thanks for your guidance on my solo flight!"

NGD: 3 Years, 2 Months, 18 Days:

Near Black Hole Danger Area C-15:

Jaime Bordeaux:

When she returned to consciousness, she found the ship in one piece and the stars filling the star screen ahead of her and to the sides. She looked down and found Hero still sitting next to her – his head still tucked between his stretched out front legs. She looked around the bridge, all the other members of her crew were passed out. Their heads all resting on the consoles in front of them. The computer had done its job and completed the escape sequence from the vortex of the black hole. *"The black hole!"* she realized as she turned to look in the rear view screen. Behind the ship was the swirling bright vortex of the black hole. In the middle was its dark center, eating all matter that came too close to its gravity well. They had made it, and although she was still recovering from the effects of their wild journey, she was ecstatic.

Halley was starting to come around, she glanced at the room around her as she cleared the cobwebs from her head. She appeared lost for a moment to Jaime, but then regained her composure, looked down at the navigational controls, checked astrometric position, turned, looked at Jaime, and smiled.

Though her voice was weakened, she was able to still convey her excitement as she said "We made it!"

"We did, Halley…we did…" Jaime replied.

Jonathan was the next to come to, then Katsumi, followed by Miriam, and finally Otter came to last – her eyes were still glowing a bright brown in the darkness of the bridge. A moment later, the computers reactivated shut down systems, and more lights came on in the bridge. Standard noises and indicators came alive, which gave a sense of normalcy to the situation once again.

Jaime looked around and verified her crew was alright and coming around, then a thought came to her. "Eva?" she asked, then questioned "What happened to Eva...War Bitch. She is Blessed...she could not take those forces!"

Jonathan smiled at her as she showed concern for her rival. He looked at his status reports then answered "She's safe. We put her into a state of suspended animation, then put her into her fighter pod and filled it with fresh gel. The gel helped to absorb the forces and kept her body intact while we hopped across the galaxy. She is still sleeping, Max said he will wake her, then give her a check up."

"Well good. Thank you, Jonathan." He gave her a look, and acted like he was going to comment, but the look on her face told him to leave it alone. He just smiled and nodded. She then looked around the bridge and asked "So, do we have any idea where we are? Are we where we are supposed to be?"

Halley rechecked the positioning, then looked at the star screens for visual confirmation. She finally announced "Yep, exactly where we expected to be! That could not have gone any better!"

"Og battleship?" Jaime asked.

Katsumi looked over the SCADAR and advanced scanner logs before saying "Not anywhere I can find." She continued looking over the scans, then said with an unusual panicked excitement in her voice "There is a ship to starboard just coming into range though...unknown identification."

"Prepare for battle" Jaime called out. "Get the bubble on line, fire up the weapon arrays, get weapons locks, look sharp everyone."

"Am I seeing an imaging ghost..." said Miriam on her weapons fire system display.

"Well, if you are...then my eyes are getting the same sort of ghost..." added Halley as she looked to the starboard star screen display.

Jaime looked to the right at the display. Her eyes opened wide as she watched the incoming ship. Finally she said "How can that be? Is that us?"

Captain Allen James:

"Take it slowly...we don't want to spook them..." he saw they already had activated defensive and offensive systems. He nodded to Alice Ansolion, his communications officer then said "Connect my Norm-Comm to them please. Send an identification before connecting."

A moment later, Jaime's face appeared on the holo-screen in front of him. She had a confused look on her face. "Allen? Is that really you? How did you?"

"Hello captain..." he interrupted. "I hope you and Hero are sitting down.

"I am...what ship is that?" she asked.

"You should know...you commissioned it. This is the Dragon class starship, Valkyrie."

"The Valkyrie? Well, I like the name...but, it was not scheduled to be ready for flight for another three months. You guys must have busted balls to get it to the point you could fly out and find us."

"We saw transmissions from your ship when you arrived in this sector. We also saw the Alliance battle logs and knew you were in trouble, so we rushed to get here as soon as possible."

"Well, I applaud your bravery...to have taken an incomplete starship into a possible hostile situation is commendable. If we still had that Og battleship on our tail, you might be in a world of trouble. By the way, have you seen the Og battleship? Did they emerge and sink into the vortex? Should we be preparing for battle?"

"Well, first things first..." he replied. "I think you should know that this ship is complete...it is totally built, and ready for not only spaceflight, but for battle." She gave him a confused look, as he expected. "I don't think you realize where or when you are at..."

He watched her look down at her command console. She looked up and shrugged her shoulders – she had no idea. He got closer to the display and softly said "Captain, you just arrived here...but it has been three months since you physically arrived in this location. We have been sitting here for a week just waiting for you to appear."

Now he could see a look of confusion and real panic on her face. "My chronometers...they say it has only been a few minutes since we exited the void."

"It appears that your chronometers are behind also. You entered that vortex three months ago. Somehow, you were stuck in time for three months. Welcome back to reality..." He tried to give her a reassuring smile, but he knew it would not really help.

He let her digest that for a few minutes. She finally began to comprehend what had happened and the look of panic began to subside. He gave her another reassuring smile, this time it did help. "You asked about the Og battleship. I think you should see this. We just noticed this in our sensors a day ago and started recording this...it ended about the time you arrived. They may be linked."

He nodded to Alice, who transmitted an image of the black hole. Jaime got closer to the display to verify what she was actually seeing. In the vortex a small dark hole sat motionless, it was then filled by the Og battleship. It squirted out as in the past...much faster than normal she noticed. Then it started its fall into the black hole. It drifted slowly at first, then quickly sunk into the black void. A second later, it was gone. Then the scenario started again.

She looked at him and said "Why are you showing it over and over? I saw it the first time..."

"Actually, that was the first image we took of that activity. It happened four times before we were able to get a fix on the position of the rift and monitor that activity. It continued until now, when you arrived here. And, you simply did...just appear...out of nothingness. You just, showed up."

"Holly crap..." she sighed. "So they had been dying in that loop over and over again?" He nodded yes. "Do you think they experienced it that many times?"

He nodded yes again. "We think that they were cognizant of the situation in each instance that the time loop occurred. If they felt pain, then they felt it during each reoccurrence."

"Damn..." she softly said. "I would not had wanted to subject anyone to that. I think just blowing up their ship and ending it quickly would have been my preferable way to rid us of them...but you have to do what is needed to protect your ship and crew. After all, it was them or us..."

He nodded in agreement "I would had done the same thing. You saved your ship and crew from an enemy that wanted to kill you. You did the right thing regardless of the consequences for your enemy."

"Yeah, but what a horrid way to go...over and over again..." she admitted.

He watched as she started going over the status of the ships systems. After a minute, she looked up, and said "It appears we have a few minor repairs before we can get under way. For one, we really need to do our maintenance on the crawler drive. We have some minor structural damage, and the crew's injuries need to be cared for. Can you loan us some assistance?"

"Of course" he replied "Kate is on board and is very excited to come over and help to get the engineering work done. I am not sure why..." he said with a snide voice as he put an impish smile on his face. He imaged on Jonathan who now had a glowing smile. "Also, I have Doctor Starling with me, she is more than willing to come over and help with triage."

"That will make Max very happy I am sure..." now Jaime had that same smile on her face.

He gave a small quiet laugh. He looked at her then suggested "Captain, how about you come over to the Valkyrie for a tour. We do have a few new enhancements you might be interested in. And, I will add a nice dinner to the invitation."

She smiled at him "How can I refuse an offer like that. Give me a couple hours to get status updates and freshen up. I guess I have three months of cleaning to do. I look forward to hearing of any changes or updates in our situation or with the Blessed. See you soon, Bordeaux out."

*　　　*　　　*

She was given the grand tour when she arrived. Allen showed her the latest updates – including a second redundant set of black box 3D computers, improved hyper-crawler drives, an even stronger bubble projector, and multiple layers of space carbon outer plating.

"This is one hell of a ship, Allen" she told him.

He beamed with pride from her compliment. "Thank you, from you that is the greatest compliment."

Behind them a woman's voice asked "Is this her? Is this the great captain?" They turned to find a woman, dressed in only a fur halter and matching brown fur skirt looking at them. She had a long face and slightly enlarged forehead. She had a primitive look, but at the same time gave Jaime and Allen an aura of intelligence. Jaime gave her a confused look, then looked to Allen for an introduction.

"Ah, Jaime this is...Patti." Patti smiled and nodded. "She was found by Kip. She escaped...thankfully...and somehow made it here."

"Not somehow, she had a plan..." spoke a familiar voice behind them in the hallway. Jaime turned and saw Jeremy standing there. A huge smile came to her face as she gave a small shriek, ran up to him and gave him a bear hug that would crush a normal man.

"Woah!" he cried out. "You have not stopped your training I see! That's good!" He looked into her eyes and smiled. "It's so good to see you, Jaime. Umm well..." he stared at her midnight face, and looked into her sparkling, electrified, blue eyes. He finally said "So, you've changed..." He reached up and touched her skin, felt the softness of the shimmering blue-black flesh. He touched her white freckles.

She gave him a warm smile. "Only the coloration has changed. I am still the Jaime you have always known. I suspect someday, you will be this color too."

He raised an eyebrow. Allen interrupted "All Normals have been going through these changes, some much slower than others."

"You wouldn't say that if you walked around my ship. We discovered that dark matter is accelerating these changes. We had...an incident...dark matter was released and now every member of the crew has either changed or is going through the process of their skin color changing. Max says it is going to happen to all of us. It is this space and something in our DNA...some energy...it is causing us to change. But, this change is for the better."

Jeremy moved the fabric covering his left arm. Now exposed was a patch of dark blue skin. "Yeah, it IS happening to all of us."

Jaime smiled and let escape a small chuckle. She turned her attention back to the dark tanned young girl. "So, Patti. You lived on Queek for how long?"

"All my life. I was born there" She replied.

"Really? If so, then where are your parents?" she asked with a bit of disbelief in her voice.

Patti just smiled at her. "They died...long ago. They left me in the cave one day and never returned. I found bones years later it was them."

"And you survived? Did you live with the Queek?"

"No, they were not friendly to me. I avoided them, and lived in my cave. That is until your people found me."

"Those were not our people!" Jaime blurted out, without thinking. "Well, they are not the same in both physical make up, and thoughts."

"I can tell..." she said and smiled. "You are nothing like them. You might survive here."

*   *   *

After days of repairs and rest, the Ladyhawk and Valkyrie were headed back to Haven. Life aboard the ship was back to normal, even the chronometers caught back up with normal time – once the ship's sensors determined the positioning of the stars and were able to detect galactic movements.

Jaime called Max, Jonathan, and Allen in for a conference. Allen was attending via holo-screen. She looked at the men for a moment before saying "Gentlemen, we have a problem...a problem in a traitor." She looked at them again, Jonathan and Max showed no emotion, Allen a slight look of surprise. "Allen, you read the logs. Someone tampered with Nova's servo motors, causing her to take the actions she did. They knew that with the proper electrical stimulation, her Blessed genetics would take over. Because of that, she almost took out the Ladyhawk. It was her Normal side that was finally able to take over once the device was disabled. Unfortunately, she also decided to take her life, as she felt she could not live with what she had almost done. Now, we are left with our lives missing one bright light. The real question...is who did this. Also, since we know someone did this, it also means that a Normal is helping the Blessed. Suggestions?"

Max spoke first "Captain, I believe I might have an idea of who did this. Let me investigate...I will report directly to you as to what I find." Jaime nodded in agreement.

"The ship has been repaired, but I need to put more safeguards into our dark matter containment. It appears to be the one weakness aboard the ship." Jonathan noted.

Jaime nodded, then added "We may have more weaknesses we have not found yet. After you correct the containment issues, please look at every system for possible vulnerabilities. We cannot have this happen again."

"I have to add however, captain..." Allen interjected "that we have to be very careful in finding security problems. We have to always be aware of the outcome of our tightening of security. Normal society is too new and fragile to go through crackdowns. We have to remember where we just came from. We cannot become too authoritarian...if we do, we might as well just go back to the Blessed."

"Your'e right, Allen" Max acknowledged. "We have to tread a very fine line between securing ourselves and becoming a police state. Our people will not stand for it...I will not stand for it."

"My Max, how strong you've become!" Jaime called out – a smile on her face and in the tone of her voice.

"He has been a lot stronger than you think." Jonathan added. The two other men gave him a slight crusty look. He shut down quickly and looked down at the notes on his computer. Jaime gave the other two men a questioning look – they added nothing.

A few more items were discussed, and the meeting adjourned. After the men left the ready room, Jaime activated her command computer and called up the history on the terrorist group, the "People Against War".

Planet Equeria 5:

Alpha Chef Monmouth Nettles:

Three days they had been on the planet. Exploring, surveying, mapping, and eating rations. This last part was what bothered Monmouth the most – he was the Chef, the cook, the person the men looked to for a decent meal after a hard day of ordering Secret Service soldiers around in their exploration tasks. They looked to him for food, for a good hot meal, for a delicious break from the exhausting work, and to prime them into a deep sleep that evening. But so far, that was not meant to be. There was only battle rations – nothing that could be used for a warm, delicious, and satisfying meal.

Today was going to be different. Today, he would find some natural foods to make something delicious, something to raise the spirits of his fellow Blessed. He was the top cook in the fleet, and thus the reason they sent him on this difficult, and dangerous mission. He was there to find food.

He was wandering around the hills that surrounded the plains that had been taken over for landing of the shuttles, and for launching of the land-based explorations. The first officer had set up camp above the plain in the hills surrounding this valley of

golden grass. The hills were a mixture of various forms of life –
there were plants, shrubberies, trees, and some small birds and
insect life. Nothing really sufficient however to feed an army, or
even a commanding group of Blessed. He was accompanied by
Beta Cook Brigham Saulsberry, a contingent of secret service
troops, and three Blessed officers.

Brigham scanned another set of shrubs housing a black
colored berry. Finally, he picked one and tasted it – then spat it
out. "Ack! That tastes horrid! Is there anything on this blasted
planet worth eating?" he cried out.

Monmouth looked at the shrub, and then shook his head.
"We have found hardly anything to eat here!" he shouted. "How
am I supposed to care and feed for our Blessed brethren if I
cannot find anything to cook? I have found one...ONE...berry
suitable for a fruit compote, but other than that, nothing! Why did
we not bring a cow with us? I could at least cook something!"

"Sir..." Tigren Marks, one of the Blessed officers
accompanying them, stood at stiff attention, and then announced
with pride in his voice "You have taken the best care within your
power. You have given us meals to keep us going. Yes, they have
not been made of the superior meats and other foods we are
accustomed to, but they still..."

"FILL YOU UP! IS THAT WHAT YOU WERE ABOUT TO
SAY?" Monmouth screamed. The young officer only shook his
head yes. "Well, we need to find *something*...scan the area
further...find me something to kill and cook!"

The crew turned all scanners to full power, no longer
worrying about the possibility of any other creatures detecting
their landing force. It was time to feast, and Monmouth was going
to give them that feast.

TIgren scanned the area to the left of them for a few
minutes then announced "I think I found something, sir." He took
his binoculars, looked down into the valley, and after scanning for
a minute handed the glasses to Monmouth. He pointed in the
direction of one of the few small green grassy spots in the plain
below. Monmouth put the glasses to his eyes and activated the
automatic zoom. Sure enough, there were animals just a short
distance from the landing site. They were standing on four legs

and were covered with short, tan fur. A black and white stripe flowed down each side of the creatures, providing some camouflage within the tall grasses. He looked at the closest one, standing in the green grass and chewing. It was oblivious to their presence – it had no idea that a superior intelligence was nearby, and was watching them.

He continued to stare at the creature through the glasses. "Yes, that has definite possibilities…" he licked his lips in anticipation. "Can you get a scan of its molecular make up? Can you determine if it is edible?"

TIgren aimed his scanning probe to the creature, studied his computer readout, and then told him "Yes, the scans say the meat of that animal is totally edible by Blessed."

Without taking his eyes from the binoculars, Monmouth reached his hand out, and then opened and closed it a number of times like reaching for something in the air. "Give me a sniper rifle…I am going to take down the kill, and feed it to our troops myself."

Tigren turned and obtained a sniper rifle from one of the accompanying secret service soldiers, and then handed it to him. Monmouth checked the scope, aimed it out over the golden plain, activated the laser sighting, the targeting computer, took careful aim, closed his eyes, and finally fired. The percussion from the blaster shot rang out and echoed over the entire valley. Winged creatures flew panicked from the trees around them. He looked through the scope again to find the creature as it lie dead on the grass, a quick formed pool of blood now spoiled the green lush turf. "Got ya!" he shouted.

He stood up, dropped the rifle on the ground, and ran carelessly down the hill as fast as his little rotund body would allow. He arrived at the spot where the dead animal's corpse lay. It looked delicious to him, and just thinking about the delicious meal he was about to cook made him salivate. His rosy cheeks smacked in anticipation of the upcoming meal. As Tigren finally caught up to him, Monmouth immediately turned and ordered "Take this creature to my kitchen tent. I want it in the oven immediately – before it even *thinks* it can spoil! Move!"

Monmouth made a feast that afternoon. He created steaks and chops for the officers, burger patties for the chiefs, and meat pies and stews for the enlisted men. It was the greatest feast ever eaten off of the planet earth. It was a feast that was fit for the Supreme Commander, if he were there. This was a day in the history of the Blessed to be remembered – the first meal of off-world meat.

They sat in the large covered mess hall tent that had been erected on the top of the hill. A view of the warm, white sunset offered additional beauty to the already delicious meal. The Blessed ate with abandon, as this was the meal they came out into space to find. They all started to think that perhaps now, they had finally found a home.

Monmouth served himself a steak out of the tenderest part of the creature. It had been seared, roasted to perfection, and covered with a light brown sauce of his own secret design. He cut into the thick brown meat, light red blood flowed from the meat as he cut, which filled his plate with even more flavoring. He put the bite to his lips, gave it a slight lick, then popped it into his mouth and began to chew with abandon. *"My god, this is the best meal I have ever served!"* he thought as he chewed the bite. He savored every chew – he did not stop chewing until the bite was totally dissolved into a mushy blob – and not until then, did he finally swallow it.

A Blessed officer walked up to him. He had no idea who it was, but he had a very large smile on his face. "You have outdone yourself, Chef" the man complemented. Monmouth simply smiled, and nodded at him. He wanted to be left alone with his meal – he wanted to savor the flavors uninterrupted.

Another noise behind him. Irritated that he had been interrupted in his enjoyment again, he turned from his plate with the look of annoyance. However, instead of an admirer, there was a dark, black set of eyes staring at him. Those eyes were sitting on the face of a creature similar to the one he was enjoying. This particular creature however had a very large set of antlers on its head, sitting between a pair of large tear-dropped shaped ears. The room became quiet as everyone realized there were noises behind all of them – skittering, and the sound of clacking shells filled the room. Everyone looked around and saw that multilegged creatures had surrounded them. Each of these creatures had blue shells and a large boney appendage on their backs. At the end of this appendage was a very sharp, wet spike.

One of the Blessed officers stood up, and pulled out his blaster. He yelled to his men "Kill these creatures!", took aim, and then fired. The beam bounced off of the shell and into the sky. Other officers and soldiers were now also taking out weapons. The spider-like creatures jumped into action before another shot could be fired however. Sharp spikes were quickly flung into the chests of the Blessed soldiers who opposed them. Human blood began to fly everywhere as the soldiers were impaled through the chest then thrown aside. The creatures moved forward to the men still sitting in their seats. They pounced on the humans, and with multiple clawed legs, tore each of the men into shreds. The mess hall was filled with the sound of screams as the entire force was mutilated into small bits of flesh by scraping claws and chewing mandibles. In the distance, Monmouth could hear the painful cries of the secret service soldiers being cut down – there was not going to be anyone left to inhabit the planet unless they gained the advantage again.

Not giving in, more of the Blessed soldiers had entered the fray. They had jumped out of their chairs, and had taken out their heavy projectile weapons. They aimed at the spiders and fired molten bolts of spent plutonium. These weapons did their jobs and inflicted damage – as large holes were cut into the spider's shells by the powerful projectiles. As the projectiles took down more of the spiders, blue blood splattered across the room. A large blob of blue muck splashed onto Monmouth's beautiful steak, ruining the color of his food, and his appetite. The soldiers turned to fire another volley into the next set of attacking creatures, but they were cut down by a multitude of green beams of energy. The soldiers splattered into small chunks of meat as the green rays arced through their armor and touched their fragile human flesh. Within a single minute, everyone in the mess hall and in the camp were dead – all that is, except Monmouth.

The creature continued to just stare at him. Monmouth's large puffy green eyes however, could not help but blink. He kept looking into the creature's black eyes, which only continued to stare. Feeling that this was the end seemed to give Monmouth a brief moment of courage. He said to the staring creature. "Well, it is obvious you are too stupid to speak. If you are going to kill me, I might as well enjoy my last meal." With that , he turned back to his plate, took his fork, jabbed it into the cut piece of steak on his plate, held up the now blue-stained meat, popped it into his mouth, and started chewing and moaning in flavorful delight. With a mouthful of meat filling his mouth he said "It really is delicious, you should try it. You creatures will make excellent meals for the Blessed."

Finally, the creature blinked and said "Biped barbarian!" which made Monmouth open his eyes wide in surprise – he did not expect the creature to actually be able to speak, and to speak in Alliance english on top of that. With a quick glow from his antlers a beam shot out, hitting his left leg and disintegrating it into a burning explosion of flesh. Along with his leg, the chair also disintegrated. Monmouth screamed in pain as he and the chair fell sideways to the floor. Then, another beam, which burned off the other leg, which was followed by a blast to each of his arms. The beam was so hot that it instantly cauterized the wound, which prevented him from bleeding to death.

The creature turned away from the now-crying Monmouth, and ordered "Take this barbarian slug to a ship and program it to return to his vessel in space. We will deal with them after that."

Starship Talon, Orbiting Planet Equeria 5:

Alpha Starship Captain Olaf Carlton:

The distress signal shook Olaf out of a light slumber. The ship had been orbiting the planet for the past three weeks. The ground troops had been exploring the surface this whole time without incident. Up until this moment, it looked like this would be the perfect planet to colonize – plenty of natural vegetables, temperate weather, and the possibility of meat food sources. This was to be the perfect place for him to settle down, or so he thought. He had thanked the gods that he was lucky enough to have been away from the battle with the Og. Word had gone out across the fleet – that a single battle took their best and most revered starship captain – Kip. Yes, he was glad to be out on an exploration and conquering mission. But now the distress signal was sounding – a transport ship was on its way up from the surface while sounding the alarm – this couldn't be good.

He snapped himself out of his slumber and into an alert state. He began checking over the ship's systems. He was the captain of this new Mako class battle cruiser. It was much smaller than both the Hammerhead and Super Hammerhead vessels, but this was still a powerful craft, and he had plenty of weapons at his disposal. He looked at the readouts on a graphical display. It showed the long cylindrical shape of the main superstructure which ended in a sharp point at the front end, the wide arced fins on each side of the craft where the main ion drives were housed, and the larger crawler section in the rear. This was a ship that was built to explore, fight, and conquer. He knew it would be up to any challenge – he just now wished he didn't have to take on that challenge.

"One Blessed is identified on board Alpha Starship Captain, and he is alive" announced the science officer.

Olaf breathed a silent sigh of relief. He hoped it was just a false alarm, and that this person used the emergency distress signal by accident – and this now appeared to be the case. "Allow the ship to board..." he ordered. He turned and proceeded to the bridge hatch, then stopped and announced "I will go and see who caused this ruckus, whoever it is will pay for their mistake, and their disruption in the normal activity of this ship!"

When he arrived at the landing bay the ship was already making its final approach. He stopped in the command deck while the ship entered through the pressurizing force fields and came to a perfect automated landing. He left the command area and walked down to the ship. There were soldiers awaiting him with their weapons at the ready. He nodded to each of the secret service soldiers and said "I don't think we will need those...but just in case."

He entered his command code and activated the hatch. When he looked in and saw the sight inside, he began to wretch. He turned out of the shuttle hatch, and then threw up on the clean metal deck, splashing vomit on the leg of one of the nearby secret service soldiers. He waited for a moment while his stomach settled, and then turned and looked in again. Lying in front of him on the deck, was his prime chef Monmouth – his arms and legs were gone, they had been burned off. He had numerous puncture marks on what was left of his body. Olaf turned and signaled the medical officer, who in turn rushed in and began a full scan on his living remains.

After a moment, the doctor told Olaf "Not good. He has had all of his limbs burnt off by some massive force beam. See each of these punctures?" he pointed to the various holes in his torso. They were now sputtering various gasses and small bubbles of coagulated blood. Olaf held back another lump of vomit in his throat as he closely looked at the bubbling holes. "There is some form of organic spike embedded in each of these holes. The spikes seem to be secreting an enzyme that is virtually eating him alive."

Between Monmouth's fat lips sat a large red ball – it was made of some unknown material that was similar to plastic, and embedded in this ball was a crystal. Olaf recognized this as a data crystal. Monmouth was breathing through his nose, and moaning with what little breath he could gather. A type of pus dripped out of his nose as he breathed with heavy, nasal gasps.

Olaf took a pair of forceps out of the doctor's medical kit, reached in, and grabbed the crystal with the plier-like tool, making sure not to get his hand anywhere close to the dissolving chef. He took a sanitizing wipe and cleaned off the slimy data crystal. "Do what you can to put him out of his misery quickly and painlessly, doctor. I am returning to the bridge." he ordered.

The doctor nodded and as Olaf walked away he heard the blast of a rifle, and the sound of brains hitting the walls of the shuttle. He stopped and thought for a second, then nodded – it *was* the quickest way to put him out of his misery, he agreed.

As soon as he entered the bridge, he tossed the crystal to the communications officer. "Decode this immediately" he barked. A minute later, the crystal had been decoded and the communications officer put the message on the main holo-screen. In the imager was the face of a deer-like creature with a large set of antlers on his head. He had dark black eyes, white and black stripes that went from each eye, around the back of its head, and down its neck. Olaf looked at the creature – he had seen images of the Flaybah before, but this one was different. This creature had those black and white stripes on its face, the antlers were configured differently also. He wondered what this particular creature actually was, and why it was apparently acting so aggressive.

His thoughts were interrupted by the voice of the creature in the holo-image – it surprised him by speaking in alliance standard English. "Biped barbarians, you have invaded our lands. You have killed our kind, and consumed our flesh. For this, we have eliminated you from the surface of our planet. Your ship is to be spared so it may warn other barbarians of your type to never enter this system again. If you do, you and your ships will be destroyed."

As the image faded and the crystal deactivated, Olaf became enraged. "Communication, have you been able to reach any of the occupation force?" The communications officer just shook his head no. This made his blood boil even hotter. "There were hundreds of Blessed officers and secret service soldiers down there…you can't reach any of them?" He quietly shook his head no again. "Science, are your scans showing any Blessed life down there?"

The science officer continued to look down on his console and simply said "No, no signs of any human life, my Alpha Starship Captain. However, I am now picking up a multitude of alien life signatures. I am not sure how they hid themselves earlier…but they are there now…millions of them!"

He saw red now. "Weapons Master, prepare all weapons – beamed weapons set for planetary attack, energize our hull, prime the nukes." With that order, everyone looked up in surprise. "If we can't have this planet, no one will…I sure as hell am not going to leave it to that race that just killed all those fine men! Prepare to attack."

The bridge was filled with the sounds of battle preparations. Alert tones sounded, targeting locks gave their normal beep each time a target was acquired, and the chatter of battle communications were broadcasting over the bridge audio system.

The science officer spoke up. "Sir, are we sure we want to do this? We do not know their capabilities, they may be more advanced and ready for us."

This infuriated Olaf, who aimed his command weapon at the young man. "Follow my orders to the letter, or suffer the consequences."

"Of course, Sir. I was just advising, not making any orders or suggestion."

Olaf lowered his arm. "Of course you were…just doing your job. Now, follow my orders." The young science officer nodded in agreement and began the process of analyzing battle preparation data. Finally, he said "We have locks on potential habitation targets. All weapons are charged and at ready. Nukes have been loaded into launching tubes.

"Very well, Weapons Master, fire when ready…" he said with an almost bored nonchalant tone.

The weapons master tapped on the various targets as indicated by his holo-image of the planet below. As he tapped, the different weapons fired their deadly load of light, particles, and energy down to the surface of the planet. Olaf could see the different explosions on the surface as the weapons hit their targeted areas. He had no idea if they were actually dealing death to the enemy below, but he hoped they were now being annihilated.

After a few minutes of firing their main energy weapons, Olaf decided to change tactics. "Fire a nuke to the most likely population center." The weapons master followed his orders, and a moment later he saw the explosion and rising mushroom cloud coming up from the surface. He squinted his eyes to the spectacular explosion and then smiled as he saw the devastation it was causing below. "Yes, excellent…burn the planet down."

A second later alarms sounded throughout the bridge – a ship was detected on SCADAR. Olaf looked to the science station. The officer looked up, and replied "A very large vessel just entered the system." He returned to his console then looked up. "It is now gone." A moment later, proximity alarms sounded as the ship somehow returned. The alarms filled the bridge with the shrill tones of an alert status. The science officer looked up again, his face had gone white. In the holo-display a ship just appeared in front of the Talon – it was large, brown, and cigar-shaped with metallic antlers at the front of the craft. The antlers were glowing a bright green. Without warning, a green beam fired from the antlers and struck the Talon in the port amidships. The ship shook violently, sparks flew from consoles, and more alarms sounded. "Alpha Starship Captain, our port-side protective arrays just went down. We already have structural damage to the port ion drive and to a number of decks on that side of the ship."

"Who the hell is this?" he barked. Before he could yell out another order, a missile of some form hit the ship, once again on the port side. The power flickered and the ship shook in massive waves. Olaf's command chair lost power and disengaged its gravity straps – sending Olaf flying across the bridge. He landed hard against the port star-screen, shattering the electronics, turning the imager into a flickering wall of static. He moaned in pain as he realized his leg was injured. When he looked down, he saw the femur bone poking through the layer of fabric of his uniform suit. Seeing the injury made him groan even louder.

The science officer ran over and quickly administered an analgesic. "We need you more than ever, Alpha Starship Captain ..." he said while he gave the shot.

Olaf managed to sit up right as another blast hit the ship – this time on the starboard side. "What the hell? They are just attacking? Who the hell are they? And why aren't we fighting back?" he snapped.

"Acquiring weapons locks, Alpha Starship Captain" said the weapons master. "Firing..."

Arcs of plasma and spent plutonium shells launched from the front of the craft, causing small explosions and fires on the enemy vessel. Another blast from the enemy ship and the bridge went dark. The holo-imager came back on after a moment.

"Is anything working?" he asked to anyone who could answer.

"Not much..." replied the engineer. "Our backup computers went down at the same time as our main systems. They are recovering, it will be thirty seconds."

"We do have communications again..." announced the communication officer.

"Hail that vessel..."

A moment later the holo-imager came on, showing a large deer buck. He had an enormous set of antlers, a uniform shirt with numerous badges, and a very visible scowl on his face.

Olaf looked at the image and recognized the creature. "Flaybah?" he said questionably.

"Biped, human barbarians..." snapped the Flaybah officer "You have violated our space, killed...EATEN one of our kind...and attacked one of our home worlds. You, have provoked us..."

"We didn't...we didn't know..." Olaf mumbled. "The creatures below do not look like you..."

"Just because they have stripes and some of us don't?" he snapped. Behind him, a stripped Flaybah officer now stood behind him. "That is no excuse. As you can plainly see, we have differences in coloration and nothing else. You have attacked us, killed many of us, and thus we now declare war on you...on the human race. Prepare for termination..." he immediately disconnected communication, then the ship fired all its weapons at the Talon. Olaf's ship, and his command ended that moment as quickly as his life.

Ten Years Ago...

"Someday, I am going to fly a giant star ship. I am going to fly into outer space" she told her friend Joan.

"Sure, sure..." she replied "Even if they somehow manage to find a way to go anywhere out of the system, do you really think your dad is going to let you go?"

"I don't care...As a matter of fact, I will be going up very, very soon...I enlisted for the Space Merchant Marine League. I will get to pilot supply shuttles for the Alliance.

"What?" she cried out "Your parents are going to kill you!"

"Maybe so, but they'll have to catch me first. And, someday...soon...I will be flying the big star ships...like, a star cruiser...you just wait and see. I will become Halley, the explorer! THEN, they will be proud of me...they will not wonder why I left without telling them in person. My ship leaves tomorrow. I will be half way to Mars before they even read my goodbye note."

NGD: 3 Years, 5 Months, 1 Day:

Haven:

Halley Cet:

They were able to make all needed repairs and get back underway in just a couple of days after their incident at the black hole. Halley was looking forward to their arrival back at Haven, and to a couple of days of rest. The trip was proceeding without incident, and they were about to arrive back at the base. Halley had returned to her place in the first officer's position while the new helmsman took the ship into space dock. It had only been a few days out of the helm seat, and she discovered she missed it – the excitement of piloting a starship could never be replaced. Being a first officer had its responsibilities, but work-wise was boring to her.

She disembarked Ladyhawk via the gangway and stopped to look out the viewports into the space harbor. The Valkyrie was docked across the way. Next to the Valkyrie were two large bulky ships in their final stages of completion, along with a long, large vessel that she recognized the configuration as that of a cargo carrier. What caught her eye however, were the two smaller versions of the Ladyhawk docked in the moorings next to the ship. They were shiny black of newly applied layers of space carbon alloy. The propulsion systems were slightly different, an upgrade she assumed. They appeared powered up and ready to take off into the emptiness of space at a moment's notice.

"Those two star cruisers are ready for flight" a voice from farther up the gangway called out. She turned to find Jonathan, Kate, and Jaime strolling down the gangway. "Those have the latest in hull plating, computer systems, star drives, and weapons. They are built for exploring, while at the same time can hold their own in a fight – hopefully, that need will never arise."

"Yeah…" she sighed "They are beautiful craft…"

"Would you like one?" Jaime asked. She turned and gave her captain a confused look. "They both need a captain, I can't think of anyone more qualified than you. You showed all of us how you would command under pressure. You handled the emergency here at Haven with calm and coolness. Halley, you have to take one of them!"

"Well, how can I say no?" She smiled and looked back at the two craft. The closest one seemed to call to her. "I want that one…the closest one."

"It's yours!" Jaime proclaimed. "Better get your bridge crew together quickly. Allen tells me that ship is scheduled to depart in just a couple days. All she needed was a captain and bridge crew."

"Captain?" she quickly called out. "One thing…I don't really want to fight. I signed on to avoid war…after what just happened, I would like to avoid a fight if possible."

"We all want that my dear…isn't that the real reason we came out here?" added Max, who was now joining them on the gangway.

"We all came out here to escape war. Take the ship and explore. We will try our best to avoid any other conflicts." Jaime looked at Max, and wondered about his bold statement.

Halley nodded at Max, saluted Jaime, and turned to head down the gangway. She was so excited, but struggled to hold it all in – she needed to get away, to let go – she just wanted to scream in excitement. Jaime called down from the gangway "You're going to have to name her..." Halley stopped and turned to give a quizzical look. She then turned and looked at the brand new ship sitting in its dock. It was clean, shiny, and new.

Jonathan ran down to catch up with her as she looked out the viewing windows. "It has all the latest technology...we put every innovation we could come up with in that hull."

"Yes, perfect!" she shouted as she grabbed him and gave him a big hug. He had a look of surprise on his face as she squeezed the breath out of him. "Handle the ship, "Innovation""" she ordered.

He smiled, nodded, activated his computer, and entered the handle into the database. "Your ship is now named, Innovation."

*   *   *

She walked down the corridor on her way to her quarters. She felt so confused, and worried. She was about to take one of the biggest leaps of responsibility ever – she was taking command of a starship – and it frightened her to death. She was scared, yet strangely excited about taking on this responsibility. As a younger adult, she always knew someday she would have such responsibility for something so important. But now, she was about to take on a giant starship, and the lives of thousands of people.

But something else also bothered her as she had the strangest feeling – the feeling she was being watched. Halley slowed her pace, slid her hand down to her belt, and then to her holster. She now wished she had a command weapon, but no one in the Normal command had ever thought one was needed. She continued to walk slowly, and listened behind her. There! She heard it...the sound of nails on the hard, black, asteroid surface of the corridor floor. The nail taps sounded like they came from a small foot. She wondered if she was being stalked by a space rat – but most of them had either been killed by the base cats, or were in hiding from the same aforementioned animals.

She finally decided to face her stalker. She unsnapped the holster as she slowly walked and put her hand around the grip of the blaster. A few more steps before she stopped, spun around, whipped out the blaster, aimed it down, and faced the stalking creature.

She immediately re-holstered her weapon when she saw the little animal that stood in front of her. It had a a long muzzle with a dark black nose at the end, fawn colored fur, big ears, and stood about eight inches off the floor. The thing stared at her with big dark eyes which were surrounded by a small lining of white fur. Its mouth hung open with a tongue that flopped in and out while it panted.

"What the hell are you?" she asked it. In reply it gave a small yipping noise. This startled her and she fell back onto her butt. The animal ran up to her after her back hit the floor, and looked into her face. It came even closer, then gave her a small wet lick of its tongue.

She laughed and the little creature yipped again. It had a little fawn colored fur tail that wagged quickly back and forth. She sat up and bravely reached out her hand. The animal didn't budge, just continued to wag its tail. She reached a little farther and put her hand on its head and lightly stroked the short fur. His tongue came back out as it started to lightly pant again – the tail still wagging ecstatically.

"My, you are a cute one!" she told it. She activated her portable computer and imaged the animal. A moment later, the computer returned the identification – it was a dog, a Chihuahua to be precise. She stood back up, and turned her back on the animal as she said "Go on home now..." She started to walk down the corridor and heard those little taps of claws on the ground. She turned around to find the little one immediately behind her, staring up at her with big dark eyes. "I guess you are not going home? Do you not have a home?" Those big eyes continued to stare up at her – that look told her this dog had no home. "Well, Jaime can have a cat on a starship, I see no reason why I can't have a dog. Okay, come on...let's go find a crew."

She arrived back to her quarters and realized how spartan the décor was. She had not taken any time to fix the place

268

up. Everything was standard issue – the dresser, bed, nightstands, and desk, all unadorned. She remembered how she lived when she was young – her room had hanging mobiles of the Solar System, there were star charts on the walls, dolls on the shelves, and pictures of her star idols on the desk. Not here however, in this room, there was nothing. She had not spent enough time here – she spent almost all her waking moments on board the Ladyhawk. She looked around and shook her head at the boring room. The tapping on the floor took her out of her thoughts as she looked down at the little animal staring up at her again with those dark brown eyes.

She smiled at the little creature and wondered. She got on her hands and knees and looked under it. "Yep, a boy...guess I need to name you something masculine." She chuckled to herself "I guess Snowflake, Princess, or Precious are not going to work...I am going to have to think of a name for you little guy..." She sat down onto the bed and the small dog jumped up and curled into ball next to her. She smiled at the little dog's action.

A moment later, her Norm-Comm buzzed. She queried to find Katsumi on the other end. "Hello...Captain?" she asked sheepishly.

"Well, not quite yet..." she laughed. "For now, just Halley. What can I do for you?"

"Well, I want to sign up for the science position on your bridge..." she replied.

"You want off the Ladyhawk? Why?" she asked with concern.

"Because of your mission. You are going to explore...explore places none of us have been to. I signed onto the Starlight for this purpose, I wanted to see new places...not fight battles for, or against the Blessed. On board your ship I can do that. I have spoken with Captain Bordeaux, she said she understood, and would happily sign my transfer. Will you take me?"

"How can I refuse the best science officer in the fleet? Welcome aboard Ms. Ito!" She disconnected from Katsumi and looked down to her new friend. "Look, we already have our first, no second volunteer! You are coming along aren't you?" The little dog gave a small yip in response.

*   *   *

The ship was loaded with supplies, and prepped for departure. She sat in her ready room, her hands shaking, and a slight sweat forming on her brow. She stood up and looked at her uniform in the mirror. She had selected a gray commander's pant suit, long straight legs, running up to her black belt, which then formed the separation between the pants and matching gray tunic. On her shoulders were metallic insignia of stars in the shape of the Little Dipper, which she chose for her ships symbol. She wanted the end of the dipper, the North Star, to always be her guiding light. On her collar were captain's stars. Otherwise, there was no other ornamentation – there would no longer be any connection or ornamentation with the Alliance or the Blessed aboard her ship. She refused, when suggested that she join the main fleet, and to have the ship christened. She did not take on the designation "Our Supreme Commander's Starship" in the title. Her ship would not have any connection with the Alliance she had decided. The Blessed had done enough damage in this galaxy, and when she met a new race, she did not want any history to taint their meeting.

She looked at her blue skin. No longer would she associate herself or her ship with the light-skinned Blessed. She and her crew were different – all Normals were now different, or at least changing every day. She had decided to no longer have that association in their past. This was the future – this was what things were to become. She and her crew were headed out into the unknown, and she was so excited to see what was out there.

One more check of her uniform, she straightened out her dark rimmed glasses, then a deep breath as she slowly walked to the automated hatchway to the bridge. The door opened and she was smacked with the sounds of preparation – announcements over the bridge speakers as various departments checked in their status – the talking filled the domed bridge. Discussions of power formulations, computer balancing, and engine statuses filled the bridge with sound. She looked around the new bridge configuration – there were still the various stations all in a circular manner around the center holo-screen. The walls and ceiling of the bridge however, were of a totally different configuration. The bridge was now built into a large domed structure. The dome took the place of the multiple star screens – as the dome was actually one large star screen. Anyone on the bridge would now have full upward views of the space around and above them. She actually worried that it might be distracting – however, she determined that in the first few days, they could adjust to the stars surrounding their heads.

Her first officer, Staci Smitters looked up and saw her walk onto the bridge. She activated her Norm-Comm and announced to all on the bridge with a loud "Captain on the bridge!" The room become totally quiet.

She looked over at Staci – she had her dishwater blonde, medium-length hair, pulled back, and in a high, flat, ponytail. She had a rounded face, which curved from her cheeks to her chin, small cheek bones above a medium sized mouth that trembled slightly from nerves. She kept her small glowing green eyes focused straight ahead as she stood at attention. Thin eyebrows were shaking slightly. Finally, she took a small glance around the bridge before saying "The ship is ready, the bridge is yours, Captain."

Halley definitely felt uncomfortable with this level of formality. Jaime was a tough captain, but still preferred her bridge crew to be at ease when working with her. That was what she wanted on her bridge too. She walked over and looked at Katsumi – her face was filled with pride and glowed with happiness at the prospect of exploration. She looked at her almond shaped eyes, they were as wide as could be, the brown color in them now glowed from her late changes. Halley noted that she still only showed streaks of the blue coloration in the skin on her neck. It was obvious that her Japanese heritage was slowing the changes that most other Normals were quickly seeing.

Throughout the history of earth, the Japanese were labeled one of the most radiated people to ever survive all of the wars of the planet. Through the many wars, the number of bombs dropped on their small country was the most any area of land had ever experienced. The damage to their society and their health was horrid – most of their people died. At the same time, the ones who somehow had survived became stronger and more resistant to external forces and radiation. Thus, her body was resisting the changes being dealt by this galaxy, and the dark matter that surrounded them.

Halley could tell she was living for this one moment, the moment they were starting something other than war. She knew that Katsumi had believed in the principles of the People Against War, and thus this was her one way of moving the Normals toward peace. She had a big smile (for her) on her face, and was not even trying to conceal how happy and excited she felt.

Halley gave her a small smile before asking "Science report?"

"All SCADAR and advanced scanners are active at low level, and will be put fully on-line once we leave space dock. Space outside the space dock is clear and ready for our departure." She gave Halley another huge smile.

Halley returned the smile. "Very good..."

She put her hands behind her back and slowly walked to the weapons station. A young raven haired woman stood at attention. She had large green eyes that glowed in the light of the holo-screen, small cheek bones, and a short upturned nose above a small set of lips. Her blue skin shimmered with a pulsing glow. She had to have just come out of training – she was so young. Halley estimated she could not have been more than seventeen or at the most eighteen years old. She wondered just how young the Blessed had been selecting their potential breeding stock. Most every Normal they took from earth were female after all...hardly any males had been taken along on their journey. Looking at her reminded her of her own roots. She remembered her chats with Jaime, and how much her future captain had taught her. Now, it would be her turn to teach these young officers.

"And you are?" she asked.

The young weapons officer snapped to attention "Weapons master Cissy Michaels, Captain!" she barked.

Halley was slightly taken aback with her quick and sharp response. She gave a quiet chuckle then said "Let's hope you are as snappy with those weapons as you are in response to a question. Also, let's hope we will not need your services...I hope to give you a quiet, boring, voyage. Carry on..."

She stepped over to the helm and looked at the back of the young woman who was reviewing and checking ships systems. She so wanted to tap this person on the shoulder as to take over – but that was no longer her duty in life. Sitting in the helm chair was Kass Fallon, the third ranked pilot in the fleet – only below the helmsman of the Ladyhawk and herself. Kass had a very dark blue skin, a few white freckles on her rounded cheeks, glowing blue eyes, large winged ears, a large grinning smile on her oversized mouth, and the brightest red hair, cut to within a half inch of her blue scalp. She saw Halley and smoothly got out of the chair and stood at attention. She stood a couple of inches below Halley's forward gaze, but even with her short stature, she had a stocky muscular build. She knew this one would have no problems taking on a much larger opponent in hand to hand battle.

She saluted sharply while announcing "Kass Fallon, Helmsman. Proud to be serving under the top rated helmsman in the fleet. I hope to learn much from you, Captain." Once again, another stiff snappy salute.

She surprised the young woman by reaching out and offering a handshake. Kass sheepishly took her hand, and at first gave it a light shake. Halley continued to shake her hand as she said "I am looking forward to seeing how you steer this craft, Helmsman. I expect you have been ready for this for a long time, and I bet I don't have to teach you a single thing." She noticed that as she spoke, her hand was being squeezed harder and harder. Finally she let loose of the helmsman's hand and glanced down at the shake. Kass looked down, realized what she was doing and let go. "Is the ship ready to leave space dock?" she asked the young woman.

"Yes, Captain. We can leave at a moment's notice. All engines and maneuvering systems are ready and at station keeping." Another snappy salute.

Halley shook her head lightly and smiled – she would have to work on her, maybe a little. She was still too tight and needed to back down a notch. "Very well, thank you.".

Next, she walked to the communication station. A short blonde actively monitored the various communication channels of the ship and the base. Even with her blue skin, her short stature and pageboy blond hair cut reminded her of Lindy. She looked up from her console and extended a hand. "Hello, I am Maxine Alta, your communications officer."

Halley took her hand and shook it. She looked at her again – her young face reminded her so much of Lindy – those rounded cheeks, round wide face, blue glowing eyes, and a warm, innocent smile that could melt anyone's icy heart. Maxine suddenly realized her protocol and dropped Halley's hand and then gave a semi-official salute. Halley chuckled lightly "You were not military before you were assigned here, were you?" Maxine looked down, slightly embarrassed and shook her head no.

In actuality, most Normals were hardly ever military trained while in space, but to help them adjust to Blessed life, the Alliance had put them through intensive speed training on military procedures and tactics prior to signing onto a ship. She knew Maxine was a late selection for the position. She secretly had hoped, and tried to have gotten Otter on her ship, but Otter refused, and Jaime and Max agreed with her decision. She was needed on the base for evaluation and training of new communications personnel. If Normals were going to explore and even colonize any other worlds, communications would be essential.

"I hope I will not let you down...I know I was not your first choice..." she said with a soft soothing voice.

"I did want the best, but I have been told that you WILL be the best. I hope you will use this voyage to hone your skills."

"Oh, I will!" she replied. "I am actually planning on some tests of extended Norm-Comm while we are out in deep space. Otter and I have a plan to extend our range of internal communications for further and further ranges."

Before giving her more opportunity to expound on her topic of conversation, Halley interrupted her with "I know you will succeed, carry on." The young woman nodded and returned to her work.

She then proceeded to the engineering station. At attention was a tall, lanky woman. Halley noted that her skin was the same dark shade of blue as herself. She stood at least six inches taller than her, and when she saluted showed long thin fingers attached to a hand that had been worked hard – fingers that told her she had always had her hands in the middle of equipment and machinery, as they were scuffed and calloused. She had a thin face, small, upturned nose, thin lips slightly shaded white, thin cheeks, a pointed chin, and small glowing gray eyes, all covered by a thin graying veil of black hair. Her face seemed almost chiseled out of blue stone as it was hard and sharp at the edges.

"Lizzie Mays, Chief Engineer..." the chiseled woman announced.

Halley looked her up and down. This was the one member of her staff she could not find a lot of information on. Her file showed she had the skill and knowledge to both build, and maintain a starship, but she wondered how she even got into space. She was so hard and cold looking – certainly the Blessed would not have selected her for breeding. Finally she said to her "Are you going to keep my starship in tip-top condition?"

"It is what I do, Captain..." she replied with confidence in her voice and spoken in a stern tone. Halley could tell she was deeply annoyed with her questioning of her skills.

She looked her up and down again, then finally said. "Very good, welcome aboard." Halley noted the tall woman slightly loosened up at that. That pleased her – she now felt that she could trust her with the running of the ship.

She looked at Staci once again, she was still stiff as a board. She put her hand on the young woman's shoulder and leaned over the console to whisper "Loosen up. No need to be so stiff." The first officer with that, took a deep breath, tried as best as she could to let her muscles relax, and gave a small smile to her captain. Halley gave a smile in return, and then said very softly "Good...good. Everything looks in tip-top condition, nice work."

She returned to her command chair and right before she sat down she heard a noise – something was scrambling behind her. She turned to look and saw her newly found friend now comfortably seated in her chair. It gave a small yip, which caused a small chuckle amongst the officers. She bent down and picked the little dog up. "Now, we will need to develop some protocols for sitting in the captain's chair..." and sat down holding the small canine in her arm. "I really need to name you..." she looked down at him and stroked the small dog's back. She felt something strange on his fur and when she examined his back closer, noticed that he appeared to have a pair of thin, clear wings on his back. To her, they looked similar to the paper thin wings of an insect, but when she stroked them they felt like velvet. She swore when she petted his little wing growths he gave a sigh. Finally a thought came to her and she said "Beau, you are such a handsome fellow, I think I am going to name you Beau. What do you think of that?" The small dog started wagging his tail with abandon.

She heard the hatch behind her, and when she turned in her seat she saw Jaenar standing in the bridge entryway. "Permission to enter the bridge?" the doe asked.

"Of course, of course...please!" she said while motioning to a chair in the rear of the bridge. The deer walked over to the chair, which detected her species, and modified its fit for a four legged Flaybah. She waited for the chair to manipulate itself, then sat down and folded her four legs into a comfortable sitting position. Halley turned away, thought for a moment, then turned back to her and asked "So, am I to assume you're coming with us?" Jaenar nodded her head yes. "Then, the question is...why? Not that I don't appreciate having your knowledge with us."

Jaenar gave a deer-like smile and simply said "Because we have never gone there. The Flaybah have only seen a small portion of this galaxy. We want to know more, and you are going there. So, we hoped we could go with you and learn. This is acceptable to you, is it not?"

Halley smiled at her and said "Of course, I will love having you on board. Your experience in the galaxy and your knowledge will be of great help. I'm so glad you're here..." Jaenar nodded in agreement.

Beau did a couple of circles on her lap before finally settling into a comfortable spot. He put his head down onto his front paws and gave a small sigh of comfort. Now that the dog was comfortably seated in her lap, she resumed the tasks of preparing for leaving the station. She looked at her command readouts to verify the ship was ready for departure. "Ok, it looks like everything is ship-shape, all systems are ready for departure. Maxine, signal the dock master we are ready for departure and to open the harbor doors. Katsumi, release the docking anchors and moorings. Lizzie, bring the engines on line. Kass, as soon as your engines are green, thruster us out of space dock." She waited for everyone to accomplish their tasks. After a minute, she could see that the ship was now away from the dock, and was about to head into space. She saw the harbor protective hatches open and the stars of outer space sparkle in the distance. Kass called out that the engines were high-by-five – reactors were at level five, and engines were ready to go to high output – everything was ready. "Ok, take her out..." Although, no one ever felt any motion, in her mind she could feel the ship move. She whispered to herself "here we go..."

The ship smoothly left the Haven space dock and moved out of the area for insertion into sub-space. Halley, looked over the ship's mission alternatives with a careful eye. Behind her she heard the soft voice of Jaenar "I would suggest sector N. Based on our unbucked probes, the best possibilities for uninhabited planets are in that sector. If there IS an empty planet in this galaxy, it might be in sector N."

Hearing her say that left Halley with a slight feeling of foreboding that this was going to be a mission with an insurmountable chance of success. She wondered if and what they would find out there. At the same time, she was excited about the possibilities – the chance that maybe, just maybe, they would find an empty habitable planet.

With as much confidence as she could muster in her voice, she ordered "Katsumi, have the computer determine the best route to sector N. Helm, once the computer has determined its calculations, insert us into sub-space. Let's go see what's out there..."

"Otter" Otterdon:

She tenderly plugged the base antenna into her still-healing comm-port. Max had spent hours reattaching all of the micro-connections needed to connect an antenna to her brain. They had given the surgery plenty of time to heal, but it was still tender nonetheless. She would have waited to plug back in, but she needed to work on the experiment with the communications array. Today's experiment was to try to get ahold of the Innovation which was still in sub-space. Her hope was to be able to work on a new thought pattern that would allow for communications through a vast amount of space, and even into and through the void of sub-space. As soon as she plugged in and initialized her connection, the signal came in. It was a signal she could not ignore either, as this request was from another controller – the only other controller in the galaxy as far as she knew – it was a communication from Lindy.

"Otter?" she said as Otter opened her tunneled channel "I'm sorry to interrupt you, but this IS important."

"Lindy, you know you can always contact me regardless of what I am doing. Now, what is it that's so important anyway?"

"First, you have to tell them...they are building something...something big. They are building something near the Devil's Throat, at the entryway from where we are to where we came from. They are keeping it a very guarded secret. Even my Jonathan program is not able to discover what they are doing. I suspect they may have discovered the program actually, and are preventing or rerouting the program's access now. I think they have found a way to hide most of their secrets. But whatever it is they are building...it is really big. That's the one thing...it is so big...they can't cover it from seeing eyes. I see it, you now see it, and now you have to show it to them."

A moment later an image came into Otter's mind. "My god, that is huge! I wonder what it is?" Through the communications array, she stored the images of the massive construction project. "I will get this to Jaime." She accepted the image packet and stored it, then said "Now, that is large and big news, but you sound panicked. There has to be something else to have you at such unease. What is it?"

There was genuine fear in Lindy's voice in what she told her next "You need to tell them to gather the P.A.W.. There is something coming, something really bad…"

Nita "Star Child" Moranda:

She watched the Innovation leave the dock and head out into the open vastness of space. She so wanted to be going out with them, but the captain told her she had a purpose here at Haven. She let out a big sigh as she watched the starship fade into the blackness and the harbor doors close.

"It's not THAT bad is it?" asked a voice from behind her. She turned to find Eva standing there.

"I really wanted to go. They are going to need fighter pilots out there, and I am one of the best." She then thought for a moment and added "Outside of you of course…and the captain."

With that Eva smiled. She looked at the Blessed woman and noticed she was looking slightly different. She was wearing looser clothing than normal, and her forehead looked slightly bigger than it did just a few months ago. Nita wrote it off to the forces of the void she had to endure. Even though she was in suspended animation, and placed inside the protection of a star fighter I.T.C. pod, she still suffered. It had to have taken a toll on her mentally and physically.

"So, you want to be the best then? If so, we need you more then ever. I want you to train new recruits in our new fighters. But first, you have to learn to pilot these new fighters yourself. Are you up for it?"

"Hell yes!" she cried out. "A new fighter? A chance to pilot it into space…am I game? Hell yes!"

"Good! Then follow me…I want to introduce you to your new lead flight instructor…"

Benedict "Messiah" Marsh:

He turned and saw the two women as they walked into the training center. Eva, was with someone he had never seen before. She was intriguing to his eye – she was much shorter than him, and actually – everything about her was small. She had a slightly flat face, small green eyes surrounding a small pointed but slightly flat nose, small cheeks on each side of a small mouth, which sat above a small pointed chin. Her head was topped with medium length hair, which was brown, had highlights of small streaks of dishwater blond, and a slight glow of red – all tied into the standard high ponytail that most Normal women were now sporting. Her face had not turned color yet, she still had olive skin, with a few small beauty marks scattered on her cheeks. She was beautiful to him – but she was also a third his age. He had no idea who she was, but somehow was familiar to him. Her beauty kept getting in the way of his memory. He tried to put it out of his mind as he watched them tour the center. But then they turned, and walked toward him.

"Messiah…" said Eva "I want you to meet Nita…Star Child…she is your new trainee in learning the new fighters."

"Holy crap!" he shouted as the memories finally came back to him

"So, you do remember me Ben…" she said as she lit up an illuminating smile on her face. She reached out and took his hand and squeezed it. He returned the light squeeze and placed his left hand on top of hers while they shook. She then dropped his hand and reached up to give him a big hug. "Man, I never thought I would see you again. When they thawed me out they told me you were sent to your death! I thought you were gone…"

"You can thank Perfecto for that…he…he sacrificed himself for me."

She pulled back and looked at him, then softly said "My god…he took his life for you? What a wonderful person…and such a good friend."

He fought back the tears, then said "Hey, you did not come here to listen to sad tales…what do you need?"

"Training..." Eva interrupted. "She needs to be trained in the operation and flight of the Firebrands. She is going to be a trainer."

"Wonderful!" he replied. "Well, how soon do you want to start?"

"Well, if I had my way..." she answered "it would be today...now..."

"Why not?" he told her. She gave him a quizzical look. "Come on...lets get you in a pod..."

She obediently followed him to where a number of I.T.C. pods sat. He tossed her a helmet and a flight suit. Get this on and meet back here. We can take out a flock of Firebrands right now. She gave him a look then jumped in excitement and ran to the dressing pod. A moment later she returned wearing the flight suit. She placed the helmet on her head and it sealed around her and attached itself to the suit.

He opened up one of the pods and motioned her in. "I will get in a pod and we can walk through the controls after launch."

"Really?" she asked, but followed his instructions and entered the pod without any further questions. The pod hatch shut behind her and the pod filled with sensory gel. She felt the soothing tingle of the gel as it transferred small currents to her skin through the suit.

Messiah came on over her intercom "Ok, launching now. Here we go."

Indicator lights flashed showing that she had been launched into space. A moment later, the pod displays lit up with the small, bright lights of the stars. She was back out in space already, and did not even notice the pod being cradled into a ship. "I didn't even feel us launch" she admitted.

He chuckled to himself as his flock was also launched out into the vacuum of space. He ran her through a walkthrough of the controls. They were very similar to what she was used to in the Wolf Pack star fighters, so she caught on quickly. "Ok, let's launch some drones and practice some dogfighting in the new fighter configuration."

"Sure, no problem with a simulation. Looking forward to getting out there and fighting the drones for real practice..." she commented.

He gave a slight chuckle, and turned the aggressiveness of the drones up to full. "Ok, let's make it a real challenge then..."

The pair bounced back and forth between covering each other's wing and being the aggressive attacker. Benedict was actually surprised how well they seemed to jell in pair formation fighting. He wondered if she would become his wing person – he decided he would ask her later. An aggressive drone took him away from his thoughts as it snuck up behind him and began trying to take him down. He made a quick barrel roll maneuver to escape the weapons fire, but the drone then moved off and onto Nita's flock. A moment later he heard her scream as she felt the fire hitting her drone. The pod was sensing the weapon hitting her Firebrand frame and was reporting the hits as real pain through the gel. A moment later, the fighter exploded.

She felt the pain, saw the explosion, and the pod went dark for a brief second. Then the stars came back and she was moving again. "What the hell?" she pondered as she looked to the left of her and saw one of her Firebrands exploding. She had lost a whelp. "Damn! I can't believe I lost one!" she yelled. She then thought for a moment and asked Messiah "Wait, I was feeling the pain as if it was my ship. What the hell happened?"

"Finish off these drones, and I will tell you..." he replied.

"But, it felt as if I was actually being shot. Not like a simulation."

"Finish these off first..." he ordered.

The pair finished off the remaining drones, and prepared to land. They saw the harbor dock doors open, and they flew the ships into the harbor. A few minutes later, they were entering the fighter landing bay. A moment after they landed, the pod lit up, quickly drained, and the door opened. She exited out of the pod into the training room. She had never left, but felt like she was actually flying. "That was an amazing simulation!" she told him.

"It was no simulation..." he replied. She gave him a quizzical look. "You were actually flying the flock. The Firebrands

282

are pure remote controlled fighters. We never have to risk a pilot in space battle again."

"What? It felt so real...You mean to tell me we will be fighting remote controlled from now on?" she asked

"I hope. I never want to lose a pilot again, and with the Firebrands, that might be the way to avoid any of our pilot's from dying."

"So, we were actually out there? The Firebrands versus the drones?" He shook his head yes. "Amazing..." Then she pondered for a moment, before asking "Won't the pilots get complacent about the job? Won't they not care if they are shot down?"

"As you saw, you felt the heat when your fighter was shot down. To make sure they don't just let them burn, the tactile controls will make the burning feeling intensify for every ship they lose. If they lose three ships, the control pod will deactivate and release the pilot from duty. I somehow have a feeling however, that if we have a pilot in the control pod, they will not be thinking about anything but the battle. However, if we run into a situation where we know we will lose a bunch of fighters, we have the ability to disable the tactile controls and loss limiters. But as you can see, it is intense in there...the pilots will not lose their concentration."

"I'll say...I actually thought we had been launched! Wow, so amazing!" She raised her arms to embrace the pod chamber, and then spun herself around like a kid in a candy store.

Benedict chuckled, then told her "We have quite a few amazing things going on here. Perhaps after you get settled, you would like a tour?"

"Yes, I would. Will you give me that tour?"

"I would be honored. Twenty-six-hundred hours perhaps?" he asked.

"Only if you buy dinner too!" she ordered. He nodded his head yes. "Okay, see you at twenty-six-hundred then...Ben. You don't mind if I call you Ben?" she said as she waved at him and walked off.

She didn't give him a chance to reply. He simply shook his head in disbelief. He never knew he would get so friendly with her. Then he looked down at his hand – it tingled.

February, 2051...

He was out of ammo, and he still had three southern taskers surrounding him. They were hiding amongst the crates and boxes in the cargo bay of the Alliance transport ship. They had snuck aboard and were planning on blowing up the star base. With the construction going on, the south thought this to be a perfect time to sneak aboard and plant their bombs. They had not counted on him being on the transport however.

For what was just going to be a time waste, ended up putting him into a fight for his life. He had gone to the cargo bay to relax and do some low to zero-g exercising, but instead ran into the five southern soldiers – two officers and three taskers. The officers were no problem in removing, he was able to flip over them using his skills, and took them down with a pair of well-placed shots. The taskers however, had been a different story. They seemed almost as adept at low to zero-g combat as he was. They had floated away from his advances, and bounced around the area with almost as much grace as himself. Each leap, sent a flurry of beamed weapons fire across the room. It was amazing to him that none of them were actually killed by all the random fire.

Now, he hid behind the crates and wondered if they too were out of battery life in their blasters. His was a worthless molded piece of junk now. Overheated and out of power, he had no need for it anymore and had tossed it to the side.

He looked at his local area for a weapon, all that was nearby was a pull bar. He decided it would have to do.

After grabbing the bar, he slinked along the floor to get a better view of the room. He saw movement opposite of his position. He took his shoe off and slid it just to the side of a nearby crate – in a spot he knew it would be seen. He figured it would draw fire and tell him if they were still armed or if they too were ready to move to the next phase of battle. The quiet told him the latter – they were ready for hand-to-hand, and he relished at that prospect personally.

He took a chance and stepped out into the open center of the room. "C'mon you southern bastards. Let's see what you've got!" he yelled. No shots – instead, the three stepped out. He felt his adrenaline flow at the thought of the fight that was about to begin. This is what he trained for all these years. It is what he trained his cadets for...at least the ones who chose him as their trainer. He would now show all who doubted him what his techniques would do when in real battle. These three would be his real-life proving grounds.

He didn't hesitate – he leapt forward and right as his foot touched the metal surface, he hopped on his other foot, then bounced back, up, and over – doing a flip as he flew over the three soldiers. He landed softly on the metal surface behind them and planted a stiff shot of the pull bar into the head of one of the taskers. The man's head caved in with the blow and he fell to the floor. The other two, surprised, then turned and jumped back. They landed, looked at the fallen compadre, and then looked at him. He shrugged his shoulders and smiled.

The two immediately leapt into action. They jumped into the air, and he followed suit. They all met at the top of the cargo bay. They pulled out flexible attack bars from their jumpsuits and began swinging them wildly at their northern enemy while they all slowly floated back down to the floor. He countered with mixed swings and blocks, which repelled each assault with ease. Right before his foot touched the ground, he fired back as he placed the bar to the head of one of the taskers. Then upon having both feet on the metal flooring, he performed a quick roll out, which led to a swing of the bar that briefly took out the knees of the other tasker. The tasker fell to the ground and he quickly followed up and put the bar to his head, crushing it.

He looked at his remaining enemy – there was fear in his eyes as they moved back and forth, trying to find some escape, or way to victory. The opening of the cargo bay hatch gave the southerner a brief moment to try to flee. He decided taking out the person at the door would be easier than his current combatant. He was not done with the tasker however, and would not give him the chance to fight anyone else. He hopped into the low gravity and propelled himself in front of the tasker. He landed softly in front of his enemy, then banged the end of the bar against the cold steel floor.

He looked at the now-shaking man and said "Did you really think I was going to let you go?" He flipped his staff around in

286

circles as a threat. The man was shaking even harder, and in addition began losing his bladder. He looked down at the southerner's pants and shook his head. "If you are going to be afraid, the least you could do is not make a mess."

The tasker without warning, lashed out at him with a hidden expandable baton. His reflexes were too sharp however, and he easily avoided the strike attempt. With just as much speed, he knocked the weapon out of his hand then swung the bar around and caved in his head.

The door was fully open now and in jumped three uniformed Secret Service soldiers. They stopped and looked around at the five dead men lying on the cold steel surface.

"Too late boys..."

"What should I put into my report?" asked one of the soldiers.

"Just tell 'em Jeremy took care of their precious star base...You know...The guy who can train anyone to fight..." he said, then dropped the bar on the floor and walked out of the bay.

NGD: 3 Years, 5 Months, 3 Days:

Haven:

Jeremy Ponds:

It was a great dinner, and he found her fascinating. He looked at her face, and into her dark eyes. There was such mystery in those eyes, so much unknown. She had such a primitive look, her long forehead and sunken eyes, but it was not unattractive. On the contrary, she was extremely attractive, and he found himself losing his thoughts as he stared into her dark brown pools. Ever since she had stowed away onto his transport ship he had no other thoughts but her. She was hypnotic, and he was totally addicted to her. He thought, and hoped she felt the same. In the same manner, she had spent all of her free time with him – so he had high hopes.

She picked at, then took another bite of her food. "This material always fascinates me. I have never eaten anything like it, but it really is good." He looked down at his plate of protein fungus – yes, it did taste good, but he did not nearly enjoy it as much as she did. She took another big forkful of the yellow colored loaf and chewed vigorously with an open mouth. "So, what do you want to do after dinner? I have no plans, I like spending time with you, and so I think we can spend it together, don't you?"

Her bluntness always surprised him. She definitely had primitive roots, the way she spoke and her abrupt mannerisms. She was a fighter, and she had proven that many times to him in the gym. She had been joining him daily for workout and sparring sessions. She was now starting to surpass him in skill – he sometimes wondered if perhaps she was holding back.

"Well, we could watch a vid...perhaps go to the gym?" he suggested. He seemed to know she already had something planned for him – she seemed to have a way of doing that to him.

"I have a better idea..." she said.

"Ah, here we go..."

"How about we go to your place?" she said with a devilish smile on her face.

This totally took him by surprise. His mouth opened and he could not force it closed. He was not really sure *how* to react to her forwardness. But something came over him – something animalistic. He felt urges grow inside him, urges he was finding he could not control. He did not understand what was coming over him.

She continued to give him that smirk with total confidence. "You want me, don't you?"

In the back of his mind, he fought for control. His logic center told him no, as she was an alien. But the primitive, animalistic side of him said yes, take her now. In the middle, he was trapped – trapped between maintaining control and letting go. He felt himself slip to the animal side, he could not understand his lack of control – he never had a problem like this before. Something was affecting him. He had no idea what, but he could barely keep control now that she had taken this suggestive manner. There was something sweet in the air, or at least in his

288

head. It was preventing him from controlling himself. He could not understand what he smelled or felt, but he kept fighting it. "Patti..." he mumbled out. The smell got stronger, her mischievous smile even bigger, her eyes drilled into his mind.

"I'm hungry, aren't you?" She reached out and took his hand, stood up, and nodded toward the door. "Come..." she ordered. He could not help himself, all he could do is obediently follow.

Jaime Bordeaux:

Otter had contacted her with two important messages. First, the Blessed were building something big. No one was sure what it was quite yet, but it was two large structures near the opening to the Devil's Throat. They had to have been using every resource from every planetoid in the area of the five gravity wells. But even more disturbing was the second message – or its lack of message actually – something big and bad was about to happen. She would need guidance, and the only place she could get that would be if she would reform the leaders of the People Against War. This group was the focal point of Alliance resistance years ago. They were considered terrorists, and hunted down. It was believed they had been all caught and killed – or that or they just gave up and disbanded. As she travelled out into the depths of space on Starlight however, she realized that they were just in hiding. She now suspected that they actually had *planned* much of what had happened – that she was put where she was so that she could become one of their leaders.

For years before Starlight took off, she always felt fate was controlling what happened to her life. But now she wondered if that in actuality, *they* had been guiding what she would be doing, from the moment she entered the Star Patrol, until now – or even farther back than that. Now, Otter told her that something was happening, something really bad. She needed to somehow find and reform the leadership of the P.A.W., that she needed to both determine and somehow reform the organization.

She sat at the desk in her quarters and stared into nothingness. She activated the holo-image of Dex. She stared at his face and wondered what he would tell her to do in this situation. Did he know about the People Against War – was he part of it? Looking at his image again brought a tear to her eye, it always did as she missed him so. Finally, she gave a loud, heavy sigh and turned off the image.

She activated her computer, and resumed her continued search of historical records regarding the organization. Until recently, she did not have what she needed to figure out their structure – as it had been censored the Alliance. Jonathan recently had given her a personal copy of his search worm program. She had been using it to find the actual historical records of the group. Upon activating her computer, she received a message that more data had been found.

She read through the secret documents – the Alliance had more information about the group than anyone probably thought. The only thing they did not have, were the names – the organizers were good at covering their tracks in that aspect at least. Or, did they actually allow for the structure to be discovered and documented in this manner? Thus someday, someone like herself would search out and find this information – the information this selected person would need, to reform, or discover the group. In these new documents, it was revealed that somehow the Supreme Commander had discovered the group's internal structure, this structure was all listed in these documents. Their structure was broken down based on skills and tasks. There was the leader, the administrator, the recruiter, the trainer, the mechanic, and the proctor. Each position in the leadership structure had a purpose to the entire organization, but at the same time, the organization could run without one or all of them. This way, plans could still be made and executed, ideas could be spread, and people recruited.

The leader made the hard decisions, he or she would determine what the group would do and how they would do it. The administrator would put people and resources together for the common good. The recruiter would seek out new dissidents, discover a person's loyalty, and convince them to join if they agreed with their thinking. The trainer would develop the new recruits, make them strong of both body and mind. The mechanic provided the resources for achieving the group's goals. The proctor was to test any new recruits, for both loyalty and mettle

– anyone that did not pass the test, or was not found to be truthful in their conviction, or was discovered to be traitorous to the cause, was dealt with by the proctor. There were backups and redundancy in the event one or all of the leadership was caught or killed. Everyone knew their part, did their parts, worked their tasks, and yet somehow they all managed to avoid being discovered all these years.

She assumed she was to be the leader, she wondered if she was a replacement, or perhaps only a backup, or a backup that needed to be activated. Since she determined she was to be leader, that left the other five positions of the command structure. She thought about it and four people came to mind – she really was not sure why it did not come to her before.

Now, she had decided to take the chance. She had decided now is the time to flush them out. If her suspicions were correct, they would show up and she could confront them confidently. If not, she might jeopardize herself and any actual members she correctly identified – especially if a wrong pick brought in a Blessed spy. However, if any of her choices were actually a spy, she would need to know and deal with that person quickly.

The chance was worth taking the risk – one by one she contacted them via Norm-Comm, and scheduled a meeting. She would confront all of them one at a time. She would discover if she was right, or deadly wrong.

*   *   *

The door slid open. "Ah, there you are…come in" she said as she waved her hand toward a chair at a small round table. The table was white, and had an illumination panel that shined brightly down onto the surface. There were six black chairs that surrounded the bright white table. The room appeared dark compared to the brightly lit table. Jaime sat in the farthest chair from the door – she motioned toward the chair to the closest left of her.

"What can I do for you? Six chairs…what's going on?" the person asked.

"Actually, I think it is what I can do for...you" she quickly replied. "I have a suspicion...I think I was meant to be the leader, am I wrong?" she asked.

The shadowed person looked at her, then answered "Of course, you are the captain. You were meant to lead."

"Oh c'mon..." she blurted out. "I think you know what I mean...Max." she leaned in to look square into her doctor's eyes. "You have known for years. And now, I know..."

"What the hell are you talking about Jaime?" he asked with annoyance in his voice.

The annunciator surprised him as his eyes darted toward the door. "I think our next guest has arrived." She pressed a button on her command module, and the door slid open. "Come in...Allen..." as soon as the door closed behind him she added "Or should I call you recruiter?"

He had his mouth open about to ask what was going on before she said that. He kept his mouth open for a moment while he thought about it. Then closed it and looked at her before saying "Are you sure you are speaking to the right person? I am simply another starship captain."

"And the man who recruited me. Please, don't insult my intelligence by lying about it." She motioned to the chair on the right of her. "Sit..." she ordered, then added "recruiter..."

As Allen sat down, Max said "Jaime, you've got this all wrong..."

"Do I, administrator?" she added. He quickly closed his mouth and went quiet. She looked at her command module before saying "Well, any moment now..." the door annunciator added to her confident demeanor. "That should be...the mechanic." Both Allen and Max gave a slightly pained look – Jaime knew she had them. She commanded the door to open and there stood Jonathan. "Please come in Jonathan..." she motioned to the next chair on the left.

"What...what's going on?" the younger man asked.

"Looks like the gig is up..." replied Max.

"She knows..." added Allen. Jonathan gulped.

"Now we need the trainer..." she said as she looked at the time on her command module. The door never buzzed. She waited for two minutes, looked at her module again, then gave a troubled look. "He should have shown, even if he suspected something. This is not like..."

"Like who Jaime?" asked Max. "Who do you suspect it is?"

"I...I thought it was Jeremy. But even if it wasn't, why isn't he here?" she queried.

"She's right, it's not like him..." Allen added. He tapped on his Norm-Comm and signaled him, but got no reply.

"Who saw him last?" Jaime asked.

"I saw him with Patti earlier this evening." Jonathan answered.

"Damn!" she softly said as she activated her Norm-Comm and signaled him. She waited a moment and signaled again. "Guys, I'm a bit worried...we really don't know much about..."

She was interrupted by the presence standing at the open door. To their surprise, none of them even heard the door opening. "About who?" Jeremy, standing at the open door asked. Patti stood next to him, her arm in his.

"Jeremy!" Jaime called to him. "Well, when you did not answer your Norm-Comm, we got worried. Since you were last seen with Patti, and she IS after all from an alien planet...we were a bit concerned that..."

"I ate him?" she quizzed with a smirk on her face. She let the thought sink in before saying. "I may not be like you, but I do have feelings just like any sentient being. I like Jeremy, and I wanted to be with him...you can understand that I hope. Well, once we went to his room, I guess him being with me must have shorted out his communications? I really would not know..."

Jaime looked at her with suspicion. However, she relaxed slightly once she looked up at the smiling man. He did look totally happy and content. "Very well, please sit here..." she said and pointed to the chair on the right. She then looked at the young girl, she was still wearing very casual clothing – a crop-tank top, and short skirt. She walked over and took a seat in one of the chairs in the darkened corner of the room.

She continued to study her until Jeremy reached across Allen, put his hand on hers, and said "I trust her, so can you."

She sighed. "Very well…So Jeremy…as you can see, I have brought together four others…three and you…who I suspect are four of the six organizers of the People Against War. I suspect you are the trainer. Am I correct?" He looked over to Patti who smiled at him, then turned back to Jaime and simply nodded yes.

"I knew it!" she cried out. "It was in front of me the entire time, and I missed it…until now! All my trusted friends and allies…you all organized this so…"

"So, we could get away from that burning war-torn mess called the planet earth." Max said, finishing up her sentence. "We were failing at our attempts to interrupt the government and the war. The machine was too strong and we were losing. So, when the Supreme Commander came up with this idea to send the Blessed into space, we started planning. We knew that if we could get out here, we could somehow find a way to escape, and to find a planet for ourselves. For years, we planned and organized. Many of the Normals that were on this ship originally were already part of P.A.W.. Leaving the others to spend time with the Blessed brought even more around. It brought YOU around…"

"It did, my friend, it did…" Jaime said as a small tear came to her eye. She always had a suspicion, and secretly hoped it would be her friends that had organized this. She placed her hand on his. She thought for a moment…organizer, recruiter, mechanic, trainer, and. She looked around "The proctor…that was the one person I could not figure out. Who is the proctor?"

"That would be me…" a voice called from the other side of the dark room.

She recognized that voice, she vowed to never forget that voice. She tapped on her command module to instantly turn the illumination panels on full. Standing in the corner, was Eva – with that standard shit-eating smirk on her face. "Damn you!" Jaime cried out as she quickly lifted her arm, aimed, and fired her command weapon at her. She fired once, twice, three, and finally four times. The screams of the four men cried out over the noise of the blasts emanating from the organic weapon on her arm. To Jaime's surprise, the beams were absorbed without doing any damage.

A strong arm grasping above her wrist pulled the weapon down and out of firing position. "Jaime, stop!" yelled Jeremy as he tugged on her arm. "Believe it or not, she is with us!"

"She is BLESSED!" Jaime spat out.

"Only in genetics..." Max said softly to her. "In mind and soul, she is one of us."

Eva yipped, then pulled out a smoldering box from her uniform pocket and tossed it onto the ground. "Damn, you stopped her just in time. Jonathan, you have to figure out a way to make these last longer. Captain, I knew you would be mad...but not that much!"

"Mad is not a proper description of how I feel!" Jaime blurted out. She looked down at the small black box smoldering on the ground. "What is that?" she asked.

Jonathan answered "That is a piece of tech Eva stole from the Blessed. It is a force projector that they are giving to their soldiers and secret service personnel." He got up, walked over, and picked up the still smoldering black box. "It sends out a small personal force field which will protect the user for two or three blasts. They had to have found this in the salvage...there is no way they would have come up with this on their own. Anyway, its only problem is that the circuit can only last long enough to stop two or three blasts, then it fries under the stress."

"You did some good...that took four of her blasts. I have to say captain, your new organic weapon really lets loose a wallop! I really thought I was done for..." Eva added.

"Well, sorry about that..." Jaime mumbled. "Eva, all those years you harassed me, and taunted me..."

"Was both a test and preparation..." she said, finishing her sentence. She then added "my back-blasting you in that final dogfight was the push you needed to leave the Star Patrol and join

Star Force, thus getting you on Starlight. Then, when you found out it was me who took you out, you accepted my duel...the final test. You let your compassion and logic take control, instead of your rage...and you let me live. It is the perfect combination we needed for command. YOU became our hope to lead us to freedom and our salvation."

"But, you are BLESSED..." she said again.

Eva replied "The Blessed were never my people. The moment I was born, I saw who and what they truly were. I decided when I was young that I could never be what they had become. I knew I would have to somehow be different. Maybe it's because I am one of the few female Blessed? Anyway, I ran into Max during that critical time of my life, when I was deciding what and how I would live...I met him after I was injured fighting a group of Blessed. I was trying to stop a group of Blessed men from raping a young Normal woman. I stopped them from raping her, and took a few of them down...but in return they almost killed me. They figured I was almost dead, so they raped, then left me for dead. Max found me, took me in, and healed me. From that moment on, I was indebted to him. I was finally able to convince him of my conviction, and he confided in me. I swore allegiance to the People Against War at that time, I am still sworn to their goal. I am one of their warriors, and now you are too!"

"You assume I am going to go along with you. You put a lot of faith that I would actually agree with your values..." she warned.

"You're here now" Max admitted. "I know you believe what we believe, you would not have gathered the organizers if you didn't. You have proven time and time again that you are one of us...you just never admitted it to yourself."

She deliberately let a long period of silence go by. Finally she said "Well, now I have...Am I the leader?" They all shook their heads yes. "Then we need to spend some time together...here...now. I need to know what I have available to me, and what to expect."

"Let me start with this..." Eva injected. "Almost every Blessed vessel has a secret weapon on board...at least one, and maybe more. They will activate if needed...like they did to Kip."

"That was you?" Jaime called out. "You caused Kip's vessel to lose to the Og?"

"No, not us directly" Eva answered. "However, it is an...asset...that we now have. An asset that we did not know about until Kip died with his ship. The moment they think it will benefit their...how should I say it...ability to get revenge...they will activate. They are not our asset...they are Blessed...but, I believe that if they think they can cause damage to them, they will."

"Good, what else do we have?" Jaime asked.

"We have tons of new tech" Jonathan answered. "The ships are being upgraded as new tech is tested and proven. I may have some changes in place on the Ladyhawk soon. Once in place I will give you a run through, Captain."

"Very good, thank you Jonathan. What else?"

"Trouble..." Patti blurted out.

Jaime looked at her with a grizzled look. "What do you mean, and why are you here...now that I think about it."

"I am here because I want to be. I know what you are doing, and I actually think that is good. I can be of help to you...but I know bad things are coming." She stood up and walked over to Jeremy and put her hand on his shoulder. "I want him...and you to be safe."

"Ok, then..." Jaime added "so what trouble is on its way?"

"Can't tell you...but you should know real soon. Maybe even before you leave this room..." she answered.

"Come on Patti..." Jaime started to berate the young savage girl, but was interrupted by Norm-Comm. She answered and listened for a moment with a pained look on her face. She now looked at Patti with a confused look. "It appears that Oomha is here...as an official ambassador of the Flaybah. He says he needs to see us immediately. I have requested he be brought to us here. How did you know?" Patti just shrugged her shoulders, not admitting to anything.

Five minutes later Oomha was standing before the six organizers. "Ah, all of you are here..." he said.

"You knew too?" Jaime blurted out. Oomha nodded his head softly in acknowledgement.

Within an instant, his face changed to the most stern look a deer could give, and with a serious, monotone voice, Oomha announced "I am here as an official representative of the Flaybah civilization. As you are humans and members of the Alliance, I am here to give you notification of our declaration of war on you, and your race."

The six shouted out in astonishment. They all started blurting out "Why" and "What did we do to start a war?"

Jaime waved her hands to quiet them down. "Oomha, we have been friends ever since we arrived. We are STILL friends. Now, tell me why we are at war with your people?"

"It's the Alliance, Jaime..." he answered. "They came to one of our home worlds and killed our people. Jaime, they ATE one of us! They are barbarians, and they must be eliminated from this galaxy. You are associated with them, and thus by this association are grouped into our declaration of war. That is...unless you are no longer associated with both them, and the human race."

"Oomha, you have always contended that we were not human. But what are we if not human?"

"Jaime..." interrupted Allen. "Have you looked in a mirror lately? None of us look...human...anymore. With this blue skin, our ears, our eyes, our hair..."

"We really are no longer human" added Max. "My scans indicate we have evolved well past being homo sapiens."

"Okay, so what are we then?" she asked.

"More than human?" Jonathan softly said. Soft chuckles filled the room.

"Well, yes. We really are the metamorphosis of Normal humans" Max commented.

Jonathan started thinking wildly out loud. "So, Metamorphed Homo Sapiens...Meta Homo Sapiens...Meta Humans...Meta Normals...Meta Homos...The Meta?" He looked up and gave the room a bright, excited, wide-eyed look.

"No that just doesn't sound right..." commented Jaime, causing Jonathan to give a sad, disappointed look.

"Well, we are definitely evolved humans." Max added. "Evolved Homo Sapiens is more like what we have become."

"Evolved...no Evo Sapiens!" blurted Jonathan. The whole room stopped talking and began to think about what he said. Some heads began to nod in affirmation. Finally, he added "Maybe just shorten it to...The Evo? It is kind of catchy if you ask me."

Jaime thought about it a moment before saying "You know, it IS kind of catchy...AND it would give us the real difference in identification when dealing with other races. What do the organizers think?"

They all agreed with nods. Eva even nodded her head yes, but had a sad look as she felt she might be left all alone again.

"Very well...Max, will you write up a proclamation establishing us as Evolved or Evo Sapiens, also known as the Evo, and then write another proclamation officially withdrawing us from the Alliance." As Jaime spoke, Max nodded his head in agreement.

"You know" Eva interrupted "the moment you announce those proclamations, they will attack us here."

"Eva, does the Blessed know how much we have changed?" Jaime asked, and Eva answered with a shake of her head in the negative. "Okay, good...then the least different we look, the better. Jonathan, I am going to announce our breaking away from the Alliance. I will need you to make me look like the old Jaime...the way I looked before evolving. Can you do that?" The young man nodded his head yes. "Good, then we will write up the proclamation, I will announce it to the Blessed, and we will break away."

"Break from the Alliance, and you will have the interstellar confederacy here to protect you." Oomha announced.

"We Flaybah will have at least one ship stationed here at all times. I doubt they will attack you. They would be foolish to try at least."

"They have done stupider things..." said Jaime, who then looked at Eva "Present company excepted." Eva nodded her head.

Jaime stood up and ordered "Jonathan, have all Alliance logos, numbers, identification, and insignias removed from our ships. Remove all Star Force decoration from our uniforms too."

"I may have something just right to replace the Star Force uniforms with..." Jonathan said, then continued "I will get right on it...if that's ok with you Captain." He stood up, Jaime nodded at him, and he quickly left the room.

"Jaime" Oomha interrupted "You have ships out in space. You will want to get a message to them. They will need to know of the breakaway."

"Damn! That's right..." she activated Norm-Comm "Otter, can you get a message to the Innovation? It is really important we let them know about events here."

"They have been out of touch for a week now. I was able to sub-space communicate with them during their last insertion, but since they left sub-space, no communications at all. I will have to send a standard transmission and a sub-space message and hope they enter sub-space before the standard message reaches them. What should I tell them?"

Jaime gave her the details of the meeting, and the war the Blessed started with the Flaybah. She then told her "Tell them we are free. The Evo are now in control of their own destiny."

13 Years Ago:

She looked up at the stars, no matter how many times she looked, she thought they were beautiful.

"They still twinkle, every time we come up here, they're still twinkling. Thank you, daddy."

He rolled onto his side, brushed her hair aside, and gave her a kiss on the forehead. "You're welcome, my little stargazer."

"Someday, I am going to go there...I am going to see one of those stars."

He looked at her, and said "You are, eh? Well, if that is what you want, then you will do it. Just keep working at your star studies. They might need an astronomer on a space flight someday."

She loved her father with all her heart, but she also knew he did not mean a thing he said. He never wanted her to leave the earth, never wanted her out in space. He intended for these trips to the star base to be the only times for her to be out near the stars. Coming up for use of the Alliance space telescope were the only times he intended for her to be out in space. But she had other plans – she had been practicing her piloting skills. She intended to rocket into outer space someday. She was going to find those other planets hidden in those twinkling lights that were the stars.

NGD: 3 Years, 5 Months, 12 Days:

Sector N, System C567, Planet 4:

Captain Halley Cet:

The landing team found nothing but rock and ice below their feet. Advanced scans detected tunnels and passageways, and they were hoping that there was something underneath the ice that might sustain a colony. However, the returns from their scans so far were disappointing. The Scans showed no life, or any ability to sustain life – this was a barren world.

Halley, Katsumi, and Jaenar stood at the opening to a cavern structure. Halley had landed the shuttle as close as possible to the opening, but the walk to the shelter of the cavern opening had still been long and painful thanks to the wind. The bitter cold wind howled, and pushed the cold air through the intricate, protective, webbed layer of their environment suits. Their faces and heads were protected by a clear acrylic shell. Heat packs were strapped to their arms to provide warmth to their suits, and to heat the air the suits took in from the outside to keep their atmospheric supplies fresh.

"Why did we want to land and explore here? Outwardly, I see nothing of interest and not sure any colony could ever survive here." Halley asked.

Jaenar answered "Your scans show that this area was populated at one time."

Katsumi added "Also, scans found cellular traces that closely match humans."

This made Halley stop to turn and look at Katsumi with a raised eyebrow before saying "Well, let's stop standing out here in the cold, and go see what's in there!"

The trio entered the small opening which led into a much larger cavern – much larger than they thought. Inside, they noticed that the original opening of this portion of the cavern had been closed off by the encroaching ice to a size just big enough to walk through – but at one time however, they could tell the opening was quite large. Outside light somehow managed to sift through the ice, which illuminated the large cavern with filtered light. As the three began to wander around the interior and sides of the large cave, they noticed residue on the floor and walls.

Katsumi used her hand scanner to analyze the soot on the wall. After a moment of scanning she analyzed the readouts then said "This residue is from an engine blast – possibly an ion drive."

"So, whoever lived here was space faring?" Halley asked. Katsumi nodded yes. Halley looked to Jaenar "Your people knew nothing of this planet?"

"No" the deer replied. "We never ventured this far into our galaxy...we had no need to explore. There are so many races and species in our galaxy that owned so many nearby planets...we figured we were lucky enough to have the three planets we had. We never really ventured out past a few sectors...definitely never to this part of the galaxy."

Katsumi continued her scans, she was now waving the scanner probe along the floor. She stopped and looked up at Halley. "These marks...they are from some form of anti-gravity energy. Nothing like I have ever seen, and I have seen anti-gravity energy before. So, I am not totally sure WHAT powered whatever landed here..."

"So, basically whoever lived here was more advanced than either humans or Flaybah" Halley said.

"It would appear that way..." Jaenar answered.

"Then I suggest we explore further..." Halley said.

"Halley, we should leave a marker here and leave them along our route as we venture forth. I do not want to be lost here." Jaenar suggested.

"Good idea" she agreed.

They left an RF marker signal device and ventured into the cave system via a smaller opening on the far side of the larger ice-filled cavern entrance. On the floor were what appeared to be some form of rails. Activating their suit lights they proceeded to wander farther and farther down into the icy maze of caverns. They left marker signals every hundred feet so they could find a quick way out and to avoid traveling in circles. Eventually, the ice succumbed to rock and the walls opened to a larger network of cavern passageways. Soon, it became evident that the widening walls were caused by excavation.

They travelled for miles through the winding passageways. All through the caverns were the signs of mining. Rock had been cleared out of sections of the cavern, signs of tool marks and digging were all around them as they passed through the empty caves. Finally, they came upon a room that had been dug into the rock wall. In this room, and to their surprise, they found sleeping cots.

They shined their lights around the room. Dust filled the air as they entered the area, and reflected in the lights of their suits. There were hundreds of cots that littered the floor. Halley recognized the cots as similar to the ones they slept on while they worked on the excavation of Haven. She realized that these cots were shaped for a human. "These are for humans to sleep on..." she announced. "Why would they have cots for humans to sleep on?"

"It may have been a race that is similar in shape to humans" Jaenar replied. Halley grumbled at that suggestion.

They wandered around the large excavated room. Halley on one side, Katsumi and Jaenar on the other. Katsumi looked under one of the cots and spotted a number of pairs of small, ivory- colored, round, plastic-looking, cylinders. Approximately three quarters of an inch tall, an inch across, with a small rounded bump on the top. She started to reach for one and felt the teeth of an animal on her arm. She turned her head to find Jaenar – her mouth around her arm, pulling her back.

"You must not touch that..." she said. "Not with your hand..." she added.

"Ok then..." Katsumi gave in and took out a pair of scientific tongs. She picked up the cylinder with the tongs and held it up to eye level to examine. "So, what is so dangerous about these?"

"Hold your finger no closer than six inches from the device." Jaenar instructed. When Katusmi did this two dozen small tentacles shot out of the bottom of the device toward her extended finger. Katsumi gave a shriek and pulled her finger back, causing the tentacles to withdrawal back into the ivory plastic surface.

"How did you know?" Katsumi asked.

"Yes, I would like to know this too...how you knew it would do that" added Halley.

"Because the race that mined here also attempted to do the same with the Flaybah home world. They made an attempt to enslave us, but we were lucky enough to have the strength to repel them. I do not know of the name of the race, as it was before my time, and much of our history of that time was deleted. But I know something of this race and their effect on our heritage nonetheless. The creatures that used those devices were insectoid, according to the history records that do exist. I had read that after their defeat at the hands of the Flaybah, they had gone into hiding. Becoming scavengers of other, less advanced races. Stealing individuals of these various races as slaves and making them mine for wealth and resources. I guess the stories were true. That device, it is called a "fear mod". It appears to have a taste for human flesh."

"That would also explain this..." said Halley who motioned the pair to her location. When they arrived they both gasped in shock. In front of Halley was a pile of skeletal bones – human bones. "This explains many of the stories of alien abduction. They came to earth and took us as slaves. Put those devices on us and worked us to death. Tell me you did not know of this Jaenar!"

"If I had...I would not have suggested we come down here. I only know of the stories, and those devices. They left those on our planet in their haste to leave. They were attuned to Flaybah flesh. They left anyone unlucky enough to find, and touch one with an insanity we were unable to cure."

"I'm taking these..." interrupted Katsumi. "I want to study them, captain. I'll be careful."

"Very well. As long as you isolate them I see no reason not to take a pair."

"Or two.." added Katsumi.

"Or two."

She took four pair.

Space Ark Starlight:

Boral Oldham:

Even before he was sent the message, he had the feeling this was going to be a horrible day. He never slept very well anymore – seeing the loss of Kip was almost too much too much for him to bear. He was after all, only one man – sure, he was Blessed and was bred to handle it – but still the burden was becoming heavy on his soul.

He got out of bed and scratched the growths in front of his armpits. *"Did they move on their own?"* They had become long the past couple of months. They now hung down to his waist, and they had grown finger-like digits that now appeared to be moving independently. It was becoming harder and harder to hide them in his normal uniform, and because of that he had changed to a looser fitting tunic for normal wear. He looked in the mirror – his hair appeared to have receded even more than the day before – that or his forehead had grown. The way things had gone of late, nothing would surprise him.

So when the two messages arrived, this also did not surprise him. The first, the declaration of war on the Blessed by the Flaybah. This worried him a little, as they appeared to have a fleet of big ships. He wondered however, was how big was their fleet?. He had never seen more than three Flaybah battleships at any one time. Maybe that was all they had – maybe their fleet was only three ships.

He flipped his computer from the Flaybah message to the fleet status. The Blessed had taken the lead in manufacturing superiority. They had salvaged practically everything from most of the planetoids that blocked the gravity wells, which made up the six portals to other galaxies. All but Plug had produced vast amounts of materials and technology. These materials were used to build and amass his fleet. Plug however, was already stripped clean. He wondered if there had ever been anything on that planetoid. He wondered if perhaps the races of that galaxy knew better than to fly through their version of the Devil's Throat – perhaps they knew what awaited them on the this side.

Yes, they had done well. His fleet status now showed thirty five ships making up the growing fleet. The last three partially being built from the salvaged remains of Kip's doomed vessel. He looked over the inventory of his weapons of war: Starlight, Ultimate, ten Super Hammerheads, fourteen Hammerheads, five Makos, and two of the newly designed Great White battleships. It was an impressive fleet.

Then, there were the new battle stations being built to protect the Devil's Throat. They had not been named yet, but they were two impressive protective structures. Once they were built to almost completion, their force fields would be activated and the Throat would be gated – with the Blessed holding the key.

Yes, the fleet and the bases were in good shape. It was everything else that was going to hell. The Flaybah were an annoyance, but they could be handled. He would have to send spy drones, and try to discover their forces and numbers.

Now the Norms...he read over the report...they now called themselves *The Evo*...those traitors would have to be dealt with. They had been nothing but a thorn in his side ever since the day they left earth. He activated the message to see...her. There she was again, her stupid pale face and reddish blonde hair in that ponytail that still brings pain when he thinks about the damage it did to him years ago. Those bright blue eyes and those damn stupid freckles. There was nothing about her that appealed to him any longer – he actually wondered what he saw in her all those years ago. No matter - now she and her Norm followers were traitors. He activated the transmission and watched her message.

"Because of the activities of the Blessed, we the Normal humans formerly from the planet earth can no longer be aligned with them or their actions. We, the Normal humans in this galaxy, now officially withdrawal from participation in the activities of the Blessed, and the Alliance of Northern Order. We are becoming an independent people, free from the tyranny of the Alliance, the Supreme Commander, the Council of Order, and more locally the Blessed. We renounce our relationship from the Blessed, and announce our independence as a free people and society. As a way to identify and segregate us from the Alliance and Blessed, we are asking the races of this galaxy to know us as The Evo. In addition, we do not align ourselves with the activities of the Blessed in regard to the Flaybah. We are attempting to stay independent from the war between these two peoples, but at the same time are accepting the protection and hospitality of the Star Confederacy. We hope that the Blessed will respect our independence and leave us in peace. Thank you."

He picked up, and tossed the holo-projector across the room. "Traitorous bitch! After all I did for her, this is how she thanks me for bringing her traitorous ass out here." He stood up and walked to the window to look once again at the star bases under construction. Each of the two future base sections looked like giant cubes connected by a central tube – that tube connector was to house the new field projectors that would be used to seal the gravity well. Looking at his two new battle stations comforted, and calmed him.

Finally calmed, he turned and activated his view screen to his first officer. "Get my contract writers to put together a proclamation...a proclamation of war against the Evo. Those bastards will not get away with their traitorous behavior. Send signals to the ships in the fleet – any Norm...or Evo...ships spotted may be fired upon at the discretion of the captain. They are free to indulge their need get their aggressions out by damaging or destroying the hulls of the Norm...the Evo ships. Also, round up any Norms still on any ships in our fleet. We will put them back in the freezer tubes...lower the scanning prevention screens so that anyone will be able to see them in the tubes...they will make a nice human shield for the Starlight."

He shut down communications, then returned to the window and looked out at the massive battle platforms again. *"No, those traitors will never see the other side of the Throat. They will never return to their home or be allowed to make this their new home. They will be removed from both old and new galaxies."*

19 Years Ago...

War games – the time when the men come to shine, and officers are picked from that group of the very best. All of the most well-known Blessed were at this event. He was able to get his name into the computer selection banks – never mind that it was through the threats and intimidation of the computer operators that he was selected. So, here he was, and he was ready.

"Men..." announced the games commander "you have been selected as the cream of the crop, the best of the best. You have been selected to show what you are made of. Many of you will leave here defeated at the hands of more capable Blessed. But for those of you who will survive this test, you will move into command positions. You will lead our troops and Normals into battle with the scourge of the south. Your job on this exercise is to survive...survive and conquer your fellow Blessed. If you have the opportunity, you are to mark your victims with a special paint when you capture or simulate killing them. This paint will signify your kill, you will be given credits for each kill, but more importantly, you will still be alive, and in the game. Being at the end of the game, alive and well is what you want...so do what you have to do to take out the weaker of your comrades. You also will be given a bag...this bag will have one item. This one item is your survival gear. Use it well...fight hard...and good luck."

The bags were to be randomly given out to the participants. In each bag was one item of survival. He could hardly wait to see what his item would be – it could be a weapon, or some other needed item of survival. He was so excited to get his bag, open the contents, and see his survival item.

Delray Utles came up to him with his two pals; Slim Marpole and Conrad Stakes. The three looked down at him and glared – they never did like him. Each of them had a evident look of disgust on their faces. Delray said to him "I don't see how you managed to get into this game. You are so down in the rankings, such a low-life. It must have been a mistake." He threw a bag at him, and he caught the light weight canvas bag with ease. He looked at it with curiosity, and with some confusion as it was almost too light. "You should be working a latrine squad and not competing with the cream of the crop. Well, in any case you have your survival item. See you on the battlefield Morty..."

With excitement he opened his bag to find – a five foot piece of rope. He looked at the small piece of rope with disgust. They had rigged the game for him, and somehow fixed the bag to only contain this worthless item. He never felt such anger before. They were rigging the game against him, all because he was considered a lesser officer.

When the game started – all contestants were led into an underground cavern area. This cavern had everything a person could need to survive. There were fungus, insects, and even some animal life down there. There was artificial light that they used to grow trees and plants. They used the lighting to simulate day and night down there. It had everything, and it also had dangers – some poisonous mutated animals, poison plants and fungi, there were cavern sections that were filled with poison gas, and of course his fellow Blessed.

One by one, they were released into the cavern system. The highest ranked officers first – they got the head start to help ensure a victory for them. He was near the end of the starting order. He didn't care, he was going to survive and win regardless.

When his turn came, he entered the cavern and at first followed some of the footprints in the dust. Once he went far enough in however, he shifted his path away from the footprints and into the areas that were harder to trace, and be found. He still stayed nearby the main path, but kept out of sight and in the dark as much as possible. As he paralleled the main path, he found many of his fellow officers already on the ground, the paint sprayed across their bodies – the paralyzing effects of the paint keeping then unable to move or run. Those unlucky ones were not going to get a command this year.

As he snuck along through the trees and shrubs of one of the mid-point zones, he spotted Delray. He was hunched against a tree, as he hid behind a bush. He must have been waiting for someone to ambush – probably himself. He was holding a club in his hand – obviously his survival item.

Watching Delray gave him an idea, and he started to move closer and closer to his hiding spot. He determined if he was as quiet as could be, he would be able to sneak up behind the trunk of the tree where he hid. He took his time, moving twigs and leaves away for each step, he did not want any little noise to give him away. Finally, he made it to the trunk of the tree. He heard snoring – the moron had fallen asleep while waiting in ambush. He slowly took his five foot piece of rope and quietly moved it around the trunk from one hand into the other. He now had the rope on the opposite side of the tree, each hand holding one end tightly. He moved the rope slightly away from the trunk, and slowly moved his hands down until the rope was dangling in front of Delray's neck. Right before he made the rope taut, he coughed and awakened him. Delray gasped in surprise right as he brought the rope around his neck and put every ounce of his weight into pulling it as tight against the tree as possible.

Right before Delray took his last breath, he whispered in his ear "It's me, Mort Torsis, Delray. I wanted you to know that before you died." He put his leg up on the trunk of the tree and used the force of his leg to tighten the rope even tighter. Delray tried to let out a gasping plea, but he would not hear it as the rope was too tight, and his windpipe was already crushed. His body went limp and he let loose of the rope, the body fell lifelessly to the ground.

He walked around and reached into Delray's pocket, took out his marker paint and sprayed him with it. He walked away feeling quite satisfied and content. He decided the other two, and anyone else who stood in his way would meet the same fate. Him and his five foot piece of rope would take them all down if needed. He kept his promise – removing both Slim and Conrad from not only the game, but from the living. He then proceeded to take out another three more officers from the earth. Each time, marking the victim with the paint of one of the others that he had previously slain. The officials never discovered who murdered all of those men, and he had the satisfaction that they would never stand in his way again. After all, this really was the Blessed way to get ahead.

NGD: 3 Years, 6 Months, 4 Days:

Exiting Sub-Space, Sector J:

Captain Mort Torsis:

The small force was about to exit sub-space into a sector of the galaxy they had not yet seen. Mort's awakening unit activated and had given him the stimulant needed for him to quickly take command of the vessel. He slowly opened his eyes to the darkness in front of him. In thirty seconds the automated protocols would take over and move the ship out into normal space. He needed to quickly check the ship's systems and then wake his bridge crew.

The sub-space crew would now be so sick and exhausted that they would be worthless in the event of a fight. All was well on board the ship, so he signaled for the sub-space crews to take their places in the recuperation capsules. These capsules were created to rejuvenate any Blessed that had to work sub-space duty aboard a starship. Because of the damage to their bodies that traveling in sub-space caused to awake Blessed, most of the crew are put into a state of suspended animation during the journey through sub-space. In this state, they would spend their time in stasis fields that protected their bodies from the forces of the void. Once they were about to leave sub-space, the automated systems would awaken all sleeping crew members and return control to the Blessed.

In the event of any computer or equipment failure, a small crew of Blessed were required to stay awake during the trip. This crew suffered all the ill effects of the void – some would even die during voyages. The Alliance granted these brave men extra bonuses in their credit accounts, and they gave them staggered void shifts in the hopes it would help them to survive the job.

He scratched the growths in front of his underarms – they itched more and more every day. He could tell they had grown some during the voyage in the void, as they were now almost past the bottom of his chest. He made sure they were properly tucked into his tunic, then stood up and looked around the quiet bridge. Seeing that all was well, he pressed the button to awaken his bridge crew. They would need a couple of minutes to vomit and relax – as they would need to clear both their heads and their digestive tracts. Their sleeping shells provided the means for clearing out the sickness while keeping them and the ship clean and ready. Now all they needed was the time, and Mort was going to give that to them.

They were still feeling the effects of the void on their bodies, but they also knew it would just be for the remaining minute in the void once they had exited their shells. The groans of pain accompanied the opening of the shells as all of the bridge crew were exposed to the forces that filled the bridge from the void. Mort shook his head in disgust before saying "Come on you wimps, it's only a little pressure. Get the lead out and prepare for exiting sub-space...unless of course, you would like to stay here?" He was feeling the effects, but as captain he had to show the resolve and stamina to get the crew through, and out of the void. He kept the pain he felt deeply hidden, the crew could not see any weakness.

His first officer looked over his console before saying "Ready to exit sub-space, my Alpha Starship Captain!"

Mort checked all of the readouts on his console – all looked good. "Very well, open a hole and get us out of here."

The exit from sub-space occurred without a hitch. He looked at the SCADAR readouts, everything appeared normal, and no threats were detected in the immediate area. He watched as the starship Saber exited sub-space right behind them. This was the second craft in his small task force. The accompanying ship was one of the small Mako class battle support craft. It was slightly smaller in length than the Hammerhead he commanded. It was also a totally different shape and design. It was a tubular shape, with slight rounded flares in the middle of the craft. The front of the ship was pointed and in the rear sat a single crawler drive surrounded by numerous, smaller ion drives. The Mako may have been smaller, but it was powerful. It was filled with weaponry, including the latest innovation of death, the Incindiator – respectfully known as the the Midas Touch by the crews. They all had no idea who came up with the idea, or if it even worked – but anything that might give them an advantage over their new enemies the Evo would be useful.

313

It looked like this was to be a quiet patrol, at least he thought that was to be the case. That thought was shot right out into space a moment later as the alert signals sounded out. There was another vessel in the area. "Science, what is it?" he barked.

"SCADAR is detecting a vessel in our immediate area, my Alpha Starship Captain. It is...Evo...sir. A smaller configuration from the Ladyhawk...a Wyvern class star cruiser. They don't seem to be on alert, sir. They are not powering up their weapons or putting target locks on us. I don't think they know we are a threat..."

"OR, it could be a trick. Communications, get me the captain of the Saber." A moment later, the image of the first officer came onto his holo-screen. "Where the hell is your captain?" he questioned.

"Dead, Alpha Starship Captain" the younger officer replied. "His sleeper shell failed, and no alerts were sounded to the awake crew."

"Damn waste of a fine officer. Well...in any case...you are detecting that approaching vessel, correct?" The young officer nodded yes. "Good, how many shots of the Incindiator can your ship fire?"

The new captain looked down at his console before answering "Depending on how long of bursts, four at the most, sir. We only have enough materials for four short shots."

Mort knew that the Incindiator required gold to function – thus the name given "Midas Touch". That metal had become a rare commodity once again, at least to the Blessed. The most powerful and influential captains got the bulk of the available gold for their weapons – provided they already had Incindiators installed. His ship did not have one, and it was salt to the wound to him. Almost as bad was that not only did the Saber have one of the advanced weapons installed, but his sub-captain had enough influence to get some gold for it. At least he was only given enough gold for four shots. "Very well, it will have to do. I do not have to remind you that you must make your four shots count."

"Of course, my Alpha Starship Captain!" and disconnected.

"Any change in the status of the approaching vessel?" he asked his bridge crew.

"None..." replied his science officer.

"Good, they don't know. Make sure all identifiers are up and operational then" he ordered. The crew all looked up from their stations at hearing that order. "They do not know...then they will not understand why we named our vessel, Evo Destroyer. Carry on..."

Halley Cet:

"It's two Blessed vessels, one Hammerhead class, and one Mako class. The Mako class is armed to the teeth if our records are accurate" Katsumi announced while staring down at her science console.

"As if the Hammerhead did not have enough weapons to worry about, eh?" mumbled Halley. "Staci, I have a bad feeling...how far can we bring the weapons on-line without it showing on SCADAR?"

She looked up from her station console and replied "We can energize the Ultras...other than that, any other power applied to the weapons systems will show. If they have developed advanced scanning, then it is possible they could also detect the Ultras being energized."

"Very good. Katsumi, any other information I can work with?" she queried.

"Well, they do have their identification beacons active. The Mako is named...Saber. The Hammerhead...Evo Destroyer? I don't get that name at all..."

"Nor do I..." Halley replied "and I don't like the sound of it." She programmed some paths into her command computer before ordering "Helm...Kass...I am sending you some escape vectors. I want you to have all engines at the ready and your hand on the thrust control. If need be, use the vectors I have sent you to move around the two vessels." Kass read over the courses and nodded. "Lizzie, bring the systems on-line as much as possible without giving our suspicions away. Katsumi, monitor our ships systems with your advanced scanners. If you start to detect anything, then notify Lizzie so she can back the power levels down. Also, have the bubble energized and ready to deploy the moment we detect any treachery." She looked down at the dog sitting in her lap, his velvety, clear wings shaking slightly in fear. "Are you sensing something, Beau?" she asked. Beau looked up at her with big, wet eyes. She could swear she could feel the distrust of the approaching vessels through him as she stared into his eyes. "Yeah, I don't trust them either. You get in your kennel at the first sign of trouble, ok?" She petted the little dog, then looked up toward Maxine. "Maxine, give them a hail. Let's try to be friends, shall we?"

After a few moments, Maxine announced "I am getting a message from them, but it is not clear. It could be some localized interference."

"They are getting dangerously close…" said Katsumi. "Still no signs of aggression…" was all she managed to get out before the sensor alerts sounded. "Hundreds of weapons locks just hit us…their weapons are coming on line."

"Now Kass!" Halley ordered. The young helmsman pressed the engine controls and shot the ship on its pre-programmed route. Without any further orders, Staci activated the bubble and authorized weapons. Katsumi ordered the computer to select weapons locks and sent those to the weapons master. Halley was impressed with the clockwork-like motions of her new bridge crew.

"Incoming!" yelled Katsumi. A moment later, the ship was pelted with hundreds of beamed weapons and projectiles. The beams bounced off the bubble while the projectiles ricocheted off of the space carbon plates of the hull. "Survived the first volley…" she announced.

"Let's not give them another chance. Cissy, fire at will…" Kass turned the ship so the main weapons arrays were facing the bulk of the Hammerhead's hull. Cissy tapped on the computer-provided targeting points, firing every weapon at the cruiser. The standard weapons were repelled by some form of shielding, but the Ultras penetrated the shields and burned holes into the hull of the ship.

"Ultras are getting through, but our standard Alliance weapons are being blocked" the young weapons master announced. "Firing heavy gravity projectiles now." The sounds of the launchers being activated filled the bridge. A moment later they could see the shells hitting their targets. "Some damage, they're getting through."

"Captain, it appears they have found or developed some shield technology." Katsumi called out.

"Captain, the Mako is swinging around, using the Hammerhead as a shield." Staci announced.

"I am getting a strange signature from the Mako...I think they have a weapon we do not know about." Katsumi yelled with some excitement.

A second later a golden beam fired from the Saber, hitting the hull of the command section. It acted like a vegetable peeler, removing layers of the black space carbon away from the Faratainum sub-structure underneath.

"Captain, that blast just removed all of our hull plating in that section of the ship. Any hit on that section now will do major damage." Lizzie announced.

"The Mako is about to fire again!" Katsumi yelled in a state of slight panic.

"Kass, move us away from that ship!" Halley ordered. "Take us to..." she did not get a chance to finish her order before a bright light in the star screen showed the beam hitting directly in front of the bridge as more of the protective plating was being removed by the second golden bolt fired from the ship.

"We just lost more plating, captain!" Katsumi yelled out. "The bubble is off-line!"

"Definitely not out of the woods yet" said Staci. "The Hammerhead is coming around...firing"

The first shot pierced the exposed substructure, taking out a gravity generator. Everything in the bridge that was not tied down started floating. Beau was one of those things not tied down. Halley saw the floating dog, shut down her seat restraint field, and jumped into the zero-g to grab the small animal. She tossed him toward the built-in kennel in the back of the bridge. The dog effortlessly floated into the kennel, the door automatically closing behind him. She sighed as she saw the dog safe and sound in his kennel. Then the backup gravity generator activated, sending Halley to the floor.

She landed hard of the metallic floor, knocking the wind out of her. She fought to catch her breath, while also trying to shake the cobwebs out of her head. Her hand reached up to grab ahold of the command chair, while she swung her legs around in front of the chair as she attempted to get up off of the floor.

She then heard Katsumi yell out. "They have a target lock...firing!"

She heard a sizzling noise above her – when she looked, there was a red circle above her and the command chair. For a brief second, she felt burning and stinging, but then felt nothing. She heard a sucking sound, then something that sounded like the sealing of a leak. The ship and time became a blur to her. She looked up and saw the Hammerhead float out of view while the ship changed direction away from the attacker. Then the ship came into view again. She wondered through her blurred mind how slow the ship was turning...it should have been able to quickly maneuver away in retreat.

She lay on the hard steel, her mind struggled to maintain consciousness. She looked around the bridge and forced herself to count the crew. Staci, Kass, Lizzie, Cissy, Katsumi...they all were there. She looked behind her as best as possible and was able to see the deer still in her chair – she was trying to do something to fix systems. Then she turned her head the other way again, then to the side, allowing her face to lay onto the cold steel floor. In front of her was – nothing. Her eyes darted up and she saw nothing – but stars. Her eyes went the other direction and what was once her command chair was replaced with a large hole in the floor – she could see the many decks of the ship below. Blood floated over an invisible force over the large hole in the floor. She realized it was her blood – it was floating on a containment force field that kept the precious atmosphere within the bridge and the rest of the ship from escaping.

Then an explosion, but it was not her ship. All she could see was the bright flash of light in the star screen and through the hole above her head. She could not tell what exploded, but something did, and it was not her ship.

She heard random yelling, then one voice yelled out "They're about to fire again!" She understood that announcement, and in anticipation closed her eyes – then the sound of another explosion. She kept her eyes closed in expectation of death, but it never came. An eternity seemed to go by before she realized she was still alive, albeit barely. Instead of her ship being ripped apart, she heard other distant explosions. She opened her eyes and saw the sparking, burning remains of a Hammerhead battle cruiser in the star screen above her.

Staci had ran over to her and was giving her an injection. The young woman at first had a look that showed illness, but then it changed to worry, but just for a brief moment. Halley felt so bad for her, she was so young and this had to be hard on her. But then Staci's face turned stern and stone-like as she stood back up and began barking orders. She had picked her first officer well she thought.

"Now what?" She thought as something else came into view on the star screen above her. It was something she had never seen before, but then she realized that she actually had seen this craft in the past. It had three engines in the rear of the craft and two at the sides. It had a round command section and a hexagon shaped connecting section to the rear engineering section that held on to the three rear engines. She heard something over the ship to ship communications channel – it was a query for assistance. The other ship was asking if they needed help. She hoped they would reply yes. They were in bad shape and if these strangers were willing to help, then she was willing to accept it.

From that moment, another flash of time passed for Halley as she looked up through the hole in the star screen. She gazed at the actual stars showing through the blown out hole in the ship's hull. The alien ship had moved off to the side, and now all she could see were the stars both projected on the star screen and the ones whose light was actually shining through the gaping hole.

Someone was now crouching over her. They were shining a light into her eyes and asking if she could hear them. She was surprised she could understand them – the translator circuits were doing their job she thought. This alien had golden skin, but was still human in appearance. *What was she saying?* She could have sworn someone said something about a doctor, and dead. Could they be saying their doctor was dead? Her mind was such a blur, she had no realization of what was going on.

When the second alien ship appeared above her she thought maybe she was close to death. This had to be a near-death experience, a dream before leaving this life. This ship was so foreign looking that she knew it had to be a dream or a delusion. There were rings all around this strange looking ship – she assumed it was a ship at least. The rings actually were a combination of rings, gears, and cogs. They floated around the outside of a sphere with no apparent method of connection. She figured it had to be her being near death, as nothing she had ever seen could look like that. It was so beautiful to watch – the rings swirling around in random orbits around a silver core.

She tried to sit up but could not get the strength in her legs to move. She realized in her haze that she could not feel her legs at all. Her arm also felt numb, and thus she wondered if her back was broken. When she turned her head to the side to once again look down the hole in the floor, she saw the blood floating on the force field. She could not feel her arm, but she had a burning in her shoulder, and her mind realized she did not see any part of her arm when she looked at the hole. Finally, the reality came to her – her arm was gone, it had been burned off in the attack.

Then she saw the bright light and heard another voice – she remembered a voice like that. It spoke English also, and if her mind was not such a mess she might have been able to recognize that voice. Instead however, it was just a voice she knew she understood. She felt something pick her up. She also understood the simple words it was telling the others. All it said was "I will care for her."

First Officer Staci Smitters:

The whole battle started so quickly that she never realized what had happened until it was all almost over. The two Blessed vessels attacked them for some reason. They somehow melted through the black space carbon shielding, and then blew a hole right through the command module of the ship. They almost took the bridge out – only luck saved them all from disaster. The beam somehow had only made a small hole through the various levels of the ship. In through the top and out through the bottom of the ship the damage had went. The emergency force fields had done their jobs and instantly activated upon the detection of a breach of the atmosphere. Each level was sealed off from the other, in the event of further breaches in other parts of the ship. *The ship might make it through this.*

The one item damaged that could not be replaced was the ship's captain. She was now flat on her back on the floor, no legs, and missing one arm. She was attempting to get back into the command seat when the blast issued forth. Luck was with her though, as if she had made it back into her chair, she would now be gone. The entire chair had been burned away with the decks above and below. But perhaps death would have been better than reality, as now she was missing three limbs. More luck on her side she also realized, as the force fields activated fast enough that she did not get sucked out of the ship with the escaping atmosphere.

As she regained her sense of duty, she realized that now was not the time for panic. She reached into her console and pulled out an emergency med kit. Thinking back to her training, she opened the kit and found the injector with the pain blocking medications. She ran over to her wounded captain and looked down at her. The beam blast removed her limbs, but at the same time saved her from bleeding out by cauterizing her wounds. Halley was conscious, but she could tell her mind was in some distant place. She just stared up at the star screen without any realization of her condition or predicament. She put the injector to her neck and squeezed the trigger pumping the numbing fluid into her system. The fluid would also further relax her, allowing her to rest and for Staci to do what she needed to do – try to save the ship.

She looked down at the hole and saw a small pool of blood that had formed on the force field surface. It was her captain's blood, and seeing it almost made her sick. She gagged a couple times while she fought the battle with her stomach, forced down her bile, and prevented her vomiting. She stood up and looked away to clear the sickness in her mind. She crouched down again and looked into her captains eyes with both sorrow and worry. She was needed elsewhere she knew, and with her captain at least as stable as possible as she needed to do her job. She stood back up, ran back to the console, and put the injector back into the kit. She looked at her ship's systems – main power was down, the bubble and weapons were down, they had limited scanning – they were not totally blind at least. They still had visuals as the star screen was still functioning.

"Lizzie, where's our power?" she yelled out over the alerts.

"Working on it..." Lizzie mumbled as she furiously issued rerouting commands into her console. First she was able to shut down the alert notifications. Another moment later the console lights all flickered back to life. Alert sounds restarted and coursed their loud chiming throughout the ship.

"Can we cut the alert klaxons off?" Staci yelled out. Lizzie worked on it, and a moment later, the bridge was much quieter.

"Science, what's going on out there?" she asked.

"The Mako is coming around for another attack. I am seeing sensor signatures of that beam powering up again. If they hit us like they just did, we will have absolutely no defense left on our hull – we'll be sitting ducks."

"Great...Cissy, weapons?"

"I can fire some shells and maybe the Ultras a couple times. Provided they charge quick enough...and our dark matter containment was not ruptured by the damage..." she answered.

Staci looked at Lizzie who shook her head no. "I think our containment is alright, prepare your Ultras. Helm?"

"I have no engine power whatsoever" she replied.

"Crap..." Staci sighed, then looked at Lizzie.

"I might have a Pulsar or two up in a minute, maybe two" she said to fill in the unasked question.

"Well, we might be dead by then...do what you can..." she softly told her.

"Mako is in firing position, golden weapon is charging" Katsumi yelled out. She then looked up into the sky for a silent prayer, anticipating the worst. As if answering her, the Mako simply exploded.

"Did we do that?" Staci asked after she recovered from covering her eyes from the bright blast.

"I didn't fire..." answered Cissy.

Katsumi looked down at her sensor reports and said "That was internal...it blew up from inside."

"Did we damage it enough to cause that?" asked Staci.

"I was shooting at the Hammerhead most of the time" replied Cissy. "I doubt it was anything we did."

"Speaking of the Hammerhead, it is now coming in for an attack run..." Katsumi yelled out. She heard a beep of her sensor alert, and resumed looking at her readouts. "First officer, another ship has entered this sector of space and is on an intercept course. It is of unknown configuration. They are now within weapons range...firing...missiles..." she looked up from her monitor and said with confusion "Atomics?"

"What?" Staci yelled out right before the first missile hit the Hammerhead. It only took one shot of the powerful weapon to take down the large battle cruiser. The warhead exploded in the rear of the ship – at possibly the best place to fire a nuclear missile if you wanted to take out a Hammerhead class ship – in the engineering and propulsion section. The second missile was probably not needed, but did even more damage, causing the hull to breach and the ship to explode into millions of pieces.

Katsumi was back to monitoring the sensors. The bridge became silent as everyone realized that their battle with the Blessed had just ended – but now they had a potential new threat ahead of them. As she monitored, she told Staci "It was as if they knew exactly where to hit them. As if they knew the design of the

Hammerhead." She studied the sensor and SCADAR returns further, then looked up with a look of surprise and shock on her face – very unusual for her. She then said "First officer, the ship is of Southern Union design and markings."

"Then that's the ship that escaped earth before us..." she assumed. Katsumi nodded in agreement.

Maxine called out "First officer, they are hailing us..."

A face projected onto the holo-screen in the center of the bridge. A woman's face looked into the room at Staci. She had golden skin, her hair was colored like a rich dark cup of bold coffee, was cut short, and pulled back. She had bright brown eyes with small eye brows of matching hair color, a thick but short nose, large plump lips – currently giving a serious look as there was no smile, and a pair of thin, but rounded cheeks and matching chin. On her collar were insignias that she recognized as the rank of captain in the Southern Hemispheric Union Air Force. When the woman turned her head, Staci was caught off guard by the wings on her ears – wings just like theirs. The only real difference, now that she thought about it, was the skin tone – golden and not blue.

She looked around the bridge again, trying to pick out any possible details before saying. "This is the starship Libertad, I am captain Nina Bonaventure.

"First officer Staci Smitters. I am acting captain." She replied.

"Is your captain dead?" she asked sternly.

"No, but badly injured" she answered.

"Acting captain..." she said with a slight Spanish accent injected into her Alliance English "I believe that in THIS galaxy we are no longer enemies. Am I to assume that you are at war with the Alliance pigs known as the Blessed?"

"Judging from what we just experienced, I would say, yes" Staci assumed.

"Then, we are allies. I will send a team over there to help..." she turned to give orders, then stopped and turned back

324

to Staci and said "With your permission of course..." Staci just nodded yes. The southern captain disconnected immediately.

A moment later, Katsumi announced "First officer, a shuttle is about to dock..."

"Wow, that was fast" she remarked.

A few minutes later, the boarding party arrived at the security door to the bridge. Staci authorized their entry, and in walked three space-suited people. Their suits gleaned in bright shiny gold foil and gold helmets. They took a moment and pulled out hand scanners and started waving them around the room. Staci chuckled as she realized they were sampling and testing the atmosphere in the bridge. A minute later, they removed their helmets.

The first person to remove their helmet was a golden skinned redhead. She had bright green but very thin eyes that seemed to have the ability to fire lasers through a person. Her face was small – a small upturned nose, pointed chin, and medium sized cheeks on the sides of a small mouth. She looked at Staci, examining her before saying "So, are you the first officer?" Staci walked over to her, but before she reached her the young woman looked over to Halley laying on the floor "Is this your captain? Where is your doctor?"

"My reports are that she is dead...and you are?" she walked over to catch up with the young redhead.

"Ah, sorry...first officer Kylie Van Sycic" she gave a short snappy salute.

Staci followed with a short salute then realized "Ah, South African? I am guessing from your accent..." Staci knew that not everyone in the Southern Hemispheric Union spoke standard Spanish. Some former independents, such as South Africa and Australia did not recognize or adopt a standard language. Thus, although all children were taught and were fluent in Spanish, they also spoke in their native forms of English. The accents in her dialect were what proved her heritage – as she spoke, she definitely pronounced her words differently.

"She's definitely a fokken' mess..." she said then looked back down to her. Staci seem to catch her staring into her captain's eyes a little more excessively than she normally would expect, and she wondered why. After a moment, she reached out and moved the dark brown hair from her eyes, and stared a few moments more. She then stood up, turned to Staci and said "We do not have much in the way of supplies to help you get your vessel started, but we can assist with salvaging what you need from those wrecks out there. We assume you are the Evo?" Staci gave her a confused look. "The enemy of the northern bahstard Blessed?"

"We definitely are not their friends..." she said while she tried to figure out what went on while they had been out in this part of the galaxy. "We have been on exploration patrol and have been out of touch..." she added.

"Ah, well that explains why you were caught so off guard then. The reports are that the Blessed are at war with two races, the Evo and the Flaybah."

Hearing this made Jaenar jump up out of her seat. She loudly yelled out "What??"

This startled the golden skinned officer, who quickly turned around. She was caught off guard, but composed enough to cause her to put her hand on, but not draw her weapon. She looked quizzically at the Flaybah female before saying to Staci "What is that bok? Did you find and bring deers from earth?"

"I..." Jaenar said loudly "am Flaybah! And I guess we are at war..."

Kylie gave a small chuckle, then said "Yes, you are at war. You and your dark skinned friends here...although I guess you didn't know that until a few minutes ago." A small bark came from near Jaenar. Kylie looked down to the right of Jaenar and saw the kennel built into the wall of the bridge. She walked over and looked into the opening. Beau stopped barking and looked at the southern officer. She smiled at the little dog and held out her hand. He sniffed at it and gave it a small lick. "Well, my little friend I see your northern friends have an appreciation for wonderful animals! Perro will want to meet you..."

"Perro?" asked Staci.

"Yes, that is the captain's pet. They should get along nicely..." she replied.

Their quiet moment was broken up by the proximity alert – another ship was entering their space. "Crap, now what?" Staci exclaimed.

"Starship exiting sub-space, first officer. It is on an intercept course to us. Will be here in thirty seconds and to be honest, I have no idea who or what it is." Katsumi announced.

"Well Kylie, I hope for both our sakes they are friendly. We have no defenses on-line yet."

The southern first officer looked up at the star screen and saw the vessel as it came into view. "Fok..." she sighed.

It was a large spherical shaped vessel. The main body had the coloration of shimmering swirls of silver and gray. Wrapped all around the sphere were tens of circular rings. Some of the rings were flat bands, some were cog shaped with teeth on inside and some with teeth on the outside. They all circled the sphere in different orbits – it amazed Staci that none of the rings actually touched or interfered with each other. It zoomed in, and just as quickly stopped immediately above the Innovation – between them, and the southern ship.

A moment later, a female voice boomed throughout the entire bridge "I am coming aboard."

A second after the message, a bright glow appeared right above the hole in the floor of the bridge. Something stepped out of the light and picked up Halley with one arm. The creature appeared mechanical, humanoid, and female. Staci started to run to the thing, while reaching for the blaster in her holster.

The creature held up a free hand with an open palm facing Staci – as if to say stop. Staci stopped running and stood in place. She stepped back into the bright light and right before the light took the two of them away said "I will care for her..."

The two first officers watched as the spherical ship simply floated away unimpeded. To their surprise, they watched as the ship stopped, then with some sort of beam collected all of the pieces of the wrecked Blessed spacecraft. It then moved the pieces into a small circular area, collected a few pieces of the disassembled starships for itself, then moved the remaining parts into a loose sphere, creating a slowly spinning ball of shattered metal. Once the collecting was complete, the ship just floated away. There was nothing they could do or say.

Finally, Staci said "Well, this is turning out to be one hell of a day." She looked at her southern counterpart. "Any chance you can get a message to our base...or a tow?"

Kylie shook her head no "Sorry, our drive system could not handle the stress of tugging another ship. I take it yours is sub-space capable?"

"Perhaps we should not answer that..." interjected Lizzie.

"No, that is not how it is going to be, engineer" Staci retorted. "We are all of former confederacies...we are no longer of those alliances."

"Well, then perhaps she would like to tell me about their drives. They are totally different from our designs, and do not appear to operate in the same manner." Lizzie blurted out. Staci gave her a crusty, annoyed look.

Kylie allowed a smile to adorn her face, and then let out a small laugh. "I don't mind Staci, she is right. We do need to trust each other. Engineer, I cannot give you precise details, but our engineers call them light drives. They somehow propel the ship based on repelling light and other forms of energy by generating a field of some sort. That is about all I can tell you. You will have to ask our engineers for any details."

Lizzie nodded her head, satisfied. "Hmm..." was all she could say while thinking about the design of the engine.

Staci looked at Lizzie, smiled and shook her head. She then turned back to Kylie "So, do you have anything like our Blessed in the south?"

She gave a slight chuckle. "We have everything you do up in the north. Including our own genetically enhanced Benditos...Blessed. See, we all do the same things. Haven't you ever wondered why no one side has actually won the war on earth?"

"Now that you mention it...I had noticed one side never gets a distinct advantage...or if they do, it is only for a very short time."

"Right. The only real advantage the Alliance had was space superiority. But, as you can see we still built our own vessel, then left earth...first."

"Wait, if you have Benditos...aren't they on your ship?"

Kylie gave another small chuckle before replying "Unlike you, we were much bolder in our hatred of them. We took over and killed every one of them. Captain Bonaventure was a great leader in that struggle. She gave us what we needed to survive and eventually to conquer. There are no fokken' Benditos left on the Libertad. Those who survived the fight were spaced...we will have no more of their evil on our vessel. You might consider the same with your...Blessed."

"Wow, take no prisoners eh?"

"No, it was the only way to secure our safety." Kylie answered.

Well, our Blessed have gotten a bit farther along in the arming of themselves than your Blessed it appears. So, for now I must concentrate on the present instead of the past or future, and on getting us home." She bit her lip for a moment when a thought came to her. "Maxine, if I got you into sub-space, could you contact Haven for assistance?"

Maxine thought for a moment, then answered "I believe I could. If I can hook up our design for the new communications array, we might be able to use it to contact one of our sub-space relays. If I can contact the relay, then Haven is easy. I would like to give it a try."

"Very good...we have two transports. Take one and attach your array to it. Give it a shot. Good luck."

"Could you use some help, gal?" Kylie asked Maxine while she pointed to a tall woman behind her. She had a short hairdo of dark tightly kinky locks of thick hair, her face sported a wide nose, big wide glowing brown eyes, and large lips gracing her tall, thin, golden colored face. "This is Ife Sesay, she is from my continent and is very good at doing mechanical and electronic work. I think you will find her to be of an invaluable help in your endeavor."

"I could use the help..." said Maxine. Staci nodded yes to the young woman, and the two left the bridge to prepare.

Kylie looked up at the spinning mass of wrecked vessel displayed on the star screen and then said "You know, that thing did something really nice and helpful. They put all of the wreckage in one spot...it will be easy to collect and reuse now."

Staci looked around the disheveled bridge and ran her fingers through her hair. In doing this, more hair fell from the side of her head down in front of her face, showing how very tired and weary she had become. "Well, at least *something* has gone right then. I guess we had first better clean up what we can, start picking through that salvage, then start on what repairs we can make. We sure do have some work to do!"

Six and a Half Years Ago...

She had just taken off from a traffic light when they buzzed her hovercar. They screamed and made all sorts of rude gestures at her as they sped by.

"Doesn't that bother you?" her friend Marta asked.

"No, not really..." she replied calmly.

Another hovercar full of Blessed sped by. They passed, slammed on their magnetic brakes and slowed down until they were right on the side of her vehicle.

Screams of "Hey baby!" and "I love you blondie" rang out from the three Blessed officers in the fancy hotrod-styled hovercar. The dark hair driver then zipped up in front of her car and slammed on his brakes. She was barely able to stop in time.

This riled her. "Damn!" she swore out loud. One of the officers stood up in the convertible car and lowered his pants, showing his frosty white ass to the two women. "Ewww!" she replied as the officer spread his cheeks for their purview. Then he pulled his pants back up and sat down as the hovercar sped away.

"My god, they're pigs!" yelled Marta.

"Don't worry, I've got this..." as she pulled her hair aside, and plugged the car antenna connection into a socket in the back of her neck.

"Shit! when did you get that?" Marta asked, in shock at the sight of the enhancement.

"A few days ago, didn't want to advertise I had it. I think it's time to give it a try." She said as she pulled the hovercar over to the side of the hover-way, then concentrated on connecting to the automotive network. She squeezed her eyes shut and worked at using the new port in her neck. After a moment, she opened her eyes and said "There! That should take care of them..."

"So, with that port in your neck...does that mean?"

"I enlisted? Yes! My chance to get away from...this..." she said as she slowly rolled by the wrecked remains of the car that the Blessed officers were driving. The engine had blown up and the

three men were standing on the side of the hover-way covered with motor lubricant. Everyone that drove by honked and laughed at the three oil-covered men. "Hi boys...nice makeup!" she yelled as they passed. After a moment and another mile down the road, she laughed and said "Those Blessed should learn to never fuck with me..."

NGD: 3 Years, 6 Months, 22 Days:

Blessed base Stopper:

Lindy Light-Griggs:

She watched as the construction robots continued their tireless work on the almost complete pair of star bases. They were huge, and they frightened her. They each had two large cubes connected by a single cylinder middle section. To her, they reminded her of the dumbbells she used in the gym for her workouts. Except the weight section of these were square instead of round, and the ones at the gym never frightened her. She analyzed the structures that were being put into place, and memorized them. In a few minutes, she would be contacting Otter and sending her the latest observations, construction reports, material reports, and the measurements being taken by what few loyalists were left – lately, almost all Normals not needed for construction had been put into deep freeze.

A voice behind her startled her "Sending your spy reports, mother?"

She turned to find Janus standing in the doorway to the communications room. She wondered how long he had been there. He had grown so much, he was almost as tall as herself, his skin had turned an interesting shade of greenish gold, his face was round and plump – where red should be on his cheeks, he instead had green. His eyes were now dark coffee brown, there was no glow to them like in her own eyes. Except for the brown color, his hair was exactly like his father's curly locks. He was much thinner and more muscular than either her or his father, she assumed that was something he did via solo workouts. The one thing that bothered her were his ears. They had taken on the wings to start, but now had only grown as much as to appear to be two thin spikes jutting out from the back of his ears.

He smiled at her. "Don't worry, I have known you have been doing that for months. You are my mother, I would never do anything to harm you, regardless of how traitorous your actions may be."

She looked at him with shock. She did not know how to react to his comment. She only stood there with an open mouth.

He walked over to her and touched her cheek with his hand. It felt strangely odd and slightly cold – she assumed it was simply his body reacting to the base temperature. "Your makeup must be getting harder to apply. The base skin color is starting to show through. I will formulate a better cover up material for you. We don't want you being put into deep freeze."

This was yet another surprise for her. She turned her head to look in the mirror sitting at her work station. He was right, the makeup she had applied was not working as well. There was a slight bluish tint showing through the Normal flesh tone cover-up. He seemed to know everything – he knew about the fate of most of her fellow Normals, the ones who could not escape in time. The moment they started showing signs of skin color change they were put into deep freeze which made them human shields on the Starlight. There was nothing that Star Force Commander Oldham would not do to save his own skin she thought.

He smiled at her again, then grabbed her and hugged her. "Don't worry, I won't let anything happen to you." She felt comfort from his embrace, despite his cold temperature. He pulled back and looked her in the eye, then said. "You might want to tell them though...your Evo friends...the bases will be active before they can do anything about it – the generator will be activated today as a matter of fact. The Devil's Throat will be sealed, and the Blessed and my father will hold the key. I'm sorry mother, I am torn between two forces. I cannot refuse either of them. I hope you can understand."

Despite her deep feelings as a Normal, she did understand. She wished she did not have to put him through what his life had been so far – being half Normal/Evo and half Blessed.

It must have been and still had to be horrible for him to have lived in both sides of the battle. "I do understand my son. I love you, never forget."

He smiled and touched her cheek again. "I love you too mother, thank you for everything."

A small beeping on her communication console took her away from her torn thoughts. She looked down and tried to figure out the beep – she had never heard it before. Then she saw the blinking green light, another thing she never saw before. Then it struck her – she quickly bent down and flipped switches activating the recorder.

"What is it mother?" Janus asked.

"It is the relay...from the other galaxy...where we came from. We're receiving a transmission."

Location, Unknown:

Halley Cet:

She awoke with a fuzziness in her head that she could not clear. Everything appeared blurry, but at the same time seemed crisp. Above her was a dome, there were swirls of various shades of silver and gray mixing within the surface of the dome. She could swear she saw various small mechanical creatures floating around in the swirling mass above her. Some looked like small men, some like insects, and some she could not recognize as familiar at all.

"You're awake..." said a voice. She had no idea where the voice came from, it seemed to be coming from someone all around her. "Welcome to our craft. I hope you are feeling better."

She thought about that for a moment and realized that she did feel better. She felt no pain, and the burning sensations in her extremities were gone. Then she remembered what happened. *My arm!*

She struggled to look down at her arm. Her head was being held down by a force, but she fought it and struggled to look down her shoulder.

"It is best you do not try to look at your healing" the voice said.

She stopped for a moment upon hearing the voice. She seemed to know that voice, it was female, and familiar. She returned to trying to move her head. She slipped out of the containment for just a brief moment, long enough to see her upper arm – and a metal frame extending from her upper arm down where her hand should be – all resting in a vat of some silver-purple colored liquid. Where her hand should be, she saw a similar frame of metal. "What have you done?" she cried out before feeling the force push her head back down onto the soft surface where she lay.

"It is best you rest and forget..." the voice said as she felt something start to flow into her brain – calming and numbing her thoughts – she suddenly felt relaxed. "You are aboard the craft of the Dekrons. I am the controller, and I...we...want to help. Please relax while we heal you. We will return you home once you are healed and fit again. Would you like to see the stars while you rest?"

She had finally stopped struggling and let her head and neck relax. She realized what the controller was offering her, it was as if she knew she would feel at ease viewing the stars. "Oh yes, please!" She called out. The dome above her cleared from the swirling mix of silvers to a clear surface. Every star shone through the dome and she could see and almost touch every one of the sparkling lights of the universe – it was as if she was outside of the ship. The stars were so clear and bright, she thought they had to only have been a few inches away.. "Oh, so beautiful!" she called out. She looked at the different constellations, she tried to pick out where the Flaybah home world was located, then she looked for the location of the Devil's Throat, then she started to look for Haven. She spotted a constellation and stared at it. "Why does that look familiar?" She stared and stared at it.

The sleeping chemicals were now starting to do their work as she started feeling a little drowsy. They were putting her to sleep again. Then it came to her, and it kept her awake, fighting the drugs. Through hazy eyes she stared at a band of three stars, and right before she drifted off into her induced sleep, she muttered "I know that constellation!"

Jeremy Ponds:

Jeremy and Jaime had just finished a rigorous workout. They ran three courses of command tri-polyhedrons – technically, the game was officially no longer played. However, everyone still enjoyed it in the gym setting, as it was one of the best workouts one could do. The violence factor had been eliminated – no one got knocked onto the hard ground, or had bones broken or fractured, and no violent actions were allowed. Only self-defense and light offensive moves were permitted. Thus one had to use agility, stealth, and cunning to make it up the ramps.

Jeremy stepped out of the shower to find Jaime, who had just finished up drying, and was putting on her casual wear. She turned and looked at him and smiled. He caught her eyes looking down below his face however, and it hit him – that was not a good thing. But it was too late – she stepped over to him and placed a soft touch to his chest.

"What the hell are those? Are you ill? Were you attacked?" she asked as her hand touched the multitude of small glowing red marks that were visible even through his dark blue skin. The small red points were sensitive to the touch and he gave a slight flinch as her fingers brushed across the surface. "Your'e in pain, let's get you to Max…"

"I'm fine!" he sharply said, cutting her off. Then he realized he was showing his annoyance and calmed himself. "Really, I am fine. I ran into something…I was allergic to…and then this. I am applying a medication for it."

Jaime looked at her friend with some apprehension. "Well, alright…if you say you are ok…" She turned and went to the other part of the locker room to finish dressing. As she finished putting on her clothes, she turned and asked again "You're sure you're ok?" He nodded yes, so she waved goodbye and left.

He gave a heavy, loud sigh of relief. He turned and was startled by Patti sitting in the corner of the locker room. "How did you get in here? You really gave me a start!"

"I'm sorry…I came in and saw her questioning you. We had better…I had better find something else."

"No!" he interrupted. "You need me, and I am willing to help. It has done nothing to harm me. You need me...I can, and will help."

"It is getting hard to hide..." she replied. "There are other things for me here..."

"What, like space rats?" he retorted. "Those are not plentiful enough, and if you ran out of those, then what? We have no "random" people here. There is no one that is not worth keeping, no one that could just "disappear" like with the Blessed. No, this is the only way." He came up to her, she had a true look of sadness in her eyes. "Do you need me again?"

She looked at him and gave him a smile, but still showed some sadness. "Well, yes..."

"Then let's go back to the cabin. I think I can take it again..." he offered.

"No, I don't need you that way. I have no hunger right now, and will not need to feed for a couple of weeks. But, I DO want you..."

He leaned over and kissed her cheek. She closed her eyes and felt the sweet kiss as it settled on her face. "Then perhaps we should go?" he suggested.

A noise in the doorway startled them, the noise was of someone clearing their throat. Jeremy turned to find Eva at the doorway. "Sorry to disturb you. Patti, would you mind giving me some time to work out with your man? I really need it..."

Patti leaned into his ear and whispered "It could be months, or even years with her...she is Blessed, no one would miss her..."

He just softly shook his head at her, then said "I will see you in a while. Meet you in my cabin, say in two hours?"

"I look forward to it..." Patti said, then walked out of the locker room, stopping to look at Eva. She slightly licked her lips as she passed, smelling the life within her.

When Patti had closed the locker room door behind her, Jeremy asked "So, what is so important that you need a workout right now?" He looked at the black-haired Blessed woman. She was dressed in tight workout pants, but for some reason was wearing a large robe. The chest area of the robe was baggy, and the arms of the robe were long as they hung all the way down to the fingertips.

"I need to make these work better..." she said as she removed her robe. Underneath she had on a tight-strapped workout halter top. On the sides of each shoulder was one of her arms, and to the inside, in front of her arm pits, were another set of arms. Fully developed with an extra set of five fingered hands on each. The four arms all moved independently of each other.

"What the hell?" he quietly asked.

"They have been growing for a while...but as you can see, they are now fully developed. I was able to hide them until they continued to develop to where they are now...and now I seem to have full control of them, but they are not in the same condition as my other arms. I figure I had better strengthen them and make them the weapons they are, or could be. Can you...will you, help me?"

Jeremy shook his head in amazement at the extra set of arms. "Things just get stranger and stranger here. Yeah, I can help...let's go make you a four-armed weapon of destruction."

Jaime Bordeaux:

Maxine's transmission gave her nothing but despair. Halley was maimed and had been taken by aliens. The Innovation is down and needing repairs. The Blessed simply attacked without any warning, which meant that the Evo were now at war, but at the same time they appeared to have a new ally in the SHU starship and crew. She needed a meeting of the organizers, as plans had to be made and implemented.

Three of the organizers answered the call. Incidentally, both Jeremy and Eva reported they would not make the meeting. She was worried enough about her friend and trainer, but this made her worries grow even more.

"Well, four of us will have to do. We do not need everyone to make decisions, so let's get started. We have a disabled ship out there. The Innovation was attacked, and is badly in need of supplies and repairs."

Jonathan spoke up "We have our Naga class engineering ships, the Whale and Guppy that are primed and ready for travel. This would be a great opportunity to give our mobile engineering fleet a real shakedown."

"Good, you and Kate get moving then" she ordered. Jonathan gave her a quizzical look. She smiled and told him "You two are the captains of the Whale and Guppy. Take what you need to get them repaired, and go!"

A big smile came to Jonathan's face. "Yes captain...er, leader!" he snapped. "I will be also taking the Shooting Star...it is a salvage and supply ship."

Jaime nodded at him "Very well...oh, and captain will do just fine" she said as the young man gave a small salute and ran off. She turned to Allen and ordered "Take the Valkyrie and escort them. They might need some protection while repairs are being made. I would like to trust our new southern allies, but..."

"I understand captain, I will escort them there." Allen replied. Jaime smiled and nodded to her fellow captain.

Norm-Comm buzzed in her ear, she answered and it was Otter. "Captain, Lindy just forwarded a message that came through on the relay at the Devil's Throat. I think everyone will want, or should see it. But, I will let you decide..."

"Can you get the video feed and forward it to our display in this room?" she asked.

"No video feed..." she said, causing Jaime to give a questioning look. "Sending it to your display now..."

On the wall holo-display the Alliance News Network logo was shown, and the theme music played in the background – it was a special report. The announcer came on – she was a pretty woman, only in her late twenties Jaime guessed, big boof-like hairdo that most of the TV people liked, and bright red lipstick on her small lips. Unlike most of the news-bots she was used to watching however, she was not her normal, happy self. She looked almost in tears, her face showed terror, not the normal *"I am about to bullshit you with Alliance propaganda"* look they normally have. No, to Jaime she looked honestly worried and troubled. The transmission had been captured at the start of a special alert.

"As you can see in the images, there is nothing remaining of what used to be sector 24, the city of Paris. Only our underground studios here in Sector 1 are still operational, and thanks to the wisdom and kindness of our great Supreme Commander for allowing us this broadcast space many years ago."

"Holly shit!" Jaime gasped. "I used to live there...there is nothing left." The drone images showed nothing but a pile of rubble where the walled city of Paris used to exist. Everything had been torn down and dissolved into dust and debris. All that was left were the shifting sands of disassembled molecular remains.

The announcer continued "We now have a reporter on the scene in sector 45, the area they still continue to call Beijing City. Hongqui Xu, are you there?"

The image switched to a young Chinese man, standing on the top of a tall building. "Send up the drones!" he was caught barking to his technicians over the announcing of the in-studio announcer. He then turned and looked to the camera, smiling in the face of adversity. "This is Hongqui Xu in sector 45 and I believe we are the only external Alliance News Network broadcast station still in operation in the entire Northern Alliance. Today, we will witness the powerful impact of the ion storms wreaking death and destruction on the entire world. From our vantage point atop the ANN tower here in the former city of Beijing, we will witness the power and destruction that these storms are unleashing on our world. In the skies, we have three Mark 4 unmanned camera drones. Let's see what they are observing."

From one of the camera drones, they watched as two massive storms swirled and spun the atmosphere into a dance of impending doom. They could see from the images, that where the storms traveled, everything had been destroyed in their wake. The view switched to the second drone, which showed a second storm traveling to an intersect with the first storm. A wind current caught the drone, and instantly flung it into the center of the vortex. The image then turned to static.

They heard someone yelling in the background, the producer, she assumed. "SHIT! Quick, back to camera 1!" The announcer was then back on the screen. The young man gasped at the drone image, but then regained his composure. "As you can see, the storms are unpredictable and dangerous. We will try to give you the in-air drone images as long as we can. We can also show you the massive destruction live from our vantage point on the ANN broadcast complex. Our team of scientists have calculated the paths of the storms and with certainty have predicted that they will bounce off of each other and miss our location. This will allow ANN to bring you the closest and most in-depth coverage of this storm event – closer than any other network in not only the Northern Alliance, but in the entire world. We are all blessed, that we have the equipment and the power to continue to transmit to our orbital ANN satellites."

He turned and pointed to the storm on his right. "If the camera would zoom into that storm you will be able to see the deflector shield generators starting to disintegrate. Why the shields have failed us is still a mystery, but they have gone down across the entire Alliance and now we are all at risk. Word from our spies in the south tell us the same story. The shields are failing, and the storms are wreaking havoc on our entire planet. Yes, now the storm has begun its destruction of the first of the city's buildings. It won't be long before they are nearly on top of us."

"DAMN!" someone yelled off camera.

The district one announcer asked "Is everything alright there? Are you safe?"

Jaime thought that was really a stupid question – so typical of the press.

"Yes...but now the second storm has penetrated the formerly protected boundary of the city. With the speed of these two storms, it should just be a few minutes before they intersect each other and collide. It should be a spectacular sight – a sight that you will only be able to see on ANN."

341

A camera shot from a different drone was now on the screen. "From our third drone, you can see our broadcast location high atop the ANN tower. With the drone overhead, we should be able to get even more details in the city below as the storms hit."

There were massive bolts of electricity flying between the clouds. He looked up in fascination "The electricity in the air is almost alive – it is such a beautiful sight. I hope the drone is getting this for all of you out there." He looked to the drone video images and a huge smile came to his face. The camera switched to the drone for a moment, then back to him. He was still staring up into the sky, his mouth open in wonder and awe at the lightning show above him. They switched back to the drone image just in time to see it get destroyed, static filled the screen for a brief moment.

For a moment, Hongqui just looked into the camera with his mouth open. He put his hand to his earpiece to listen – probably his director barking something at him. Hongqui seemed to now ignore him as he just turned away from the camera and stared out across the city. Finally, without turning back to the camera he said "Ladies and gentlemen, it appears that there is something going on behind our broadcast location. If I could get the camera to turn please, you will see this amazing event."

The camera turned and pointed up into the sky above their location. A swirling mass of dark black clouds had formed above them. "As you can see…" Hongqui narrated "it appears that a new storm is forming right overhead…"

The light from the sparks of electricity lit up the screen as the lightning flashed across the clouds. The vortex was now moving at a high rate of speed, but still was forming slowly. Buildings and debris were being picked up off of the ground as the vortex slowly planted itself onto the ground.

Hongqui walked over and took over control of the camera himself. He panned one direction, then the other. The two other storms were moving in a convergence with their building. He finally said "Well, it appears that in just a moment we too will be victims of these storms. We thought we were going to witness the collision of the two storms, but it appears we will instead see the convergence of three storms."

He sighed, realizing that more than likely no one was alive to see his biggest and final broadcast. "Well, ladies and gentlemen...assuming any of you are out there...it appears that this will be my final broadcast to you. Are you out there Kelly?" He waited, no reply from sector one control. "Good, since there is no one to control what I now say, I hope I do not have to convince you of the errors that the Supreme Commander and the Council have caused, and that they are the cause of this bloody mess. To those who will survive, watch what happens here, and realize that we doomed ourselves. Our actions and wars caused our planet to decay to this state...and we acted like sheep and allowed it to happen. So, with that..." Jaime saw a tear come to his eye then blow quickly away, before he said "This is Hongqui Xu, for ANN in Beijing. Good luck to everyone left...if there IS anyone left after this..."

He turned the camera toward the edge of the building and showed the massive vortex howling toward their location. He walked up to the edge, and held his arms out wide as if to hug the means of his destruction. The storm reached him and right before the image went blank, Jaime saw him get torn into ionized molecules. Arcs of electricity and sparks flew across his body, and his flesh peeled away along with his clothing. She barely saw parts of his body fly into the storm – flesh and organs had no way to stop the vortex from tearing him apart. Then the storm moved forward, the building crumbling it like a cracker in a sandstorm. The camera started to fall right before the image went out.

The image switched to the sector one announcer, she had tears in her eyes, and her lip was trembling. She fought a battle just to get out "I...I think we are about to also go off the air. We all thought we were safe here...we..." Then static.

Jaime just stared at the now blank screen. "Holy crap. I don't know what to say?" she softly said.

Max looked at her and took her hand. "I think we might have just witnessed the end of everything. Everything...there..."

"Max, what happened to the city's shields? Let me call Jonathan back in...he can answer that..."

She reached up to activate Norm-Comm but Max took her hand and moved it down. "No, don't let him know. Let's leave him

343

in ignorance okay?" He stood up, looked at the now blank monitor and walked out.

Jaime looked at Allen with confusion. He stood up and quietly said "We think he might have written the program that took the city's shields down. It would be best if he did not know what his handiwork might have done..." Upon her realization, she nodded at him as he was right.

Before Allen got to the door, she said to him "The world is gone...is the Alliance gone?" she asked, then said "All those innocent people..." a tear formed in her glowing blue eye and dripped down her face.

Boral Oldham:

He watched the telecast again, but could not believe his eyes. He knew the Supreme Commander and the Order had survived. There was no way they would not have been protected – yes they had survived, he was sure. After all, they were in underground bunkers. No weapon could penetrate those bunkers – no force could get that far underground.

He tapped on his communication device. "Get me the captains of the main fleet, then get me the captains of the war patrols. I wish to speak to all of them."

He disconnected, then thought for a moment before he contacted his science officer. "When will Zeus and Apollo be up and on-line?" he barked.

"In approximately two hours, my Star Force Commander."

"Good...let me know the moment they have successfully brought them on-line." He stopped and looked out the viewports at his two mega-starbases about ready to come to life. He then turned back to the science officer, who was patiently waiting for his further questions and commands. "How many Norms do we have in deep-freeze?" he asked.

The science officer looked at his ship's status display, then said "We have approximately sixty thousand Norms in storage."

"That's it? Hmm...how many are female?" he asked.

The officer consulted his readouts again, then answered "About eighty seven percent female Norms, my Star Force Commander."

"Very well, keep the females well frozen in the stasis tubes for later use. But, space the males...no need for that waste of flesh taking our resources. Then, get with our cartography teams, determine if we now know the pathway through the Throat – I may want to send some ships back to our old home."

Patti:

She looked down at her open cavity...there was nothing left of the space rat. Jeremy was right, these were barely keeping her going. In addition, the small amounts she was taking from Jeremy were helping less and less lately. She found she needed more and more – what she was taking in was not doing the trick. She needed to find a source, something that would keep her going for months. She needed a whole body, a whole source of life-force, and a source of protein via meat. She knew there was only one way to get it. It was now the time to either be bold, or die of starvation.

There were guards at the door. Even on Haven, they knew they were at war and thus were protecting their space assets from potential spies and saboteurs. They knew there was one that was with them that was actually not – a hidden mole, a spy. Thus, they had guards everywhere until that person was found. If that person was a Blessed, she probably could find him or her – they had a certain smell to them. That could help both herself and her hosts – but that would take time, and time was one thing she didn't have. No, she needed to get out and away, get to a place where she could feed.

She walked up to the hatch to the space dock. The two guards eyed her suspiciously, but they also knew who she was and did not take arms. One, a light-blue skinned female looked down at her and smiled before saying "You are not allowed here, Patti. Please move on."

Patti, gave a slight pout to her, as if she had hurt her feelings. It caused the guard to return a smile – right before the small flash dazed her and the other guard. They stood at their posts, stiff as stone. Patti, unlocked the hatch unfettered, went in, and started working on the dock computer. A moment later, the harbor space doors opened just slightly. She boarded the Blackbird, and slipped the ship through the small opening in the doors right as they were about to return to their fully closed state. No one noticed the small, stealthed ship leaving in the dead of the late hour, and slipping into the darkness of space.

Nine Years Ago...

"Can it really do all that?" his study partner Franklin asked.

He nodded his head proudly. "Yep, and more. This is the most potent virus I have ever designed. It could be used to knock out any system, regardless of security protocols. It has intelligence to work its way around firewalls and filters and infect, then take down whatever it is programmed to seek and destroy. I call it, the paradigm...the model of interruption. I never plan on using it, but it is good to always have around...you never know when it might be needed."

"Well, I'm impressed. Hide it well!" His friend said before he left the university computer lab.

"You are going to give that to us, aren't you?" A voice from the server room asked. He turned to find the recruiter, standing in the shadows. "You promised..."

"Only if you keep your promise and never use it. I can stop it you know..." he warned.

"Don't worry, we will do what we agreed. We will only want you to put it into the missile command system. It will only be activated in the event the Alliance decides to use their nukes again. We are sworn to keep that from happening...aren't we?" The young man nodded his head in agreement. "Then that is what we will do. You can leave the payload in the missile command system, correct?"

"Yes, I will leave it there. It should only affect the launching of weapons."

"Very good. We will leave that up to you. We will name it the P.A.W. paradigm, and it will guard the planet from further nuclear war."

"I will set it up to disable their launch platforms in the event they turn the keys. It will be ready and injected this evening." He connected to the Alliance defense network with ease using a hack. He then proceeded to prepare the virus for infection into the command system.

"Very good...you will save the planet and the people from extinction. You and your P.A.W. Paradigm will prevent further wars."

He pressed a button and the injection of the virus was completed. He watched as it began to infiltrate the various systems of the missile command software structure.

"You are our most skilled technician. Have you thought about the offer we made? The Alliance still thinks of you as only a communications expert. They have no idea of your true skill or knowledge. Now is the time, we can cover you. If you wait, it may be too late to hide who you are and what you really can do. What say you Mechanic?"

He just nodded his head yes. He could tell the man in the shadows was smiling. He looked at his terminal, the paradigm had already totally infested the software of the missile command system. He could have sworn for a moment it had moved into the defense command system, but when he tried to verify it, the virus went into hiding. Maybe it had infested that subsystem, but without missiles it would not matter.

NGD: 3 Years, 7 Months, 4 Days:

Sector J:

Jonathan Faraday:

The Guppy was the first to rendezvous with the Innovation. He looked over the scans of the damaged ship – peeled layers of space carbon, which allowed for damage to the Faratainium substructure. Then there was that hole that went all the way through the ship. He estimated that there was damage to the bridge, and he assumed that very likely many of the vital systems were also damaged and needed repairs or replacement.

He shook his head in disbelief – had they been that wrong on the design of the ship? Was the space carbon that weak...it seemed so strong to him. He wondered how the Blessed could have peeled it back so easily.

Kate in the engineering ship "Whale" had also arrived in the area and joined him in a holo-meeting along with Staci Smitters and Captain Nina Bonaventure of the Libertad.

"Well, we're definitely a mess…" said Staci. "We have main power, the crawler is still damaged, but Lizzie is doing her best to restore the drive. Our main issue is the hull. We have substantial damage and could not do an insertion into sub-space in our current state. So, we need repairs to the hull – at least to the point where we can return to Haven."

He looked into his monitor at the Innovation, then turned his attention to, and absentmindedly stared at the floating ball of metal beyond their location. "That is one big ball of salvage metal…" Jonathan said, sounding almost in a daze. He finally came back to reality and said "I am ordering the Shooting Star to start salvage and processing operations on what is out there. We should be able to use that to at least patch the Innovation."

"Perhaps we should also sift through the rubble as we go?" asked Kate. "If the weapon they used to damage the space carbon is in that salvage, it would be useful to get our hands on it." Jonathan nodded in agreement.

"Question…" Captain Bonaventure interrupted. "How do you intend to repair the ship in this location? You need a star base so that your robots and crews can get supplies. Your crews need to be in a controlled environment to work safely. There is no way you can do that out here."

Jonathan smiled at this question. "Now you will witness the magic of these engineering ships. If you will give us about fifteen minutes, you will understand how we will be able to do repairs out here." She nodded in acknowledgement.

He disconnected from the conference and looked to his helmsman. "Prepare for repair maneuvering. Dock Master, open the shell for repair docking, please."

Outside, the starboard side of the massive ship opened like a clam shell to reveal an empty cavity. If one were to look inside into the middle of the ship while the side was open, they would see that the actual operational structure of the ship was in reality quite small. On the other side of the Innovation, Kate had maneuvered the Whale into a similar position. The shell of the Whale was now open in a similar manner, except the opening was on the aft side of the craft.

Both ships were now fully opened and the sides were facing each side of the Innovation. Jonathan ordered "Helm, slide us over the Innovation for the repair docking procedure."

Three minutes later, the Guppy had its clam shell hull now fully over the the Innovation. The Whale positioned itself in the exact same manner on the other side. A moment after that, the ships used their thrusters to slowly position themselves until they met in the middle. The two ships softly attached to each other, seals joined, and the ships enclosed themselves around the Innovation. Pressure seals engaged and provided a safe working environment for robots and crew.

Jonathan rejoined the conference. Nina had an impressed look on her face. "Very good. So, you now have a protected repair area I see. I never realized you northerners were so inventive."

Jonathan smiled at her and said "I think there is a lot we both need to learn about each other."

Patti:

The ship exited sub-space, then went into extended near light-speed running until it reached the sector where the galaxy portals were located. As she approached, she shut down the RFS, went into stealth mode, and glided into the area. She observed the two giant battle stations that were on each side of the Devil's Throat. She could see a force field that surrounded the gravity well – she surmised that it was powerful enough to block any incoming or outgoing ships.

The shattering on her view port startled her, and made her yelp. Then another shattering on the front of the ship. She came to a stop and looked through the view ports. The area of space was full of dead bodies – dead human bodies – dead Normal bodies. She examined the floating corpses and also realized they were all male. *"So they flushed their male Evo prisoners and kept the females, eh?"* Although this did not surprise her, she was amazed at how primitive these Blessed had become. All they seemed to be concerned with was sex, and procreation. She

350

decided at this point that her mission was sound, and the Blessed would provide exactly what she needed. She gave enough thrust to get the ship moving again, glided the Blackbird in near the closest starship, and using stealth mode quietly docked to a side airlock.

After breaking into the airlock computer and opening the hatch, she quietly walked down the corridor looking for something that would suffice to satisfy her needs. She finally found it, a Blessed off-duty soldier – this was exactly what she wanted. It took her no time to seduce him – they were such easy marks. An hour later, she was in bed with him, and another hour later the soldier was gone. She knew she could now survive for another two or three months – or maybe even longer. But she thought she might need to pick up something in reserve for later.

She wandered through the corridors without a care or thought, she had forgotten that she was not supposed to be there. The guard in an adjoining corridor reminded her of that fact.

"You, stop!" he yelled out as he pulled out his blaster and aimed it at her threateningly.

She slowly walked up to him and gave him a smile. "You don't really want to do that, do you?"

He gave her an even bigger scowl. "Lady, I don't like your type...I could give a crap if I shoot you or not."

She could see his finger start to flex, he was about to shoot her – so, she defended herself. He could not resist the flash of bright light that caused him to become frozen in place. She walked around the now stiff Blessed soldier. She ran her finger along his chin as she circled him. "Perhaps it would have been easier to like girls?" she asked. She looked at him, and on the back of his head was a long ponytail. She thought that was unusual for a Blessed – nothing about this one was what she normally encountered. She sighed over the effort she would now have to put out as she grabbed his ponytail and tugged on it, sending him crashing to the hard metal floor.

Like a caveman, she dragged her prey down the corridor. She knew he felt the pain, she blamed him – it was his own fault – she was not going to worry about it. She quickly dragged her captive down the corridor, hoping she would not have to deal with any more interruptions. That was not to be however, as when she turned a corner she almost ran over a woman going the opposite direction. The young woman just stood and stared at her – Patti did the same thing. Patti saw she was Blessed, it surprised her as she never actually expected to see another Blessed female besides Eva. This Blessed woman had short blond hair, blue eyes, was not particularly tall, but was very slim and attractive. Patti considered if she should be dazed and taken. But then the woman looked down at her captive and smiled. Patti decided she would not need to be killed. She smiled back at the Blessed woman.

Finally, the blond pointed to the statuesque Blessed man still being held by his ponytail, and said "You know he's gay. Not many of those amongst the Blessed – at least ones that admit it and somehow manage to live." Patti just nodded in agreement. "I never liked him. He thought I was competition for the guys...how wrong he was." She turned and looked down the corridor behind her, then back to Patti. "You know where you're going?" she asked and Patti nodded yes. "Okay, better let you get on with your business then. See ya!" she raised a hand in a wave goodbye, turned, and walked away from the primitive-looking girl. Patti gave a slight look of confusion, then shrugged her shoulders, and then continued on her way. She dragged him all the way to the airlock and onto the Blackbird.

Once inside the ship, she found a storage closet. She took his stiff body and threw it in harshly. "You, stay there." She ordered to the statue before slamming the hatch.

Minutes later she quietly disconnected from the starship and flew back to where she would kick in the RFS for the trip to the insertion point. She momentarily stopped and took advanced scans of the two new star bases. She also hacked the computer of the nearest star ship and downloaded as many specs on the new battle stations as she could find. She hoped it would calm all who might be mad at her back at Haven. Her plan was to sneak back in the same way she left, but somehow she also thought her plan might fail. So just in case, this would be her trump card. She hoped this intelligence would give her some forgiveness.

Jeremy Ponds:

She had finally returned – she had somehow managed to get the harbor doors open and slip the Blackbird in as quietly as possible. But some things were impossible to hide, like the missing spot in their bed. He was sleeping when she slipped under the sheets, reached over and gave him a small kiss on the cheek.

He reached over and turned on the lights. She looked at him with some surprise, he wondered if the look was all an act. "So, where the hell have you been the past few weeks? I hope you're not thinking we didn't notice the Blackbird had gone missing? Two guards who had no idea who slipped by them and took the ship. Then you just go missing, then you simply slip back into Haven and into bed like you stayed up late? What do you take me for?"

"Someone who will understand that I am different...and that I could not stay here...that is, to stay here, and keep you safe" she replied.

He looked at her and realized she appeared strong and healthy again. "You fed, didn't you?" She nodded yes. He shook his head in amazement. "So, you snuck off and took care of your needs...so you would not harm me any further?" She shook her head yes again. He sighed, reached over and kissed her on the forehead. "Thank you...I really was not sure how much more I could take, actually..."

"I know...and that is why I did what I did" she told him.

"Well, you're still in hot water with the captain." He got up and put on a robe. "I am going to have to go talk her out of sending you off."

"I have some information to give her...something I hope will help in receiving forgiveness. It is on a data crystal...I will get it."

He walked over to her closet. "That's okay, I'll get it...I'm assuming it is in here?" He reached the panel control to her closet. She tried to stop him, but it was too late – he activated the control, the panel slid open, and the stiff Blessed soldier came tumbling out. "What the?"

She ran over and shoved the stiff back into the closet. "Let's just say, he's a snack...for later..."

"You went and ate a Blessed? And took another for later? He could tell them everything if he escapes!"

"He won't..." she told him. "He'll never move, unless I allow it...and I won't!"

"Well, we had better find a more suitable hiding spot for him...somewhere with a good lock..."

*   *   *

Jaime was definitely not happy when he came to her. He knew why too. "She's back, isn't she?" she said with a dry tone. He softly nodded his head yes. "You know she violated every rule we have. She might have even given out secrets to the Blessed."

"I don't think so..." he said, then tossed the data crystal at her. "She said this might be useful to you...and hoped it would help to show she is asking for forgiveness. She really is on our side."

"Then tell me where she went and why?" she asked.

He hesitated then sighed. "Okay...well, let's just put it this way...she has needs. These needs can only be satisfied by living energy and flesh."

"So, she eats us?"

"Pretty much will eat anything living...but she is logical, and intelligent...much more so than she lets on. Also, she loves me..."

"Do you love her?" she asked

"Yes...and I believe she would never do anything to compromise or hurt us. Thus, the data crystal. It's her way of saying "sorry""

"Well, we might as well see what she found." She inserted the crystal into the holo-projector and activated the image. First, the images of the dead Normal males. She cringed at the images of the dead bodies hitting the view screen and shattering into thousands of pieces. She found herself being reminded of that dogfight above earth, which now seemed so many ages ago. Then they examined the scans of the two enormous battle stations. She had somehow managed to not only get very detailed scans, but had somehow raided the Blessed computers for schematics and design details. Then the scans of the fleet, the make-up of the ships, weapons potentials, on-board arsenals, and command structure. "Holy crap..." she softly said in amazement. "Okay, she is forgiven..." then stopped and looked at him "Those marks?"

"They were her taking small amounts of life force from me. I was not damaged...she was careful. But, she is satisfied now...I will no longer be needed for that."

"And so, she fed from..." she crinkled her forehead, then completed the sentence "Blessed?"

"Yes, she ate one there..." he paused, then decided to admit "and she has one in cold storage here."

"WHAT?" she blurted out. She then lowered her voice "She has a Blessed here?"

"Yes, but she has the ability to somehow stun living beings. She did that temporarily to the dock guards. But, this Blessed she has is somehow permanently stunned. She assured me..."

"I expect you to make sure of that. That Blessed is your responsibility..." he shook his head yes. "I shouldn't allow this..."

"Thank you Captain. She also told me she was discovered by a Blessed female...and this female did nothing to stop her."

"Hmm, that's interesting. Perhaps the inside asset we have?"

"Let's hope so..." he replied.

At the entrance to the command center stood Patti. She had a sheepish look on her face. She still feared Jaime, and the captain thought that was a good thing. "Come in Patti...you are forgiven..."

About Sixteen Years Ago…

Private Beacham had gone out to make adjustments on the field generator while she was getting everything ready inside the protective field. Too many minor storms had popped up on the Yucatan, and these storms were coming on shore one at a time in a parade of mayhem. Instead of trying to make a run for the base – which they knew would fail – they instead set up a shelter inside a burned down hobble that once was a place meant for family meals. The walls were partially standing, and even a small section of roof still clung to the charred walls. With the field up, it was actually feeling quite pleasant inside.

She knew they would have nothing else to do, so she removed her armored battle suit and began to clean and repair her battlefield lifeline. She was working on the chest piece of the suit when she heard the opening and closing sound of the field. "Cliff, do you have a four-ten modulator? My armor needs an adjustment and I can't seem to find mine" she said while she dug through her tool kit.

"Oh, I have a modulator Señorita…but it is of a different type…" said an unfamiliar voice.

Slightly shocked, she reached down for her blaster, but was stopped before she could reach it. Her arms were grabbed, and at the same moment she felt a quick fist to the face, which stunned her. She looked up in a daze to find a southern tasker removing his battle armor. He had a large toothy smile on his dark skinned face. There were multiple scars running all different directions forming an array of tire tracks across his pockmarked face. When he was done, he held her down while the other two men removed their battle armor.

While the third tasker removed his armor, the scarred one continued to hold her down – he put his ugly mug right next to her face. His breath smelled like fish, she turned her head to avoid the stench. He grabbed her chin, turned her face back toward him, examined her face and said "My, for a soldier you are a pretty one." He ran a dirty finger across her cheek. "I guess we had not shot at you? Perhaps your beauty made us miss? Well, my señorita…this time, I will shoot, and I will not miss." He let the other two take ahold of her arms again, and then ordered "take her clothes off."

His men tugged on her pants and uniform shirt with single hands, while they continued to hold her down. She wiggled a hand free, but in reprisal she felt another fist into her cheek. Her arm was quickly shoved behind her back and held down, all while the free hands continued to strip her. The uniform buttons and snaps resisted their attempts at removal, causing them to use even more force to open the garments, and less force to keep her down. They finally had her shirt opened, and her pants down, revealing her olive green standard issue women's panties and halter bra. While she struggled, she had managed to slip her hand under her shirt without them noticing.

"Well, those have to go..." the toothy tasker said as he removed a laser blade from his belt. "Hold that up for me, will you amigo?" he pointed at the thin spot of her panties while he asked the help from the soldier who held down her right hand now pinned under her back. He moved just enough to help hold her underpants up slightly, giving the scarred man the room to slide his blade under the material and cut each side loose from the rest of the garment. He put his blade down and peered down at her partial nakedness. The three men joined in peering, and made "oohs" and "ahhs" as they peered at the naked flesh near her crotch. The pockmarked man moved more of her panties out the way to provide better peering as he began to take his pants down. She heard the change in the respiration of two men holding her down – their breathing was heavy and filled with lust. Their minds were becoming clouded, and she felt they had loosened their grip on her arms.

It was just the small break she needed. She was able to grab the laser knife she had stashed in a holster strapped on the back of her halter bra. It was a small blade, but long enough to maim, or even kill if used in the right way. She forced her arm loose from the man holding her on the right. She swung the knife with her now free hand into the man's neck. Within the blink of an eye, she rotated her arm around and pulled, which took the knife through his neck. Blood splattered on her face and into the eyes of the man on the left. By instinct, she followed through with a wide swing of the knife into the man on the left's neck. She rotated it making a large hole and causing him to make sucking noises while he attempted to get any amount of breath through his punctured windpipe. She quickly pulled the blade out and turned toward the pervert.

The rapist tasker was taken by surprise over the quick motions and actions of his former victim. She took advantage of his confusion by grabbing his privates, and with a swift motion sliced them cleanly off. He gasped in shock and pain, as he dropped to his knees. She followed up her attack with a slice of the blade through his abdomen, up his chest, and then stopped at his right lung. The cutting-edge laser beam flowed up through the abdomen and internals like butter. She stopped her cutting motion and watched as his intestines fell out of his gut, and onto her legs.

He then fell on her, her blade sinking further into his lung. She rolled him off her now blood-covered body and stood up. His intestines rolled off onto the ground and her panties fell off of her crotch, landing on the intestines. Instead of picking them up, she just stood there and looked down at her rapist's now-dying form. "This is what you three wanted wasn't it? Well, here you go..." she said as she slightly opened her legs above him. His stone cold eyes looked up between her legs. "Good, no? AH, but you will now have to pay for the views..." she said as she reached around and took out her field rifle. One by one she blew each of their heads cleanly off with single shots. Her anger took the better of her after that as she began dissecting each one of them – throwing their body parts across the house ruins in every direction.

Throughout the night, she had flung pieces of the three southern taskers across every part of the protective field, except in the spot where she eventually fell asleep. When she woke up that morning, she looked around at the carnage she had caused. She silently stood up, tied her panties back together, put them on, took out some water and a folding towel, wiped the blood off her face, cleaned her body as best as possible, put her uniform shirt and pants back on, and then put on her battle armor. She performed each task in silence, with methodical deliberateness and accuracy. When she determined she was fully equipped and all systems were active, she stepped out of the protective field, and looked around. The storms had subsided and the field of battle looked clear once again. On the outside of the field bubble she found Beacham – a large blast hole in his helmet. His weapons and food stolen from his fallen corpse. The storms took much of the material of his battle suit with it, as he was partially stripped of clothing and flesh.

She shut down the force field, then walked a distance away from the ruins. She stopped, turned, lowered her back, and pointed her head toward the house. A moment later, a laser guided missile ejected from her battle suit's backpack and slammed into the remains of the house. The explosion rocked the area, but she also knew that now, no one would ever find the remains of either the house or those taskers.

"Rest in pieces, southern pieces of shit. I will never trust any of you, even if we somehow don't kill you, and for some reason make peace with you. I will always hate you lousy slimes…"

3 Years, 9 Months, 14 Days:

Evo Base Haven:

Jaime Bordeaux:

The ships had finally returned. Jonathan and Kate in the engineering ships Guppy and Whale, had done enough repairs to allow the Innovation to return home to Haven. Only its captain was still missing.

Then there was the southern ship Libertad. Upon exiting sub-space, Jonathan had transmitted a complete report. Acting Captain Smitters had also given reports about the battle and how Captain Bonaventure had come to their assistance, and how she had provided her own crew to assist in the cleanup and repairs to the ship. It appeared they now had a new ally in the war with the Blessed. The ships were traveling together in hopes of preventing another Blessed attack. The Libertad was not sub-space capable however, so the Evo ships did leap frogs through sub-space while the southern ship caught up using its light drives. It was a slow trip, but now, they had finally all arrived back at Haven.

She watched on the monitors in the control center as the four ships entered the harbor, and docked in the enormous cavern that had been turned into the Evo shipyard. She stood from her chair, straightened her uniform, and left the control center to meet the ships as they docked.

She felt some apprehension, as she still had hatred and pain from the ground war so many years ago. She told herself that this was a totally different group of southerners. This was a group of southerners that struggled against their own Blessed – this group not only defeated their Blessed, but then took the time and risked their lives for Halley and her crew. They didn't have to engage the Blessed, but they did. She had to put aside those feelings from so long ago. She had to make peace with herself and them – now was that time.

She had the Libertad use the guest dock, that way she could prepare a proper reception for their new friends from the south. She ordered food and drink be available for the arriving dignitaries as they disembarked and stepped foot onto Haven for the first time. She wanted to make a good impression as they may all be working together for quite a long time – or so she hoped.

Jaime watched as the large golden ship docked outside. It's long round engines so different from their ion drives – Jonathan had reported that they were a completely different way of propelling a ship in space. He had already arranged for technology trades with the engineering staff of the Libertad. She chuckled softly at the thought of the engineers breaking down the barriers so quickly, and exchanging information. She hoped it was not a mistake to trust them – she hoped they were indeed who they said they were. She believed there was no deception in their minds. Also, if they really wanted to deceive them, then this would have been way too much work – it would have been easier to have just attacked while they were under repairs. Besides, they would have to know the base would blow them to bits at the first sign of deception.

The gangway was extended to a specified point onto the Libertad, connected, and pressurized. Jaime found herself slightly nervous as she realized she was about to meet her southern counterpart. She wondered if they would be that different – they had both struggled to get where they are now. While they had managed to permanently remove their Blessed from this galaxy however, she and the Evo were only able to get away, and establish themselves and this base. The Evo on the other hand had made other allies, and were starting to grow and thrive in this galaxy.

She watched as she saw people start to exit the ship and slowly walk down the gangway. She knew they would be curious about Haven and would have to take in the views of the harbor as they walked down the gangway. She would be patient in waiting for their arrival – it had been years since they were all in one place – and even longer since they were all in one place and *not* at war. She would wait for them to admire what they had accomplished.

First to exit the gangway was a golden skinned redhead. She stopped to judge the defensive situation in the room. Her bright green eyes flashed back and forth across the room as she assessed the situation. She looked over at Jaime – she swore she was trying to shoot laser beams through her as she stared at her. Jaime recognized the first officer insignias on her gold uniform. The young woman continued to look around inspecting every detail with her stabbing eyes. After a moment, she took another step in and stood to the side of the hatch. With a loud voice, and in southern standard Spanish she announced "Captain entering the room!"

Jaime continued to stand casually, but stiff enough to show respect. Now entering the room was a tall woman with golden brown skin – the gold was much more pronounced than the brown. She had expresso colored hair that was short, and slicked down toward the back. Her golden uniform had the captain's insignias, cords looped from her epaulets around her arms, a dark brown fabric belt adorned her waist above her wide hips. She wore matching gold fabric slacks, and a dark brown set of knee-high boots that clacked as she walked.

She took slow steps into the room – each step making an echoing snap as her boot hit the black asteroid floor. Finally she arrived to where Jaime was standing and stopped. She looked her northern counterpart up and down before giving a tough smile and a stiff salute. "Captain Nina Bonaventure of the independent starship Libertad."

Jaime returned the salute and introduction "Jaime Bordeaux, captain of the starship Ladyhawk..." she thought about what else she did for a moment – she never really realized what she was now. Nina gave her a confused look due to her long pause by the time she continued. "And leader of the civilization of Evolved Homo Sapiens...the Evo. Welcome to Haven."

Nina smiled, and slightly loosened up. "Thank you Captain, a pleasure to meet my counterpart in the struggle..." she said as she extended her hand.

"A pleasure indeed..." Jaime said as she reached out and took Nina's hand in a hearty handshake. She saw her first officer relax slightly as the two of them continued to shake. Suddenly, Jaime felt heat in the palm of her hand. She and Nina both looked down at their hands still locked in the handshake. They saw that there were sparks arcing between their hands. They both immediately let loose of their shake and started to wave their hands in the air as if cooling them down. "Well, I did not expect that!" Jaime exclaimed.

"No..." Nina agreed. "Do you think we are not compatible here?"

"I would doubt that..." said Max who had just entered the room. "I would almost say that it is the opposite effect that just occurred. Is it possible you two just started reconfiguring?"

Jaime shook her head no. "That can't be Max." Nina looked confused. Jaime explained "We discovered that that when two Evo are compatible and should mate, they form a bond upon physical contact. This starts a process of molecular reconfiguring between the two people. Because it starts as a tingling at the point of contact, Max is assuming that we might be compatible."

"Fok..." Kylie softly sighed as the two captains looked down at their now-tingling hands.

Nina Bonaventure:

She woke up very thirsty. She turned on the cabin lights, got out of bed, and went to the sink to pour a glass of water. She filled the glass and started to drink, but almost choked on the fluid when she looked at herself in the mirror. Dropping the glass, she ran over to the intercom and contacted her doctor.

Mena Petri was not the most experienced doctor that a ship could have, and she showed her inexperience at every emergency. As a matter of fact, she only was the ship's doctor by proxy. The real ship's doctor was killed in the revolution, as he was a Benditos. Because of his genetics, he had to be removed – spaced to be exact. It didn't help that he tried to kill Nina during the fight. So, Mena was now the doctor. She gasped in surprise when she entered Nina's cabin. She walked around and looked at her captain. She ran her scanner up and down her, and then studied the readouts.

Nina watched her studying her scanner readouts for well over five minutes before she finally lost her patience. "Well?" she asked with annoyance.

Mena looked up from her scanner, shrugged her shoulders and said "I have no idea. The one thing I can say for sure is that your skin color is changing."

"Tell me the obvious..." she replied dryly.

"I have been speaking with the northern doctor. I think they have made some discoveries about these changes. Perhaps we should go speak with him?" Nina nodded and put on her uniform, and Mena contacted Max.

When they arrived at the Haven infirmary, Max was waiting for their arrival. He had all of the medical scanners and instruments ready for examination and treatment by the time they had arrived.

"Hello doctor..." Nina said "I hope YOU can help me with my malady."

Max chuckled lightly, slightly annoying Nina. But then he said "I don't think I can help you. I have called the captain here however, as I think she will want to see this."

A moment later Jaime arrived and said as she walked in "I hope this is important Max, we are right in the middle of inspecting the repairs on..." she stopped and just looked at Nina with an open mouth. "What happened?"

Max simply said "YOU are what happened. You two touched and reconfigured..."

"Umm, I don't think so Max. I respect my southern counterpart…"

"But, we are not meant for each other…" Nina said, completing the sentence. "You told me about the reconfiguring of mates. We are not doing that…"

Max shook his head no, then started scanning while he said "Jaime, you have looked at her haven't you?"

Jaime took another look at Nina, her mouth opened slightly in shock as she saw the streaks of black running up her neck. Her skin color was changing from the greenish-gold to the same dark shade of blue-black as herself.

"So see, I would reconsider that statement you just made. The scans will prove that you two are…" he stopped and looked at his scanner. He reset the unit and scanned Nina again.

He looked up at Nina with a confused look. "Not reconfiguring are we, doctor?" she said dryly. He shook his head no, then turned to Jaime to speak. He stopped himself however, walked over to Jamie, and without saying a word started scanning her.

"Umm, what's up doc?" she asked.

Nina looked at her counterpart, then also walked up to her. Then reached up and touched her cheeks, before saying "Have you looked in a mirror lately?"

"No…" she said, then left the two to walk over to the mirror. She gasped as she saw the changes on her face. Her skin coloration was the same shimmering shade of midnight blue, one of the darkest, virtually black, shades of blue – but her white freckles had changed color, and were now a bright gold tone. Her freckles were now the same tone that was previously the color of Nina's face. "Oh crap…" she mumbled.

Max read his scans again, then said "Well, you are right…you are NOT reconfiguring. Instead, the differences between us and our southern counterparts are merging…It's the spark in your DNA. That spark is extra energy that you somehow always had…but now something about this galaxy excites that spark. This is what is causing the changes in you and in us. And now, this spark is causing the changes in DNA of us from the north to merge with the DNA of the people of the south. And as you Jaime, are always the catalyst for change because of that spark, we can expect that these changes will affect all of us soon in the future. I would assume Captain Bonaventure, that when you change, your crew changes?" She nodded yes. "Yep...so I bet if I do a molecular analysis of your cells, I would find the spark is in your DNA too. In that case, your crew will start to show the same changes in coloration. I think I would say at this point...we will all be the same very soon...so, welcome to the Evo."

About Six Years Ago...

"So, do you think that there are others up there? Other races, beings, we know nothing about?" he asked while they lay on the simulated grass and looked up at the stars through the viewing dome at the star base grid.

"I do...I look up into those stars, I have hope. Hope that there has to be something better in this universe. Has to be something or someone we can look to as a friend. Someone that does not always want to kill us like those in the south."

"Ah...for a soldier, you really are a dreamer..." he reached over and kissed her on the cheek.

"For a..." she sat up and looked at him "What the hell are you anyway?"

"Well, you could call me a Jack...as I don't seem to have a single thing I am an expert at. But, I do have a lot of things I do...pretty good."

"So, jack of all trades, but master of none, eh?" she chuckled.

"Maybe so...but you sure have a trusting heart for people...or beings that you have never met. How will you know if they really want to be friends? Maybe they will just kill you...or worse, maybe eat you?"

"Eat me? Really?" she blurted out laughing.

"Well, you are quite tasty..." he said as he rolled over and lightly bit her neck.

"Stop that...I'm serious...I really hope I somehow get out there and meet other races. I know there are some out there that will be our friends."

"Dreamer..."

NGD: 4 Years, 3 Days:

Evo Base Haven:

Jaime Bordeaux:

Jonathan had asked her to come to the Ladyhawk to see the changes the engineering staff had made to the various systems. He was very excited when he contacted her, and it made her wonder what was up.

She and Hero arrived at the gangway to the Ladyhawk and was met by the young man. He had a large smile on his face as he gave her a small salute. "Thanks for meeting with me Captain...you too Hero. We have added a number of new features that I wanted to run through with you before you take the ship out for a shakedown."

"It's my pleasure, Jonathan. You may start your...tour" she told him.

"First, let me point out the changes to the outside of the craft. We analyzed the data from the attack on the Innovation by the Blessed. We also THINK we have found the weapon they used in the attack. It appears that they have discovered that molten gold will melt the space carbon of the asteroid. This was how we mined the materials here, and it is how we created Haven out of this solid piece of space carbon. I am still not sure HOW they discovered this, but they did...and this weapon takes advantage of that one weakness."

"Interesting. Do you think our potential spy gave them that information?" she asked.

"I don't think so" he replied. "We kept our mining process a complete secret. By the time people started arriving at Haven, we had mined most of the current base. All of the mining equipment is now deep inside the lower levels of the base. We have moved into a mining purely for materials mode – it is pretty much automated. I doubt anyone would be going down there to discover our mining techniques. No, I don't think it was our spy...but the Blessed got that knowledge somehow." He shrugged his shoulders in surrender. "Well, in any case the new hull configuration should take care of the initial blast from that weapon. The hull is now comprised of multiple layers of space carbon and Faratainium. If a layer of space carbon is removed by their weapon, the Faratainium will provide protection to the layer below...if that layer is destroyed, then the next layer of space carbon will protect the next layer of Faratainium, etcetera, etcetera. We hope this will make it harder to reach populated levels like they did with the Innovation. In addition, we have added particle deflection field generators – much like the personal protection field generators we have been adding to our uniforms. Oh, also we have new uniform suits." She gave him a look of surprise. "They are made from the materials left over by those alien insects you brought back from Queek. They build a hive, utilize it fully, and then leave to build another hive. I am still not sure about where they find the materials to build it, but they do. In any case, what they leave, we slice and turn into fabric. This fabric is resistant to blasters, will protect us from the vacuum and cold of space, and will provide connection to the gel used in I.T.C.'s. It's perfect! I have a suit ready for you inside."

She raised an eyebrow to him, she was surprised by how much he and Kate had accomplished in the short few months. She looked at the space carbon on the outside of the ship. It shined with the look of being new – it had none of the dulling that occurred after a ship had been exposed to the harshness of space. She turned back to Jonathan and said "Okay, let's see what you've put together."

He showed her the upgrades to the main star drives. "These are no longer ion drives. We replaced the main R.F.S. with light drives – the same drives that are on the Libertad. They operate by generating an energy field that originally would use light waves to push the ship. By doing this, the ship will practically reach the speed of light. What worried me however, was that there may be times when the light is weak or nonexistent. The engineers on the Libertad told me they had ran into that situation a couple times. To remove that weakness in the drive, we modified it to use cosmic rays instead of light energy. This should prevent any failure, but just in case, there is a small pair of R.F.S. installed. That, along with the pulsars, gravitons, and the hyper-crawler...well, we should have no lack of means for propulsion."

369

"Are you providing these improvements to the Libertad? I would hate to leave them out, especially since they provided the initial design for this star drive."

"Already done, Captain. We have installed the new light drives on their vessel. They have not tested them at full force yet, but they anticipate they will experience faster-than-light travel with this improvement. In addition, we are installing the hyper-crawler, pulsars, and gravitons to the Libertad, so we will all have similar propulsion configurations.."

She nodded her head, impressed with the advancements. "Very good, show me more..." she requested.

They went to the bridge where he handed her one of the new uniforms. She looked at the one-piece suit. It was black-colored and she noted a slight honeycomb pattern in the material. It had an opening in the back that would allow her to slip in easily. On the front, over the heart was the new insignia of the Evo – a circle with a wing in the middle – the wing started on the lower left of the circle and the wing tips extended past the circle on the right. No other ornamentation was present on the suit. "Captain, if you would go into your ready room and try this on, I have the next improvement to show you."

She did as he requested and put on the black suit. She walked back out onto the bridge where the young man was still waiting. He motioned to the round metal plate in front of her command chair. "If you would step here, I would like to show you the next improvement." She did as instructed, and as soon as she and Hero stepped on the round plate, it lowered itself below the floor. It stopped in a round pod that reminded her of an I.T.C. of a Wolf Pack star fighter. She looked up at Jonathan, confused. He looked down at her – she noticed he had a slight look of fear on his face.

"What's going on, Jonathan?" she asked sternly.

"Well...first my apologies..." he said as the hatch above her closed.

Living gel began to fill the pod. It reached her feet and she felt the connection to the single cell organisms. She remembered how much she enjoyed the feeling and gave a small sigh. Then reality struck her – she called out on Norm-Comm "Jonathan, I don't have a helmet. I won't be able to breathe!"

On Norm-Comm he replied "I'm sorry Captain…it will be uncomfortable for just a moment, then the discomfort will leave."

"What?" she yelled, but got no reply.

The gel was now to her knees. She became slightly afraid – the gel flowed into the pod at an even faster rate. It was now up to her chest – then to her neck. She struggled to keep her head above the rising goo. It was up to her chin, and she started to panic. In her struggle she realized Hero was in the pod with her. She started calling out "Hero! Hero!" She looked down and saw the cat down deep in the gel. She started to cry out again "Hero!" Then the gel rose above her mouth and nose. She held her breath while she tried to find a control that would release her from this death trap, but there were no controls or indicators active or visible. She now knew she would be facing death in here – but she wondered why. Why would Jonathan do this to her? What happened that would cause him to want to assassinate her? Had he become a spy…was he always a spy? She held her breath as long as she could, but finally her need to breathe overtook her, and she let out her remaining used air in a final large puff. Without being able to stop it, her lungs took in the living fluid. She coughed and choked for a moment, then realized that she was still alive. She looked down at her feet and Hero was looking up at her while he paddled around the pod.

A moment later, Jonathan appeared in front of her. He was being projected in front of her inside the pod. "Again, I'm sorry I had to introduce you to the new gel that way. You would have never entered the pod if you knew what was going to happen…and you would not have believed you could live in the new gel without a helmet. The psychologists came up with this immediate immersion method to get the crews used to the new pods. I was just following their directions."

She found she actually could speak in the gel as without thinking she said "Remind me to kill a psychologist the first chance I get." She realized it felt really strange speaking in the gel – and was actually surprised she could do it. She looked back down at Hero, he calmly lay at her feet on the round platform. *"He seemed to know what was happening the whole time..."*

Jonathan was now smiling at her. "So, as you can see...the gel has also mutated while we have been here. No longer do we need a mask to breathe. The cells of the gel can now survive and provide a breathing environment inside our bodies. Now, for the rest of the tour in your pod..." and suddenly she was surrounded by the openness of the space harbor.

She gasped at the sight. In front of her, controls and displays lit up. Everything that she had on her command console was now located within reach in her pod. "Oh sh...are you telling me that I can command the starship through an I.T.C. pod?"

He nodded yes, then added "Not only command functions, but ALL functions. I too am speaking to you from an I.T.C. pod. There is one for every bridge station – engineering, science, communications, helm, weapons, and the first officer all have a pod. There are other pods for any extra personnel you wish to add to a voyage...even a Flaybah can use one of these."

"You're kidding?" she asked, but knew he was serious, despite the smile. "Well, I'm impressed. So, when do we take her out for a test run?"

"Anytime captain...whenever you want to assemble the crew. They have all been...indoctrinated...to the pods."

"What?" she questioned loudly. "Why was I the last to..." She was interrupted by the alert signal.

Otter spoke to her via Norm-Comm "Captain...base scanners are picking up an unknown ship entering our sector of space. Allen has called alert status."

"Let's head up to command...umm, how do I get out of here?" she asked.

"Green light to your right. Grasp it like a ball and squeeze to exit. It was setup that way to prevent accidental exiting."

She squeezed the ball of light and the pod opened above her. The platform below her raised to her feet and started lifting her back out into the open area bridge. As her head left the gel, she coughed from the fluid still in her lungs. The gel flowed out of her lungs and back into the pod as it cleared itself out of her body. When she was finally out of the pod she looked down at her feet to find Hero still sitting in a relaxed position. She also noticed her new uniform suit was no longer black – it was now a dull red. She looked at Jonathan with a confused look and pointed to the now red suit.

He gave a sheepish smile before saying "Well...the material in the suit reacts to the heat and emotion of the wearer. Normally, it's in its normal black color. However, when it turns blue it is indicating you are happy, purple when emotionally or sexually excited, green means you are scared or concerned, and red...well, it means you are angry. And the brighter, more distinct the color, the more intense the emotion."

"So, pretty much what you are telling me is that it is showing my annoyance for you dunking me in the pod without warning, eh?" He gulped and nodded yes. She put her hand on his shoulder, smiled, and said "Don't worry...Now, let's go see what's going on..."

They ran to the command center. Her uniform had turned back to black by the time they arrived. As they entered, Allen turned to them, and waved them over. "Captain, it appears a ship of unknown origin and configuration has...appeared...in our sector. It is headed this way."

"No identification?" she asked. Allen nodded no. "Any idea how they arrived?" Once again, he nodded no.

Jonathan looked over advanced scans and SCADAR readouts. "I don't recognize anything about this ship. It is totally unknown to us...but it will be here in three minutes."

Jaime ordered "Arm weapons, prepare all ships and fighters for launching. Get our allied ships on guard patrol to be ready. Everyone get ready for a fight...Give me the status..."

She was interrupted by a voice on Norm-Comm, a very familiar voice. "Captain...Jaime?"

"Halley?" she said, slightly confused.

"Hi!" Jaime could hear the excitement in her voice. "Yes, it's me. The ship headed toward Haven is not aggressive or a threat. I am on board…they healed me and are bringing me back home. I promise nothing will happen…please don't fire on us."

Jaime turned to Allen, and whispered "Stand down the launch order. Keep the base weapons active and notify our allied guard ships to maintain alert for the moment." He nodded in acknowledgement.

"Okay, Halley…we are standing down…somewhat."

"I understand completely. Keep some of your defenses on alert. Have to protect the base. The ship will stop within a half light second of the base. Then I will come over…with your permission of course."

"Halley, you are always welcome here." She warmly replied.

Within a minute the ship stopped exactly a half light second from Haven. A light was reported at one of the dock boarding areas. Jaime, Jonathan, and Allen ran down to the boarding area to find Halley already standing there, wearing a gray jumpsuit – and having all of her limbs intact.

Jaime looked at her with amazement. "I thought…well, I was told…"

"That I was missing…parts? I was, but the Dekrons healed me.

From the doorway, the four heard someone say "But, you were missin' you fokkin legs…and an arm!" They all turned to see Kylie standing in the doorway, her eyes firing laser shots through the now-returned Halley.

"As you can see, the Dekrons have the technology to regrow lost limbs. They somehow used my cellular structure and duplicated it in mechanical form. So, they were able to manufacture or regrow my limbs. They feel perfectly normal…I can feel a touch, sense pain…everything I could do before, and yet they are now stronger and tougher than they were…or so I am told." She walked up to the golden-skinned redhead and asked "Who are you, anyway? You look familiar…like you were looking over me at some point."

The young woman looked into Halley's eyes and instantly loosened up her stiff stature. She looked at Halley for a moment before extending an open hand and saying "Kylie Van Sycick, first officer of the starship Libertad."

"Nice to meet you, Kylie. You had a really concerned look on your face when we first met…" she took her hand and shook it – she felt something like sparks in her palm. Kylie felt it too, as she slightly jerked her hand away after the shake, and stared down into her palm. Halley looked at her palm, then into Kylie's eyes. She now understood the look she got from her on the Innovation. Kylie looked at her, smiled, and gave a small chuckle before saying "What the fok was that? Felt like standing in a fokkin' reactor there for a moment. Thought I had burnt my hand."

Jaime and Jonathan looked at each other. The engineer gave a small smirk and chuckle. Kylie looked down at her hand again and gasped. "What the fok?" Her palm had changed color from gold to deep blue.

"Umm, perhaps we should talk about that…" Halley said while looking at her changing palm. "Meet me for dinner perhaps?" Kylie just nodded yes, then turned and walked out of the room – still staring at her changing palm.

Halley turned and looked at Jaime with excitement in her eyes. Jaime let out a small chuckle at her friend's excitement. "Well, your back…but what about your friends? The ones that put you back in order for us?"

Halley turned serious for a moment, then said "I never really met them. They spoke to me, and the voice sounded so familiar. Yet, everything I saw in their ship was alien."

A voice over Norm-Comm interrupted them…it was the Dekron controller. "I can explain everything. May I come over and meet with you?"

"Yes, of course. Anyone who helped my officer is welcome here." She immediately saw a light near the wall closest to the harbor viewing ports.

In the corner of her eye, she spotted Yuli standing in the doorway. She turned and looked questioning at him. He looked at Jaime and smiled.

When she returned her attention to the light she now saw a humanoid woman emerging from the shaft of light. As soon as she stepped out, Jaime saw the silver shimmering skin, the female face, the metallic flowing hair, and recognized her immediately. "Nova, it's you…" she softly said.

"Hello Captain, Jonathan, Captain James." She looked over to the doorway and a warm smile came to her face. "Hello, my love."

Yuli slowly walked into the room and stopped right in front of Nova. He stared at her metallic face, her shimmering features, and her flowing waving hair. He started to reach out to touch her, but then stopped himself.

She smiled at him, and said "It's okay…I am not dangerous to touch. Please, touch me…" He reached up and felt her skin – like quicksilver it flowed around his touch. It felt smooth and liquid to him as he stroked her cheek. She closed her eyes and relished in his touch. "I thought I would never feel that again. Never experience the feel of your hand on my face, your breath flowing around my face and in my hair. It's wonderful…"

He asked her softly "But how? How is it you are here?"

She reached up and took his hands in hers and lowered them both to their side. She said to him "In a moment, there is something else that first needs to be said…to them. Then, I need to say something to you." She dropped one hand but continued to hold the other while she led him over to Jaime. She looked at her and smiled before saying "Jaime, the Dekrons are a race of intelligent machines that live in the void. When I ejected myself out of your ship and into sub-space, they found me. They were fascinated by my combination of living matter and machine…by the way, thank you Jonathan." He gave her a weak smile. "I think I was dead…they revived me, and then improved me. They were able to change me, improve me even more. I am now a being consisting of both living cells and machinery. From me they learned of the universe outside of the void. With my help, we left sub-space and have been wandering this galaxy. Since we left, I have been showing them all the wonders of space outside the void. They have been fascinated by what is out here. We...the Dekrons and myself...are planning on staying here. We are going back to the void only if and when needed. However, as we have travelled, we have been seeing and experiencing the pollution that the Blessed have been leaving in their wake. The Dekrons...not me...decided they were a blight that needed to be cleansed. From my knowledge of our journey, they knew of your plight with the Blessed...thus, my reason for being here. Well...one reason..." she said as she looked into Yuli's eyes. She returned back to look at Jaime, and then continued "The Dekrons have decided to be here as allies of the Evo. We are here to help."

Jaime looked over to the healed Halley, then back to Nova. "Well, you saved my best friend...perhaps helped to save one of my ships...I see no reason we cannot be friends." Nova gave a smile and a nod.

The Dekron controller then looked at Yuli. "That brings me to the next reason for coming here...you, Yuli. Despite my changes, I still need you...we still need you." Yuli looked at her confused. "Your child...your daughter...she lived inside of me when I jumped into the void...the Dekrons saved her also. She needs her father. Will you join me...join us?"

Yuli had a look of shock and curiosity on his face as he considered what she said. He finally answered her with a question "How? How can I live there? We are different species now."

"You don't have to be. You can become a Dekron with me and your daughter...your daughter...she needs you to help me pick a name" she replied.

He now had a worried look on his face. "Become a Dekron?"

She smiled and touched his cheek. "You felt my cheek, touched my skin. You saw how I enjoyed your touch. I would not have been able to even feel your touch before. I can tell you are enjoying my touch now. I am enjoying your touch more now than when we met. You will too. We will be able to touch and feel each other. Hold each other in our arms, love each other like when we met and got married. Touch our daughter, enjoy the feeling of being a family. The Dekron will keep us strong and healthy. It is beneficial both ways as we can help by giving them direction and providing the means for them to explore. Won't you consider it?"

He now had a smile on his face. He looked over at Jaime who smiled and nodded at him before saying "If this is your wish, follow your heart."

He looked at his wife, touched her face again, and then asked "Will it hurt?"

She smiled, gave him a kiss on the cheek and said "Not at all…" A column of light came from out of nowhere, and scooped the two up and away. A few minutes later, the Dekron ship left the sector as quickly as it arrived.

"Wow…" said Jaime "This is turning out to be quite a day!" She turned toward Halley again. "Are you ok? Nothing wrong or out of place?"

"No…" she answered. "I feel great."

"Will you still stop by and see Max anyway?" she insisted.

Halley Cet:

She left the boarding area and walked down the passageway to her ship. She promised Jaime she would stop by the infirmary, but first she needed to check on the Innovation. She walked the long passageway thinking about what she saw while on board the Dekron ship. She would need to investigate that too. She had so many things to do, to catch up.

When she arrived at the gangway to the ship, she found Staci waiting for her. The young woman looked at Halley, a tear formed in her eye – but she was fighting hard to keep the tears in check. Halley stopped and looked at her, unsure what to say. She finally smiled, and opened her arms to her first officer. She, without speaking ran to her and the two embraced in a warm tight hug.

After a moment, Halley pulled back and looked at her once again. She looked tired, she could tell that Staci had been working way too much trying to keep things together.

She looked at the ship as it sat in the dock. It still was having repairs performed, the robots were quickly running around the outer hull, replacing old hull pieces with new layers of materials. The hole in the ship was gone – repaired while still out in space. The hole still showed in Halley's mind however, she would have to make that repair herself. She still felt the pain of the burning beam in her mind – the damage it did would take longer to heal mentally, but she was determined to fight the mental anguish to the end. This visit was going to start the healing process.

"Looks like you took good care of her. Perhaps better care than I did…" she told the first officer.

"I only kept it together. You made us a crew that could take care of her while you were gone. I also had the southerners to thank…" she replied.

"Ah, yes…I met Kylie. She's a hellion, eh?" Her hand still tingled at their meeting.

Staci nodded yes. "She has been very helpful in getting the ship back together though. Her and Captain Bonaventure…the Captain heard you were back and is on board waiting for you. Are you ready to see the ship?"

She paused for just a moment while she remembered the pain she felt the last time she was on board, but then said "Yes, let's go see your work."

They took the grand tour. Staci showed her all of the improvements and changes that Jonathan and Kate had made once they had gotten the ship back to port. They had just finished installing the new light drives, improved R.F.S. and the new layered, shielded, space carbon hull plates. The ship looked as good as new. They rode the lift up, then walked down the corridor to the bridge – the closer to the hatch they got, the more she felt the temperature rise on her forehead. She felt the moisture from the sweat that formed in her palms. She was starting to wonder if she could make it through this – but she was determined – she would do this.

The hatch opened and Staci boldly walked onto the bridge. Halley was tentative however. She looked around, looking up at the domed star screen first – it had been repaired – the hole was not at all evident, the hole in the floor also gone, and had been replaced by a brand new and improved command chair. She slowly stepped onto the bridge, looking all around with each step.

She heard a yip behind her and recognized the noise. A smile came to her face and she turned around. "Beau!" she shouted. She looked for her little friend, but when she had finally located her dog, he did not look like the little companion she had lost her limbs over. The Chihuahua's coat was still slightly fawn color, but now had a shimmer similar to her own skin. The small velvety wings she felt that fateful day had grown into a small set of full wings. They flowed like fabric in the wind, the clear flesh always in a slight state of motion. "Oh my, you've changed..." The little animal ran up to her, his tongue hanging out of his mouth in excitement – that had not changed. She reached down and picked up her little friend. She noticed he was not that little anymore either – he had grown and was no longer the little teacup she remembered. He was now a good foot and a half tall, and now weighed at least a good fifteen pounds. "My goodness, someone has been feeding you well!" she said as she picked him up. He yipped and gave her a wet lick on the cheek. She giggled in delight at the affection being given by her friend.

"He has changed a little, no?" said a voice behind her. She turned to find Captain Bonaventure – from the descriptions of her, Halley had determined she had changed too. No longer did she have golden skin – instead it now was a dark blue, just like Jaime's. She also had a few golden freckles on her dark face. Her hair was still the dark coffee color, with some lighter undertones, and it was still slicked back in the same style as she saw in the images. Her brown eyes were such a deep shade, but like all Evo, they now glowed – but the glow in her eyes was so dramatic. She also wore a black Evo space uniform, her muscular frame bulged through the tight fit of the suit. The large woman walked up to her and extended a hand "We have not officially met...I am Captain Nina Bonaventure, and you are Captain Cet, no?"

"Yes, Cet..." she replied as she took the large hand in a hearty shake. Halley thought she was going to lose a hand to that powerful grip. "You can call me Halley. You and my first officer have really done a super job putting the ship back together."

"We did it for you. We were not sure when or even if you were coming back. But after what the bastards did to you, we felt we had to make the ship right in the event of your return. I am glad you approve."

"I do approve, you all have done a marvelous job!" she replied.

"Glad you like it, Captain..." a familiar voice called out behind her. She turned to find Lizzie at the engineering station. She had not changed, still tall and lanky, and her face still as hard as steel. Captain Bonaventure had not done anything to smooth her roughness. "I've been working with Jonathan to make some improvements." She pointed down to the circles on the floor, next to each command station. "When you get a chance, get with Jonathan for your orientation to those."

She looked curiously at the round, metal plates. "Okay..." she said cautiously.

She heard a noise behind her and turned back to Nina. Standing next to her was a larger version of Beau. The transparent wings flowing just like her little dogs'. Its fur were dark shades of brindle, and the colors seemed to shimmer as it sat next to the captain, The larger animal looked down at her little Beau. Nina reached down and scratched behind the dog's ears. "This is Perro...she and Beau have become good friends. They must be the only two in this galaxy, I imagine."

She looked and noticed that Beau was also looking up at Perro with the happiest smile. She realized they were at least friends. She then wondered if they enlarged Beau's kennel...she looked over and indeed they had.

Nina realized what she was looking at. "Yes, we made it bigger to accommodate your changing friend."

Halley suddenly felt guilt, as she realized these women had done so much to repair and upgrade the ship. "Well, I should let you get back to your work..."

She had a sheepish look on her face and Nina saw through it. "Actually, I think it is YOU who should start getting to work. You need to reacquaint yourself with your ship." Halley gave another look of desperation, so Nina continued "This is YOUR ship. I have the Libertad, and Staci...well I believe she has had enough of command for now."

Staci nodded her head yes. "It's your ship, Captain. You should stay onboard and get reacquainted with her. I am very happy to be a first officer again." She gave her a snappy salute, then smiled, and right before she walked away said "Yes, I have loosened up...thank you!"

"Take your first officer's advice. Stay onboard..." Nina suggested.

"I will..." she said, then realized "for a little while..."

"You have a date or something?" she asked.

Halley thought for a moment, then said "Yeah, something like that..."

*   *   *

She was late to meet her at the Harbor View Diner. By the time she got to the restaurant Kylie had already arrived and was waiting for her at a table next to the large bank of windows. She was wearing the now-standard issue Evo hive-produced, one-piece, stretch suit. She stood up to greet her, which showed how the purplish-black. tight suit showed off her curves and muscular frame. She quickly glanced down at herself – she was still wearing her older-style, gray tunic and matching pants outfit. She didn't care, she was not quite ready for the now-Evo-standard issue. She reached out to shake her hand, then hesitated. She noticed Kylie giving the same hesitation. After that brief hesitation, they both chuckled then took their hands in a soft shake.

They dined on an excellent selection of native plants harvested from one of the recent expeditions. That, along with a textural protein base made for an excellent meal. As they dined, they chatted about their various adventures.

She looked at the young South African, then asked "Kylie, how is it you were able to navigate the Devil's Throat to get here? From what we saw, that void should have trapped you..."

"Tell the truth, I have no idea. They had been shadowing your ship for the whole voyage. We figured they were planning a sneak attack on your vessel, and when you went into the Throat, they decided to follow you through to keep pursuit...we would not have done that. Somehow, the light drives got us through it, and out to the other side. Once there, they took off to hide and plot."

"So then, how is it you were able to take over the ship? You had to have been outgunned."

"We were..." she replied, while still chewing her food. " However, they piloted the ship into an asteroid storm. We suffered major damage, it killed quite a few of us...but it killed even more of them. Captain Bonaventure found the armory lightly guarded during the emergency, so we took advantage of the situation. We quickly took control of it and armed ourselves. They were unprepared for an armed force, and thus we were able to take over the ship quickly. We were unkind to them. We gave each of them a speedy trial, then spaced them."

"My god, that seems a little...well, barbaric."

Kylie looked both pained and annoyed at her comment. "Would you have let them live then?" She stood up and said "Maybe I misjudged you..."

Halley reached out and grabbed her hand. "No, don't go...I actually don't know what we would have done if it had been us. After what happened to me, I can now say I would probably do the same thing. Please, forgive me...don't go."

Kylie looked down at Halley holding her hand. "Do you feel that?"

"Yes..." she softly said. Then looked up at her again and said "Don't go..."

She sat back down and looked at her. "Okay, I am here, and staying. What do you want to do?"

Halley thought for a moment, then said. "How is your knowledge of astronomy?"

"It's only OKAY...why?"

"I saw something aboard the Dekron ship...I could use another set of eyes to figure it out. Want to take a look?"

"So, you want me to stargaze with you...well, that actually sounds...pleasant...really pleasant...alright."

They stood up and Halley noticed that Kylie's jumpsuit had changed – it was now a deep shade of purple. Kylie looked down at herself. When she looked back to Halley, she noticed that her cheeks showed a bright red through the now deep-blue shade of her skin. She looked up and the two giggled.

Kylie softly said "Oh, fok..."

Halley softly said "So, we still show embarrassment through this dark skin, eh?" They both laughed again, then, Halley reached out and took her still tingling hand. "Come on, let me show you my first love."

Six Months Before Starlight Launch...

She read the digital memo again:

"You have served your Alliance well. We thank you for all of your hard work and service to the cause. As of this moment, you are relieved of active duty status. Your new permanent position will be located on the Alliance star base grid. You will be a reservist for the Alliance Star Patrol, you will maintain your flight training status on the – Wolf Pack Star Fighter – and will operate the – Quadrant 15 Spy Monitor – when you are not on flight duty. Report to Monitor Command at 2530 hours in three days."

"Crap..." she sighed. It finally happened...they've put her out to pasture. She is to be a spy satellite monitor for the rest of her career.

"The rest of my career..." She thought about that over and over. She knew they would never put her back into a Wolf Pack. She was too good, and they wanted only Blessed to be the wing commanders now. The Alliance had won the space war – they were superior and forced the south back to earth-based warfare exclusively. She was no longer needed, as it was safe for anyone to fly a fighter now. So, she had been put on permanent satellite station monitoring. She would probably only get simulator time, or at the very least some minor flight practice time. But she knew the real meaning of the memo. She was going to be an administrator...a desk jockey. She would never fly anything faster than a touch pad, do anything more dangerous than answer an email from a pissed off general.

She had been put out to pasture...

NGD: 4 Years, 1 Month, 5 Days:

Evo Star Base Haven:

Jaime Bordeaux:

She sat at the desk in her quarters, catching up on her reading the hundreds of emails that sat in her inbox. She had reports, status updates, ship condition reports, battle action reports, and other miscellaneous items that needed to be read on a daily basis. If only she had the time to have read them daily. She hated desk work.

It had been a fairly quiet month. There had been only a few skirmishes with the Blessed since they declared war on the Evo. The Evo fleet was powerful, and between them and their allies they had been more than capable to repel any space attacks. She read a recent report of a Hammerhead that made just that mistake as they took on a Wyvern, and Flaybah star cruiser. The new layered reflective hull plating appeared to be able to take a few good shots from their weapon, so that was a good thing. Also lucky for the Evo, they had not been so bold as to attack Haven.

Then a message caught her eye – it was a Norm-Mail from Halley. She wondered why she had sent the mail message, and not made a personal call. She had been quite aloof to her of late, and she wondered why. Jaime had worried about her best friend since she was injured in the battle, was taken away, and had been returned healed and repaired. Jaime wondered if she had done something to upset her. She had not kept in touch enough lately, as life had been way too busy for her as the leader. She at one point realized she had not seen her much, but she also had not had the time to find out what was wrong. She felt bad about having ignored her friend.

She knew that the repairs on the Innovation were complete, and she had taken her out a few times on patrol. She assumed that was where she had been all this time. Then she looked at the email again. No, she had been on base quite a bit, so Jaime had ignored her and had not realized it. Reading the message gave her some hope however, as it had the tone of excitement – maybe she had been forgiven, or maybe she was never mad at her. Jaime actually had a spare moment, she could either find out more about the message, or continue to read emails. She decided she wanted to find out what had gotten her so excited to send the message. She decided it was a good time to go on a house call to see her friend.

She and Hero went to her quarters and rang the annunciator. She didn't expect Kylie to answer. At first, the sprite South African girl seemed surprised and embarrassed by her unexpected visitor. But then quickly adjusted as Jaime asked about Halley's whereabouts.

"Anymore, she is in three places...here...with me...in the Innovation...or in Astrometrics."

"You two been seeing each other long?" Jaime asked, now realizing what had taken her away all this time.

Kylie now showed some red tinges in her dark blue face. This was something that she never expected out of this spitfire-of-a-first-officer...embarrassment. "Since I arrived here. Actually, when I first saw her on the Innovation. She was injured, but something about her...well, attracted me."

"Well, that is actually a relief to me. I was worried I had angered her somehow" Jaime admitted.

"Oh fok...er...no, Captain. All she ever talks about is how great of a friend you are. I'm sorry, I think I have kept her too occupied of late."

Kylie bent down and petted Hero. He cooed, then started a loud purr. Jaime was now pleased – if Hero accepted her, so would she – and as they had reconfigured, obviously Halley had accepted her too. She smiled at her, then said "As long as you both are happy, I'm happy. Her welfare is my priority...she is my best friend after all...and if she is happy with you, then we can be friends too." Upon telling her this, Jaime noticed she had loosened up her stature, and had relaxed enough to return a light smile. "Well, I will go check Astrometrics, I really want to know what she's discovered."

"Perhaps, I can join you?" she asked.

"Of course! Mind if we jog it though?" Kylie shook her head no. "Good, come on."

As they ran down the corridor Kylie told her "So, she told me she thought she loved you..."

"She was infatuated, we are best of friends and she was young. She got the two mixed up. I will never be joined...it is my fate. I was to be joined, then the Blessed took that from me."

"Then you have a reason to hate them...more reason than them warring with us" she said and Jaime nodded yes.

She thought about what she just said, then replied "You know, I like hearing that...them warring with us...we really have unified. After everything that has happened to us on earth, the battles we fought against each other, the death we caused to each other...and yet, we can still come together years later and join to fight a common foe. Wow, just amazing how far we Normals...now Evo...have come."

Kylie nodded in agreement. "I think being forced to fight each other...yeah, it caused us to hate each other on the battlefield, but once the oppressing forces of the Union and the Alliance were removed, we no longer had a reason to hate each other. We really are the same after all."

"Were you a soldier?" Jaime asked.

"No..." she replied. "I was a ground-based technician. I'm good with electronics and computer circuitry. But I was also top in my class in battle tactics, and the school boxing champ... so, to the Union I was perfect as a mate to the Benitos."

"Familiar story..." was all she needed to say in reply.

The two ran down the corridors through the interior of the base until they had jogged the five miles to the opposite side of the asteroid. Here the Astrometrics lab was located at an outside wall of the base. This location was selected so that all of the space telescopes and viewing domes could be located on the outside walls of the base, but still near the computers that would control the telescopes, and provide viewing for the occupants of the lab. As they suspected, Halley had her face glued to a computer screen – on this screen were a line of three stars.

"Halley?" Jaime asked softly, not to startle her.

She turned and saw her and Kylie walking toward her. A look of slight panic flowed across her face. She softly muttered "Fok..."

"Now, where did you pick that up?" she said as she turned and glanced at Kylie. The first officer blushed again. She turned back to Halley. "Don't worry my friend. I know...and I am happy for you two." This brought a small smile to her face, but Jaime could tell she still felt slightly guilty. To break the ice, she then said "Now, what is it that caused you to...email...me?"

388

"Sorry to have not Norm-Comm'd you...but I knew you were busy, and I wanted to make it so you could read and respond when you had the time. So, come over here...let me show you what I found...While I was healing on the Dekron's ship, they gave me the opportunity to use their technology to stargaze. During that time, I did nothing but concentrate on the stars...once when I was awake and doing my gazing, I saw this."

Jaime and Kylie walked over to the computer display and looked at the line of three stars. She stared at the image before finally saying "Ok, it is a line of three stars. Is this of significance?"

"Significance?" she softly cried out "Of course it is significant. Don't you recognize it?"

"Obviously no..." she replied. It was simply a band of three stars. On the right of the three stars, were another smaller line of two stars and a dull glow on that went down from right below the line of stars.

"Ok, let me point these out...up above that line of stars is Betelgeuse, below to the left is Rigel..."

"No, wait..." she interrupted. "This, I DO know...but Rigel is on the right and Betelgeuse is on the left."

"When you look at it from earth...but if you were or ARE on the opposite side of the galaxy..."

"You mean?" she nodded yes.

Kylie interjected "Well, my astronomy sucks...I am a battle tactician...what the fok does this mean?"

Halley replied "It means my dear...that this is the constellation Orion...while looking at it from the opposite side of the galaxy. And so..." She refocused the telescope to a single star before saying "THIS is the Solar System, OUR Solar System...and THIS is where earth is located. If we wanted to go back, we could simply perform a number of insertions and be back, without using the Devil's Throat.

"So, if we decided that we needed to go back...like if the war goes sour, or we can't find a new home..."

"We could return home?" Kylie added. "You know, with our new technology...and our fleet of ships..."

"We could easily remove the Alliance, AND the Union..." Jaime said.

"And remove the bahstards from the fokkin' planet..." added Kylie.

Boral Oldham:

It was an impressive battle station. He was being led around on his tour of Zeus by Fitchburg and Janus. They looked through a viewing portal to a bright ball of plasma that was generated between the gaps of two large, shiny metal, points.

"How does this work?" Boral asked.

Janus, now as tall as Boral answered "These two points focus massive amounts of black energy into a ball. Once the energy is accumulated to where it can no longer be contained, it escapes into the focus lens. When it meets the plasma beam from Apollo, it collides and repels, which forms the protective bubble.

"So this is dark energy?" he asked.

"No, black energy...totally different. It is quite unstable, but our design allows us to capture, and utilize it before it stays in containment too long. Thus, we use it before it could possibly harm us." He then looked at Fitchburg, and said "Isn't that right, father?"

He was briefly caught off guard, but then replied "Uh, yes...yes, that is how it works. Nice job at explaining the complex operation of my design."

"Yes, you do know quite a bit about your father's design..." he told the young man. He looked at Janus – to him, he seemed freakish. That strange skin color, those ears that were not even properly developed for a Norm, his growth at such an early age – there was nothing about him that was "right".

A loud explosion startled them and made them cover their ears, as the entire station shook at the same frequency of the explosion.

"What the hell is going on?" Boral yelled out.

Janus was already on the computer, and had checked the status of the base. He turned and smiled at the two men. "It appears that we have caught something. A ship just exited the Throat...it ran into the barrier and we now have something to salvage."

"Really? So, how do we enter the field to get it? That is, if nothing can get through the barrier?" he asked the young man. Fitchburg was showing some frustration over Boral's ignoring him.

"We will readjust the focus lens, this will cause the beam to change shape, which will create an opening in the guarding bubble. Ships will be able to enter and exit through this opening."

"Good, good...so we can salvage what we just caught then?" The two shook their heads yes. "I am thinking we may want to remove the other asteroids in that case, and build more of these bases to capture anything that might come through. It would be like stealing candy from a baby."

Janus looked confused. "Why would we do that?" he asked. "I like candy..."

"It is only an expression, son." Fitchburg replied.

They went to a nearby viewing deck and looked out into the protected area of the base. There floated the remains of the spacecraft that had just attempted to exit the throat. It was nothing but rubble and fragments of what was once a medium-sized star ship.

"We should get some good salvage from that wreck." Janus said.

"Perhaps some tech?" Boral asked.

"Maybe..." Fitchburg replied. "Let's go to the control center now..."

The three started to walk away from the viewport and back to the lift, when Boral stopped and looked around back at the viewport. He then asked "What happens if one of these bases is destroyed? Do we lose our gate protection?"

"Yes, my Star Force Commander" replied Janus, who now was taking the cue from his father. "However, this base is so armored and weaponized, I doubt any force would be able to crack its shell." Boral nodded his head, apparently satisfied with the answer.

He thought for a moment, then said "Make a project plan to build more of these bases...I want to get another set on-line within a year. We will need to expand the fleet...because part of the main force will be returning to earth. After the broadcast we all saw, we need to see if the Supreme Commander requires our assistance. He will be too proud to ask if he is in trouble. Thus, we will need the salvage and tech to build a fleet expansion to protect our claim on this galaxy."

"Yes, my Star Force Commander!" Fitchburg snapped. Janus just looked at the two in curiosity.

About Eight Years Ago...

As an experiment, he was running a communications beam from earth to the moon – that was when he discovered it. He had ultra-charged a radio wave for hyper transmission, thinking it would speed the transmission time from point to point. This experiment was to be for his upcoming Bachelor thesis for his communications degree. He was determined to find a way to get a message across greater distances in shorter amounts of time. This hyper beam experiment would prove his theory. He even wondered if he could sell the idea to the military – they certainly would want a way to instantly communicate with say, forces on Mars.

He powered up the transmitter and verified the receiver that was located on the broken surface of the moon was ready to receive. He tested the message that he was going to send for the transmission, then set the frequency of the transmission to match the receiver. All appeared to be ready.

He activated the ultra-frequency and activated the recorded message:

"Hello Mars...Earth calling...Hello? Hello? Can anyone hear me? I am the radio man..."

It was a silly message, but it was original at least.

He checked his receiver on the moon – no transmission received. He furrowed his brow as he wondered what could have gone wrong. Then he heard the reply.

"This is Mars Alliance base...who the hell is radio man?"

"Oh shit..." He checked the transmitter, everything looked correct. "How could it have transmitted to Mars? That was too far away, and it happened much too fast" he wondered.

He then checked space for any anomalies and was shocked as to what he found. Where his hyper-transmission had travelled, there was a small point of damage to space, like a scuff or a cut. He called a friend at the observatory.

"Halley, can you check something. I am beaming over some coordinates. Can you run a full spectrum scan on that area? Sure, I will wait..."

She did the scan and sent him the results while saying "What did you do? It's torn there!"

He read over the scans and said "A micro-tear, in space? Wow, I have no idea...but I am going to do it again!"

"You're so reckless!"

NGD: 4 Years, 5 Months, 13 Days:

Starbase Haven:

Jonathan Faraday:

He knew what was about to happen when he rang the annunciator at her office door. As he expected, she was surprised by his announcement. "Captain, we are short of star ship fuel. Actually, we are short of fusion materials...boron and free hydrogen."

This caught her totally unprepared. "Okay, so how did we get to this point?"

He now had a pained look on his face – he knew he messed up. "Well, I kinda forgot that when we built all of these ships, we would need fuel for them. I was able to move and skim reserves off of the other, existing craft...but now I can't do that as we are pretty much out. We have plenty for small trips, but anything longer than a single long insertion...well...I would advise against it."

"Crap, Jonathan..." Jaime sighed. "What do we need to do to go find some?"

Now, his face brightened up having been asked that question. "Actually, I have discussed this with Oomha and Jaenar. They know of a planet that is uninhabitable that will supply the boron. The hydrogen, we can scoop off of a gas giant. Once we have those supplies, we will be in great shape. The fusion reactors just need those two materials and we can produce all sorts of energy – more than enough to power both our ships and the reactors here at Haven."

"So, you have been skimming from Haven too?" she asked. He gave a sheepish nod of his head.

"Well, it's settled then…Jonathan, I believe the Innovation is on station patrol. Tell Captain Cet to accompany you. Perhaps the Marcole could join you?"

Jonathan nodded his head yes. "Oomha has already suggested that. Jaenar will be on the Innovation."

Jaime thought for a moment, then contacted Allen on the holo-imager. "Do we have any confederation patrols still here if the Marcole leaves?"

"We have the Xillomartak cruiser. It is small, we don't really know their ability to hold out in a fight, but it's better than nothing. We can get the Flaybah to send a ship to relieve the Marcole…but it will probably be a day before they arrive."

"Captain…" Jonathan interrupted. "We will need to take the Shooting Star for storage. That ship is armored, but not weaponized. We are building another, but for now we cannot afford to lose that ship yet. I would highly advise that you let me take the Marcole as protection."

She sighed "Very well. I will prep the Ladyhawk for base patrol." She contacted Allen again. "Allen, please have La Lucha prepare for departure as additional base patrol. We should be alright with three ships protecting the base until the supply convoy returns. Besides, three ships is about all the fuel we can expend on patrol." Allen acknowledged and signed off. "Well, Jonathan…let's hope it will be a quiet few days."

Alpha Starship Captain Belleview Blythe:

Finally, all this time waiting in hiding had come to fruition. The battle patrol had been sitting in a nearby nebula, just waiting. Now, the spy drones he had sent out to monitor Haven were providing the news he had been waiting to hear. The guard patrol ship had left and only a single ship was guarding the Evo's starbase. He watched from the bridge of his Super Hammerhead as the images from the spy drone were received, and displayed on his holo-screen.

"They are leaving. The base is only lightly protected." He tapped his fingers on his command console while he watched the ships leave the area for sub-space insertion. "Notify the Scimitar that we attack in five minutes."

"Alpha Starship Captain?" questioned his first officer. "I thought our orders were to monitor the base and report back any weaknesses shown. Is attacking the base wise?"

"Are you questioning my judgment?" the first officer shook his head no. "I thought not. No, the orders were to monitor, and if needed take advantage of any weaknesses that might be seen." He lied on that part of his orders – with a victory, no one would question him. "So, we will take advantage of their lack of defensive ships and attack...while they are vulnerable. Prepare the fleet for battle, first officer."

"Yes, my Alpha Starship Captain!" he yelled out and began battle preparations.

The sounds of alert tones filled the bridge. Men ran around checking their stations, and prepared for battle. The weapons master checked his targeting locks on the distant base and its single defensive starship. He felt the excitement, it stimulated him in ways he never expected, ways that also slightly embarrassed him. He shifted slightly in his seat while he attempted to get control himself – but it was difficult with all the battle preparation going on around him.

"Alpha Starship Captain, the Scimitar reports they are ready. All battle preparations are ready here. We are prepped and primed for battle. Command us to victory!"

"TO VICTORY!" the bridge crew yelled.

He felt the pride in his crew, and it made him even more excited. He stood up from the command chair and ordered "Helm, take us out of the nebula. Take us into battle!"

Captain Allen James:

It was only a few minutes after the supply convoy left that the proximity sensors sounded. He looked at advanced scans – what he saw was not good. "Shit..." he muttered as he watched the two ships leave the nearby nebula. "They were waiting there the whole time…sound base alert."

He patched the scans to the Ladyhawk. Jaime appeared on the holo-screen. "So, they were waiting for us to let our guard down…crap, I should have known this would happen."

"Don't beat yourself up about this, Jaime. We check that nebula every few days. They must have found a pattern in our patrols, and were able to leave the nebula before the patrols discovered them. How long till you can get out into battle?"

"Reactors are not high yet. I am being told that it's going to be another ten minutes…they were fully shut down for maintenance."

"Very well. I will get more of the fleet powered up and ready for battle. James out."

He turned to Otter and ordered "Make a base-wide announcement. Have all personnel put on pressure suits. Get everyone to their stations. After that, get yourself to the Ladyhawk. It's the safest place we have, as Jaime's commanding her." She nodded in agreement, then proceeded to use her calming tone to prepare everyone on the base for the imminent attack.

Allen and the rest of the staff also donned pressure helmets – the clear acrylic forming over their heads – sealing to the fabric of the new Evo uniform suits made out of the hives left over by the insects that were the gift of the Queek. To him, everything was now in preparation for the incoming attack – if only their starships had been powered up in advance.

The enemy ships charged into battle quickly. It only took a minute to completely dispatch the Xillomartak cruiser. Allen felt bad for the overwhelmed allied vessel, but at least they did cause some damage. Scans indicated the protective fields on the attacking Mako were lower than at the start of the attack. He saw Otter leave the command center, then heard his science officer yell out "They're firing!"

He looked out through the viewports across the harbor. He saw the harbor space doors turn red and melt away. A large gaping hole had formed in the lower center part of the door. He looked at his console, scans were showing another buildup of power in the Mako. He then saw the golden beam fly through the hole in the harbor door and head right at them. The explosion rocked harbor control.

The concussion of the blast knocked him out momentarily. Only his newly developed Evo recuperative powers brought him back quick enough to realize the emergency. He jumped up and quickly read over the base status reports. Scans showed that atmospheric pressure was leaking out of the room. He heard the slight hiss of atmosphere escaping, which supported the scan reading. He worried that the leak would become worse, and that they might all be sucked out into the harbor. The rest of his staff was coming to from the concussion, so he barked out "Everyone, evacuate the command center, now!" He helped a couple of the staff to their feet and pushed them to the door. He himself ran to the door, heard a noise, and turned to see the glass of one of the viewports cracking. Everyone ran out of the room, and got the door closed just in the nick of time. As soon as the door closed, he heard the rush of the remaining air escaping through the closed hatch. He could feel the force of the air escaping through the vibrations in the floor and the shuddering of the door.

"Everyone move to the emergency command center in the center of the base." Another shot hit below them, the floor shook like an earthquake. "Let's hope the base survives this."

"Captain?" Messiah called out on Norm-Comm. "Permission to launch fighters. We need to start striking back at these bastards!"

"Negative, any fighters leaving through the hole in the harbor door would be picked off like target practice. Even in our numbers, our fighters would not survive. Hold until we get a couple of capital ships launched and somehow get them into open space."

"Hate to disagree, but we have a better launch point..." he corrected him. "The idiots just shot a hole right through the entire base. Not only will we be able to fly a whole squadron of fighters through it, I bet you can get a cruiser through that hole...it is that big."

"Well in that case, proceed with launch of wings one, two, and three" he ordered.

By the time he got to the secondary command center, Messiah had launched the three wings of fighters. They were zooming through the hole in the back of the harbor, and coming out the back side of the base. They were now stationed in the shadows of the back of the asteroid, hiding while they prepared to take on the enemy fleet.

The Super Hammerhead was now coming into firing range, its weapons were powering up. He looked over the base defense systems, base status, and weapons – many of the base's communication systems had been severed by the first attack. He said "This isn't going to work here. I think it's time we moved command…" He activated his Norm-Comm "Jaime, I am switching command to you. You're the flag vessel for the base. We will be moving to the Valkyrie as soon as all command functions have been transferred." SCADAR indicated that the Hammerhead was about to fire. "Shit, hope we survive this. Prepare yourself, another blast on its way!"

Captain Kylie Van Sycic:

Her first chance at being the Captain of a starship, and in her first command, she now faced possible or even certain death. She sat in the command chair of the La Lucha and checked the status reports coming into her command display. The ship was ready for launch and for battle – all weapons were active, engines were ready, and reactors were at full power. She read over all the status reports, realized she was about to take her crew into battle, and sighed quietly "Fok…"

Her science officer announced "All systems are go, we are ready to depart Captain."

"Very well, release dock moorings, Helm slide us out of harbor dock. Wait for the fighters to clear the base – they will be using that back door the Blessed just made and once outside will be giving us navigation telemetry." She watched as the hundreds of Firebrand fighters shot out of the launch bays of the base's hangar deck. They immediately headed into the large hole in the back of the harbor. A moment later, the fighters began sending back information about the battle going on right outside their home base as they all sat in hiding on the back side of the asteroid.

"Course Captain? The harbor space door is still under attack..." the helmsman announced.

Kylie changed the helmsman's display to show the back of the harbor. "See that hole in the harbor wall?" she asked. The helmsman looked at her visual display and requested scan readouts on the blast hole. She gave a pained look before saying "Umm, yes..."

"Take us through there..." she ordered.

"Umm..." she continued to look at her scan readings.

"Is there a problem going through there? Shall I take over? I can navigate it if you can't" she mockingly stated.

"No, I can do it Captain!" She said as she slowly took the cruiser to the back of the harbor.

"Stop here for a moment, we need to get some assistance here" she ordered. She activated Norm-Comm "Captain, we are prepared to attempt using this back door to enter battle. Do I have any backup or assistance once I get out there?"

Jaime replied "Affirmative. We will "distract" the enemy here at the front door while you, Tigresa, and Nimbus go out through the back and hopefully catch them off guard. We are hoping they will not expect cruisers to navigate the blast hole for escape. If we're lucky, they haven't realized how far their blast actually travelled. In the meantime, we are going to try to find a way to get the harbor door open...Dragons and the other larger ships are trapped in here like rats in a cage. Tell me you're able to navigate that hole."

"We think so..." she said without asking her helmsman.

"Are you using your pods?"

"Negative Captain. My crew is not ready to use them. My helmsman is more comfortable using her nav console. I am willing to let her make that decision."

"Very well, good luck to us all. Bordeaux out."

Her helmsman took the cruiser to the opening of the blast hole at the back of the harbor and pointed the front of the craft down the tunnel. Jagged, curved, stalagmites and stalactites jutted from the walls of the tunnel and pointed down and back into the direction that the blast had travelled on its way through the asteroid. The dark hole sparkled with small glimmers of light as the ship's navigation beams hit the small flakes of gold that pitted the space carbon material of the base. The helmsman made a small gulp as she peered down the small opening in the wall.

"Ah, that's nothing!" said Kylie as she came up behind her, put a hand on her shoulder, and gave her a reassuring squeeze. "It has at least twenty feet on either side of the ship...piece of cake!" Then coldly ordered "Proceed..."

The ship slowly entered the tunnel. The helmsman inched the throttle controls a little further and propelled the ship down the narrow passageway at a slow but constant speed. She constantly monitored the SCADAR readings, looking at measurements and judging the best positioning of the ship.

Kylie watched intently until she was interrupted by her science officer. "Captain, I have reviewed the scans taken by the fighters, we have a problem..."

"All stop!" she ordered and walked over to the science station. "What is it?" she asked.

Maria Espinosa, her science officer was a tall young woman. Even through her now-blue skin, her Hispanic facial features and heritage stood out. She had worked with Kylie since they escaped from earth. Kylie had nothing but the utmost trust in this young woman, her knowledge, and her abilities. She walked up behind her and peered down into the reports from the fighters. In the display was a very large stalactite hanging down so far that Kylie could see there would be no way to get past it.

She softly said "What damage would it do if we hit it? Just enough to knock enough of a piece of it to get by..."

Maria thought about it for a moment, then answered "Well, either two things will happen...one, we sustain some pretty heavy damage, but knock enough of a piece off to get through..."

"I don't think I really want to hear possibility two..." Kylie interrupted.

Maria ignored her and continued. "Possibility two is that we take such massive damage from the collision that the ship decompresses, and explodes."

"Fok, I told you I didn't want to hear that." She thought for a brief moment. "Okay, let's hope it is possibility one. Figure out the best spot to hit it with the ship that will cause the least amount of damage. Work out with Iffe any details, evacuate that section, seal it off totally, and when you are ready, we'll give it a go." She looked over at Iffe, who was now her engineer and said "Sorry 'bout what I'm 'bout to do to your ship..." The tall African woman, just silently nodded.

Kylie then looked at her communications officer and said "Patch me into ship-wide Norm-Comm." She felt the connection, then announced "*Attention all hands, this is the Captain. We have an obstacle in front of us that is preventing our exiting the base. This will cause the assault fleet to not be available in the defense of our base. For this reason, we are going to use the ship to try to clear the obstacle out of the way. Our plan may work, or it may not. In any case, we are going to try. We will clear out all personnel from the affected portion of the ship...but we still might damage the ship to the point where we may all die. Just wanted to let you know. I know this is our maiden voyage and this is to be our first battle. We all want to go show those bahstard Blessed just who we are. I am hopeful we will have that chance. We named our ship "La Lucha" for a reason...we must always fight the battle and overcome the struggle if we, as evolved humans are to survive...and we WILL survive this. Keep your fingers crossed anyway...prepare for collision. Captain out.*"

She looked around at the nervous faces on the bridge, then questioned "Helm, is course set?" The helmsman nodded yes. She looked at Maria "Is everything prepared? Sections evacuated, calculations made?" Maria nodded yes. Kylie again looked around the bridge at her crew – every one of them were now wearing uniforms of green rubber-like fabric – they were afraid, the uniform material changed with their mood, and she understood why. She looked down at her own jumpsuit and it had a slight tinge of green showing through the normally black material – she was afraid also. She ignored the feeling she had and announced "Ok, let's do this. All hands prepare for collision. Helm, proceed at calculated speed, an' take that fokkin' thing out of our way…we have a battle to get into!"

The helmsman guided the ship quickly down the dark tunnel. The holo-displays showed the approaching stalactite, dangling down from the ceiling, and blocking their path. It was very thick at the base, but wiggled down into only a small pointed sliver at the end – the end they were hoping to remove. It got bigger and bigger on the display, alarms started to ring in alert. The closer they got, the louder and more pronounced the alarms chimed out.

Kylie yelled out "Hang on!"

The ship hit the hanging column of space carbon, which caused a loud crash that was felt throughout the ship. Without the protective strapping fields everyone on the bridge would have flown across the room with the sudden shift of momentum. More alarms rang out as the hull took the brunt of the damage and caved in under the collision. Everyone on board could hear the sudden evacuation of atmosphere in the damaged areas of the ship. The loud swooshing sound was loud and impossible to miss. During that moment, everyone had a slight look of fear on their faces. Lights flickered, and went out as power couplings overloaded briefly – returning a moment later. Random consoles blew out their electronics from the impact and sparked and smoked before the automated systems calmed the damaged circuitry.

When the ship finally calmed from the collision, Kylie looked around and said "Tell me we did it?" She waited for the holo-screens to reactivate, and when they did she was shocked to see the damaged section of the ship. The starboard side of the command section now had a large "V" shaped indentation. There were sparks flying out of the damaged section as various plasma conduits released their energy out into the space beyond. And to Kylie's dismay, the ship now wrapped itself around the still hanging stalactite. "Fok…" she whispered in despair. Suddenly, the ship moved away from the hanging space carbon and started slowly down the remainder of the tunnel. The tip of the stalactite still firmly attached to the damaged section of the ship.

"We appeared to have succeeded in breaking the tip of the obstacle, Captain" announced Maria. She continued "However, it appears that tip is now embedded into the hull of the craft."

"So, it's part of the ship?" she asked. Maria shook her head yes. "Well, I guess it is better than a big hole...proceed with the mission as planned. Helm, take us out and once we are in open space, park us in the shadow of the base while we wait for the other two ships. Iffe, get a crew down to that section of the ship and do a quick analysis of the damage...but be quick...we will be in battle soon."

She was contacted by Captain Sheba DelMonaco of Tigresa. "Captain, are you all okay there? You took quite a bit of damage. Should we ask for a replacement for the lead cruiser?"

"Absolutely not!" she retorted. "We may look like someone punched us in the fokkin' nose, but the damage is now plugged, and we can still fight...and fight we will!" She calmed a moment before continuing "Join us in the shadow...cruiser Nimbus, you also rendezvous with us in the shadow. Do not continue out into the fight...I have an idea..." She switched to the fighter command channel on Norm-Comm. "Messiah, Star Child, we are going to make a small maneuver...when we do, you will need to send your fighters into the attack. I wish to say no more as we don't know if they might have broken our Norm-Comm communications."

Messiah replied "Roger that. We'll figure out when to charge in. Messiah out."

She typed navigational plots into her command console, then sent them to the helm and to the other two starships via tunneled protocol.

The helmsman looked over the plots and turned and looked at Kylie "Really?" she questioned, not expecting an answer.

Kylie simply nodded her head and said "Let's just hope that the Ladyhawk can get out of the harbor before we perform that maneuver..."

Starship Ladyhawk:

Jaime Bordeaux:

She floated in the command pod – Hero swam around her without a care in the world. All around her was her bridge crew, also all floating in their appropriate pods. They all maintained the same positions as when they sat in bridge console chairs, but instead of sitting, they were standing – actually, floating in their appointed positions. Most of her original crew was gone – almost everyone was now a replacement. She still had Otter, and that was good. Lizzie had taken engineering, since Jonathan was now the captain of the Whale. Micha Reynolds was at the helm, Aimee Maderia from the south was her new weapons master. She even now had a Flaybah as a science officer – KayOolah – a brilliant doe who had turned out to be such an asset to her team. Jaime chuckled slightly at the doe trying to adjust to the gel-filled pod. Despite her great bridge crew – in the back of her mind, she missed the old days and all her friends – but they had all gone their own way. Still, she felt fortunate to now have such a great replacement crew.

Apart from the visions of her crew, everywhere else around her was the openness of the space harbor. The ship had pushed out of the dock and even with the protection of the pod, she could hear and feel the sound and vibration of the engines as they kicked in. It was quite a sensation, the hull of the ship was only a ghostly outline in her vision – she knew it was there, but for the most part it felt as if she was commanding a spirit.

Dead ahead of her was the harbor space doors, or what was left of them. The blasts had created a large gaping hole in the middle of the former protective doors. She looked behind her at the large blast hole in the back of the harbor – the three Wyvern cruisers and the hundreds of Firebrand fighters had already made their way through the artificially created back door. She looked to her left, at Lizzie. "Engineering status?" she asked.

"Reactor is only at level 3, output is low. We still have a few minutes before we can kick in the ion drives to full power, light drives will be on-line a minute after that. We have some power for some maneuvering speed...that's about it" replied the hard, light-blue-faced woman.

"It will have to do then..." she sighed. "Helm, take us to the left side of the harbor doors. Keep us behind the door and do not let us be seen in the damaged opening." She thought for a second before asking "Otter, do we have that changeling software Jonathan created?" Otter nodded yes. "Good! Activate it to show me the way I was, then send a signal to the attacking force." A moment later, Belleview Blythe appeared on the holo-screen. "Belleview, this is...well, not really a surprise. Are you really sure you want to attack us?"

The enemy Captain gave her a look of slight confusion, then he smiled with confidence. "I think it is you who should be reconsidering. We see your ships powering up in there...we know you were unprepared for our attack. I think it is YOU who should reconsider...surrender." He looked at her carefully in his viewer screen, then asked "Why is your uniform now red?"

She gave a small smile, then said "My uniform? It reflects my mood...and I am really...really pissed off! Disengage in 30 seconds or it will be more than your jaw that I break this time. Bordeaux out."

After she disconnected from Belleview, Otter announced "Captain, I have Captain Bonaventure..."

She nodded in acknowledgement and a second later Nina appeared in front of her in her pod. She looked stern, but also quite worried. "Captain, need I remind you that now that the door is damaged, it will not open enough for me to take the Libertad out. I am worthless and a sitting duck to the pot shots they are taking out there. If I could get out there, the weapon they are using would be useless against me."

She nodded to her counterpart from the south. "Will do the best I can to get that door open for you, Bordeaux out. Micha, get us to that harbor door, best speed."

Before they reached the harbor door, another shot blasted through the hole and into another area of the harbor wall – and another large, melted hole formed in the structure of the asteroid.

"Shit, I guess he is not going to give up. We need to get out there and into battle before they totally blast Haven to bits! Weapons, prepare to fire a volley of the rail guns as soon as you have targets. You will only have the frontal launchers pointed at your targets, and I will be moving the ship quickly...so be ready" she instructed to Aimee who nodded, smiled, and then prepared her weapon gloves for firing." KayOolah, can you get firing points for Aimee using our base externals?"

"Yes, determining the best firing locations now...despite my having to use these primitive SCADAR and "advanced" scanning readouts." She gave Jaime a deer smile...she always joked about the fact that the Evo's scanning was much less advanced technologically than the Flaybah's.

"Well, you know how to fix that...just get your superiors to release some better scanners to us..." she knew they were not going to do that. She looked back to the helm and ordered "Ok, initiate maneuver H-23, now!"

With that order, Micha swung the craft forward facing the door, then using the side thrusters moved the ship quickly into the blast opening. As soon as the ship entered the opening, Aimee fired the heavy gravity projectiles. As the ship moved farther into the opening of the damaged harbor door, she fired more and more of the rail guns. Slight popping noises filled the pod as she fired the projectiles. As the ship moved to the opposite side of the harbor door, she stopped firing the starboard guns and started firing the port guns until the ship was safely hiding behind the opposite side of the harbor. Now away on their course, the weapons of destruction travelled toward their targets with no indication of danger – no beams, lights, or flares to give their approaching position away. The heavy projectiles quietly shot their way to their target – the Mako positioned immediately outside of Haven.

"If they make it without being seen, they will hit their targets in thirty seconds" announced KayOolah.

"That's a big if..." muttered Jaime. At that moment, her indicators showed that the Mako's golden weapon was once again powering up. "Crap, a bigger if..."

"Some might make it…ten seconds. The beam should fire again in about the same amount of time."

"Give them something moving to shoot at…" Jaime ordered. "Move the ship across the opening. Aimee, fire everything we've got."

"Captain that will give away our position and make us a target…" cautioned KayOolah.

"Yes, but we will be a target that is moving…away from the projectile shots." KayOolah nodded in agreement. "Now, activate our thrusters, move us into the hole and fire when you have a target. KayOolah, activate every external base weapon for automatic firing…let's give them yet another thing to think about."

Micha moved the craft back across the hole and Aimee immediately fired every weapon at her disposal. Multitudes of beams, arcs, and shots bolted out into space. The Mako detected the shots and moved the craft slightly to adjust the position of the Midas Touch, which now gave it the ability to fire at the Ladyhawk. When it fired, the beam hit the hull, some of it being repelled by the new protective hull fields, some peeling back the first thin layers of the space carbon, which exposed the Faratanium underneath. The enemy Mako followed up with its own volley of beams, which took out some of the exposed Faratanium down to the next layer of space carbon. The Mako turned slightly to adjust to the course of the Ladyhawk and immediately fired a second shot of the golden beam – this time it followed the Ladyhawk as it passed back behind one of the remaining pieces of harbor space doors. That part of the door melted away, exposing more open space to Jaime. At that same moment, the previously fired shells hit their target. Massive explosions rocked the Mako, and sent flames of escaping atmosphere into space. Cheers rang out across the bridge pods as the explosions showed on the image of the Mako.

"Okay, we have a big enough hole…please tell me Lizzie that the reactors are?"

"High by five…we are ready to fly!" she answered without letting Jaime finish.

"Then go, go, go...get us out into space!" she ordered. She then nodded to Otter who activated fleet-wide Norm-Comm. "We now have gotten the enemy to expand the damage in the harbor space doors, which should provide a hole big enough for most fleet ships to pass. If you can, get out into space. We will divert their attention from your escape. Good luck all, Bordeaux out."

At that exact moment, the three Wyvern cruisers flashed into the space behind the two attackers, and the hundreds of fighters flew out from behind Haven into the fray. The three ships threw everything they had at the two attackers as the Ladyhawk slid its way through the opening in the damaged space harbor door.

Both enemy vessels launched tens of Wolf Packs to repel the swarm of Firebrands. The small numbers of Wolf Pack ships were totally outnumbered by the hundreds of small Firebrand fighter craft – when the Wolf Packs shot one down, two more flew out of Haven to take their place. The older-style Wolf Packs were no match for the endless supply of modern Firebrand remote controlled fighters. What also was to the Wolf Pack's disadvantage were the pilots behind the Firebrands – most of them expert dogfighters and experienced pilots – the Blessed pilots were no match for Messiah, Star Child, and the other Evo pilots. Every enemy fighter was destroyed within five minutes of the attack. From there, they turned their fighters and added their small firepower to that of the attacking starships.

Jaime had no time to relish in the small victory, as the Mako was once again firing its golden weapon, this time on the Valkyrie. Allen was attempting to get the Dragon starship out of the harbor and was a sitting duck to the waiting Mako right outside. "We need to take some heat off of Allen. Take us closer to the Mako, Micha."

"Captain..." interrupted Lizzie. "May I suggest keeping the rear section to the Mako? We have stronger reflective field generators back there. We can take a few more licks than in the command section."

"Noted..." she replied. "Micha, show 'em our backside..."

The Ladyhawk glided in front of the harbor opening and began to turn back and away from the Mako – exposing the engineering section to the attacking craft. While turning, they fired a full barrage of weapons at the heavily armored vessel. Predictably, the Mako redirected its golden weapon onto the rear of their ship. The reflective fields did their job, leaving a small foil of gold floating in space. They only lost a very small portion of their top layer of space carbon. Like an angered animal, the Mako turned to pursue the Ladyhawk in revenge for the stealing of their prey.

Another shot of the golden weapon. This time, they all felt the blast even in the protection of their command pods. Jaime looked at the damage reports – the last hit did some real damage. She looked over to Lizzie, who said "Okay, we need to avoid shots on our back sides...at least until I can reenergize the reflective fields.

Jaime looked at Micha. "Can we turn and avoid another shot?"

Micha began readjusting the ship's course, then told her "It would be best to engage the light drives and get some distance."

"That would just put them back onto Valkyrie and Haven. No, we have to keep them busy until we can get some assistance."

"They are preparing to fire again...I suspect we will sustain major damage" announced KayOolah.

Jaime held her breath while waiting for the next hit – but it never happened. She looked at the readouts, then to KayOolah. The deer read her scans, then said "Hmm...they powered down their weapons..."

"Take advantage of it...Micha, turn us around...Aimee, fire the moment you have acquired targets."

Seconds later they were almost right on top of the Mako. Aimee fired every weapon that was even near the enemy ship. Ultras tore through their hardened titanium hull and caused massive internal damage. Plasma arcs burned the outside of the hull – bubbles of metal now showed the weakened sections where the weapon had just hit. She followed up with the cutters, rail guns, and finally another round of ultras.

410

"Her reactor is about to breach..." announced KayOolah in an unusual tone of excitement.

"Light drives, now Micha!" Jaime ordered.

The ship zoomed off in a flash of light moments before the reactor breached and exploded in a bright white fireball. Everyone on the bridge cheered in their pods at the sight of the bright explosion of the enemy vessel.

"Don't get too comfortable. We still have that Super Hammerhead to deal with. It will be much harder to take down than that cruiser. Micha, slow us to battle speed, turn us around, and take us in."

"Captain..." Otter interrupted. "Message from the Hammerhead...incoming only.

"Show me" she ordered.

Projected on her pod wall was Belleview. He held a blonde, Blessed girl by her hair. She dangled weakly as she had been beaten close to the point of death. "I suppose you are hoping that your spy will help defeat us too? Well, she will be no help to you as we now know of her treachery. They only discovered her counterpart on the Scimitar after she had disabled their power systems. We now know of these traitors...this one will no longer help you..." he said as he took out a laser knife. This knife was a large metal blade with a small glowing laser beam on the cutting edge – it was a fearsome looking weapon. He put the blade to her neck and quickly slit her throat. She moaned in pain and agony as her blood spurted out from her Jugular vein and Carotid artery. "By the time I am done here, these bitches will never harm another Blessed again. But for now, I am going to do the same thing to you...once I catch you Bordeaux." He dropped her to the floor like a rag doll and disconnected the transmission.

"Bastard..." she gasped as she watched the image. "Otter, can you block their transmissions? I do not want them reporting anything about the assets to Boral."

Otter nodded while saying "Yes, but if I do...you will not have the ability for asynchronous communications during battle...you will have to direct every message individually."

"It's worth it" she acknowledged. "Block them. Micha, Take us in...Aimee, prepare to fire." She looked ahead at the battle that ensued. La Lucha was damaged, but still fighting. Tigresa appeared to be dead in space – a large hole in the engineering section told her they were out of the fight. Nimbus was still fighting, sending another volley of weapons fire at the large battleship. Valkyrie was now joining the fray, circling the ship and firing its first round of weapons as they attempted to weaken their protective fields. "Let's lend a hand, fire at will Aimee."

First, they avoided a blast of Midas Touch and circled around to fire the port weapon arrays into the engineering section of the ship. The enemy's reflective barriers finally sputtered, which allowed Aimee to pierce their heavy armor with a few select shots from the Ultras. The small fighters – who were buzzing the ship like angered insects – took advantage of the opening in the hull, and flew into the ship on Kamikaze runs. They fired their weapons and crashed into whatever internal working asset they could find. Hundreds of small explosions rocked the Super Hammerhead. Lights on the ship flickered, indicating to Jaime they were making progress – the enemy was close to being defeated.

"Keep hammering them" she ordered. "Any signs of escape pods?"

"None yet..." replied KayOolah. "I am getting some readings of power overloads. I think the ship is about to lose power..." she continued to monitor advanced scans before saying "They are powering up the one engine that is still functional...I think they are trying to escape."

"Keep firing..." Jaime ordered. "Take out all their engine pods...keep them from being able to escape." She followed up her orders by contacting each of the vessels and giving the same order.

Moments later the ship went completely dark. Scans showed no power readings at all – it was dead. KayOolah read over the advanced scans, then announced "Captain, there were no escape pods launched. No one appears to have escaped, and I am no longer reading any power or atmosphere being generated. If there are people alive, they won't be for long."

Jaime sighed "Leave it to Belleview to kill his entire crew for his own failure. Let's take a shuttle and go see if anyone is left alive. I will lead the party…KayOolah, you have command." She activated her platform and exited the command pod onto the old bridge. It was odd seeing no one at the command consoles – and yet, the bridge was fully manned. She left the bridge and ran to the docking bay. She had a contingency of fifteen Evo soldiers waiting for her. When she arrived, the lead soldier, Cathy Drexel tossed her a clear acrylic space helmet. She put the helmet to her head and it wrapped itself around her face and head and sealed itself to her hive uniform jumpsuit. She felt something flopping from the back of her head, and when she reached around she found her long ponytail still exposed. She looked at the soldiers – they all had their ponytails hanging out of their space helmets. She looked at the various colors of hair dangling down from the tops of their heads with confusion, then asked "So, how is it our hair is going to survive in a freezing vacuum?"

Cathy replied "Oh, you didn't hear? They discovered a couple things…for one thing, our hair has changed so that it grows long on every female of the Evo, thus we all have hair to braid. But they also discovered that with its ability to grow, it can also handle extreme conditions…even the cold vacuum of space. So, since we all have our ponytails, and they are all weighted with heavy gravity pellets…"

"You expose them to use as weapons?" she finished the sentence for her. Cathy nodded yes. "Interesting…" She then nodded toward the shuttle, and said "Okay, let's shove off."

They were aboard the Super Hammerhead after a short flight from Ladyhawk – the shuttle encountered no resistance when attempting to land. Inside, they found nothing but death. Floating bodies littered the launch bay. The atmosphere had evacuated so quickly, the soldiers waiting to be launched as boarding parties had been caught completely off guard. Their faces swollen and puffed – frozen blood had flowed through their noses and mouths from damage to the blood vessels in their lungs. Their blood vessels popped from the changing pressure due to holding their breath.

Jaime looked at the death that floated in the zero gravity. "We will need to collect them when this is done. They may be

Blessed, but they deserve some form of burial. Perhaps launch them into a sun?"

"How about a black hole?" remarked Cathy. Jaime looked at her surprised for a moment, then after another moment of thought, slightly shook her head yes.

They left the launch bay and ventured down the corridors of the now dead vessel. Finally, they reached the bridge. They scanned the entrance portal...the mantrap lasers were still active – Jaime assumed it was Belleview's last booby-trap joke on her. It required them cutting into the wall to find the power conduits for the hatches and beams. It took them over an hour of cutting before they could verify the entry was safe for passage. They entered the bridge and looked around. The power was still out, no controls were active. There were a number of human shaped containers that were attached to the floor. When she peered into the window of the first officer's pod, she saw his face. He was alive – his eyes darted back and forth in fear as her light flickered into the small glass portal. From what she could see, he was only wearing his standard bridge uniform – no pressure helmet or space suit showed. If that shell opened, he would be dead in moments from cold and suffocation – he was no threat.

"This one is alive..." she announced. "So, is Belleview...?" her question was answered by the hissing of air, and the noise of the clam shell of the status chamber servo motors as they opened in a rush. It opened so quickly that the soldier that was next to Belleview's chamber was flown across the bridge and into the wall. Belleview jumped out and fired a quick blast of his command weapon into the next closest soldier. Then he turned to aim at Jaime and fired. Her reflexes kicked in faster than his moving arm as she raised her weapon and fired before he had even fully turned toward her. The shot hit his helmet, which split in half, and then flew off of his face. His cheeks turned puffy as he held his breath against the vacuum. As his lungs expanded from the changing pressure, a small dribble of blood slowly dripped from his nose and froze on his face.

At the same moment he came out of the shell, all of the other stasis chambers opened, and the rest of the bridge crew jumped out brandishing weapons. Despite their surprise attack, the fast reflexes and reflective force fields of the landing party allowed them to repel the attack and react even faster. Before the first member of the enemy bridge crew could even fire, they were all taken down in a firestorm of beams. Only seconds elapsed before every Blessed on the bridge was dead. The first officer was actually the unlucky one – Belleview must have designated him the decoy – hoping to fool Jaime and her party into thinking that none of them were in pressure suits. Belleview had ordered him to not wear a helmet, and thus, he now struggled in a vain attempt to hold his last remaining breath in the vacuum. He suffered a slow death while his companions died quickly in the firestorm. While he died, he realized his death was in vain as the ruse did not fool Jaime – she knew her opponent and was prepared for deception.

When the last shot was finally fired, and the last Blessed crewman had lost his air supply to the vacuum of the bridge, Jaime looked around at what was left. Dead bodies now littered the bridge – frozen blood floated in the zero-gravity along with the bodies. "Let's get more troops over to survey for any survivors...clean up any corpses found and prepare them for a proper space burial...all except this one..." she pointed at Belleview. She walked over and looked at the science console. She thumbed through the various displays until she arrived at airlock status. She reviewed the status panel until she found what she was looking for, then said "Ah there! Take the Captain to that airlock..."

One of the soldiers looked at the display. She then asked "If I may ask...why an airlock, Captain?"

She smiled at the young woman and said "I am taking him for a very special ceremony." The soldier nodded at her and took his corpse away. She activated Norm-Comm "Max, how is it?"

"Not good Jaime..." he replied.

"How many dead? Can you estimate?" she asked.

"Yes, we have a count. We lost twenty six thousand in that attack."

She felt her head tighten as she thought about the number of dead for a moment. She actually thought she was going to pass out from the shock of the news. She could not believe they had lost so many. She felt a tear start to roll down her cheek under the acrylic helmet as she thought of all the lives lost. Finally, she regained her composure and asked "How many children?"

"We were lucky..." he replied. "We only lost fifteen..."

She gave a small sigh. "Well, that is one piece of good news...I guess. One life lost is too much – and each child is a major loss. I am not sure how many we lost on the ships yet...be prepared for the worst." She disconnected and connected to Kate "I know things are crazy there...but our ship's engineers are going to need the assistance getting the ships running and back to port. Can you get to Tigresa and La Lucha?"

"Will do Captain. I have a crew working on clearing the harbor door...Captain Bonaventure is having kittens with the Libertad being stuck in harbor. But even with that going on, I have a few engineers I can spare. They will be on their way immediately. Kate out."

She looked around the bridge, then told the soldiers "I have something to do...carry on here with the search of the rest of the ship."

She left the bridge and walked until she got to the gymnasium. Once there, she scouted around until she found a lightly padded sparring glove. Padding covered the knuckles, then thinned down to a thin layer of metallic mesh. She examined it again, then said "Perfect..." and put the glove over the material of her space suit. She left the gym and walked down the dead corridors to the air lock she designated. Floating in the lock was Belleview – the soldier had removed his helmet and pressure suit. He still was wearing his Alliance uniform – metals decorated his chest, his insignias were stained with his own blood. She opened the hatch door, walked in and looked at the corpse. She then walked circles around him, and shook her head slightly in amazement and disgust. "Ah Belleview...you were such an idiot in life...I guess this fate for you is justified. You were a failure...you took lives, and you gave nothing. I tried to warn you, but you didn't listen...and now, I am here to send you to the depths of space in your final humiliation. Fortunately, no one is here to see your final defeat...but trust me, I will spread the word of your humiliating defeat. So..." she reared back and swung the

416

gloved fist into his cheek. His flash-frozen head shattered into a cloud of frozen dust with the impact of her fist. She then swung her foot around in a roundhouse kick, causing his body to fragment into thousands of small bits. She stepped back and looked at the floating debris that used to be Belleview Blythe. She opened the airlock hatch and stepped back into the corridor. She closed the hatch behind her then activated the pressurizers. The chamber filled partially with atmosphere – then she opened the outer hatch, allowing the escaping air to send his fragments to open space. "Good riddance..."

*   *   *

She stood in a corridor at the edge of the blown out tunnel that used to be the back side of Haven. She had been joined by Kate, Halley, and Jonathan. "Shit...what a mess! So, what's left here?" she asked.

"Not much, Captain. The side areas of Haven are still intact. The attack pretty much took out everything in the middle though. We closed pressure doors, so the main living areas have atmosphere...but..."

"But, all of our people are trapped in there, most still wearing pressure suits. Are there not airlocks we can use to get in there?"

"I am working on it, Captain...I am working on it" she replied.

"I know, thanks Kate" she said as she patted the engineer on the shoulder. They stood in what was left of the corridor. She looked down, and below her was nothing but the large cavern that had been blown out in the attack. Between her and the continuation of the corridor was just – nothing. The base had almost been cut in half by the multiple attacks by the Midas Touch. There were no connecting corridors below the damage, and the corridors above were too damaged to be used. The base had technically been cut in half.

She looked at Jonathan – he had a look of pure guilt on his face. He was blaming himself for the loss of the base. She put her hand on his shoulder and squeezed while she gave him a reassuring smile. "Come on, you guys...let's figure out what else we can do..." Jonathan gave her a small nod in acknowledgement.

They activated their personal propulsion units and floated out into the vast cavern blast hole. She looked out into the harbor – the space dock doors had finally been removed and the rest of the fleet was able to leave the harbor. Yet, another reminder of the attack and the damage inflicted. She just hoped that their attempts to block any Blessed messages was successful. If Boral had found out about the damage they had inflicted, he would surely send another task force to finish the job. They needed to make repairs before that ever happened.

The engineering crews and robots had been working constantly to clean up what they could, and repair anything possible. The robots would have connecting corridor tubes built soon to provide a means to free the inhabitants of the two halves of the base. Deep in her heart, she knew the reality of the situation – Haven was no longer viable – they needed to find a new home. She sighed and softly said "It's gone...Haven cannot be resurrected I fear."

Behind her on Norm-Comm she heard "I agree, I think it is a lost cause." She turned to find Max coming up behind her along with Allen.

"So, where do we go then? We have not found a suitable planet to colonize...without Haven we have nowhere to repair and refuel. We cannot win the war if we do not have a base."

"We go back..." Halley interjected. They all turned to look at her, and she continued "Come to the Innovation...I have something to show you."

*   *   *

The five were joined on the Innovation by Nina, Allen, Jeremy, Eva and Kylie. They looked at the star display on the holo-screen. Jaime stared at it with the same level of curiosity as the first time Halley showed her. "So, you're sure of this?"

She nodded her head as she zoomed the display further and further into the field of stars. "Yes, I have studied and studied this set of stars. I am positive that this is the view from the opposite side of the constellation Orion. I am zooming in where Earth should be. Using the Flaybah's advanced telescopic instrumentation, we are able to see much farther with much more detail than ever before. Here." She zoomed in on a small system then, farther into the system until a green planet showed on the display. "This…is earth."

"Impossible!" Max cried out. "Earth is a burning mess! This planet is green…possibly lush. There is no way that could be earth."

"I disagree…" she replied "You saw the video of the destruction of the earth's cities. The storms cleansed the planet…it has recovered. I am sure of this!"

"In any case…" Jaime added "Even if this is not earth, it is a planet…and it is habitable…and it is far enough away from the confederation that it may not be inhabited. It is worth a shot at least. Halley, how long would it take for us to get there?"

"I estimate 45 maximum insertions into sub-space. That many insertions, would take…"

"About eight years…depending on how long of insertions we tackle" added Jonathan. "Taking into account, time to maintain the sub-space crawlers…and we might have to find additional supplies and fuel on the way."

"The light drives will help there…and give us some fast travel time when not in sub-space."

"We will need for you to finish the installation of the crawlers…" Nina added.

"So, am I to assume you agree with Halley's assumptions…and you are wanting to try this?" Jaime asked. Nina and Kylie both shook their heads yes. "Any objections from the organizers?" Allen, Max, Jeremy, and Eva all shook their heads no.

Jonathan thought for a moment "We were building a large salvage transport…I think we should convert it into a people transport. We need to keep the battleships military. I estimate that we also have enough materials to build a second people transport. Should have more than enough materials after salvaging the Blessed attack force ships."

"I agree…" said Nina and Jaime nodded her head yes in agreement.

"Then, I have no objections…" the young man said.

Jaime nodded and announced to the group "Very good. Then we return to earth…"

About Four Years Ago...

"When I used to dream about being a mother...YOU would have been the last person that I would have selected to be my child's father."

"Well, whose fault is that?"

"Hey, shithead...YOU were the one that raped me and got me pregnant. I didn't pick you...you chose me! I would have never picked a loser like you. I would have picked...a Normal!"

"Well, had I known you would have produced a freak...I would have reconsidered mating with a freak Norm like you."

"Well, now you have a son...you had better learn to love him as he is yours. I don't give a crap if you think he's a freak...he is us. He is part Blessed and part Normal...and he is showing the signs of both. So, deal with it and learn to love him, damn you."

"I don't think I will ever love him. Thank god, mother Griggs will never have to see the son I produced..."

NGD: 4 Years, 7 Months, 28 Days:

Battle Station Zeus:

Lindy Light-Griggs

He was drawing something for his father, again. At least now he sat at the table when he would draw. He also now used real pencils instead of crayons. She leaned over his shoulder and looked at the drawing – it was amazing to her what ideas came out of his head. This drawing was of a canister – it had a dark area in the middle, circuitry in the front, and some small propulsion unit in the back. She really was not sure what it was, but she knew Fitchburg would be so interested in this drawing – thus, it had to be something bad. Every idea Janus had come up with, Fitchburg had turned it into something bad. She wished she could keep him from giving it to him, but she knew she had no chance of that.

"That's interesting...what is it?" she asked him.

He just smiled, then said "Something for father..."

She resigned herself to the fact that he was not going to tell her the purpose of this. He knew she was still connected with the Evo...he had picked his allegiance she feared.

He took his drawing, and said "I have to go...dad is waiting for this..." Without saying another word, he stood up, started to walk toward the door, finally stopped, waved at her, said "Bye", and walked out. She shook her head, wondering what she would, or could do about him. Her thoughts were interrupted by the buzz from the communications console. The blinking green light told her there was another message being relayed in from the other side of the Devil's Throat – from the home galaxy.

She ran to the console to try to intercept the message before it was sent out to fleet command, but it was too late. Since her interception of the ANN broadcast, they had installed a instant routing system for any relay message. They wanted to stop her from being able to prevent home-galaxy messages from being forwarded to Boral. The software they installed definitely did the trick. Now that her Jonathan program had been discovered and eliminated, she had no way to work around the new software – by now, Boral had the message.

She sat at the console, and retrieved the message for herself. She plugged herself into the console, and listened. Her eyes opened wide...she could not believe what she was hearing. Once the message was over she contacted Otter. "Otter, we just received a new relay message. It is hard to believe...forward this to the organizers."

Otter said "No Lindy...not yet...don't send it yet..."

Evo Star Base Haven:

Captain Allen James:

The two women caught him off guard. "Ahhh, what? You need a what?"

"A father..."

"Uhhh..."

"Speechless?" he was asked.

"Well, yeah...I am honored, but confused."

"It's like this..." Kylie finally spoke up. "Obviously, we can't have them without some help. We are asking you for that help. You are a starship Captain, we are starship Captains...it should be a genetic match. Not sure what else you need us to say..."

"Well...I guess so then. So, what...do we like meet for dinner first or something?" Now he was smiling.

Halley shoved two small plastic tubes at him. "Not quite..." now she had the devilish smile. "Take these and go see Max. He can help you with what is needed."

He put on a disappointed look, then smiled at them. "Very well...I'll head over there now." He placed the two tubes in his uniform pocket. They bulged slightly, but he figured it would only be until he got to the medical bay. No one would see or figure out what he was doing.

He left the two and walked to the medical bay. The doors slid open and he walked in. "Doc, I was told you could hel..." he stopped in his tracks when he saw Max and Jaime standing in front of him. The two were discussing some topic of importance – and he had just interrupted their conversation.

She looked down at the bulges in his pocket. "Happy to see the two of us?" she jokingly remarked.

He tried to adjust the tubes, but it only made it worse. Jaime giggled at him, which caused him to uncomfortably pull the two tubes out of his pocket. He held them, while he tried to hide them in his hand. Jaime looked down into his hand and said "Max, I think he..." she looked down again and with a bit of surprise said "are those Pleasure-Matic collection tubes?"

"Uhhh..." was all he could get out.

"It's ok..." said Max, as he took the two tubes of embarrassment out of his hand and placed them on a nearby counter. "We can deal with that in a while. But first, there is something we need to discuss...come over to the computer..."

This helped to take him away from his moment of being discovered. He tried as hard as he could to relax in front of Jaime after the ego shattering moment. He straightened his uniform, and calmly walked over to the computer display. Jaime was now pointing at one of the readouts.

"See…" she said. They were examining a display of transmissions logs. "Otter has been blocking these transmissions for months now. Fortunately, she is quite capable of multitasking. Every few days, someone has been attempting to get a signal out. It is quite well hidden…but luckily for us, not hidden enough for Otter to discover and block. And, look at what it is…it is a Blessed encrypted signal."

"The spy…" Allen filled in the blank. Jaime nodded yes.

"It's time we flushed this person out. Allen, we are taking the Ladyhawk out on a secret reconnaissance mission to get a look at the new Blessed space stations. I want you to softly…leak…the information."

"Will do Captain" he replied. "We will add a few notes to files here and there. Some messages regarding the mission in open protocols…it will be a soft information leak…"

"Speaking of leaking…" Max added, then shifted his eyes to the tubes on the counter. Allen looked over at the two tubes and blushed bright red through his dark blue face. "Come on…" he said and motioned him to a private room.

Starship Ladyhawk:

Jaime Bordeaux:

The ship was prepped and ready to go. She entered the bridge and looked at her crew. "Are we ready to head out?"

"Yes Captain…" announced Allen who had taken the First Officer's position.

"Shall we enter our pods?" asked KayOolah.

"Negative…" she replied. "We will be operating in the old manner. Stay seated…use the old controls." The deer nodded in acknowledgement. "Helm, take us out of space dock."

The ship left the harbor and quickly arrived at the sub-space insertion point. As quickly, they entered sub-space.

The bridge hatchway opened and Jacob walked in. Jaime looked at him with confusion. "Jacob? I thought Max was coming with us on this mission?"

"He fell ill. He sent me a message and asked me to come along. He's on board though...I'll bet he's in his quarters." She looked at him with some scrutiny. He continued, "In any case...I am here to give physicals and to give supplements for the voyage."

"Supplements? That's unusual..." she questioned.

"New protocol...I have the order..." he took out his computer film and presented a medical order. It had been signed by Max. "See, he ordered supplements for the crew. I can come back..."

Suddenly, she felt that feeling in her again. A slight tingle and pain in her head. She rubbed the back of her head, trying to remove the small pain she was feeling. She looked at Jacob, but could not see anything in the look on his face. "Very well, you may proceed."

He began to give small injections to each of the bridge crew starting with Micha. He moved on to KayOolah, then Aimee, and was moving to Lizzie and Otter when Max popped onto her Norm-Comm. He was using the emergency activation signal. "Jaime, where is Jacob?"

"He's on the bridge. He's giving..." She stopped and looked up at him. She quickly stood and yelled "Stop!" Allen taking her cue, flew up from his seat and ran to the young man. He grabbed Jacob by the arm, but was as quickly flown across the room with small a fling of his arm. He turned again and gave Lizzie the injection. Suddenly, everyone who had gotten a shot passed out.

"Damn!" she yelled as she elevated her arm and fired her command stunner at the young man. The arc of electricity hit him squarely, dazing him for a brief moment. But what surprised Jaime was how briefly he was stunned. He immediately jumped at her, injector in his hand, aiming it for any part of her body.

She quickly jumped and avoided his attack. But he just as quickly turned and grabbed her arm with a strong vice-like grasp. He reached at her, with the injector in the other hand and quickly moved to give her the shot. The sizzling sound of a beam filled the air – a bright red flash of light hit his arm and burned a hole through the wrist. Black fluid spurted out of the new hole in his arm.

He turned to look at Allen, now standing on the opposite side of the bridge, his command weapon smoked from overheating – he would not be able to fire the beam again. Jaime took advantage of his distraction and shook free of his grasp, then made a twisting leap backwards. She landed squarely, then with a fast and small jerk of her head, sent her long braided ponytail into the face of Jacob. It hit squarely on his chin and jaw. The blue flesh caved in under the force of the heavy gravity pellets embedded in her braid. His head flew back from the impact – she thought perhaps she had hit him so hard his neck might have snapped. But after a second, and to her surprise, his head returned to its normal position. The side of his face was still caved in, but somehow, he was able to continue smiling.

He reached out with his good arm in a surprise attempt at grabbing her again. He managed to grasp her left arm with a powerful grip, just above her command weapon. She gasped in pain as he squeezed her arm like a hydraulic press. She started to feel her bones weaken under the assault. Not even the chair to the back of his head – swung by Allen – helped to get him to release her. He simply ignored the other Captain and continued to crush her arm.

In one desperate attempt to regain her freedom, she fired a point blank burst of her command weapon. Putting every ounce of power her reactor could provide, she shot the deadliest beam she could produce into his chest. More black fluid flew across the room as the beam went in through his chest and shot out of his back. He released the grip on her arm and dropped her to the floor. He then staggered, and fell to the floor – black fluid now oozed from his mouth.

"Damn you..." he managed to mutter as he fell to the ground. His arms and legs convulsed in small spasms. He spat small globules of black fluid from his open mouth.

"Shit..." she said as she rubbed her bruised arm. She looked down at him, then reached down and felt the blue skin of his bashed-in cheek. Rapping her fist on his face, she decried "He's not human...he's made of metal!" She stood back up, pointed at him and ordered "Keep an eye on him." Allen nodded.

She looked around, and saw that some of the crew he had injected with the drug had already started to come around. It then occurred to Jaime that Otter was missing. She walked around to the back side of the communications console and found the young woman hunched tightly in under her communications station. She smiled and offered her a hand in getting up. Otter took her hand and stood. Then, Jaime noticed her belly – it had grown. "Are you...pregnant?"

Otter nodded yes. "Ted Salmon...he's the communications officer on the Nimbus."

Jaime smiled and gave her a hug. "Wow, how lucky to have found one of the rare men...and he is in communications too...congratulations! Now, we need..." she was stopped by that nagging pain in the back of her head. She rubbed her neck, trying to massage the pain away.

Otter hooked herself back into the antenna array and concentrated on the signals flowing around the ship. "Captain, I was tracing something when the trouble here started...when did this pain start?" she asked.

"Well...since we took off from Haven..." she replied.

She did some quick port scans, then she looked over to Jacob, and then up to Jaime and said "There is a signal being beamed to, and from...him...and it started as soon as we left Haven..."

"The source...can you trace it?" she asked.

"I think so..." she entered a firestorm of commands on her console. Finally, she looked up with a surprised look on her face. "The other end is in engineering!"

Jaime contacted Max, got Allen to his feet, and then ordered up a contingent of soldiers. She headed down to the engineering section. When they arrived, they did a thorough search of the area, but found nothing. She contacted Otter "There is no one or no device here, Otter. We can't find anything out of the ordinary."

"Check the engine room" she replied. "The signal moved a minute ago."

"Odd..." Jaime replied. The contingency moved to the engine room. Inside were the massive chambers that housed the hyper-crawler drives. Above them were separate deck levels, each level had rooms off of the upper catwalks that housed the various Pulsar drives. Enormous wave guide conduits ran from the reactors outside of the room to the three large, drive cylinders. The wave guides glowed and surged with raw ion power that was being provided by the reactors. The room was filled with a low bass sound – low toned pulses filled the area with sound that could be felt in addition to heard. Jaime walked up to the center, main crawler drive. She looked at the engine housing – it was clean and shiny white. A round smooth surface gave no visible signs of the complex workings that were housed below its ceramic coated metal surface. "I see no one here, Otter" she told her upon inspection.

"I have triangulated the signal...it is fifty feet in front of you, and a little to the left..." she replied.

Jaime looked at the end of the engine pod and estimated fifty feet. "Impossible...that would put them INSIDE the engine...no way...Otter, are..." she stopped and thought for a moment. She turned to the left and walked around to the side of the engine housing. Embedded in the surface of the smooth cylinder was a small door used for maintenance access when the engine was not running. "There is a door to the inside of the engine housing, but the crawler is running...full cycles. No one could be inside there..." she pondered out loud.

"It is a two layer door" said Lizzie who had just come up behind her. "There could be someone in the mantrap which is between the doors...but I don't know how they could survive in there very long. There has to be ionization leaks...I never go near that door unless I have completely purged the engine."

"Do we have a way to look in there?" she asked.

"We do. We placed cameras and holo-projectors inside every dangerous entry point...I don't like going anywhere that I can't see inside first."

"Wise move, Lizzie. Please activate the camera, and send the feed to my command module" she requested.

A moment later, the holographic image appeared as it was projected from the command module on the back of her hand. In the image was a man...Blessed...sitting on the floor of the mantrap. He looked familiar to Jaime, but he now had a very sickly skin tone. It was a whitish-blue tone instead of Blessed flesh. It appeared that small crackles of ionized particles were arching across his face. In his hand was a controller – she surmised that he controlled Jacob, and that Jacob was nothing but an advanced robot.

She stared closer at the man, then her eyes opened as she recognized who was trapped inside the compartment. "Jacoby..." she said quietly, but loud enough for Lizzie and Allen to hear.

"Jacoby?" Lizzie asked.

"Yeah, Doctor Jacoby...the one who did the implants on me...without anesthesia..."

"That does not sound good" Lizzie added slowly. Jaime shook her head no.

"I have waited years for this moment..." she said softly. Lizzie now had a slight look of worry.

Behind her Jaime felt others arriving. She looked around and saw Allen and Max standing behind her. Max asked "Is that the one...the one who operated on you without anesthesia?" She nodded yes. "Crap..." he added.

"I have waited a long time for this..." she added as she reached for the controls to the interior door that opened into the compartment of the running engine.

Allen reached up and stopped her hand before she activated the door control. "That's the way the Blessed handle things. We are better than that..." he insisted.

She started to force her hand from his grasp, then paused, and finally moved her hand back away from the control. "You're right Allen...we ARE better than that" she said as she started to move her hand to the exit door control.

This time she was stopped by Max. "You can't do that either." She scrunched her forehead in confusion. "Look at him...he's been ionized. He's pretty much dead already. Also, if you let him in, he will be like walking death...he will spread the ionization to all of us. He is now like an infection. One touch to any part of you, and you will ionize like him. It spreads that easily"

"Okay, so do we just leave him?" she asked.

"We could...he would eventually die in there." Allen answered.

"He might not die, actually." Max added. "Studies have shown that ionized humans actually continue to live. They develop a hunger for living energy and will eventually do anything to obtain it. If he can figure out how to leave there, he would hunt every living being in this vessel, and try to consume our life energy. Also, every living being he touches and takes life force from would also be infected by the ionization. Thus, the disease would spread...eventually, we would not be able to stop it...we would all become, like him."

"Okay, so if you ask me...there IS only one choice." She activated the communication port into the mantrap. "Jacoby...it's me...Jaime Bordeaux. Remember what you did to me?" He looked up with mild fear in his eyes. She knew he remembered, and she knew he still feared her retribution. "As much as I would like to get you out of there, tear you limb from limb, and slowly space you, I can't. You took that away from me when you decided to hide out in there...and now, you are already pretty much dead." His eyes opened wide as the realization of her words hit him. "So instead, I am going to do the humane thing..." He now had a small smile of relief on his face – until she cracked open the engine compartment door. The ions filled the compartment, his mouth opened in pain as the ionization increased – but he could not scream as he realized he was no longer breathing. She then continued "I have quickly killed you – if I had not done that you would have been alive for hours or days in pain...now instead, you will die fast. I will leave you with this however...your last few seconds of existence WILL be that of a dead person. You will experience what it is like to have no life...that is what you have done to others...maimed them, and left them slowly waiting for death...or you tortured them and left them wishing for death...now, it is your turn. So, now I leave you with those thoughts and feelings. When you are finally dead, I will release you from the pain of being dead and yet still being animated." She re-closed the engine access door and watched as his skin turned an even brighter shade of white-blue. Crackles of energy flowed around his body. His eyes took on a look of stone – he now looked straight ahead into the monitor – no fear or thoughts at all showed in his eyes, or in his facial expression. He turned toward the inner door as he sensed the life forces on the other side. He tried to open the hatch, but Jaime had secured it, which prevented him from opening it from the inside. He began to scratch and claw at the door like a hungry animal. He opened his mouth as if to wail, but the lack of air in his lungs prevented sound from coming out. She watched the dead Blessed man as he tried with all his energy to get to the living Evos on the other side of the hatch. She realized he no longer would understand a word she said, but she told him anyway "You probably don't even realize what is happening now. You are now just a lifeless mass of animated flesh...and with this thought, I now relieve you of your torment." She opened the outer hatch to its fullest. The change of pressure sucked his body out of the chamber and into the engine compartment. His lifeless form somehow managed to grasp ahold of the hatch frame and he hung on. His body flailed in the stream of energy while the ions flowing past him disintegrated him into nothing but disassembled molecules. Within seconds the remainder of his hand grasping the frame was all that was left. Seconds after that, even his hand was gone.

They all watched as his form disappeared into the engine thrust stream. Finally, Jaime closed the outer hatch, and turned to the group. She looked at Max and smiled, then silently walked away.

Space Ark Starlight:

Boral Oldham:

The fleet had been split up – twenty of the star force ships had been moved into the task force that would be bound for the return trip to earth. Starlight and four other starships were already within the safety of the protective field surrounding the Devil's Throat. The other fifteen ships would be granted passage once the initial five ships passed through, and were safely on their way. The other eleven ships that were to remain would defend the bases and ensure that no vessels followed them. This was especially true for the Evo – they were to be prevented at all costs from entering the passageway. They were never to return to their galaxy of origin, and absolutely never to return to earth.

Boral was in his ready room with his first officer preparing plans in anticipation of their departure.

His first officer asked "Are we sure that a meager force of eleven ships can hold off the Evo threat? They will outnumber us."

"You mis-underestimate the enemy, and our fleet. Although we have only eleven ships stationed here, one of those is a Great White. No Evo ship, not even their mighty Dragon class ships can defeat that. In addition, we have Zeus and Apollo...no mightier gods could we ask for to defend the Devil's Throat."

"Of course you are correct, my Star Force Commander" he replied.

The communications officer interrupted their work. "What is it?" he barked as he scratched his long hairy face with two of his arms.

"My Star Force Commander, I have the Norm Lindy Light-Griggs on the communication channel wishing to speak with you. She said it is vital..." he replied.

"Somehow, I doubt it..." he grumbled. "She is lucky she is the only one fortunate enough to have mated with us successfully..." he sighed "Very well, put her through. What is it

Griggs?" He knew addressing her by her husband's name would unnerve her.

"My Star Force Commander...I know you are preparing to go back to our part of the galaxy and back to earth..."

"Don't state the obvious, get on with it...what the hell do you want?" he demanded.

"Well, I would like you to take my son, Janus with you. He will be a valuable commodity...he has helped in designing many of the new weapons and technologies you are using."

He looked at her and tried to conceal any confusion. He always assumed Fitchburg had a team designing all of the new tech. "You don't say..." he said as he continued to attempt to hide his surprise. He thought for a moment about her request, then answered "Well, sorry...but we don't have room to take him. He will have to stay and follow in the next voyage. Don't worry...there will be more trips. We are just going for more forces and supplies."

"No, you must take him!" she shouted.

Her burst of emotion caught him off guard. He quickly regained his composure and dryly said "How dare you speak to me in such a manner. I should have you spaced for speaking to me that way."

She calmed herself, then said "Apologies, my Star Force Commander...but he can be of valuable assistance to you. He thinks he can help you navigate the Throat. He tells me he somehow knows of all of the different passageways. You need him!"

He gave her a stern look. "Decision has been made...he stays. Star Force Commander out."

"Other passageways?" his first officer asked.

"She is delusional..." he replied. "We have no record of other passageways. We recorded one gravity well that led to a void, then on the other side of the void the only other passageway out. She and her freak son have no clue..." His officer gave him a concerned look, to which he waved his two right hands at him and said "There will be no more discussion of this. We know the way, we will be fine. Now, prepare for departure...after the first five ships depart we will move five ships at a time into the field. Each of those five will go in one by one, one ship every twenty minutes. We will use the relay to communicate back to the waiting force. Starlight will be the first to return to our part of the galaxy. We depart in an hour, prepare the crew."

About 7 Years Ago...

"I don't know, I think she is a loyalist" said the Proctor.

"No, she isn't. She just needs to be convinced of the evil of the Alliance" the Recruiter replied.

"We have her boyfriend with us don't we?" asked the Organizer.

"Yes, and he has vouched that she will come around" said the Recruiter.

"Then, we need to get her on Starlight. Otherwise, if we can't get her on that ship, we are lost at the start" said the Organizer.

"I can do it. I will give her a reason to join the mission, then I will test her...she will either show her compassion or she will be unfit and will have to be killed. But, I hope we will find her to be the person we need" said the Proctor.

"And, I can get her on the Supreme Commanders "special officer's list". That will get her in as a starship Captain" said the Mechanic.

"She will lead us..." added the Recruiter *"I know she will. She will become the Leader..."*

NGD: 4 Years, 10 Months, 23 Days:

Starship Ladyhawk, Orbiting Haven:

Jaime Bordeaux:

The ships had all been repaired. The small fleet was as good as it would ever be – four Dragons, ten Wyverns, Libertad, the two engineering ships, two supply carriers, and two civilian transports. They had a big enough fleet to carry all of the Evo back to earth. Jaime met with the rest of the organizers and fleet captains in one of the Ladyhawk's conference rooms as they developed the final plan.

"So, Halley tells me that with luck, we can make forty insertions to get back to our side of the galaxy. Once there, we can return to earth."

"Forty...can we survive that?" asks Max.

"We think so..." answers Allen. "We think we can find enough planets on the way to mine materials for the reactors, and to forage for food. We can also take our fungus farms from Haven, keep them reproducing, which will provide a food source regardless of what we find."

Max shook his head in agreement, then asked "How long will it take to get back?"

"We think twenty years, give or take five to ten years..." answered Jonathan.

Max whistled. "Wouldn't it be easier to just take back the Devil's Throat...faster at least?"

"Faster, but the losses are unacceptable" Jaime added.

"I suppose you are right" Max agreed.

She looked at her command module, it showed various readouts of ships and base status. "Well, am I reading this status report correctly? Has everything been moved from Haven onto the ships? Is there nothing left on the base?"

"That is correct, Captain" answered Allen.

"Then I see no reason to stay, do any of you? I say we plan to leave immediately..."

Only Eva noticed Patti, who was sitting in the corner – she gave the primitive girl her normal suspicious look. To Eva's surprise, the strange woman jumped up, left quickly, and without saying a word.

The group left the conference room and proceeded down the corridor to the launch bay. They turned a corner to find Patti standing in the middle of the corridor, her arms outstretched.

"You can't do it. You can't go there..." she said with urgency in her voice.

Eva started to step forward to take on the alien girl. Jaime stopped her and motioned her back. "We have to Patti...it's our home...we have to go back" she replied.

"No!" she yelled at her this time.

"Out of our way Patti...we are leaving..." Jaime insisted.

They walked around her and proceeded down the corridor until an alert sounded. Klaxons filled the ship with the sound of urgency. Jaime shut down the alert tones with her command module then contacted the bridge. "What's going on?" she asked.

KayOolah replied to her query "Captain, an unknown...thing...just entered our space."

"Thing? Is it a ship?" she asked.

"Unknown. It is nothing even the Flaybah have ever seen. It appears to be a ship, but then again, it also appears to be composed of living crystals...so, it could also be an entity."

A light ahead in the corridor took her away from KayOolah's information. Standing in front of them were two creatures – they were shaped like trees, but made of a white bony-appearing crystal material. They each were covered in bony, crystalline appendages, with the largest and longest mass of the spiky crystals on what she assumed were their heads. The apparent head was slightly more rounded than the stalk, and had two glowing lights, which she assumed were eyes. Each appendage on their heads had what almost appeared to be a small snake-shaped head – they each had small mouth openings that opened and closed independent of each other. The appendages seemed to wave to and fro, like long grass in the breeze. It was both a beautiful and frightening sight to her. She raised her arm to prepare her command weapon, when the flash froze her in her tracks. She could not move a muscle, she was barely able to breathe.

In her mind she heard the creature on the right say "These creatures are much weaker than we anticipated, and they are evil. They want to travel to the forbidden area...they cannot be allowed to do so...it is time to destroy them..."

"No…" said Patti in her mind. "They are a good race. They are nothing like the ones who inhabit the portals…like the one in the back…" she pointed at Eva. "They have broken away and are looking for a home. I was trying to explain it to them…"

"No, they are too dangerous to exist in this galaxy. They must be destroyed." Said the creature on the left.

"What…what is going on?" Jaime asked.

"She speaks?" said one of them – she thought it was the creature on the right. Then another flash and she froze once again.

"Let me talk…reason with them. They will understand…" Patti told them from behind her.

"I think you have become…too attached to these…Evo" the creature on the left told her.

"She speaks the truth" said a voice from…somewhere. Jaime had no idea who that was and where they were.

The one on the left looked down. Jaime could have sworn its eyes lit up brighter than a moment before. It then said "You? You are with these creatures?"

"I am…and I CAN vouch for them" said the small voice. "They are good, we live with them…"

"But they are planning to go where it is forbidden by us. You know that…you were going to allow this?" said the one on the right.

"We knew that you would show…that you would convince them to not go. We did not know that you would judge them without cause."

"It was a mistake…" said the one on the right. "We now look to your advice as to what to do…We are to spare them?"

"Yes…Patti will tell them of their mistake. They currently do not understand."

"No…" said Jaime "We absolutely do not understand…we do not know what is considered forbidden in this part of the galaxy and why. The planet we are going to is our home…"

"She speaks again?" said the one on the right. "Amazing…how can she break the dazzle?"

"It is what makes them special…" said Patti. "It is why they need to be saved. Just let her talk…"

"Very well, since she is once again breaking the dazzle, and the wise ones request it. Speak Evo, why should we save you after you defy our wishes and plan to travel to the forbidden area of the galaxy?"

"Why is it forbidden? It is our home…"

"No…" said the one on the left "It is not…"

"But there is a system, with a planet that is where our home world should be. It has to be our home."

"You have to go through the portal to get to your home…that is where you came from" said the creature on the right.

"Then, what is that planet?"

"Forbidden…" said the one on the left.

Jaime felt the control of her body returning. She was now able to move her arms. Patti stepped in front of her. "See Jaime…this is what I tried to warn you about. You cannot go there…that is not your home world."

"What are you Patti?" Jaime asked. "You are not what you seem…" And with that statement, a bright light appeared around Patti. Her skin separated from the middle of her abdomen and opened up to her head, down around her crotch, and at the same time also split down her legs and arms. Then, her skin turned inward and wrapped around the back, revealing a similar colored crystal material. The skin finished folding back upon itself and the same bony appendages sprouted out from the crystal stalk. Her legs merged together to form the lower stalk, and her arms shrunk into the upper part of her body. Like the two standing behind her, the appendages waved back and forth independently of each other. Jaime gasped.

"I am…we…are the Mayoola. I was sent here to observe, and to judge. What I found of the Blessed, needs to be purged from existence. However, you...you Evo...well, I have found not only an advanced race...but a race that does not want to destroy everything it touches just to survive." She looked a Jeremy whose eyes were showing just a small bit of shock through the dazzling. She walked over to him and with a small flash he unfroze. "You knew...you knew and yet you still loved me." He wanted to reach out to touch her, but was unsure what to do. Her appendages reached out to him and softly stroked his cheek. "You were willing to sacrifice yourself for me...and this is so typical of this race. They would do anything to help the other races in this galaxy. They need to be allowed to live."

"Mayoola..." Jaime said. She looked at the creatures standing before her. Their thin stalks of white crystal, and the appendages on what appeared to be their heads – waving back and forth independently...like snakes. "No, not Mayoola...we knew you...long ago...you visited earth didn't you? We saw you then...and wrote about you. But we did not call you Mayoola...we called you Medusa. That was you...you came to us, and we feared you. You turned us to stone...but it was not stone...you somehow froze us."

"We call it dazzling...it is one of our gifts of protection, and is also a weapon if need be" said the one on the right. "But, you were able to break it...you are different from your ancestors...when we dazzled them, they never came back."

"Which is why they need to be spared...they are different." said Patti. "They have not even noticed..."

"Noticed what?" asked Jaime.

"Do you feel your voice when you speak? Do you ever feel it?" Patti asked.

Jaime thought for a moment, then answered. "Now that you mention it...no...how am I speaking to you?"

"Mentally..." answered Patti. "As a matter of fact, you have been speaking to each other mentally for years. You never even realized it. Your Norm-Comm...it has turned into a pure mental network. You never realized you stopped activating it to communicate...think about it."

Jaime thought back over her talks with everyone over the years. Her eyes opened wide in the realization, and said "Your right! I have been using Norm-Comm for so long without ever activating it...and never even noticed. You mean we have been speaking to each other telepathically all this time and never realized it?" Patti nodded yes.

Jaime heard the rest of the organizers coming around, except Eva. The Mayoola on the left said "They are all breaking the dazzling...amazing!"

"See, they are special...they need to be saved" said Patti.

"We agree" said the small voice below her. She finally was able to look down and to her astonishment she saw – Hero.

"Very well, we will let them live...provided you can convince them to abandon their journey to the forbidden areas of the galaxy" said the one on the right. The one on the right then asked her "Do you wish to come with us after your task is complete? There is no need to stay now."

Patti had already reverted back to the "woman" they knew. She looked at Jeremy and shook her head no. "I wish to stay...provided they understand and abandon their foolish mission." She walked up to Jaime and said "Do you...do you still want to make that journey?"

Jaime looked at the others, then turned back to Patti and the two Mayoola and said "No, if that's not our world...then we have no reason to go there. We will have to go through the Devil's Throat instead. We have to find, and get back to our planet...save who we can."

"You will have to hurry...in sixty years, the passageway will be resealed." Said the one on the right. The two Mayoola then gave what she thought to be a small bow, and then in another beam of light disappeared. The crystal ship as quickly as it arrived, moved away at a massive rate of speed.

Jaime looked down at Hero. "How long...how long have you been able to understand us? Why have you not spoken all this time?" Hero looked up and meowed.

"They only speak in the presence of similarly advanced civilizations. Cats have lived on your world for generations...and they have been there the whole time to observe. Cats are the wisest of races, dogs come close...but still have a long way to go. The dogs Perro, and Beau for example...they are now, near where they should be in the evolutionary scale...but still nowhere near the cat, as the cat is near perfection. But even closer to perfection is the Siamese. They were the ones chosen to venture out into space."

"Well, I'll be damned..." she said softly while looking down at Hero. He looked up with bright blue saucy eyes, and gave a small squeaky noise in reply.

The group heard a small sob in the back. Jaime and Patti looked back behind them to find Halley crying. Kylie held her hand and was trying her best to comfort her. They walked back to her. She looked up to the two and Jaime gave her a soft smile.

"I failed...I thought...was so sure...it was our earth..." the tears flowed more with each word.

"No, you were right..." said Patti. "It is earth...just not *your* earth." That quickly closed the valve on Halley's tears. She looked up at Patti and weakly smiled.

"Then, this is not the same place...the same galaxy. We have no idea where the hell we are, or even when, but we are not where we thought we were. So, what do we do now?" asked Max.

"I don't know..." said Jaime. She looked behind Max and noticed Eva still frozen, stiff as stone. She looked at Patti and asked "Can you do something about her? I need my security leader."

Patti nodded yes. "But, it will take me quite a bit of work..." and gave the Blessed woman a smirk.

A moment later, Otter contacted them. "Captain, I have been monitoring the situation down there. I have just received some information that may make a difference."

"What is it?" she asked.

442

"It is a message…from the relay. Lindy just sent it and thought it might make a difference in what we now do…" she told them.

"Odd she is sending that now…play it back please…" Jaime requested.

"To anyone that can hear this. We are under siege…we are what remains of the free colonist of Mars. We are under attack and we don't think we can hold out much longer. We are going into hiding…hiding to survive…we will strike when possible. Our home planet is gone…we have nowhere else to go. If you can hear this…if you can help us…if you are human…a Normal…we know you are out there…please come to Mars, please help us."

"That's the message…it repeats every few days now." Otter told them.

"Thank…thank you Otter" Jaime said. She looked down to the floor for a few minutes. When she looked up, she appeared unnerved. She quickly regained her composure, then looked to the group, and said "Ok, now we reconvene…"

"What are we going to do, Captain?" asked Allen.

"It's time to take down the gods. We need to plan our attack on Apollo and Zeus. We convene in five minutes." She quickly turned, and stormed down the corridor like a person possessed, Hero hot on her heels.

Max looked at Allen confused. Allen said "It was the person in that message…" Max shrugged his shoulders, and again gave another confused look. "I recognized his voice…I recruited him, a long time ago…She knows that voice too…it's Dex."

About Seven and a Half Years Ago...

She was the first to step off the transport onto the surface of the moon. Her platoon was right behind her and all of them were ready to fight. She looked around the landing area, checked the readouts of her external scanners, and looked for any sort of heat or movement signatures on her heads-up in her helmet. It was quiet, too quiet.

Right behind her was Messiah and Perfecto – each had their assault squads, and also joining them was the Blessed sergeant Conrad Donnason. Even though Conrad was Blessed, they put him and his explosives squad under her command. She thought that to be odd, but who was she to question Alliance Command and their troop deployments.

After a short moon walk, they arrived at the base. She and Messiah took the northern wing of the base while Perfecto and his squad escorted Conrad's squad to the south end of the base. The objective was to find and destroy a force field generator that had been installed on this particular base. The generator was only partially operational, but once it was fully on-line they could block anything incoming to the moon – this was to be prevented at all costs. Alliance Command also suspected that the southern forces on this part of the moon had been building a secret particle beam projector – one that could strike at Alliance cities or military earth-based forces without reprisals. Command determined that if this weapon existed, it must be eliminated.

They entered the base though an access door at an uncompleted section of the base. They only made it a hundred yards down the north corridor when the southern forces attacked. The enemy had taken up a defensive position in a small unlit courtyard at the end of the corridor, and were waiting in ambush. The southern defenders put up a valiant battle, but the superior armor that her troops sported, along with their training was the detail that made the difference in battle – that and their leader. She deployed her gunner troops so that they had established a cross fire on the opposing forces, pinning them down. In attempting to create their own pincer move, the southern fighters tried to get a new position of advantage both above and behind. However every time one of them tried to get that advantage, they were cut down before they could even get a shot off. Blasters flared in the vacuum, and bombs were launched that took out the southern fighters quickly – they never even had a chance to hop into a new attack spot before her troops took them out.

She could hear a similar battle going on over her intercom in the south end as Perfecto and Conrad were gaining a similar advantage at the opposite end of the base.

Once they had cleaned up on the southern soldiers in this section, they proceeded on to clear out what remaining forces were left further into the base. They eventually reached the control center, cleared it of any forces, and took out the technicians that were operating the equipment that controlled the force field. They shut the field down, which would allow for more troops to storm the moon, and would eventually lead to the establishment of a new Alliance base. The Alliance would then have control of the entire spatial area of the earth, and could start building the star base grid over the earth.

Over the radio, Perfecto notified her that they had completed their mission and had cleared the southern end of the base. No super weapon was found, but Conrad was doing one final sweep for the location of the super blaster and would meet the rest of the platoon at the extraction point. Her squad had found the force field generator, and had placed explosives to remove it from existence. The small bombs did their task and left the generator as a pile of rubble.

She met up with the other two squads as the shuttle landed near the now-empty base. Her squad boarded, then Perfecto and Messiah followed with their troops, but Conrad and his squad had not arrived. She called out for him on the radio, but no response. She was about to send a party to search for him when he returned with all members of his squad intact. He had no explanation or excuse for his tardiness. He was a Blessed, so she could not press him.

They finished boarding and took off from the cold moon surface. Within minutes, they were on their way back to the forward attack base which orbited the earth. She felt good that they were able to clear the base, remove the threat of the force field, and discover that the weapon was not to be found. Perhaps intelligence was wrong she thought. She looked over at Conrad who kept checking his watch. "Something wrong?" she asked him.

He smiled and put his watch away while saying "No, not anymore..." At that moment, the shuttle rocked, and the deafening noise of an explosion filled the entire cabin. Everyone yelled and screamed, but no one could be heard over the noise of the blast. She yelled over the intercom to find out what happened, and then she glanced out the viewport. What she saw shocked her – the moon was tearing apart – the lower half of the moon floated away from the top half. The two halves floated away farther and farther from each other before the gravitational force of the earth finally stopped the explosive motion of the now-split natural satellite. Massive clouds of dust began floating around the surface as no gravitational forces were holding the loose materials down. She gazed in shock as she watched the destruction of the planet's only moon. She turned to Conrad who shrugged his shoulders and said "I had my orders. I was to make the moon uninhabitable to southern forces. I did that job – however, I may have overdone it a tad..."

NGD: 4 Years, 11 Months, 5 Days:

Starship Ladyhawk, near the Galaxy Portals/Devil's Throat

Jaime Bordeaux:

She looked at the fleet status – everything was in order and ready. The drones were out in force and all in stealth mode as they were performed reconnaissance over the area of battle. Patti had taken the Blackbird out on her own reconnaissance mission, but only found ten of the thirty one ships of their fleet – ten ships of the massive fleet that were originally stationed at the star bases. Lindy had been correct in her force assessment report – Boral had taken a good portion of the fleet through the Devil's Throat. He was overconfident and miscalculated her fleet's power – she hoped they would be able to capitalize on his mistake. The Blessed did that at Haven – her tactical error cost them the base. She would never forgive herself for that mistake, she only hoped that this battle would help to ease the pain she still felt over the deaths of so many. One miscalculation endangered and killed so many – she could not get that thought out of her mind. But now, she *had* to block that from her mind, as it would cloud her judgment – she needed to be sharp and ready for anything.

She floated in her pod and analyzed the fleet status reports. Hero swam around her feet without a care in the world. She wondered how such creatures went so long without ever revealing their true selves. She smiled at the young cat as he swam and enjoyed the feeling of the gel in the pod.

She looked around and saw all of her crew ready for the upcoming battle. They looked slightly nervous – except KayOolah – she could never tell what she was feeling. The Flaybah were very good at hiding their emotions. In any case, she and the rest of the crew were prepared and ready.

She looked at the reports from the drones. There were Super Hammerheads stationed at each base along with three Makos. Standard Hammerheads were on patrol around the perimeter. The one ship that was missing was the Great White. She had only seen the reports and images sent by Lindy on this battleship. Was it as massive as Lindy had described – she wondered if it would shock her to actually see this behemoth of a ship when it would join in battle as she knew it eventually would.

She contacted all of the captains for a final strategy gathering. They all appeared in front of her as if they were all in a large room. Every ship now used the I.T.C. pods on their bridges. They felt it gave them a tactical advantage over the old-style bridge controls on board the Blessed vessels.

"I think we are ready...let's review our strategy. We will perform a trident attack – Nina, you will take your ships and attack Apollo. Allen you take Zeus, and I will take the heat from both stations in the middle."

"Do we have any help coming from our allies?" asked Allen.

"I don't think so. They say it is our problem to deal with..." she replied.

"Of course..." blurted Nina "never any help from...*allies*...when you need them."

She looked at Halley, who appeared very nervous. "Are you ok?" she asked. Halley smiled and gave a half-hearted nod of yes.

"All, remember that they have been as busy as us...they have developed weapons that not even Lindy could tell us about. Be prepared for anything...be prepared for any weapon...be prepared for boarding."

"They do that and we will be ready Captain" said Eva. She was actually standing on the bridge and not in a pod. The imagers picked up her form and projected her as if she was standing out in space with the rest of them. Her four arms were proudly displayed, armored in dark black hive material and protective plates of space carbon. Her jumpsuit bore the winged circle logo on her chest and had similar plates of space carbon applied across her body for extra protection. She had two laser swords strapped to her belt, and four blasters – two on each side of her body – strapped in front of the swords. Her face and head had elongated, she had grown hair on the sides of her face and her forehead had expanded up. She really no longer resembled a Blessed or a Normal. She looked familiar, but Jaime could not place where she had seen a person or being like that before. Looking at her gave Jaime a slight fear – she was formidable now, and she was so glad she was on *their* side. "My soldiers are stationed on all ships and will take out any attempt at boarding" she assured her.

"Ok, well...let's do this...prepare for battle everyone. Let's take 'em in."

Starship Libertad:

Captain Nina Bonaventure:

Using the ships enhanced sensors, she could see their target even from their very remote location. It was enormous – it loomed over the small blinking point of light which made up the entrance to the Devil's Throat. Along with the other station, the twins of destruction awaited unafraid. Not even the entire

449

Blessed battle force was stationed nearby – they were confident – and maybe they had a reason to be. She wondered if they had made proper plans – it seemed sound at the time, but now she wasn't so sure. She stared at her target one last time, then looked around at her crew. They all had expectant looks on their faces – looks of both excitement and fear – all of their hive uniforms bore a slight tint of green – the uniforms gave away their fears. But this was not any different than the other hopeless battles they had faced in the past. But this battle was of such a large and grand scale. To lose, would be to both die and never get home again. She thought about that – getting home – she never really wanted to go back there until now. Now, it was all she wanted to do, and she wondered why.

She activated a meeting with her battle wing. Kylie, the captain of Nimbus, and the two other starship captains in her wing appeared in front of her in the gel. "Let's quickly review the battle plans" she ordered.

Kylie replied "We will be taking on Apollo head on. Using our weapons to try to take down the shielding."

"I must stress…" Nina added "I only have two atomics at my disposal. We have to take down or weaken the shields to the point where the atomics will do their damage. If they don't take down the base, we will have lost." She looked down for a moment, then asked. "Do we have any other assets? I am hoping our Ultras will weaken or take down their shielding…but I am not certain."

"We have fighters…" said Kylie. "Let me get our wing commander on." A second later Star Child appeared in the gel.

"Captains, I have two thousand fighters that can be quickly and constantly deployed. If the shielding can be weakened, we can run fighters into the base to try to take out weapons or armor plating. Of course, we will take on any of the opposing ships and fighters."

"Very well, that covers the fighters. How about the golden beam…have we considered if they can extensively use that weapon?"

"We've thought about it…but I have no fokkin'…ah…pardon me Captain…no clue as to how to stop it. All we can do is try to keep our hulls constantly turning and hope our reflecting projectors can recharge quickly and not burn out."

She chuckled to herself at her former first officers continued brash attitude. "Okay, my ship will try to take the heat from the golden weapons...we can handle it...if you can take some of the other weapons fire."

"We will do what we can, Captain" replied Kylie.

"That is all I can ask...Very well, I think we have it covered. Prepare your crews...we are go for battle in five minutes."

She disconnected and waited. Five minutes seemed like hours to her. She was primed for battle and was as edgy as a caged animal. She floated in her pod, examined the command statuses, fleet deployments...then she just couldn't stand it any longer. "We are ready...all ships, engage the enemy."

The wing activated their light drives and quickly zoomed into the theater of battle. Just as quickly they were being fired upon by the Hammerhead and the Makos. The Super Hammerhead was as quickly swooping in to join in the fray.

La Lucha was already attacking and taking a number of volleys of the golden beam. Kylie was moving the craft in a constant motion, hoping to stave off any permanent damage from their weapons.

"Get us in there to take the heat off of them" she ordered. The helmsman obeyed and swiftly move the Libertad in between the base and the ship. Apollo pummeled them with a massive array of weaponry. "Launch fighters...Kylie, take the on cruisers, and take them out. Annie Oakley, stay with me and attack the base."

Annie Oakley was the Dragon battleship in her wing. She commanded the two ships to flip back and forth, in the hopes of providing an inconsistent target for the base. The pounding of plasma bolts on the hull made deafening sounds, even in the pods. They were returning fire...every beam was being levied upon the square blocks of the battle station. Heavy gravity projectiles were shot at the spinning bulk of the station. Everything they fired however, seemed to have no effect on the heavily armored bulk of Apollo.

"Damn, what the hell do we need to do to take down those shields?" she looked over her attack reports – no damage at all from their standard weapons. "Ay, caramba! Tell the Annie Oakley to back off, then I will fire an atomic at close range and hope we can get out of the way."

A few seconds later, the Annie Oakley engaged their light drives and zoomed off to a safe distance. The Libertad moved a short distance away, fired an atomic missile at the base, and engaged their light drives moments before the missile fired its engine, which thrust the weapon into the upper large square bulk of the Apollo station. They disengaged their drives and came to a stop to watch the massive fireball engulf the top half of the station. When the explosion cleared, Nina looked to find that the station still appeared to be perfectly intact.

"Science...tell me we did something...anything?" she pleaded.

"Aye, a tiny bit Captain...not much...but we did weaken its external force fields. We may have done some radiation damage to the occupants...if we were lucky."

"Well, let's go find out. Helm, return to the station. Weapons, target the area we just bombed...see if there is any weakness. What is the status of the rest of our wing?"

"We have taken out the Makos...we may have gotten some help from the inside assets" replied the science officer. "The rest of the wing is now moving in on the Hammerheads."

"Captain..." called the communications officer "Annie Oakley is asking to engage the Super Hammerhead."

"Granted...at the least we can take out their fleet and regroup for another assault on the station. Weapons, fire at the weakened area of the station upon receiving target locks."

Another volley of weapons from both the Libertad and Apollo. Some small explosions showed on the surface. "Ah, we have caused some damage...fire more." More small explosions, then they stopped.

"It appears their shields have gone back up" announced the science officer.

"Shit...one atomic left...can't use it yet. Wing status?"

"Nimbus has lost power and is barely holding out. La Lucha and Annie Oakley are taking on the Super Hammerhead...but they are taking substantial damage. We are not getting any help from any inside asset...they may have been discovered and taken out."

"Helm, take us to their location...weapons, open fire on the Super Hammerhead as soon as you have target locks. We can't take down Apollo yet, but let's at least remove the external targets."

"What about Apollo?" asked the science officer.

"We will save our atomic...use it later, and pray for a miracle."

Starship Valkyrie:

Captain Allen James:

The battle was not going well. The captain's had all given into the strategy of removing the Blessed fleet first, then regroup for another attempt at the two battle stations. Jaime had moved her wing into formation with his wing and had joined in taking down the smaller craft. The bubbles were still holding the standard Blessed weapons at bay, but their rail guns were doing damage, as it appeared they found a way to enhance their destructive force. They also had found a strategy that seemed to be doing quite a bit of damage to the Evo fleet – they would fire a volley of rail gun projectiles, which took down their reflective field generators, then immediately followed up with a blast of the golden beam – Midas Touch. Every ship's hull was starting to show a mix of patches of black space carbon and the silver of the Faratanium layers underneath. His ship, and the Ladyhawk were tackling the Super Hammerhead while the rest of the two wings were making the attempt to take out the Hammerheads and Makos.

At first, they appeared to be getting some inside help from their assets – but since the first efforts at helping the Evo in the initial attack, the interruptions in power and weapons had stopped. He assumed they figured out the identity of the assets

453

and eliminated them, as Belleview had done when attacking Haven.

"We're wearing them down...continue your fire, Weapons Master. Pound them with the Ultras as soon as they recharge. Helm, take us around to their backside. Bordeaux has them concentrating on the Ladyhawk...let's take advantage of that. Science, give weapon fire points that target their engines. We need a victory, now!"

The ship pummeled the Super Hammerhead's engine section. The blue light of engine exhaust from the ship's ion drives began to sputter. More shots and they saw the drives explode. Cheering filled the pods as they realized their small victory.

"Don't stop now...they aren't out of it yet. They still have power, and are still firing at us." He looked over to communications "Can we get some fighter cover here? They're launching..."

"Captain Cet reports they are launching Firebrands from the Innovation now Captain" the communications officer replied.

"Good, Halley...good!" He knew Halley was having problems getting back into the saddle of the command pod and worse, going back into battle. To help her, he and Jaime had decided to put the storage of many of the fighter wings onboard the Innovation. They thought that would both give her and her crew purpose while giving them a little lighter involvement in the battle. However, if things continued as they were, she might have to join in and get into the thick of the fray. He called up the Innovation on his Norm-Comm "Halley, you doing ok? Getting the fighters launched without problems? I know your ship was only retrofitted yesterday for this duty."

The young woman appeared on his pod's holo-projection. She was still wearing her old square glasses, even though the Dekron's had repaired her eyes to perfect vision. "Yes, Captain. We are handling the launching with ease. Messiah says that we can keep launching a hundred fighters every few minutes if needed."

"Very good, hopefully that won't be necessary...but be prepared, just in case. Allen out." He mostly contacted her to make sure she was alright, and to hopefully give her a confidence boost. He hoped he could keep them out of the main battle.

Another explosion on the side of the ship told Allen that they had defeated the Super Hammerhead. Debris filled the space were the ship once fought. More cheers filled the bridge pods. Allen started feeling slightly hopeful. Three more Makos and a Hammerhead, then they could figure out how to take down Zeus and Apollo.

His proximity alarm took his thoughts away from finishing the battle. "What the hell is it?" he barked at his science officer.

"Something is exiting sub-space right on top of us..." she replied.

The ship that appeared above them was enormous. It was long and round, and ended with a curved pointed nose in the front. It had a super structure on the top, which appeared to be the command center. On the bottom was a giant maul-like structure. It glowed with the eeriness of red death – he knew that had to be a weapons port of some form. The rear sported an attached engineering section, with three crawler drives, and a number of smaller drives that did not quite look like ion propulsion, but something totally different – something they had never seen before.

He looked at the ship and heard the calls of the other captains as they tried to regroup and reorganize the force – ignoring the last three ships and preparing to concentrate all their fire on this one massive bulk of a battleship.

"My god, what is that?" asked the helmsman.

"That..." answered Allen "is a Great White battleship...and we may be screwed..."

Starship La Lucha:

Captain Kylie Van Sycic:

"What's our status? Do I have engines yet? They need us!"

"Not yet Captain…" replied her engineer.

"Fok…we're a sitting duck out here!" She looked over and saw the Mako coming in for another attack run. "We need engines…please!"

She looked at their position – they were close to joining the main battle force. Command had changed their objective from that of the bases, and instead were taking on the remaining Blessed support vessels. They were headed to join the main fleet, but the attack of the Mako had stopped them, and they were now stuck in the thick without propulsion. The attack had taken them out of the battle, and out of the range of any assistance.

"We're working as fast as we can…" snipped her engineer.

"Tell me we can activate our bubble?" she asked.

"Aye, we have the bubble…" she replied.

"Thanks for something…keep working it. If we have any weapons, use them now."

The weapons master fired what few weapons they had. The dark matter containment tanks were dry, they were almost out of heavy gravity shells, which left them with only plasma and beamed weapons. The Mako fired upon the La Lucha, mostly beams and some rail gun shells. Only minor damage occurred.

"Thank the stars we have some luck…they appear to be out of weapons materials also…no Midas Touch" she softly announced.

"Captain…new problem…" said her science officer. "To your right…"

She looked and there was a sub-space tear that had been formed right next to the ship. Above them was the Hammerhead – they had taken advantage of the Mako's distraction to fire their ram beams, which quickly created the tear without their noticing. The Mako now swooped in, and then made a quick turn only miles away from them. They kept their forward momentum however, and continued to float toward La Lucha at a high rate of speed. Right before they would have slammed full speed into them, they fired their ion drives and changed their direction. The Mako slammed into the La Lucha, then fired their side directional engines and pushed away, and then lurched forward. The La Lucha drifted away from the impact point, and toward the sub-space tear.

Kylie looked at the approaching tear. She looked down and saw her uniform had turned bright green – she was scared to death. "This is it...fok...I'm sorry all..." She watched the approaching sub-space rift, and quietly thought about her life and what meaning it had as she waited for the nothingness of the void to encompass them.

The next slamming force sent her flying through the gel and into the pod wall. "What the fok?" she yelled out, then noticed their direction of travel had changed.

"Captain, we have been knocked off course and away from the sub-space tear. Another ship bumped into us to save us."

"Who?" she asked.

The science officer looked at her console then looked up, not wanting to say. Kylie gave her an expectant look. She softly said "It was the Innovation...and it is now drifting into the rift."

She activated Norm-Comm. "Halley! Why? Why did you do this?"

"Why do you think?" she said softly as a grainy image of her lover appeared in the pod "to save you..." Her image went dark as the Innovation was pulled into the void of sub-space. Tears came to her eyes and floated free in the gel.

"Captain, we have engine power. Give me a few minutes of travel and we can recharge the dark matter containment for a few shots..." said the engineer.

"You have it...fill the tanks...then we are going after the Mako." She looked down, her uniform was now bright red.

The engineer got her five minutes, then the La Lucha took out not only the Mako, but also the Hammerhead that caused her to lose her Halley.

Starship Ladyhawk:

Captain Jaime Bordeaux:

It was like shooting spit wads at a brick wall. No matter what they threw at the Great White, it was not doing enough damage. She had seen La Lucha take out the two smaller ships, the last Mako had retreated to the safety of the shields behind Zeus and was now parked at the station. She did a quick count of ships – everyone was still accounted for – except the Innovation. She wondered where Halley had gone. That took a good portion of fighters away from the battle. She didn't have time to worry however, as the Great White did not allow her any spare time to think.

Another hit from their rail guns, followed by a shot by the Midas Touch. They were being shredded while the Great White's hull was only showing small holes. It looked like a piece of fine Swiss cheese – definitely had not done enough damage to remove the threat.

"We're not doing anything to that hull..." she decried.

"That hull, is extremely thick and is made of alien metals. Obviously something they found on a salvage and were able to analyze and replicate" said KayOolah. "I fear we will not be able to penetrate that thick of a hull enough to cause internal damage."

"What about that opening in the front? Can we take the ship in there and do any damage? What the hell is it for, anyway?" she asked.

"Trying to scan it...but the thick hull is preventing our advanced scans and SCADAR from penetrating and getting any sort of an accurate image of the inside."

"I wonder if we should just fly up in there?" she muttered while she rubbed her chin in thought.

The enormous ship was slowly turning away from them. A moment later, an orange beam fired out from the large maul striking one of the Wyverns in the distance. The ship's engines went completely dark. The beam continued to fire upon the hapless vessel, pulling it closer to the much larger vessel.

"Captain..." said KayOolah "that beam has hit the Columbus. Their power output is now zero and they are being pulled in by the beam. It appears that beam is an energy neutralizer that also contains a gravity attraction component."

"But, what the hell are they going to do with the Columbus? Board it?" she asked.

"Unknown..." replied KayOolah.

The fleet continued firing upon the behemoth in a hopeless attempt at forcing it to release the Columbus. As the ship got closer, the beam added a powerful Midas Touch component, slicing up the vessel into smaller chunks – those chunks were then drawn inside the large opening. A minute later, the entire ship had been broken apart and pulled inside the large glowing maul.

Jaime looked over at KayOolah who was studying the scan readouts. She looked up at her after a moment with a surprised look – something Jaime hardly ever saw on a Flaybah. KayOolah said "The Columbus...is gone."

"Gone?" she replied. "How gone...taken inside?"

"No, gone as in disintegrated." Now Jaime had a surprised look on her face, along with the entire bridge crew. "It appears that that glow coming out of that opening is being generated by a consumptive matter reactor. It takes in matter, and converts it into energy. I knew they existed, but had never seen one until now."

"And the Blessed have one...and worse know how to use it..." she added. KayOolah nodded, and Jaime noticed a slight glow on her antler stubs.

Her conversation with KayOolah was interrupted by Nina, her image now standing inside her pod. "Captain, we can't defeat that thing...it eats our ships! We have fired everything but our last atomic and it still pursues. I am seeing defeat following us..."

"I can't believe we will lose to the Blessed...I won't believe it. There has to be a way!" she decried.

The ships proximity alarms rang out once again. Nina looked at her command readouts. "Caramba...now what?" A second later, four Flaybah battleships appeared surrounding the Great White. Another moment later, two silver globes emerged from sub-space – Dekron vessels.

"See Nina...we DO have allies. Now, we have a chance."

To everyone's surprise, another sub-space tear formed and out popped the Innovation. "What the hell?" Jaime asked rhetorically.

"Halley! I thought you were fokkin' gone!" blurted Kylie on the open channel. She then realized her error "Umm, sorry Captains..."

Halley replied "It's good to be back in the battle too Kylie. The time I spent with the Dekron's provided more than just healing...I also learned how to navigate the void. I no longer need a chaser, or a door knocker. I simply find where I want to go and fly there...then, open a tear and exit. I never realized it was so easy until today."

Four Flaybahs appeared in Jaime's pod...she was starting to feel cramped in there with Hero and all those holo-images. There were now three starship commanders, and Oomah. Also joining them were Nova and Yuli of the Dekron. Yuli was now the same silver color as his wife. Their skins both flowed as if they were composed of Mercury.

"We are all here to help, Jaime" said Oomah. "Engaging the enemy now. Benedict, if you would guide your fighters in after we break down their defenses that would be helpful." Messiah sent a non-verbal acknowledgement.

The four large ships moved in and pummeled the Great White with their advanced weapons. The two Dekron globes used sprays of living machines to coat sections of the vessel. Once the living machines contacted the hull of the Blessed vessel, they began devouring the hull metal like acid. Messiah followed up by sending Firebrands into the holes kamikaze style. Now the Great White was showing signs of real damage. It no longer was concerned with the Evo vessels, but attempted to apply all of its firepower against the six vessels that had just joined the fight. It tried to turn and use its consumptive reactor, but the larger ships were too fast, and their engines too powerful for the beams to strike or grab hold, much less pull the larger ships in.

"Yes, NOW we have a chance..." Jaime said.

"Captain...we have incoming bogies launched from Zeus. They are of unknown configuration and design..."

"Another mystery eh? Weapons and all Evo ships...fire at will at the incoming objects. Let's not take any chances."

Zeus began firing massive barrages of its weapons at the Evo fleet. They were determined to protect the incoming objects. Their crossfire did the trick as the cylindrical objects approached the nearest of the fleet – the Nimbus and Ladyhawk.

Jaime noted that the objects were of two sizes. The larger sized objects slowed, allowing the smaller objects to reach the two ships first. The ships fired at the small canisters, but they somehow shifted out of phase – allowing the beams to harmlessly pass through.

"What the hell?" she said as she heard and felt the small canisters attach themselves to the hull. "Eva, I hope you are ready for anything up there..."

"Yes, Captain. We are in pressure suits and are armed to the teeth for small fire and hand to hand" she replied.

"Good...I will notify the other ships that their external crew members should also put on pressure helmets." She immediately had Otter send a broadcast message to all personnel on all ships.

She activated a holo-image of the empty bridge. She watched as the ends of the small canister passed right through the hull and become embedded in the star screen of the external bridge. The end of the canister then opened, and she heard a whooshing of air passing from the canister into the atmosphere of the bridge. The air in the bridge took on a slight yellow haze. Her command alarms indicated the atmosphere of the bridge had become toxic. She looked to KayOolah who had already started an analysis of the bridge atmosphere. She looked up with big dark eyes and said – those canisters are delivering ancient chemical-style weapons. The materials delivered by those phasing canisters are of the VX gas and vaporized mustard type of weaponry of the nineteenth and twentieth centuries. I guess they hoped that if the VX did not instantly kill you, the mustard agent would burn your eyes, skin and internal organs, thus disabling you. They really are barbarians..."

"They are, KayOolah, they are..." she shifted her Norm-Comm to Eva "Are you and the crew alright up there?"

"Yes Captain. Because we took the time to put on our pressure helmets, we lived. The mustard agent appears to not be able to penetrate our hive suits...but in any case, we will be disinfecting as soon as it has dissipated and the crisis is over. Engineering is ventilating the ship now. I sure hope the larger ones are boarders...I am really itching to give a little punishment to my former kin..."

"She will have her chance..." said KayOolah. "Scans indicate that there are life forms inside those larger phasing canisters. They will be attaching themselves to the hull in a matter of moments."

"Get ready Eva..." She watched as twenty of the most hard core Evo fighters entered the bridge, and joined Eva. They were a hardened crew – the Evo in her team were all decked out in black hive uniforms, with black space carbon armor plates covering their bodies. Each Evo had their long braids hanging out of their helmets. She assumed that each braid had heavy gravity pellets woven into the intricate weave. Each assault member carried two blasters, and at least one laser sword. The laser sword was of a polymer make-up ending in a sharp piercing point, with a laser on the edge that provided a means of quick cutting. They were a fearsome crew of the twenty, toughest women she had ever fought alongside. Seeing this force brought a little bit of terror to her own heart. Then, she remembered she had trained most of them.

Eva had three braids coming out from her helmet. Her elongated face had the look of pure rage – she was allowing the Blessed in her to take over. They would regret bringing her to this state. She held two laser swords in two of her hands, and a blaster in each of the other two hands. She stood at the ready, itching for the battle that was about to occur.

Then she watched as the star screen went black on the aft side of the bridge. A large yellow door appeared where the screen went dark. A hatch flew open and thirty Blessed soldiers poured out. She was now receiving similar reports from all over the ship that boarding parties were attempting to take over the ship.

The things that jumped out of the boarding vessel no longer looked like Blessed – or human for that matter. They all had elongated heads like Eva, hair grew down the sides of their faces, sharp teeth filled their large-lipped mouths, and then there were those four arms. She stared at the invaders and then realized who they had become.

"Og..." she softly said. KayOolah looked up at her with confusion. She looked over to her and pointed to the invading Blessed. "They have turned into...Og. They look exactly like the Og when we fought them. Is it possible that, when we evolved, they DE-evolved? They seem to have gone backwards in evolution. I thought Eva's condition was just due to being with us...but now, I see it's every Blessed. What do you think, KayOolah?"

"It is very possible. We have scans of the Og...I will scan the invaders and see if they match."

She nodded at the deer then went back to watching the fight above them. At first, the boarders were confused by the lack of a bridge crew, but then saw Eva and her force. Upon seeing them, they immediately charged into battle. Even with four arms, they could not compete with the athleticism and skilled fighting of the Evo soldiers. They swung their swords, but were met with similar matching parries, then the Evo soldiers either flung a fist or a foot into them, took out their blasters, and quickly removed them from battle.

Eva was not using her blasters at all. They fired upon her, and with personal shields on her arms, she easily repelled the shots fired from the enemy. She then charged in with her shields active on two arms, and swinging swords in her other two hands. She picked up a Blessed soldier and flung him in front of an Evo fighter, who quickly dispatched him with a plunge of a laser sword. She then swung around and applied her two swords into the chests of two Blessed fighters. She spun around and pulled out a blaster and took out two more.

Another Blessed went down from the hit he took from the swinging braid of one of the Evo soldiers. Eva caved in the head of one with a swing of her hair – three heavy gravity weighted braids were a superior opponent to the bone of a skull, even when protected by a pressure helmet.

The fighting only lasted ten minutes, and it ended in a blood bath. The Blessed boarding parties were no match for Eva and her Evo security soldiers. After taking out the bridge boarding party, they moved on to help in other parts of the ship.

She checked the ship status – they had lost a few crew. Some did not get their helmets on in time and succumbed to the chemical weapons, and some fell prey to the boarders. She assumed a few losses were to be expected. For the most part, she was pleased that the crew had performed so well.

"Captain..." said KayOolah "I have the DNA results of the scans of the boarders. They are indeed an exact match...for the Og."

"Shit...glad I am not Blessed..." she joked. "Pass your findings to Max please." She activated her holo-imager to the still fully-functional battle stations. She rubbed her chin while she pondered what to do about them. Then an idea came to her. "Otter, get me Halley please." A moment later, Halley appeared on the holo-image. "Halley, you said you can accurately navigate in the void?"

"Absolutely, Captain. I can bring the Innovation within inches of a targeted area. Why?"

"One moment..." she looked over the status of every ship in the fleet. "Do you mind giving up command for a few minutes and getting yourself to the Valkyrie? I have an idea..."

Battle Station Zeus:

Lindy Light-Griggs:

"Sure, I can do that Jaime. I do have a favor to ask."

"Name it…you deserve anything we can do for you." Jaime replied.

"I want you to take my son, Janus. He is not like us, or like the Blessed, or what they've become. He needs to be safe, and I fear for his life."

"We'll take him. Send him out the first chance you can. Thanks again, Lindy. Bordeaux out."

She made some adjustments to the station's communication systems. Then tuned it to broadcast. She watched as the battle continued between the Evo, Flaybah, Dekron forces, and the Great White battleship. Her people were winning, but by adjusting the visuals from the base, it would be impossible to tell who was actually winning the battle. She had set the Blessed channels to block any communications from the Great White to the station – they would not know what was going on out there.

A moment later, the transmission came in. She picked it up, then contacted Fitchburg. "Fitchburg, the…queen…of the rebel fleet wishes to speak to you. She is offering an alternative to any further fighting."

"The rebel queen? Put her on…" he replied. She switched the transmission to the station-wide broadcast channel. Everyone on board the stations would hear it.

A picture of Jaime in a flowing pink dress came on the holo-screens. She had her previous flesh tone and her hair flowed like it was blowing in the wind. "To the superior Blessed forces, this is the queen of the rebels. We are admitting defeat…we should not have attempted this foolish venture. We wish to talk terms of surrender."

She heard Fitchburg reply "We will consider your offer of surrender. You finally learned that we are the superior ones did you?" They had become as primitive as they suspected, and they had taken the bait. They had mixed up the fantasy of the simulator with reality.

"Oh please! Let us surrender to you. I, the Queen of the Rebels will be eternally grateful to you…and can reward you in any way you see fit."

465

"I will accept your offer. You may come aboard the station...but only you."

"I will be right there..."

She ran into Janus' bedroom. He was in bed resting. She ran to him, gave him a small shake to fully wake him, and took his hand. "Come on...we need to go!"

"Where mother?" he asked with sleepy eyes.

"You have a ship waiting for you. I need to get you to an escape pod."

"Escape? But we will win...won't we?" he asked.

"Whatever you do...where you are going, never speak like that" she scolded.

"Are we going to the Evo? I've always wanted to meet them!" and with that he jumped off of the bed with an enthusiastic leap. Grabbed his drawing materials, and put them into his backpack.

"Janus...I have to tell you again. NEVER tell them about the things you drew for your father...NEVER...do you understand?" He shook his head yes. She took his hand and ran the two of them out of their quarters and down through the winding corridors to an escape pod near the dock. At this dock sat the last remaining Mako on this side of the Devil's Throat – Fitchburg's last route of escape.

She opened the hatch and led him into the pod. Behind her, she heard a chilling voice. "What the hell are you doing, bitch?" She slowly turned to find Fitchburg standing behind her, rage in his eyes. "Why are you putting our son in there...why now, in our time of victory? The Rebel Queen will be arriving any moment. I want my son to see our final victory over you idiot Norms. Bring him out...he will be riding in the Mako if he goes anywhere." He turned to point at the docked Mako – that is when the tear in sub-space appeared in the middle of the protected area of the stations force field, and the Valkyrie slipped out. "What the hell?" he yelled.

The Dragon fired every weapon at the remaining Mako. With its protective fields down, its hull failed quickly as the projectiles and beams tore through it like a paper airplane. The explosion of ship gave her the time needed. She turned and reached for the door control. Janus yelled "Mother, you have to come!"

"I'm sorry, my son. I have something that I have to take care of...I will not make it...you be good and grow up to be someone I can be proud of. Goodbye my love..." and with that she activated the door control. He screamed and cried as the door closed. He was still screaming when the escape pod shot out into space toward the waiting Valkyrie. The pod was captured and recovered into the docking bay. A minute later, the ship fired a volley of weapons into the station's field projectors, then ripped another hole in the fabric of space and disappeared, only to appear back with the fleet a minute later.

Fitchburg got over being dazed by the explosion, turned, and looked at his wife with pure hatred and rage. "You bitch...you...you sent our son to...them!" He started to raise the arm with his command blaster.

"Oh, I have something else to request, Fitchburg..." she calmly said.

"What's that, bitch?" he replied, causing him to lower his arm.

"I want...a divorce..." she said while she pulled out a blaster that was hidden behind her back. She raised the blaster and aimed it at him. He replied by raising his command weapon at her. She fired, he fired. The two blasts hit each other in their chests simultaneously. He looked down at the blood spurting out of the hole in his chest. She too looked at him, then down at the matching hole in her chest, and laughed as she fell down. He followed right behind her, falling to the floor. He died quickly. She however did not die until she saw him spit his last breath at her. She smiled, and closed her eyes as she passed into a content, eternal sleep.

Starship Innovation:

Captain Halley Cet:

The plan worked – she had piloted the Valkyrie into one of the best ambushes that could be devised. Jaime had taken their attention away from the battle, which allowed them to sneak off unnoticed, they slipped into sub-space, and she piloted the ship into the gap of the force field generated by the two stations. They destroyed the last remaining starship on this side of the Throat, made an attempt at taking out the field generator, collected Lindy's son, and escaped by using another tear in sub-space. Now, she was back on her starship, and she actually felt much better for her little excursion into danger with Allen. It was the confidence builder she needed to get herself back on track. Now they needed to determine a way to take down the two stations. With their allies finishing off the Great White, they needed to have another holo-meeting to decide their next move.

"I am open to suggestions on how to take down those two stations...the field generator was not even affected by an internal attack..." Jaime said with deep concern.

"I have one atomic left..." said Nina. "It weakened their force field...but it will take a lot more than that to take those stations down. Why couldn't we just pop in there by sub-space and attack there again?"

"Wouldn't work" replied Allen "We attacked and scanned while we were in there. The bases are shielded even on the inside of the force field...our attack did nothing...we would not have any advantage, and we would be trapped in there...inside the force field...getting pounded by both stations. We were lucky that time, as we had the advantage of surprise on our side. I checked my inventory...I have a couple of atomics...now that we removed the threat from their star force, I think we can use them."

"Anyone else have any WMD's?" Jaime asked. The other captains shook their heads no. "Well, let's see if we can make a big enough dent in their field to get some weapons fire through to them. All it will take is one hole, and we have a good shot at taking both stations down. We really only need to take one down, and access to the Throat will be ours. Any questions? If not, good luck all."

She disconnected and looked around at her crew. Staci asked "Plan Captain?"

"The plan? Don't have one yet...we are going to wing it. Follow the other ships in formation...wait for them to launch atomics, then run in after the explosions and hope there is a hole to shoot through. Be ready all...look sharp. Take us into position helm."

As planned the Libertad and the Valkyrie zoomed in and both launched their weapons – three massive explosions followed.

"Take us in...Weapons Master, fire at will..." she ordered.

They rushed in along with three other Evo vessels and fired at what appeared to be a weak spot in Zeus' force field. The weapons did not do damage however.

"We made a little more of a dent..." said Katsumi as she constantly watched her advanced scans of the attack area. "Maybe another run?"

"Yes...take us back in for another..."

She was interrupted by a voice in her head – it was Nova. "Halley, tell the fleet to back off...more help is on its way...you have to be far away..."

"Who?" she asked, but did not get a reply. She looked to Maxine "Get me Captain Bordeaux, immediately!" she ordered. Jaime appeared in her pod a moment later. "Captain...Jaime...you have to trust me on this one...back the fleet off immediately. Take the fleet as far away from this area as quickly as possible...do it right now, please!" she pleaded. Jaime looked confused, but then nodded her head and disconnected. A moment later, a fleet-wide message was broadcast, move away from the area of battle – disengage, and back off.

A few seconds later, Katsumi called out "Captain, you are not going to believe what I am seeing on SCADAR..." She looked over at her with a raised eyebrow. Instead of saying anything else, she switched her SCADAR images onto the holo-projectors.

Halley gasped at what she saw – ten green glowing missiles headed in from another sector and bearing down at the stations.

"My god...it's the Queek. They're helping us?" Halley gasped.

"It appears we impressed the Queek enough to be worthy of their assistance" Katsumi replied.

"Well, let's hope their weapons are strong enough to take them down."

When the missiles hit, they caused impressive of explosions of green force that were too bright to watch. When their vision finally cleared from the flashes, they discovered that the Queek had weapons that were definitely strong enough. The two earthly gods Zeus and Apollo, were now nothing but rubble.

NGD: 5 Years, 3 Days:

Near the Devil's Throat:

Captain Jaime Bordeaux:

She looked out the observation window in her ready room. The fleet was repaired and in tip-top shape. Jonathan, Kate, Lizzie, and Iffe had done such a good job on repair operations. Allen had worked with Nina on salvage operations. From their efforts, they now had enough materials to build another salvage and storage ship.

For the most part, the two bases were a total waste. The Queek missiles had left only radioactive waste in their wake. Jonathan discovered however, that those waste materials could be used to build more atomic weapons, and also would provide fuel for the old-style reactors that they used for certain practical uses.

Jonathan also got his hands on the consumptive reactor from the remains of the Great White battleship. He had mounted it on the new salvage ship. His hopes were that they could use it if, and when power and resources were scarce. *Ah, a boy and his toys...*

She had met Lindy's son, Janus. He was a strange mixture of Human, Blessed, and Evo. She shook his hand and – nothing. No changing, no reconfiguring, nothing, just coolness in his touch – he was different from any of them. Then there was his size for his age – he looked and acted like a fifteen year old at the young age of just over four. He was nothing like the Evo children and would not interact with them. Also, she was not sure where his loyalties lie – was he Blessed, or Evo, or worse – both. She would keep an eye on him – besides, she promised Lindy she would.

The message from the relay of Dex repeated every few days. It was definitely a recording n a repeat loop, but she stopped her day each time to listen as if it was him actually speaking. She feared the worse for him based on the message – but she always hoped for the best. He made such a mess of things sometimes, but at the same time managed to always turn things around – like how he managed not to die during the launch of

Starlight. She would soon discover his fate – as today was the day they were returning to their galaxy. With luck, they would be within the orbit of Mars in a year, or if luck was not with them, a little longer. She looked down at her hand – the dark blue color reminded her of another problem. What would he say if he saw her like this? She wondered if she could actually ever face him – maybe just sending down Evo troops to help out would be enough to save him and put her mind at ease. He would be safe, he would not know of her fate, and her changes.

She stepped away from the window to find Hero waiting for her near the door. He gave a small meow, then walked over to rub her leg. Was it affection, or did he do it to try to trip her. She always thought he purposely ran directly in front of her for tripping – probably some cat game they liked to play – "Trip the Human", or in this case, "Trip the Evo".

"Are you ready to try this?" she asked him. It appeared to her that he might have smiled at her. She knew he understood, but for some reason they refused to speak to Human or Evos. He did seem to be as excited as she was to go back through to the home galaxy.

They walked out onto the bridge – it was empty, as her crew were in their pods. She and Hero stepped on the platform in front of her command chair, and it lowered into the pod. She thoroughly checked all of her ship's systems while the pod filled to the top with gel.

"Otter, connect me with the organizers, the Fleet Captain, and the Wing Captains please." She looked over at Otter, who was very close to having her child – a boy. She was so happy for her, and happy that they would be getting another male in the fold, as they were so short of them.

A moment later, they all stood in front of her – Allen, Max, Jeremy (with Patti surprisingly), Jonathan, and Eva – the organizers. Then there was Fleet Captain Nina, and Wing Captains Halley, and Kylie. Every one of them had always been, or had become her most trusted friends.

Also in her pod was Perro and Beau, the space dogs. This galaxy had caused them to change also, as both now had shimmering fur and thin clear wings that always appeared to

472

wave in the wind. Standing around Allen, Max, and Jonathan were the other Siamese – they had all found their places in the fleet, and were all headed home.

Then Oomah and Yuli joined them – she was starting to feel a little claustrophobic in her little pod.

Now that everyone had joined the meeting, she cleared her throat, and began. "Well, unless there are any objections...this is it. We head back to our galaxy today. I have no idea what we will find when we return to earth. We know the planet was ravaged...at least it looked that way based on the telecast. We also know that at least a small band of Normals made it to Mars and somehow took over...at least for a while. The message said that they are now in trouble, so they will need our help. If there are any Normals left on either planet, we have to save them. I have no idea if the Alliance was still in force in the northern hemisphere, did they take over the planet...are they even in existence? Same mystery regarding the Southern Union. We really have no idea what we will find. We do know that Boral has a head start however...so we need to expect resistance from him and his remaining force...which probably includes another Great White battleship. I believe we gave everyone the chance to stay? To take one of the Wyverns and go back to Haven. Has anyone taken up our offer?"

Everyone shook their heads no.

"Yuli, do I take it you, Nova, and the Dekrons want to come along too?"

"Don't forget Star!" he said as he held up a small silver-skinned humanoid girl. "She, and the Dekrons want to see where we came from." She smiled at his daughter, then nodded in agreement at him. The little metallic girl smiled, and then giggled.

"The Marcole will be joining you also, Jaime" said Oomah. "We Flaybah also want to see this planet of yours. We have heard we may have had some roots there once."

"Good, then we are all in agreement that we need to go back and at least *see* what happened to our home planet. After we pick up any leftover humans, we can find somewhere in *our* galaxy to colonize. So, if we are ready..."

473

She was interrupted by the proximity alarms.

"Ack! Can we ever have a moment that those damn alarms don't sound?" said Nina with real spite in her voice.

Jaime looked over to KayOolah who checked the SCADAR. She looked up and said "Mayoola vessel is approaching at their normal high-rate of speed.

"Getting a hail Captain…" said Otter.

"Put them on, please…" she replied.

One of the Mayoola…she had no idea which one spoke to the group. "We know you are leaving and wish you success in your return back to where you belong. As there are still Blessed left alive in that galaxy, we wish for you to destroy them. We do help lesser races to remove diseases to their home area. The Og for example…"

"You helped the Og to try to defeat us?" she asked.

"Yes. They told us about what you…or in this case, the Blessed had done to one of their worlds. They also told us they were unable to defeat you. So, we agreed to help. Thus, we gave them the ship, with the weapon."

"Plasma slime…" Jaime said as she filled in the blanks.

"Yes, if that is what you want to refer to it as…In any case, we gave them the ship design and the weapon. We still limited them to how they could use it…after all, we could not upset the balance of power. We just wanted to give them a small bit of help."

"Glad we survived your help…" Jaime said dryly.

"You survived…you proved your superiority over the Og. They are in their place now…and it appears that your Blessed have devolved into a facsimile of the Og."

"We noticed that too" She agreed.

"So, for this reason…we wish to help you to remove them." A bright light flashed onto the Ladyhawk. Jaime and the bridge crew had to cover their eyes in protection from the brightness. When the light subsided the Mayoola said "There, it is done. Now you have a limited weapon to help in defeating the Blessed from your galaxy."

"Captain?" said Aimee. "I appear to have an extra weapon on my selector now…"

"What?" Jaime asked, confused.

"We have given you the ability to fire "plasma slime" from this ship. You only have four shots however…so do try to make them count" advised the Mayoola. Jaime could have sworn there was some sarcasm in its voice. Seeing Patti giggle didn't help to conceal the hidden attitude she felt they had toward them.

It looked down at Hero and asked "Are you sure you want to go with them? You can stay with us if you desire. Consider it, please."

Hero surprised her once again by saying to the Mayoola "No, I prefer to go back with them." The Mayoola nodded at the small animal.

It returned its gaze of those bright glowing eyes to Jaime. "We will now leave you and wish you luck in your struggle. Should you fail and have to return…remember this, that we are already sending a new asteroid to block your way back here. It will be here in…thirty, to thirty-five of your years." With that, the Mayoola vanished from their holo-projection, and the crystalline ship zoomed off as quickly as it showed up.

"Captain, I am showing four bolts in this weapon. I guess it was telling the truth" said Aimee.

"I could try to analyze it…make a copy, or figure out a way to generate more shots" said Jonathan.

"And if you did…" interrupted Patti "you would destroy the weapon permanently. We have built those so you cannot reverse engineer them."

Patti now sounded so different from when they first met. She acted like a primitive back then. Now that they all know she is far advanced than them, Jaime assumed she no longer had to give the façade.

Jaime thought of something. "Patti, you said you are going with us. But, how will you feed?"

"Oh, I took care of that when you attacked the bases. I kind of snuck aboard a few of the starships and...acquired...some food for the trip."

"Some?" she asked with suspicion.

"Ok, quite a bit. Just don't ask where, so I don't have to tell...if you ever find a door you absolutely can't open...don't" and with that she gave another small giggle.

Jaime shook her head. "Okay, we start down the Throat in five minutes. We will go in one at a time...use the relay as your directional source in the event you get disoriented in the void. Also remember, you must have your Graviton coils fully active, using dark matter on the way in, then dark energy in the void and as you pass into the exit tunnel. Then, you will need to reverse it again so the dark matter will push you out. If you don't follow those procedures exactly, you will be stuck in the void. We can't go back in and save you...so please be careful. Are there any questions?" Everyone shook their heads no. "Good! See you all back in OUR galaxy. Good luck all..." and with that she disconnected the conference.

"Okay...Helm, take us to the Throat..." she ordered.

Otter called out "Captain...Janus wishes to speak with you."

"Put him on..." she acknowledged.

He appeared in her pod a moment later. "Captain, my mother said I should help you with the navigation...that is, if you want it."

"Thank you, Janus...we have been there before. I think we will be alright." She gave him a small reassuring smile.

He shrugged his shoulders. "Okay...I did what mom asked me to do. Can I draw while we go through?"

"As long as you stay safe and secure...I don't see why not. Do you have enough drawing supplies? Have enough snacks? It may be a while before I can check in with you again."

"Yeah, I'm okay..." he said and immediately disconnected.

"Strange child..." she muttered. The ship was now located directly in front of the bright, blinking light that was the opening of the Devil's Throat. She took a deep breath of living gel before saying "Okay, take us in..."

The Throat opened up and swallowed them down just as quickly as the first time. They fought the forces pushing on them on the way down. It was the total opposite from what a normal space navigator would expect traveling through a gravity well like this. They felt the forces start to ease, and Jaime ordered "Okay, start to back off the dark matter and switch to dark energy."

They started speeding up again and quickly shot into the void that was the center of the Throat. Inside were hundreds of alien vessels stuck in the gravity void like fly paper. She wondered how long some of them had been trapped in there. Were there any beings still living in any of those ships? Could anyone even live here? So many things made her ponder what this mysterious place actually was – was it created, was it natural? There were too many questions that could not be answered.

She felt the change in the forces again and noticed that Lizzie was changing back to dark matter for entering the tunnel on the other side.

"Umm, Captain..." said Micha.

She looked at the path ahead and understood Micha's confusion. There were five tunnels ahead, each of them looked the same. She wondered if she should have taken Janus' offer of navigational help. She passed off the thought and said to Otter "Can you get a fix on the relay signal?"

She closed her eyes while she concentrated on finding the signal. A moment later her eyes opened wide, and she said "Ah, there! Yes, Captain...I have it...sending the signal to KayOolah for triangulation."

A minute later, one of the tunnels was blinking red. KayOolah said "I have highlighted the passageway that the relay signal is broadcasting through."

"Follow that light then, Micha." Jaime ordered.

They passed through the tunnel entrance and once again fought the opposite forces of gravity to the end of the Throat. The phenomenon spat them out as quickly as it sucked them in. A moment later, the stars began to appear in their pods.

They travelled a little farther from the Throat and came upon the relay. Small red marker lights and transmitters that had operated so far away from home for so many years, still in perfect condition. It was a welcome sight to the bridge crew. Seeing it reminded Jaime of Perfecto – she still remembered the day he set the relays. It was the day she lost her good friend.

"Okay Otter...tell the rest of the fleet to come on through." Within moments the first ship appeared...it was La Lucha. Then the Innovation, and then Nimbus. After the initial ships passed safely, the rest of the ships came through every couple minutes.

The first thing Jaime noticed was the chronometer. It showed:

Date: February 26, 2075

"Wow, we are back to normal date...and we've been gone a long time!" she admitted.

Halley was the first to transmit to the Ladyhawk. "We made it! Our navigation systems have not orientated themselves, but it is great to have made it through and know that we are back in OUR galaxy again. We will be back at earth in just a year...hard to believe."

"Umm, Captain..." interrupted Micha. Our navigation system just finished its orientation. I think you should look at our positioning.

She examined the navigation readouts. "Halley, take a look at this..." she said as she transmitted the readouts.

"This can't be...if this is right, we are light years away from being anywhere near our Solar System. But the relay is here...it has to be a glitch!" she decried. "Wait, my navigation system is coming back on-line. Let me see what it says..." She looked at her displays with a look of desperation. Then she got a pained look on her face and said "It reads the same. We are in a totally different sector of our galaxy. If I am seeing our position correctly, it could take up to ten years to get home. Assuming of course, this really is OUR galaxy..."

Jaime thought about that possibility, sighed, then nodded her head and said "Yes...that's what I am seeing also. We may be able to cut some time using the light drives in between insertions...but I fear we still have a few years to travel."

The Libertad had just passed through and was getting updates on their discovery. It was quickly followed by the passenger transports, the cargo ships, the Dekron ships, and finally the Flaybah battleship Marcole. Nina contacted Jaime "Is it true? Are we that far away? If so...what the hell is this relay?"

"Yes, its true..." she admitted. "I have no idea what is with the relay...it functions as if we were near the earth. It is a mystery we will probably never figure out...it may be getting its signals through the Throat, directing signals from our original entry point to it, then onward to the relay on the far side."

"We could try to go back in..." Nina suggested.

"Not a good idea..." said Jonathan. "That trip puts quite a strain on these ships. Without some maintenance, we would probably explode going back in...or worse, get stuck in there. I can do maintenance...but we might be halfway there by the time we have fixed all of the ships and gone back in to try again."

"So, then I take it we need to head out?" asked Nina.

Jaime nodded her head. "Yes...as soon as possible...the Blessed have a head start."

February 2080:

Jaime Bordeaux:

"Hello, it's me. I thought I would send you a message. I was chatting with friends the other day, telling them about you, and mentioned this personal communication channel and encryption code. One of them suggested I try it...I thought "what the hell" and here I am. I am not even sure it will reach you before we return...I'm not really sure about sub-space transmissions to earth...will it reach you at all. Well, I am giving it a try nonetheless. I have so much to tell you...and should you get this message, then at least you will have some idea about what I have been through since we left. Hell, I don't even know if you still monitor this channel and encryption code...but in the hopes you still do...well, here goes.

So, we just finished our second set of sixteen sub-space insertions...we have some downtime while they do the required maintenance on the crawler drives. So, this really is the perfect time for me to tell you I am near and coming home.

I don't really have time to tell you where we've been this entire time, but let me just say...it was somewhere totally different from where we expected to be going. But now we're back, and headed back to earth. When I see you I can tell you all about the adventures you missed after Starlight took off. As a matter of fact, we are no longer even aboard Starlight...another story for another day.

When I think about it, it really is hard to believe it has already been five years since we arrived back in our home galaxy. Halley...she is the best astronomer and navigator I have ever known...said we are about half way between where we returned to our galaxy and the Solar System. I really hope she can find a way to shave a few years off of our return.

When we exited from this last sub-space insertion, Halley used one of her advanced telescopes to view earth. To our surprise, the planet went from the red coloration that it was when we left to a planet that appears to be covered in ice. We have no idea what has happened there...but it sure doesn't look like the planet we left. I asked her to find Mars, but I guess you are on the other side of the sun right now...so I guess I don't get a chance to see you from here.

481

Instead, I am talking to the holo-image I have of you. You have been with me all these years...you will never leave me. Well anyway...

Part of our journey took us to another galaxy...for another time...While we were there, we've made a lot of new friends...most of them are not human. We have our good friends the Flaybah...they are a race of super intelligent deer. I know, that's hard to believe isn't it? Well, in addition to them, we have the Dekrons...they have a couple of our kind with them. They're now part human, part machine...but are acting like a normal human couple...they're happy and are reproducing and growing...so that is a good thing. Then there's Patti and she is...well, hard to really describe...but she is in love with my good friend Jeremy...you remember him don't you? Anyway, because of her feelings toward him, she joined us...and I actually am glad to have her with us.

We have grown too...we have had many children in the past five years. The one couple I would have never guessed would have gotten together is Allen and Nina...the captain from the south...yes, we have even made friends with our former enemies from the south. I would have never figured those two as mates, but they ended up together and already have a child. Domino is a wonderful girl and at four is already developing into a future starship captain. She is serving here on the Ladyhawk and...wow...she has the skills. I can hardly wait until she is ready to take on a ship.

As a matter of fact, all of my friends have gotten together and had children...Max and Annette, Jonathan and Kate...hell, even Halley and Kylie have had children. Oh, and ready for this...Jeremy and Patti are trying their hand at reproducing...and they think they will succeed! Me...no...I don't see how it will work, but stranger things have happened on this adventure!

Oh yeah, then there is Lindy's son, Janus. He is a mixture of Normal and Blessed. He is...different...He tends to avoid most people, I think because he looks so different. I will say however, he is brilliant. It's just...well, I just don't know where his heart is...I have to keep an eye on him all the time. And when we finally reach earth and the Blessed fleet...well, that's when I will really have to keep him on a short leash.

And speaking of which, we also discovered that animals we always thought of as pets...namely cats and dogs...are really advanced beings. Not sure why they allowed themselves to become extinct on earth though. Maybe they were just caught there when the hemispheric war broke out...who knows?

Oh Dex, I want to get back to the Solar System, and get to Mars so badly...but I have to face the reality of two things. First, I HAVE to take the fleet back to earth first. The remainder of the Blessed fleet will be there. If there is anything left of the Alliance then we have to stop them from regaining power. Second, and even harder for me to face is that you probably are not alive anymore. I am still hearing your messages...I have no idea how long ago you actually recorded it. But, somehow I doubt that you are still there or still alive. If you do get this message...please, change your recording and let me know you are still there.

If I find out you're still alive and struggling there...I will head right to Mars as soon as the Blessed are defeated. We will win too...I guarantee it and promise.

My only worry is what you will discover when I find you. I have...changed...I don't look like the Jaime you knew when I left so many years ago...but inside it is still me. I hope you will understand and not turn me away. I don't know what I would do if that happened...so...well, just don't okay?

Alright, I had better stop using resources and maybe get a little rest. Please, if you are alive...keep living...hold out. We are on our way and will help. I will find you. I will try to send another message during our next maintenance cycle. Until I find you my love...and if at all possible, I WILL find you. Stay safe and alive..."

The end of book 2 – Metamorphosis of Normal

Meanwhile, back on Earth, many years ago…

He thought to himself while waiting for the procedure to begin. "Here we go. I wonder, will this be like death? I wonder what death is like? I might just find out today…maybe that would be for the best?" Despite being on the cold steel table, he was nervous enough that sweat formed and rolled down his forehead.

In the control room Edward sat in front of a large computer console. "Begin phase 1 A, molecular decomposition…activating the array." He activated virtual switches and typed onto the computer console. A loud hum filled the room as the reactor began the process of energizing the molecular disintegration array. In the monitor they could see the array light up in bright colors that illuminated the subject's naked body.

Edward announced "Phase 1 B, obtain DNA sample for computer analysis." He flipped some different switches and entered commands into his computer console. The disintegration array lit up slightly, the hum intensified, and then returned to its previous state.

"Phase 1 complete…beginning phase 2, obtain DNA sample of bonding animal" he called out.

Without any additional noise or effort, the computer located the sample in the enormous repository located in another building, and removed a sample set of cells. The computer indicated that a successful sample had been obtained.

A display on the main console illuminated and showed the computer representation of the subject's DNA and other information of his genetic makeup. On a second screen a breakdown of the bonding animal's DNA and genetic makeup was displayed.

"Your friends DNA donor is listed but not shown on my screen. I hope you two picked wisely – for his and your sake" he said with disgust in his voice.

His words sent a shiver up her spine, she now had goose bumps across her entire body. "I am sure he will be successful due to this choice. He will use this donor to his best advantage" she replied.

He smiled as he said softly "That's good...as I would hate to have to destroy your lover...and please don't deny it. We have cameras in that room, and I saw your activities last night." An evil chuckle escaped his lips. "I really enjoyed the show."

"You bastard! How dare you!" She was livid with rage, but at the same time she dare not provoke him at this stage of the process.

"You should have remembered that every room in this complex is monitored" he cautioned her. "I would have thought you would have been more professional. However, that is a discussion for another time...I have more important things going on right now. Besides, if this does not go well...it won't matter..." He returned his attention to his computer console. "Ah, the computer has determined the best splices and bonds...we are ready for phase 3."

"Begin phase 3" Edward announced as he flipped more switches and entered the commands to begin the sequence that will reduce his subject to individual molecules. The light intensified and began to break apart his body. Small bubble-like spheres of light bounced off of his body and were lifted into the array. His eyes opened wide as he was able to feel his body being torn apart. A tear rolled down her cheek as molecule by molecule his body was broken apart and moved into the joining matrix of the computer. Within seconds there was only a light outline of the body left on the table.

On the main computer screen, a display of the progress of the bonding process was shown. When it was working at full capacity as it was now, a loud hum was heard everywhere. In the control room this was no exception as the loud hum and vibrations were both heard, and felt. The entire supercomputer complex was fully dedicated to the splicing and bonding process it controlled inside the matrix.

60 percent complete she noted on the main console. Sweat was dripping down her forehead and onto her cheeks. She felt the sweat but ignored it, and instead focused on the computer monitor as if her constant stare would help him to survive this ordeal.

"75 percent and so far so good" Edward commented, pleased with the progress to this point.

The process continued for what seemed like hours to her, but was actually only a single minute. Without warning, the loud hum of the computer stopped. "What happened?" she gasped.

Edward laughed at her fear, then reassured her "The bonding process is complete and successful. Begin Phase 4, reintegration."

The computer complex churned to life once again, this time the machine gave off an even louder hum. The array in the chamber once again lit up – a bright red color emanated from the emitters. A loud high pitched noise began as the array started its work. A light outline of a human body appeared on the table, red bubbles of light floated out of the array emitters and down onto the outline. Bright red beams of light bounced across the outline of his body as molecules were brought down and placed back in the proper position in his now reappearing body.

His face had the same facial expression as when the disintegration process started – his eyes wide open almost popping out of his head. It was obvious he had not only felt what was happening, but was almost in a state of shock from the process. The beams of light continued to dance across his body, as he became more and more whole. After a few minutes, the lights stopped, and the array darkened. The high pitch whine quieted, and the computer hum lowered.

"Process complete and if my readings are correct, he lived." Edward said, pleased with himself. *"Now, to see what we end up with."*

He spun around in his chair, and looked at her with a smile on his face. "This is the part where the real magic occurs" he told her "I hope we get a good bonding and your training actually does some good."

She did not care about what he was saying, and really was not listening. She was too concerned with the man in the other room. She watched and waited for any changes. "Perhaps the bonding did not hold, maybe he would not change?" She said to herself almost hoping for a failure in Edward's process.

Suddenly, his body began to convulse – still being held down by the restraints, he flailed like a fish out of water. The room was filled with the sound of his body pushing up, and then slamming down on the stainless steel surface of the table. After a few moments, the noises of his body flailing on the table stopped. The quiet only lasted a second however, as then the room became filled with the sound of his screaming. The screaming caused by the pain he felt in his body as it began to change.

Look for more in Starlight Series Book 3, coming soon!

www.ingramcontent.com/pod-product-compliance
Lightning Source LLC
Chambersburg PA
CBHW071216250626
47163CB00001B/7